PENGUIN BOOKS

MAKING GOOD AGAIN

Making Good Again, first published in 1968, is
Lionel Davidson's fourth novel. His first, *The
Night of Wenceslas*, won two literary awards in 1960,
and his second and third, *The Rose of Tibet* and *A Long
Way to Shiloh*, were, respectively, best-sellers of
1962 and 1966. All his novels are in Penguin, have
been acquired for filming, and have been published
in several foreign languages. Lionel Davidson was
born in Yorkshire, and now lives with his wife and
two sons in Israel.

LIONEL DAVIDSON

Making Good Again

PENGUIN BOOKS

Penguin Books Ltd, Harmondsworth, Middlesex, England
Penguin Books Australia Ltd, Ringwood, Victoria, Australia

—

First published by Jonathan Cape 1968
Published in Penguin Books 1970

—

Copyright © Lionel Davidson, 1968

—

Made and printed in Great Britain by
Cox & Wyman Ltd, London, Reading and Fakenham
Set in Monotype Garamond

wieder, adv.   again

gut, adj.   good

machen, v.a.   make

Wiedergutmachung, n.f.   making good again, reparation

New German Dictionary

IN RECOGNITION
OF THE FACT

THAT a wrong has been committed against persons who, under the NS terror régime, were persecuted for reasons of their opposition to national socialism or their race, religious faith or ideology,

THAT the resistance offered to the NS terror régime from conviction, for the sake of faith or for reasons of conscience, was a service rendered to the welfare of the German people and nation, and

THAT democratic, religious and economic organizations too have been injured by the NS terror régime in contravention of the law,

THE BUNDESTAG, by and with the consent of the Bundesrat, has enacted the following law . . .

Preamble to the German Federal Indemnification Law (*Bundesentschädigungsgesetz*)

PART ONE

A claim to indemnification for loss of life may be asserted if the persecutee has been deliberately or frivolously killed or driven to his death. It shall be sufficient if there is a probable causal nexus between death and persecution.

German Federal Indemnification Law
(*Bundesentschädigungsgesetz*)

Chapter 1

A TRICKY ISSUE OF STANDARDS

'What you've always got to remember about these chaps,' Gunter said, 'is that they've got no sense of humour. Absolutely none. So I personally wouldn't raise this anti-semitic thing, even in joke. They simply wouldn't get it – even old Heinz, whom even after thirty years I wouldn't presume to – oh, my word, very nice. Get younger every year, don't they?'

'Yes,' Raison said. They were walking through Lincoln's Inn Fields to the Tube station, and every evening at about this time the senior partner would inflame himself at sight of the tennis players. Summer as a whole seemed to inflame the old man. It couldn't be good for him, Raison thought. His already rubicund face and full lip had taken on since May a somewhat gorged appearance, and even his personal aroma, normally fruity, even wholesome, seemed now distinctly gamey, no doubt to do with his pipe, constantly clogged with saliva.

It was necessary to talk further about the case – the ostensible reason for Raison's having been clobbered in this way – but the moment seemed propitious for getting something even more urgent out of the way before they hit the train. Raison had had experience of Gunter in trains. Some words of the afternoon had given him a reasonable expectation of what topic might well occur to him the moment they were aboard.

'About the Wilkinson annulment thing,' he said. 'Wasn't there something you wanted to raise?'

'The Wilkinson annulment?' Gunter said, lifting his bowler and mopping his head slightly as they continued. 'I don't think so. Was there? What is there special about the Wilkinson annulment?'

'Wife already living *in adulterous relationship with other man*,' Raison said, raising his voice slightly as he checked over in his mind every factor that might have brought it to the other's summer consciousness. 'The action is to void the marriage, owing to the husband's incapacity.'

'Quite, quite,' Gunter said mildly.

'We are acting for the husband. Of course we are saying that there was no incapacity at the time of marriage.'

'Of course you are. Naturally you are. Do I understand you are admitting a bit now, though?'

'Of a purely temporary nature.'

'I see.'

'He's unfortunately under treatment for it.'

'Quite right,' Gunter said firmly. 'In certain people the thing comes and goes, nothing final about it. It's quite a common occurrence for a young wife to be attracted elsewhere, not necessarily seriously, and of course it puts the husband off his peck. It doesn't mean he loses the desire to have relations, or that he won't be able to again. It is a young wife, isn't it?'

'Yes,' Raison said. He suddenly remembered that Gunter had a young wife, a pale but surprisingly boisterous young wife, and in the same moment found himself transfixed by the other's somewhat wild brown eyes.

'There's rarely anything final about it,' Gunter said.

'No.'

'Science usually has a cure.'

'Yes.'

'The thing is to keep trying with the wife.'

'He can't,' Raison said. 'She's left him.'

'Well, it's a pity. He shouldn't have let it go so far. It's quite a common occurrence,' Gunter said.

'Yes.'

'Yes. How's your wife, James?'

'Fine,' Raison said. He was accustomed to these sudden leaps, and kept on his toes for them. 'Quite mad, of course,' he added, recollecting how Hilda liked to be described.

'Such high spirits. It's a shame she doesn't come to work any more. I think of her often. Tell her that.'

'Thanks. I will. . . . Quite sure there was nothing about the annulment, then?' he said, persevering.

'Not that I can –'

'Well, good. I'm afraid I interrupted you, Rupert. Sorry, Rupert. You were saying something very interesting about the Germans.'

Gunter resumed being interesting about the Germans. He was still being interesting about them – loudly, of course, but at no great embarrassment to Raison who had immediately stopped listening – as they burrowed westwards under London. He was thinking about Gunter's wife, and realizing why he'd been landed with the trip. Gunter wasn't making trips lately.

'. . . Nazis, of course there are Nazis,' the old man was saying. 'You don't surely expect solid family men to turn their backs on a whole period of their lives without finding some merit . . .'

'True. Absolutely,' Raison said from time to time. He was trying over a few specimen interviews with Hilda. Was there an absolute need to tell Hilda?

'. . . nonsense to group Heinz with them . . . his record plain for all to see . . . to whom a case is simply a . . .'

'Of course,' Raison said. He'd be back after all in the evening, no bother about the week-end. It would be concealment, though. He didn't know how he felt about concealment. There was a tricky issue of standards here.

By Knightsbridge, Gunter had managed to get himself a seat and Raison hadn't, and so had to submit to some slight increase in the embarrassment level as the old man merely shouted up at him a little louder.

'I was forgetting, of course, that you'd met Heinz. I suppose you would call him a happy man, wouldn't you?'

'Well, Rupert, I haven't given it a lot of –'

'You'd be wrong. He ought to be, of course. Most of us ought to be.'

'Ah, yes,' Raison said. He had spotted a seat, apparently soon to become vacant, which would put him well beyond range of Gunter.

'Yet something in our nature always seems to prevent us. We want something more, or something else. We feel ourselves robbed. I expect you do yourself,' Gunter shouted.

'I expect so. I expect we all do,' Raison said, trying to keep his nod at once rueful and vigorous.

'We should try to count our blessings. We should try to appreciate what is still left to us.'

'Quite.' The train was running into South Kensington. 'Do you know,' Raison said, 'I think somebody over there is getting up.'

'Of course, his sister makes him unhappy,' Gunter said.

'Does she?'

'The widow of the SS general. They have had a great deal of trouble with her.'

'Yes. If you don't mind, I think I'll take the weight off –'

'Naturally, it's worrying for him in view of his work with the prosecuting agencies. Still, she had her own money, which is something.'

'Yes.'

'From the mother. She divided it between the daughter and the granddaughter, Heinz's girl.'

Raison sighed. The seat had become vacant, the doors had opened; those going out had gone, and several large school-girls had swarmed in, one of them taking the seat, and the rest lurching with their briefcases on either side of him as the train started again. He took a tighter grip on the handstrap and nodded rather more seriously at Gunter. The man had given him, it was true, a relatively easy ride so far, but schoolgirls were now about. They were talking and laughing among themselves, and Raison was himself getting off at the next stop. But it was a long way to the next stop.

'. . . one more headache for him,' Gunter was shouting as the train picked up speed again. 'I don't know what's happening now, but last autumn when I was there she had taken up with a deformed Hungarian Jew and was living with him.'

'I see,' Raison said. This line of talk would have to be watched.

'Heinz's girl. Living with the fellow as his mistress.'

'Yes,' Raision said. His ear had detected a certain pause in the schoolgirls' conversation. The man had very often to be handled like a dangerous lunatic. 'What was the weather like when you were there?' he said.

'The what?'

'The weather.'

'The weather? It was all right.'

'Yes. It can be very changeable, of course. I expect it's the effect of the Alps.'

'I expect so. I am her godfather, you know.'

'Are you?'

'Oh, yes. What worried Heinz particularly –'

'Of course, they take that kind of thing very seriously, don't they – godfathers?' They must have gone over half-way by now, he thought. With any luck he should be able to hold him off till Gloucester Road.

'Yes. Although it was not the religious aspect that bothered Heinz so much as the nature of the fellow's deformity. I can't recall exactly – good lord, yes. Do you know, I've just remembered what it was about the annulment – the wife's case.'

Raison did the first thing that came into his head. He broke into amused laughter and began waving his arms to indicate that the noise of the train was making conversation impossible. As if decreed by fate, the train immediately stopped. All conversation stopped with it.

'What they are claiming, of course,' Gunter said, modulating his voice in the perfect silence to a more comfortable level, 'is that your impotence prevented the consummation of the marriage.'

Raison felt himself beginning to sweat. He could feel it breaking out instantly beneath his bowler and trickling all over his body. His impulse was to assert at once and loudly that the reference was not to him but to his client. In the face of the other's total unconcern with the audience, he couldn't bring himself to do it. It seemed best to say nothing at all, to try and pretend that Gunter was either drunk or eccentric and engaged in a long and well-modulated conversation with himself. The train was bound to start again at any moment. Hanging on the strap, he turned his head. He found everybody looking at him.

'Of course, now that she is living with the other fellow it is doubtful if she will have any physical evidence of her own to support the case, so yours will be examined pretty closely. Are you perfectly certain there is no evidence of malformation?'

'No,' Raison said, the word torn from him almost like a groan.

'What does the doctor say?'

'I haven't spoken to him. Not yet,' Raison said, his desperate mumble sounding in his own ears worse even than a more damning admission.

'Good heavens, you ought!' Gunter said. 'I honestly think you ought.' The train had begun to chunter slowly along again. 'That sort of thing needs looking at. I'll have a glance at it myself if you like. Heaven knows what medical evidence she's got hold of. Doesn't the 1937 Act allow her to bring communicable venereal disease to support a nullity suit? Not, I suppose, that that is very likely in the present case.'

'No.' Raison said. 'Not very likely.' Some masochistic part of him was beginning to extract satisfaction. 'Not if I am malformed and impotent,' he said. He sought for further indignities to heap on himself – leprosy, bestiality – but could think of nothing suitable as the train, as if to emphasize the chance nature of his ordeal, chuntered at no more than a walking pace into the station – it had stopped a bare twenty yards outside.

'What, Gloucester Road already?' Gunter said. 'Goes quickly doesn't it? I'll look into the matter, then. Have a good trip. See you on Monday.'

'Yes. Right. Thanks,' Raison said, scrambling blindly out of the carriage. He was aware that the schoolgirls were making way for him with alacrity and studying him with close interest as he passed. But something kept him on the platform, all the same, beaming and waving his umbrella in a jolly fashion at old Rupert until the doors closed. He'd never been able to take himself quickly from the scene of a humiliation. The tricky issue of standards was always present.

Raison crossed Gloucester Road and walked along Stanhope Gardens, still perspiring. He let himself into the house, and loped slowly up the dark stairs, umbrella and briefcase swinging, to his flat. It was a rather loathsome flat. He'd taken it in a

16

hurry six months before. In the depths of winter, with the main idea being to cut out the daily journey to and from Boreham Wood, its true character had not immediately struck him. It had been striking him ever since. There was a single enormous room, chillingly dismal, and a small one off it that was a bath-room-kitchen. All of it was too dark. He had put in more lights, but even with the lights on it was too dark. He seemed to live a mole-like existence in it.

He noticed a few letters on the floor as he went in, but didn't bother with them. He needed a drink first, and then he needed another, sitting on the sofa with his bowler, briefcase and umbrella beside him and looking around the room.

He was a tall man, slim, with a bulging babyish forehead. His general coloration was copper. His face was copper, his hair was copper, the hairs on his hands and at his wrists were copper. His copperish sandy eyelashes blinked slowly around the room as he sipped his whisky. When he flushed – he was still a bit flushed – he seemed to be overheating, and the grey eyes to be liquefying in their whites; he looked then like some mutely suffering animal peering through the eye sockets of another alien body. A medium seeing him like this one day had told him he was an incarnation.

His babyish face and generally honest manner had always had the effect of drawing people to him with a view of confiding in him and involving him in their affairs. Raison found this an unwelcome effect. He knew himself to be a person totally unlike the one suggested by his face, a far less pleasant one. But he was honest enough. His easily blushing skin made him a bad liar, so that he was forced mainly to tell the truth; he nearly always told it to himself. This was not necessarily an advantage in his profession, and his occasional appearances in the lower courts, always dreaded by him, were not a success. But he loved the law. He loved the idea of it. He was happy with the arrangements regulating oyer and terminer, tort and trespass, malfeasance and misfeasance, and with the conceptions of hotchpots, emblements and estoppels. He particularly liked estoppels, that legal convention that barred a man from taking one course of action when he had already committed himself to another. He was trying these days to order his own life on the theory of estoppel.

It wasn't easy. A lot of people were around. And more and more these days people bemused him. All too often he seemed to understand what they were up to only in retrospect. Sometimes, listening to them from behind his desk in Lincoln's Inn, he was disturbed and astounded by the things they got up to. He couldn't imagine himself getting up to these things. There seemed to be a lot of viciousness about.

His slowly-blinking eyes paused on the telephone. He rang Hilda every night when he was in London. There was no reason why he shouldn't ring her tomorrow night, too, if he was held up for any reason. Why should she suppose he wasn't still in London? What possible difference could it make to her, anyway?

He finished his drink and went into the kitchen and absorbedly cut himself two slices of bread. He couldn't think of any difference it would make to her. He put the kettle on and got out his teapot and his cup and saucer and spoon. He couldn't see the milk and sugar. Where were the milk and sugar? The woman was always shifting milk and sugar about. He found the sugar but not the milk, and started buttering his bread. It was a problem to know what kind of questions might arise. Quite often she wanted to know what work he was engaged on. He could tell her. He'd been engaged on it all the week.

He licked butter off his thumb and remembered the milk and had another look for it. It wasn't in the fridge, or in the cupboard, and there was none in the jug. Where had the woman put the milk? The kettle wasn't boiling yet. He took his plate of bread and butter over to the window and ate, looking down on Stanhope Gardens. Sometimes, for instance, she asked what the weather was like and if it was raining. Well, he could tell her what the weather was like and if it was raining. She wasn't, after all, interested in the general weather picture, only in that part of it that concerned him. What deception was there?

The kettle was singing, so he warmed the pot, an inch and a half of water, carefully swilled round and poured out of the spout. He put two spoonfuls of tea in and took the pot to the

18

kettle and poured the boiling water in, and stood the pot to infuse. Deception, of course, he couldn't allow; this was an old position, well debated. Deception infringed fidelity, and was thus a clear case for estoppel. No argument about deception. *Was* it a deception? If she asked him if he was in London and he said he was, that would be deception. If she asked the question and he evaded it, that would be deception, too. If the question never arose, if it could be shown to be quite clearly outside the area of discussion, then he would have thought that there was no deception. He would really have thought so. Concealment, perhaps. But was there a duty on him to volunteer information of no relevance to her, which might provoke tiresome and objectionable scenes? He would have thought not. But it was a question.

He poured out the tea and looked for the milk.

Where the hell was the bloody milk?

His tea was *out*. It was getting cold. What had the mad woman done with his milk? He ran into the living-room. Perhaps it was still outside the front door. He opened the door. It wasn't there. Coming back in, he picked up the letters. Under the letters was her note – left there plain for him to see on entering, but left there before the post came.

Milkman never left you again today. Will pop you 1 in downstairs from Dairy if Time – Mrs Law.

He ran downstairs. No milk. Evidently no Time. She hadn't popped him one in, anyway.

He went bitterly upstairs again. The dairy would be shut, of course. He'd have to get a carton later from the machine in Gloucester Road.

He hated tea without milk, but he had poured it, so he drank it. As far as possible, he liked to complete actions.

He had his dinner at Dino's on the corner of Gloucester Road, and took his coffee outside under the awning. It was a heart-stopping evening and girls were all around; pulling up on the pillions of scooters, laughing under the awning of Dino's. The world seemed to be full of them. He'd got a spot of Gunter's trouble, of course, only with a difference; with a practical and mind-reeling difference. It was June and the sap had risen. He finished his coffee and left.

He'd meant to ring up the air terminal, but he walked there. It was only five minutes away in the Cromwell Road. There was nothing wrong with a walk on such a magnificent evening.

The big steel-and-glass structure stood bloodshot in the last of the day, like some cindered relic of the last of all days. He made his way through the confusing building and found the desk. They spotted each other before he got to the desk.

She said, 'Hello,' smiling.

'Good evening.'

'Back again?'

'I wanted to check the return flights,' Raison said. 'From three o'clock onwards. On Friday,' he said.

'Yes. Munich, wasn't it?'

'Munich.'

He couldn't keep his eyes off her. She had a white shirt and straight blonde hair and eyes that were not quite even. She had the most beautiful breasts. He hadn't been wrong. He hadn't known she'd be on. He hadn't known it. Perhaps that made it worse. In some ways it might be worse. He thought that it was worse. He stared hungrily at her as she wrote down the times for him.

She said, 'It's a beautiful city, Munich.'

'Yes.'

'It's beautiful there now.'

'Is it?'

'Beautiful. You're not staying long.'

'No.'

'Back for the week-end.'

'Yes. Good night,' he said.

It was definitely worse. He decided to tell Hilda. He decided to walk first. He walked to the High Street and along it to the Albert Hall, and crossed at the Memorial and walked through the park. The park was sinking in dark maroon light, couples all about, getting up to God knew what in the warm gloaming. He walked fast to the statue of Physical Energy and back round it to Palace Gate. He was sweating as he loped upstairs again in Stanhope Gardens. He took the phone over to the sofa.

She said, 'Hello,' quite brightly.

'It's me.'

'I didn't think you'd be ringing now.'

'It got late.'

'What have you been doing?'

'I was busy,' he said. She sounded all right. She certainly sounded all right. 'Rupert asked to be remembered,' he said.

'Who did?'

'Rupert. He was talking about you and your high spirits.' He suddenly realized he shouldn't have said it. 'He was going on a bit,' he said. 'He was rambling on. You know Rupert.'

'What made him say that?'

'I don't know. He was just going on. He was asking how you were.'

'What did you say?'

'I said you were fine.'

'I see.'

'No, really. I said you were fine. I said mad as ever,' Raison said.

'Did it come out all right?'

'It came out beautifully. It came out very nicely. So what kind of a day have you had?'

'Didn't you get my letters?'

'They're beautiful letters,' he said. He was frantically trying to read them in the terrible light.

'That's the kind of day I've had.'

'I'm sorry, Hilda. I'm really sorry.'

'But I mean it about the week-end.'

He couldn't see anything about the week-end. It must be in the other letter. 'I love you Hilda,' he said automatically.

'Do you?'

'I love you.'

He'd found it.

. . . to leave at the week-end . . . that I am inadequate and of no use to society, but it isn't right the doctors should have such powers. If you loved me you wouldn't leave me in their power . . . could

live for a while on a small island I am sure I could pull myself together . . . definitely do not want to go home.

'I see,' Raison said. 'Yes. You don't fancy coming just for the
week-end, then, Hilda?'

'I don't think so, James.'

'Not just Saturday night?'

'Not honestly, James. Not really. I know you love me.'

'I see,' Raison said. So that had come up again. Although he
loved her, he might all the same be driven by kindness to kill
her if they spent a night in the house together. It had been some
time since this had come up. She'd spent the week-end at home
a fortnight ago. A few people had come in for drinks. Nobody
could tell when she was at home that there was anything wrong
with her.

'Well, let's sort it out at the week-end,' he said.

'I've got a book about islands. We could arrange something.'

'All right.'

'There are pictures of Skokholm.'

'Skokholm, eh?' He couldn't think where the hell Skokholm was.

'Off the Pembroke coast. It's a lovely book. If you want, we
could stay at an hotel on Friday night.'

'All right, if you'd like to.'

'On the way to Skokholm.'

'I see,' Raison said. 'Yes. I see. That might be very nice.'
They'd evidently changed her drugs. He wondered why. It
was certain she wouldn't be going anywhere this week-end.
She probably wouldn't be conscious. There was no reason to
tell her at all. Because there was no reason he said quickly,
'While I think of it, don't worry if I'm a bit late on Friday. I've
got to go to Munich in the morning. It's a Bamberger thing.'

'What? What do you say? What do you mean? Mr Gunter
handles all the Bamberger things.'

'Not all, Hilda. Not all of them. It's not very important. It's
this business with the Swiss money. Do you remember the
Swiss money? It looks as if it's coming up soon, so we have to
get the German probate certificate in the form the Swiss want
it. It isn't anything important.'

'If it isn't important why are you going?'

'It's the Bambergers. It's Mrs Wolff. You remember Mrs Wolff. You know they don't trust Haffner. They have this idea that German lawyers are anti-Semites. They always insist we have somebody there for a court hearing.'

'Look, I don't understand. James, why have you got to go? Why can't somebody else go? What will happen to me if you don't come back? What will happen to me if something happens to you?'

'Nothing is going to happen, Hilda. It's my job. I'm going in the morning, we're seeing the probate judge at noon, and in the afternoon I'll be back. I'll see you in the evening.'

'What do you mean, we? Who are you taking with you?'

'I'm not taking anybody. I mean Heinz Haffner. And there is an Israeli lawyer. Do you remember there was some Israeli interest in the money? It's very simple, really. I'm sorry I told you.'

'James, you *are* going to Munich?'

'Of course I am.'

'Send me a postcard from there.'

'All right. I'll be with you before the postcard.'

'Send it, though.'

'All right. Now have a good night.'

'Yes.'

'I love you, Hilda.'

He put down the phone and blew out his cheeks. There'd been some rough spells on the whole, today. He sat for a moment looking at the phone. He thought of the wild brown eyes of Gunter. He thought of Gunter discussing aspects of unhappiness in the Tube. He thought of the grounds mentioned by Gunter as allowed by the 1937 Act in the matter of the nullity suit. There was another ground that Gunter hadn't mentioned. Recurrent insanity, unknown to the petitioner at the time of marriage, was also a ground allowed by the 1937 Act. Raison sighed. It was a beautiful thing, the law. It was in many ways far more beautiful than people. But it was made to fit people, and some of them it couldn't quite fit.

He took the Bamberger papers to bed with him, but he put

the light off early. Something had been bothering him, and he couldn't think what it was. He tried again in the dark. Something not done that he ought to have done. . . . No.

Just as he drifted off to sleep he remembered.

The bloody milk.

Chapter 2

'LET THEM KILL YOU – BUT DON'T CROSS THE LINE!'

'*Asher natan lasechvi vinah*,' Grunwald said, gently sniffing at his phylacteries as he took them out of the bag. They still smelt new. He didn't like the smell very much. He had liked the smell of his old phylacteries, a slightly musty delicate old smell. But phylacteries got worn out like everything else. '*Lehavchin bein yom*,' he added, '*uvein layela*.' He was thanking God for giving the cock intelligence to distinguish between day and night. Then he thanked him for not making him a heathen, and for not making him a bondman, and for not making him a woman.

He liked to take his time over his prayers. It was permissible in time of sickness, terror or flight, or if time were short for some other reason, merely to cast the eyes over the words. Grunwald was not short of time. He allowed time. When he woke in the morning, he allowed time for thinking over the day ahead. When he got up and went into the bathroom he allowed time for a careful toilet. When he went into the front room to lay his phylacteries, he allowed time for that, too. There was a time for everything. This was the time for prayers, and he said them.

Besides, he liked saying them. He liked a little more each day the way the old words were put together, psalms, Talmud readings, scriptural passages, the last cries of martyrs, immaculately dovetailed to make a formal morning address to the Creator, a reminder almost, a signing-on for the new day. He felt not quite ready, not quite complete, in a sort of limbo, until

24

he had signed on in this way. He always allowed plenty of time for it. Also the new phylacteries needed an airing. It would be some time before the new phylacteries would be really nice. He didn't like new things.

Grunwald began to lay the phylacteries. He strapped the first phylactery, the little black box with its tiny scroll inside, on his bared left bicep, and wound the strap seven times down the arm, blessing God for commanding him to put it on. Then he strapped the one on his forehead, and completed the arm strap with three turns round the hand and the middle finger. 'And I will betroth thee unto me for ever,' he said. 'Yea, I will betroth thee unto me in righteousness, and in judgement, and in mercy. I will even betroth thee unto me in faithfulness,' Grunwald said.

He breathed easily and swayed pleasantly on his feet. He went comfortably into the morning service.

'Blessed be he who spake, and the world existed: blessed be he. Blessed be he who . . .'

A lot of banging about was going on in the kitchen; far more banging about than was necessary. Grunwald heard it, and knew about it, and went equably on with his prayers.

'He reigneth. The Lord reigneth. The Lord hath frustrated the design of the nations: he hath foiled the thought of the peoples . . .'

Was she calling him? Was she actually calling to him, during his prayers? No disturbance showed on his face. He continued swaying gently there and back. But Grunwald was disturbed.

'The horse and his rider hath he thrown into the sea. . . . The enemy said I will divide the spoil, my hand shall destroy them. But thou in thy loving kindness hast led the people which thou hast redeemed; thou hast guided them in thy strength to thy holy habitation . . .'

She was not calling him. She was not nominally calling him. She was nominally addressing some third party or herself. But she was in fact calling him. He knew the declamatory style. She was Rumanian. His first wife had been German, Frankfurter born and bred, like himself. So had his three children been. This one was Rumanian; very declamatory; very rhetorical. It seemed to be something about the defective gas tap on the stove.

'He knows I break my fingers! He wants me to break my fingers. He wants to claim the benefit for my fingers.'

'And for slanderers let there be no hope,' Grunwald said without pause. 'Let all wickedness perish as in a moment. Let all thine enemies speedily be cut off . . .'

'He can go without his coffee. Let him go with his tongue hanging out. Does he do anything to please me? I'm the dummy that cooks and washes and sews. Without me he could go with his backside hanging out!'

'. . . that we may not be put to shame,' Grunwald said. 'For we have trusted in thee. Blessed art thou, the stay and trust of the righteous.'

He was disturbed. This had not happened before, not during his prayers. She should be given some extra and early attention today. When he had time he would do that today. But today was Wednesday, the fourth day of the week, so the psalm for the fourth day of the week had first to be read. Grunwald read it, carefully.

'. . . to the proud their desert. Lord, how long shall the wicked, how long shall the wicked triumph? They prate, they speak arrogantly; all the workers of iniquity are boastful. They crush the people and afflict thine heritage. They slay the widow and the stranger, and murder the fatherless . . .'

She was still banging about and shouting in the kitchen. She was upset, of course. Today, undoubtedly, she was very upset. It was to be expected. He would say a few words to her, some timely words.

He was suddenly aware of the extreme timeliness of the words he was reading.

'They say, the Lord will not see, neither will the God of Jacob give heed. Give heed, ye brutish among the peoples: and ye fools, when will ye be wise? He that planted the ear, shall he not hear? He that formed the eye, shall he not see? He that chasteneth the nations, shall not he punish . . .'

Amazing. Grunwald had rarely read a word of the morning

service that was not, from some aspect, appropriate. But he marvelled at the extraordinary appropriateness of these words. It seemed almost as if some divine clockwork had so ordered the running of the universe that his business in it and the psalm of the day should at this point of time coincide. For a moment he felt quite lifted up; above his flat in Hayarkon Street, above Tel Aviv even, above the entire Land of Israel, poised like some heavenly agent in the sky, scanning the lands of earth and especially that foulest of lands whose crimes had so reeked with their smoke to heaven.

'Hath the tribunal of destruction, which frameth mischief by statutes, fellowship with thee? They gather themselves together against the soul of the righteous, and condemn the innocent blood. But the Lord is become my stronghold, and my God the rock of my refuge. And he bringeth back upon them their own iniquity. O come, let us exult before the Lord. Let us shout for joy to the rock of our salvation,' Grunwald said. It was so extraordinarily apt he read it again, nodding to himself, and at the end almost did shout. He shouted as loud as his damaged larynx would let him. This was not loud. But he was deeply moved. He took his phylacteries off and kissed them and put them away, and went into the kitchen.

'So what's the matter with the gas?' he said.

Nothing seemed to be the matter with it at the moment. The coffee was steaming gently away. His wife wasn't even talking now. She was crossing and recrossing the kitchen in silent rage. She was a large handsome woman, high-coloured. She wasn't as handsome as she had been; overweight; all the time now altering her hair. What did she want with pink hair? But he understood her, he loved her.

'What can I help with the gas?' he said mildly. He picked up his *Ha'Aretz*. 'It's a job for a gasman. Get a man in and he'll do it. It won't cost a fortune.'

He went out to the balcony and took his morning breath of sea air till she came out with the tray.

'There is the pain in my breast again,' she said.

'It will go away,' Grunwald said.

'It won't go away. You think I'm imagining it?'

27

'Rivkin said it would go.'

'Rivkin should have it,' she said, slamming the tray down. 'Have I asked you for anything else?'

He could hear Miron breathing at the other side of the canvas. He had put up the canvas between the balconies so that he shouldn't have to see Miron. He nodded to the canvas. He said, 'We'll talk of it later. Another time.'

She sat down in the other chair and said intensely, 'Listen. It's the only thing I'll ask you. Everybody has an assistant. Why can't you have an assistant? I help in all sorts of ways. My passport is in order. If I'm crazy, indulge me. Can't you indulge me in one thing, to satisfy me?'

'Let me eat,' Grunwald said. He was already eating. He took cream cheese, olives, cucumber, radishes. He took a few strips of green pepper. 'I'll talk to Landsberg today,' he said.

She said furiously, 'Can't you understand? I'm not interested in Landsberg.'

'Landsberg's son-in-law', he said, buttering his rye bread, 'is without question one of the finest doctors in the world. He has told *them* how to do things. He's lectured to them in Germany. Where are you going to get better?'

'In this they're better. For some reason I'm sure of it. It's a wonderful opportunity. It may never happen again. If they can set my mind at rest, why can't you indulge me?'

'I want my black hat,' Grunwald said. 'Remember to look it out today.'

'What?'

'The round black hat. It will need cleaning. Take it in this morning.'

'Are you mad? They'll laugh at you. What do you want with that hat?'

'It should be somewhere under the shoes,' Grunwald said. 'In a bag. It will need a good clean-up.'

'It's green with age. It's mouldy!' she said. 'Where have they ever seen hats like that? In the Nazi papers they saw hats like that, in the cartoons. They'll shriek with laughter when they see it. You never wear it here, even.'

'I'll wear it there,' Grunwald said. 'If there's any coffee, I'll have it.'

But he didn't want it. He felt a sick excitement, a small pain almost, inside him. Suddenly he had no appetite. But it was breakfast-time, so he crunched a radish and looked over the headlines of *Ha' Aretz*. He didn't like excitement. He knew that he was slightly off-balance this morning. He had slept badly. The words 'And spit upon my Jewish gaberdine' swam into his mind. From where? Of course. He had been reading Shakespeare last night. He had been reading *The Merchant of Venice*. The words must have nested there in his mind all night long. *Hath the tribunal of destruction, which frameth mischief by statutes, fellowship with thee? . . . He bringeth back upon them their own iniquity . . .*

He felt very slightly dizzy, very slightly breathless. He stopped crunching for a moment and pressed the back of his hand against his shirt, but took it away again immediately. Rivkin had said quite specifically not to do this. He had said to leave it alone. It will go on ticking, Rivkin had said. He reached in his pocket and took a pill all the same. He swallowed the pill with the radish.

'Excuse me, good morning, Dr Grunwald,' Miron said.

'Good morning,' Grunwald said. He didn't look up from his paper.

'It's a beautiful day for a journey.' Miron's leathery tortoise face was peering round the canvas.

'Yes.'

'So today you are going to Munich.'

'No,' Grunwald said.

'You're not going to Munich?'

'Not today.'

'One day, another day. Dr Grunwald, if it wouldn't be an imposition, there's a small favour – well, for you small, for me big –'

'I handle no business while away,' Grunwald said.

'Certainly not. What business? It's my nephew, my sister Fegele's boy – perhaps you remember him – not that it matters,' Miron said hastily, as Grunwald immediately denied it. 'He's in Frankfurt – with a very small box, which weighs nothing, which he can deliver to your hotel – '

'I shall be in Munich no time at all. I shall be in and out of Munich,' Grunwald said.

'Wherever you are, he'll come. Fegele's boy,' Miron said.

'I'm afraid – '

'It would be a charity. When does he see a face from home? It would be a charity.'

'Excuse me,' Grunwald said. He went in the kitchen. 'I'll go now,' he said.

'Your coffee!'

'I won't take the coffee. I have to see Landsberg. I have an early appointment with Landsberg.'

'Not on my account. Don't trouble yourself.'

'It's the conference. I have to see Landsberg before the conference. I'll be home early. I'll be home very early this evening. And put out my old tallith – the oldest, the one I came with. I'll go to synagogue. Before a Journey,' he said.

'I want to talk to you.'

'We'll talk. It'll be all right,' he said. He kissed her. He patted her cheek. He kissed her pink hair. 'You'll see,' he said.

He didn't have to see Landsberg all that early. There was time to walk. He felt a little bit too dizzy to walk. He walked through to the bus stop in Dizengoff Street. There was a queue at the bus stop. He felt suddenly too dizzy even to stand. What was this? There was a chemist along the street. Should he go to the chemist? But a Sherut taxi came up then, and he took that instead. Five passengers were already sitting inside. He nodded to them and squeezed in.

He got out at Dizengoff Circus and felt better. His liver had needed a shaking-up, that was all. He walked to the Tel Aviv cinema in Pinsker Street, and round the back to the office block in Glickson Street. It was a good block. They'd had to buy, not rent, their offices in it. But it was a good investment, an excellent piece of real estate which he had strongly urged against Landsberg's disapproval. So who was the rash spender now? Any time they wanted to sell, they could get treble. This was the way to look after funds. It needed a feeling for

30

people and growth, and also for knowing when the time was right. There was always a right time for doing something.

Landsberg didn't have this feeling. He was a small-minded man. In his small-minded way he had crept into the general-directorship. Grunwald didn't grudge him it. Let him have his glory. With a brilliant son-in-law Landsberg needed the glory. He couldn't shame his son-in-law. Grunwald had nobody to shame. He had only his second wife, whom he would like to please. He would like to please her in her latest obsession. He didn't see how he could bring himself to. It was a piece of foolishness. She knew in her heart it was foolish, that some of the best doctors were here. Why not? Who had given German medicine its lustre? All the same, he would do it if it didn't somehow conflict with one of his basic rules: accept nothing from them that was not yours – no kindness, no favours, no services: nothing. It was one of the rules he had to keep, it was so basic. He had a small collection of such rules, assembled in a short column in his mind, as though from a scroll of the Law. They summed up certain standards that had to be preserved. He could always visualize the column quite clearly. It stood on the left, in the north-west corner of his mind. To the right of it was a straight vertical line. To the right of the line in black Hebrew lettering was a rabbinic aphorism he had come across one day in his reading: 'Let them kill you – but don't cross the line!' He quite often looked at the words standing in the north-western corner of his mind.

He unlocked the postbox in the foyer to see if he was the first in. He was the first in. The post had not been collected. He took it up in the lift with him to the fifth floor. It was a crowded building; advocates, tax consultants, patent agents, small film companies. Several directors of these small organizations were briskly unlocking their doors as he walked along the corridor. The small Perspex plate on his own door was inscribed:

KEREN HANEEMANNT LIKEHILOT DROM GERMANIA
(Süddeutsche Kultusgemeinden-Stiftung GmbH)

They had four rooms looking out on to Glickson Street, nice

rooms, very nice. He left the post on Mrs Katz's desk, and went through to his own office. He took off his hat and slipped on his yamulke. He had never served as a rabbi – he had gone right away into his legal studies, and later on to private practice – but he had received *semicha* from the Rav of Frankfurt, and was still a religious man. He liked to keep his head covered.

He had left late last night, and there were no new papers in his in-tray. He opened the safe and took out a photo-copy of the codicil, and then thought better of it, and took out the original instead. The members of the conference were entitled to see the original. It would be better if they didn't touch it. It was falling to pieces already, dirty, torn, much folded. It was perfectly visible through the plastic envelope. He got together the few other necessary papers and slipped them into a new cardboard folder. Something was missing. His recommendations were missing. This was strange. He had left the sheet in his out-tray for Mrs Katz to type and distribute, and Mrs Katz had gone before him. Who else could have come and taken his recommendations?

He knew who else could, and went through to Landsberg's office. His recommendations were now in Landsberg's out-tray. He saw through a faint mist of fury that Landsberg had amended them, in red ballpoint. This was surely too much. Landsberg didn't have the right! Or if he did – all right, technically, he *had* the right – who but a *mamser* of the first water would do it? He picked up the list and returned with it to his own office.

He felt a little palpitation under his shirt and he sat down to examine the amendments. Under the reference to his flight, Landsberg had inserted 'by tourist class'. Grunwald quietly burned. Why should he go any other way? Why should the conference members care which way he went? All Landsberg was showing was how the all-seeing eye looked after the funds.

There was something more serious. For 'removal of the sum deposited', Landsberg had written 'for liquidation of the account'. And Grunwald burned again, for he saw how Landsberg's mind worked here also. Landsberg was trying to force a position. He was trying to imply entitlement to something they might not be entitled to. He was trying to imply that the Bamberger family in England would trick them if they didn't watch out. Why should the Bambergers trick them? They were, like those the agency represented, survivors of a holocaust. What a fool! He thought that by making a statement he could bully others into believing it – put them on the defensive, undermine their position, put himself in a position to grant favours. There was here a neurotic drive for dominance, deriving from insecurity, that Grunwald feared and detested. The man thought like a German; it was exactly the way a German would think.

But nothing of the matters disturbing him showed on his small pale face with its neat clipped beard: not his fluttering heart, nor the tyranny of Landsberg, nor the journey he must make, nor the recurrent pain in his wife's breast. There was no sign even of the old disturbance – that he had nobody on whom to reflect glory or shame, that his blood had turned to dust.

He simply crossed out Landsberg's amendments and put the list back in his out-tray for Mrs Katz to copy and distribute. There were forms. There were meanings. One must never cross the line.

He was back early, as promised. He was quiet – quieter than usual. His wife saw it and made him a glass of tea. She said, 'So sit down,' when he started rooting about.

'Did you get the hat cleaned?'

'It's done.'

'Where is my old tallith?'

'It's out.'

'Good.' He sat quietly on the balcony and looked at the sea. He could see the Sheraton Hotel and the little Independence Park. He would take a short walk tonight before going to bed. He needed sleep tonight.

She brought him his tea on the balcony, and a glass for herself. She said, 'He forgets his prescription, even. He needs looking after like a child.'

'You got it?'

'Of course.'

'Ah.' He loved her. He could appreciate her virtues more than those of the wife of his youth. He was in some sense responsible for those earlier virtues, as for the defects. He had moulded them. He had not moulded these. They had come to him as strange qualities, with many strange contradictions. It had been a fascinating voyage of exploration for a man in his sixties; at times desolating, on the whole rewarding. They were in important ways alien still, partners only, with frontiers: how could it be otherwise? But both had lost a life, and been given another, unexpectedly. The best had to be made of it. For schematic reasons, Grunwald had tried to love his wife, and later found he could do so quite easily, for no reason at all.

'Also the syrup,' she said.

'Good.' He needed the syrup to lubricate his throat; he still woke up sometimes choking.

'What did you do for me?'

'Well,' he said. He'd wanted to get to this in his own time. He wasn't sure if it was the right time. 'I want you to look at these,' he said.

'What is it?'

'Cuttings from the German press.'

'I am not interested in Landsberg's son-in-law.'

'First read, then talk.'

'What difference what they say? What difference if they say he's the greatest genius in the world?'

'They say he's the greatest diagnostician. Read.'

He drank his tea while she read. Landsberg always kept a selection of cuttings in his office. No matter how bitter the atmosphere he was always ready to supply the cuttings.

'So?'

'I want Landsberg's son-in-law to see you.'

'I'm not interested.'

'If *he* thinks there is anything, and if there's the smallest chance of better treatment in Germany, whether with equipment, knowledge, whatever, you'll go. For the sake of health and life, you can go.'

He could see she was impressed, but she said, 'So why not

have done with the mishmash and go now? Even days are important.'

'To a failing person they're important. You're a strong healthy woman.'

'Mr Miron's sister-in-law was a strong healthy woman. He told me today. She was a strong healthy woman and today she lies in the Hadassah hospital with one breast.'

'Mr Miron, of course,' he said, 'together with all his relations, can go wherever – '

'Mr Miron is an intelligent man. He advises I should go.'

'Did Mr Miron tell you about his nephew with the box in Frankfurt?'

'What box? What nephew?'

'Mr Miron is an unprincipled pest!' he said. He was suddenly very angry. He couldn't tell if Miron was there. He couldn't hear him breathing. 'An unprincipled pest!' he said. 'He wants something smuggled back from Germany, that's why he thinks you should go. He knows I won't do it. Let him understand, you won't do it, either! I have no dealings there, I make no use of my time there, I will do nothing there that I have not absolutely got to do! Let him understand that. Let everybody understand it!'

'All right, all right. Don't get so hot,' she said.

He could see she was abashed at his sudden passion, and he knew she'd already settled for his proposition. He hadn't meant to get angry. He was simply exhausted. Landsberg had exhausted him.

'Was it such a bad day?'

'He wears me out, that man,' he said simply.

'Landsberg?'

'Stop him here, he comes out there. It's an attitude of mind. Well, he can't help it. Life has made Landsberg what he is,' Grunwald said. He didn't believe this. Landsberg was what he was because he was Landsberg. Plenty of people had shared Landsberg's experience without turning into Landsberg.

'Anything in particular?'

'Ach, it's all the time nonsense with him. It needs energy to cope with him. He's telegraphed already altering instructions to Amiron without telling me.'

'Who is Amiron?'

'In Switzerland. The Swiss-Israeli Bank there. They're doing some work for us. Before I get there with the certificate of probate from Munich they must enter a statement of particulars. But Landsberg meanwhile cables altering the particulars, which I then have to cable re-altering. . . . It's a long story, too complicated to go into.'

'So forget it. Don't give him the pleasure. All right, don't choke. I can come back for the glass,' she said. 'Rest.'

He rested, and thought over the day. It had not been a good day. On the whole it had been a bad day. But no day that brought nearer the related matters of *rachmanut* and his heart's desire could be altogether bad. He concluded it had not been altogether bad.

Later, he went out to the synagogue. He went with his oldest tallith, the one he had come with. He didn't normally put on a tallith for the evening service, but he put it on tonight. He put the prayer shawl over his head and said the Prayer Before a Journey.

'May it be thy will, O Lord our God and God of our fathers, to conduct us in peace,' Grunwald said, 'to direct our steps in peace, to uphold us in peace, and to lead us in life, joy and peace unto the haven of our desires.' He prayed to the end, and went into the Psalm Before a Journey.

'. . . Thou shalt not be afraid of the terror by night, nor of the arrow that flieth by day; of the pestilence that walketh in darkness, nor of the plague that ravageth at noonday. A thousand may fall at thy side, and ten thousand at thy right hand; it shall not come nigh unto thee . . .'

Thousands had fallen on either side of Grunwald; and it had not come nigh unto him. He did not see the working of Providence in this, and he didn't want to see it. He didn't want to feel that the Watcher of Israel had had any part in the things that he had seen, and in his mind was still deeply confused as to the role of the Watcher of Israel in these events. Sometimes he fell into a state of disbelief. But he had never lost belief in the conception of Israel, and found in the ancient affirmations of faith and trust something wholly admirable, and also, in the communal 'we', something that prescribed a part not totally without meaning for one whose blood had turned to dust.

Chapter 3

'A KISS FOR ALL THE WORLD'

HE was in such a fury that he passed one space without noticing, and then spotted it in his rear mirror and jammed on his brakes and reversed. He saw a little BMW nipping into it. It was a woman. He could see her hat. There were no manners any more. Nobody cared any more. It was all grab, to the devil with you; an entire order disintegrating, frightfulness. In his fury he had reversed right up alongside, and he leaned over and wound down the window.

'I was backing into this space. Couldn't you see me?'

'So sorry. I'm in a hurry.'

'I, too, am in a hurry!'

She'd come in nose first. The car was askew. She couldn't straighten it while he was alongside. Fine. He would stay alongside. He would give her a much-needed lesson in manners. She collected her bag and got out the other side. She got out and left the car askew. She had never meant to straighten it. It didn't bother her that it was askew! What was the *matter* with everybody? Was he the only one who noticed the rottenness? He was enraged, and at the same time frightened. He slammed the automatic gear into Drive again and cruised on down the Prinzregentenstrasse, past the unbroken line of parked cars, till he found space—not much of a space, too short perhaps for the big Mercedes. He didn't care any more. Why should he be the only one to care? He got the big fat backside of the car in. He sweated at the wheel. So it wouldn't go quite in. All right. Everybody did it, he would do it. To the devil with everything.

He got out and locked it, and hurried under the trees to the Haus der Kunst. Crowds were already there on the steps; very elegant in the warm evening. He adjusted his silk Cardin tie and smoothed down his beautiful silk mohair jacket, soothed a little by the sight. He was simply hot and bothered, and with work unfinished though he'd left late. Too late. She would be waiting on the steps. He walked up, through the crowds, looking for her. He went all round, from one entrance to another. He had said the main entrance. She knew which entrance. He could feel fury beginning to nag away at him again, spoiling the elegance for him. Why should everything be constantly spoiled for him? He decided he wouldn't worry any more, he wouldn't look further. Besides, they could be going about missing each other. He stationed himself beside a pillar at the main entrance, and lit himself a long mentholated cigarette. He knew some of the people; the best people were here, of course. He nodded and smiled, but took care not to become involved. With such a crowd one needed eyes in the back of one's head. She could come from any direction.

He looked at his watch. He had a little double vision. He had been working too hard. He wiped his glasses. Seven forty, for God's sake! Has she perhaps gone in already? But how could she go in? He had the tickets.

He went into the main entrance and saw the head commissionaire.

'Excuse me, I am looking for a lady. She hasn't a ticket.'

'Without a ticket she can't get in.'

'I have the tickets. I thought perhaps she might have had a word with you and decided to wait inside. My name is Haffner – Dr Haffner.'

'Without a ticket nobody can come in, Herr Doktor. It's not possible to wait inside without a ticket.'

Haffner saw sense in this, and was glad of the understandable and reliable man. He became at once calmer. 'Of course. With ladies one has to think of every possibility.'

'Ah! Ladies are not sticklers for rules, Herr Doktor. I'll keep an eye open for her. Be sure she won't get past me.'

'Good. I'll wait outside – immediately outside, by the pillar.'

And that's where he would wait, without budging, blessed order and arrangement falling on him like a benison. He had liked the cut of the fellow. Well, it was a fact – beneath all the nonsense and the swinishness, the solid structure of society remained intact, an inherent responsibility and decency in people. And now he could relax; and now feel guilt for the disorderly way he had left the car. He knew that the image of it, poking out there under the trees of the Englischer Garten, would prick at him all evening. He shouldn't have done it – a momentary aberration, a momentary lowering of standards. He could see all about him the faces of well-known citizens, some of them associates, even schoolfriends. He knew they would not have left their cars in this way, and this thought, too, brought solace – and, suddenly, powerful feelings of unworthiness that he should have done so himself, together with an appreciation of the basic decency in himself that caused such remorse. He felt a rush of love for all those he had blindly accused of rottenness. For no reason – or for the reason only that school faces had brought back school days – some lines of Schiller's swam into his mind.

Seid umschlungen, Millionen!
Diesen Kuss der ganzen Welt!

'You millions, I embrace you! This kiss is for all the world!'

He waited without budging till five minutes to eight, and nearly went out of his mind, and approached the commission-aire again. He had a fair enough idea now where his wife would be, but couldn't bring himself to suggest it to the up-holder of order. He said, 'My wife is obviously delayed. I'll go in myself now. Perhaps I may leave her ticket with you.'

'Perfectly in order, Herr Doktor. I'll keep a good look-out for the lady. Will you be in a particular room?'

'Just circulating.'

He went in and circulated, hating her. The rooms were crowded – but with the best people. It was the preview of the summer exhibition.

'How crowded it is, Herr Doktor!'

'Around you, Frau Generaldirektor. You are as beautiful as ever.'

'Ah, good evening, Haffner.'

'So good to see you, Herr Baron . . . Herr Geheimrat . . . Herr Professor . . .'

'I don't know why we stew in this scrum every year, Herr Doktor.'

'Because it's our duty, gnädige Frau,' Haffner said whimsically, kissing her hand.

It was all very nice, it was all quite delightful, except. . . . Suddenly he saw her, through a doorway, and froze. She was with somebody, a younger woman. She had her arm through the arm of the – wasn't it Elke? It was Elke. He saw at the other side of Elke a lock of greasy hair and something in a velvet jacket, and his stomach turned over. She had not brought the Hungarian monstrosity with her? No. Thank God, it wasn't him. It was some other monstrosity – with its arm, he noticed, linked through Elke's other arm, and thus, indirectly, with his wife. This was shameful, sickening. Where did the girl get this scum? How could she be attracted by it? What business had the invitation committee to let it in at all among polite society?

The situation was decidedly ticklish. He couldn't cold-shoulder his wife. She had no business putting him in such a situation. It was unlike her, totally unlike her. He saw that she had seen him, and walked over, his face stiff.

'I met Elke outside, Heinz, I'm sorry. I came in with them. Did you wait long?'

'No, no.' She was flashing him some sort of look that he was too enraged to interpret. He kissed her coldly, and then his daughter.

'This is Franz, Father, a friend of mine.'

'It rejoices me,' Haffner said formally, bowing stiffly. At least, the young swine had not attempted to shake hands with him. He was just nodding his greasy curls in a friendly manner.

'We're appraising Franz's pictures, Father. He painted these two. Give us your opinion.'

Haffner examined the pictures. As he might have expected!

40

'What do you call them?' In his rage he'd not even bought a catalogue. 'What are the names of the compositions?'

'Red,' the young swine said, smiling tolerantly. 'And black.'

'Yes. Very interesting.'

'It's apparently done with his hands,' Klara said. 'He applies the paint directly. And with a knife.'

'Indeed.' He'd noticed the extreme filthiness of the man's hands. He could smell him now, a smell of garlic and cheap brandy. His own lips felt unclean after kissing his daughter's cheek, imagining the other man's lips there. What else hadn't he done to her? It defeated him completely how the girl, so short a time before an angelic child of astounding delicacy and purity, could allow herself to be ravaged, probably twice a night, by this – he had been going to use the word *Unter-mensch*, and experienced the familiar recoil in the mind: *Untermensch*, sub-human, a word from former times. It had struck him right away that the fellow, like the one before him, was probably a Jew, too; but this thought also he did not allow to come to the surface of his mind.

He said abruptly, 'Well, there is a good deal to see. Perhaps we will see you later, Elke,' and nodded again briefly to her companion. He drew Klara firmly away.

'Must you do this to me?' he said softly through his teeth. He was shaking with rage.

'What else could I do? Did you want to meet him on the steps, a family group? Elke had her own ticket. He had an artist's ticket that admitted a guest. He invited me and I went. They'd only have waited with me otherwise. It that what you wanted?'

'All right!' There had been no word left for him with the commissionaire; merely an arrangement broken and nothing left in its place. He knew from whose blood came the careless wayward streak in Elke. Perhaps Klara would have gone the same way herself if he'd not married and taken her in hand early. The Viennese had so little fastidiousness. All the same, she was a credit to him. She always looked right, beautiful bones, a straight back, the intelligent look that so many of the Viennese women had. It had taken him no time in their marriage to learn that she was not intelligent at all, and had no backbone to speak of. Who had wanted to run all the time to the Party dignitaries' soirées, in former times? And to the Americans', in more recent times? Still, she was a credit to him, silk wrap, blue-rinsed hair, her diamonds. Her figure was good, legs good, a credit to him. And there was much to be said for her quick-wittedness in a social crisis. She had acted intelligently, according to her lights. He could feel his rage going, and once more thought of the car so badly placed under the trees of the Englischer Garten.

They joined this group, and that group, and looked at some hundreds of pictures. It was warm, very warm, but Haffner was enjoying himself and they stayed on later than the nine thirty they had already agreed. It was gone ten o'clock as they came out into the dark.

'I said we would go in for a drink to the Kelsdorffs.'

'I told you I had work. I have an hour or two to do in the study.'

'All right, it's not important. Trude was very pressing.'

'Well. For half an hour, perhaps,' he said. It wasn't simply the Kelsdorffs: it was the von Kelsdorffs. It pleased him that the women got on so well together. She was always a credit to him. 'When did you see Trude?'

'At the hairdresser's. It doesn't matter if you're busy.'

'For half an hour,' he said.

They stayed over an hour. It was getting on for midnight as he swung the big car into the plump and prosperous suburb of Bogenhausen across the river, and he was yawning.

'Who is it coming tomorrow? You said it wasn't Rupert.'

'He couldn't get away. It's Raison – you've met him.'

'The tall shy one who blushes?'

'Yes. It wasn't necessary to send anybody.'

He had a good idea why they were sending somebody. He had met Mrs Wolff of the Bamberger family in England. He had knocked himself out trying to be nice to her. She wasn't easy to be nice to. An unpleasant woman, distrustful. He thought of the hour or two's work he still had to do tonight to convince this woman that her affairs were in good hands.

'Do we have to have him to dinner?'

'No, no, he's going back in the afternoon.'

'I asked Elke in for Sunday. We see so little of her. She's thinner.'

'I don't want to talk about Elke now.'

'Her looks are going. We'll have to talk soon. I don't think she gets enough sleep.'

Haffner brooded unpleasantly on the probable reasons for this, but made no comment. He put the car away and kissed his wife good night, and went into the study. He poured himself a Scotch and opened his briefcase. Then he took his Grundig electronic notebook from the drawer and started immediately, as he always liked to do in business. 'Make this the first thing in the morning,' he said into it. 'Two copies only. Mark the top one Mr James Raison. Heading Bamberger Estates.' He switched off to collect his thoughts for a moment, and in the same moment heard it. He thought he heard it. He remained perfectly quiet. He heard it.

He got up and switched off the lights and softly opened the french windows. Out of the dark it came again, and then again, and then a beautiful, wonderful, unbelievable flood of it, falling like liquid grace from the pines. He was at Schonbach; fourteen; the spice of cones, and from heaven, from twenty metres:

He remained silent, trembling in the dark. Should he, tonight? He hardly dared tonight. It need interior purity; it needed a parabola of exultation, several parabolas, a declension of them, relating the tenses and the parts of 'I soar', 'I descend', 'I rest'; eyes full of skies, of night leaves.

He crept back in and went to the file and with his pen torch found the folder. *Lullula arborea arborea*, the woodlark. Several entries from Schonbach, 1913 to 1918; 1923 to 1933; then a gap and then three more, all Bogenhausen, all last week. He couldn't be mistaken. He checked the notation again. He checked the phonetics. Didloi didloi didloi tüttüttü-wiiuui diduli diduli diduli lululu-u dwüid dwüid dwüid pii-iiüu-ui. Not mistaken. Could it be tonight? With trembling fingers he felt for his reeds and warblers and assembled them and crept back.

The ripe and luscious notes of the bird still hung like black grapes in the garden. He controlled his shaking hands and the muscles of his mouth. 'Pii-iiüü-ui,' Haffner said to the woodlark. 'Didloi didloi didloi.'

The woodlark packed in.

'Diduli,' Haffner said. 'Diduli diduli. Tüttüttü-wiiuui.'

Not a peep out of the woodlark.

'Dwüid,' Haffner said in a panic. But he didn't say it again. The woodlark might go away. It was an incredible thing that it had come at all, here, to his garden in Bogenhausen; of all things, a woodlark! None of the birds answered him now, he didn't know why. He didn't care so very much. But a woodlark. Well. He was tired. There was strain. It needed purity. These things could be sensed. He didn't want it to go away. He went quietly back in and drew the curtains and switched the lights on and made the new entry. Then he gave himself another drink and got back to work.

He played over what he'd said on the Grundig and collected his thoughts again. It was a matter of how to put it. Whatever he said, the Wolff woman would see anti-semitism. If he said nothing it would be a dereliction of duty which she would also, in time, see. Well, it would have to be done. He had a drink and switched on again.

He said, 'One. Today's proceedings. The petition is being presented by Ansback, Levy, acting on behalf of S.K.S. GmbH. of Tel Aviv, Israel, whose executive officer, Herr Yonah Grunwald (a former practitioner at the Frankfurt bar) will be present in court. The petition is initially for a new Declaration of Death (*Todeserklärung*) – in English and German, please – of Herr Helmut Wolfgang Bamberger, as requested by the Swiss Fiscal Authority examining the assets in Switzerland of former Persecutees. The claim with regard to the assets

44

in Switzerland of the late Herr Helmut Wolfgang Bamberger was advanced in the first instance by S.K.S. GmbH. with our knowledge and approval, immediately on the formation of the Swiss Fiscal Authority, it being understood that claims from Israel would have priority.'

He switched off and took another drink. Damn the woman. Any other lawyer would get the point without explanations – no doubt Raison would – but this memo was only indirectly intended for Raison. The person it was intended for would need very careful explanations indeed. Damn her. He switched on again and had a shot at it.

'Two. Experience of claims of former. . . .' He switched off, ran back and re-recorded. 'Experience of restitution claims has shown that claimants frequently overstate. . . .' Damn her. What he meant was that very often they were crooked little swine who claimed far more than they had lost, they always put in for more than they were entitled to, everybody knew it, it was an attitude of mind. But this was no good, of course. He had another drink and tried again.

'The practice has grown up, in view of progressive legislation which has tended to increase claimants' entitlement, for lawyers acting on their behalf, to enlarge the area of claims in order to protect their clients' future interests. Our colleagues Ansbach, Levy – a firm that enjoys the highest repute at the Munich bar – are of course specialist restitution lawyers, and may be expected to present the type of case mentioned above, well understood in the German courts but less well understood perhaps in Switzerland where the case will no doubt later come to court. It will be necessary therefore to examine very closely *now* the exact nature of the claim which is being made – so far, for technical reasons, with our approval – against the estate of the late Herr Helmut Wolfgang Bamberger.'

He switched off and ran it back, listening carefully. It sounded all right. What could there be that was anti-semitic in that? And yet it made the point that these very specialist gentlemen had to be watched like hawks. Fine. Very good. Very delicate. He had another drink.

'Three. The evidence to be brought by the other side. . . .'

He switched off and ran back. '. . . to be brought by S.K.S. GmbH. consists of the document described as a codicil purporting to be a bequest by the late Herr Helmut Wolfgang Bamberger to the Hilfsverein der Juden in Süddeutschland, the South German Jewish Relief Fund (to which organization S.K.S. GmbH. is the legal successor) of one million Swiss francs. So far neither the Swiss Fiscal Authority nor S.K.S. GmbH. have supplied any information relating to the bank into which this sum was allegedly paid, whether a new account was started for it, or whether it was paid into an existing account.'

He switched off and got up and poured himself another Scotch, rather a large Scotch. He had had a few drinks this evening. He seemed to be needing one or two this evening. He lit a mentholated cigarette and collected his thoughts again. This was a tricky bit.

'Four. While for tactical reasons we have allowed. . . .' He ran back. His speech was becoming a little slurred, and he didn't like 'tactical'. 'While, for technical reasons, we have allowed S.K.S. GmbH. to proceed with the claim, it seems now necessary not to let them run away with it.' Was there anything wrong with that? He was becoming less able to detect if there was anything wrong with it. He paused a while to clear his mind, and while he was doing it, poured himself another drink. What was it he wanted to say? It was becoming something of an effort to clarify what he wanted to say. He'd better get the situation clear in his mind.

The situation was that nobody had even known of this money in Switzerland. Thousands of Germans had illegally kept money there during the Nazi régime. In the nature of things the deposits had been secret. When the depositors died, the secrets had mainly died with them. Even if surviving heirs had found out about the money, they couldn't get at it. Swiss banking procedure precluded the giving of information about accounts – even the admission that accounts existed.

It was only after years of protest, from Israel and elsewhere, that the Swiss government had set up the Fiscal Authority to examine claims. Then along had come this claim from Israel

46

with the photostat of the filthy bit of paper Bamberger was supposed to have signed, and Bamberger Estates had let them go ahead with it – why not? It would be years before all the claims could be dealt with, and those from Israel had priority. Meanwhile, the estate could acquire further information about the money, and before the Israelis laid hands on any of it, could perhaps take over the claim. It could at least put in its own claim. If Bamberger had laid aside this sum for a bequest, who knew what else he had laid aside in Switzerland?

There was another point. What was it, now? Ah, yes. *This* sum of money, the nature of the deposit. He'd better get it down. It was a little out of order in the memo, but he could tidy it in the morning. He switched on again.

'Paragraph. Inquiry will have to be made as to the nature of the deposit, whether payment was made into an investment or a deposit account. If into the former, the sum will certainly have multiplied several times. Our position in regard to it seems most insecure. Our contention would have to be that whoever is the rightful owner of the one million francs, all sums over and above would belong to Bamberger Estates. But the position is debatable, and to strengthen it my recommendation would be that application should be made on behalf of Bamberger Estates to liquidate the account in its entirety. This would put us in a position where those who have counter-claims would have to bring them to us ...'

His speech was very decidedly slurred, and his whisky had gone. He poured himself another, and sat back in his chair and admired for a moment the triptych of photographs at either end of the bookshelf: at one side his mother and father and Uncle Albrecht, at the other himself, Klara, Elke; a handsome collection. Elke had been fifteen, already so like her mother, good bones. Would Klara have gone like this if he hadn't taken her in hand, would Elke have gone some other way if somebody *had* taken her in hand? To such questions there were no answers. Personality was a mystery, the working-out of life a mystery. There in the photograph he could love her; and he loved her now in the photograph, a wonderful entity of eagerness and innocence, and felt his eyes grow misty. He took off his glasses and wiped them.

Who could say that this entity of the photograph was the creature he had met in the Haus der Kunst this evening, the thing that adored to be ravaged, probably twice a night, by the – by the, all right, *sub-human* with its greasy curls and insolent smile? They were not the same. Even physically, biologically, they were not the same. He'd read somewhere that the body cells renewed themselves every seven years. Every part of the body was renewed. No part of it was what it had been. It was not the same. It was something different. It was a different person.

This remarkable – he could almost say *inspired* – observation struck him suddenly with the force of revelation. It needed another drink. How true it was, how true on the metaphysical as well as the actual plane. *People were not the same.* Identity did not continue. What was true of one time was not true of another.

He knew he had to grasp this truth, had to hold on to the incredibly beautiful and mysterious perspective suddenly opened up to him. Through the chinks of everyday experience he had been vouchsafed a glimpse into the secret essence of things. What was it again? He focused on the photographs. Yes. People who acted in a certain way at one time could no longer be said to be the same people in some other time. Everything had changed. The context in which they had acted had changed. They themselves, every part of them, hands, ears, brains, had changed, evolved into something else. They were no longer the same people who had performed the actions.

It answered so much! It explained so many things in himself of which he was – not ashamed, but perturbed, uneasy; not so much things he'd done as things he ought to have done. He was judging by the standards of the being that he was today, instead of by the standards of that historical person he had been, of all those historical people. It explained the underlying contradiction of how one could reconcile the good decent people who were around with the horrifying things they had . . .

48

Well, it was a fact, terrible things had been done, barbarous things. The mind reeled at some of the things that had been done. It was totally impossible sometimes in a courtroom to accept that the ordinary decent-looking fellow in the dock had actually . . .

And of course he hadn't. *He* hadn't. Not that ordinary-looking fellow. His former self, of Former Times, had done them. This was the explanation – so blindingly clear suddenly. Of course, society had to take account of the actions of the former person. Laws had to be obeyed, even retrospective ones. Dual standards, untidiness, could not be permitted. The slate had to be wiped clean. Nobody understood this better than himself. Something had always driven him to action in this field. The slate had to be wiped clean! But he saw now with beautiful clarity that the whole thing was totally symbolic. Justice was being symbolically done to culprits who were themselves symbolic. It was logical therefore – he wondered why it had ever given him trouble; he took another drink while he wondered – it was logical that the punishment, too, should be symbolic.

It was not only logical, it was moving. The whole idea of society acting in this symbolic fashion through the judiciary moved him. It moved him so much he choked on his whisky, and had to replenish it a little. It occurred to him that he was probably getting drunk. He spilt whisky on the Grundig and realized he *was* drunk, quite drunk. Never mind. *In vino veritas*.

Something had been achieved tonight. He was experiencing a feeling of tremendous release that he was sure would last this time.

After all, decency survived! The urge to wipe clean the slate, to make recompense. And by God, they were doing it, the decent millions, in every factory, every shop, every home in the land, shouldering the burden of the past, paying and paying for what had been done – even those who had been babes in arms, even those who had not been born; through their work and their taxes making this massive act of expiation, un-exampled in history. What a giant sweeping of the slate was

49

this! He felt one with them, a pulse in their pulse, loving them, loving them all.

Seid umschlungen, Millionen!
Diesen Kuss der ganzen Welt!

'Heinz! What are you doing? It's gone half past two.'

It took him a moment or two, focusing dazedly, to see that his wife was there, in her maroon dressing-gown. The kiss for all the world sounded huskily in his ears. Had he said the words aloud?

'Notes. I am making . . . for tomorrow. . . . For today.' He was having some difficulty with his lips.

'Come. You'll be in no condition in the morning. You have to go to court.'

She slipped the Grundig in his briefcase while he levered himself up, and wiped the desk with her sleeve, and corked the bottle. Almost another full bottle gone, she noticed. She made a mental note to replace it. The whisky bills were getting exorbitant. They always became exorbitant when he had to work over former times.

'Give me your arm.'

'Quite capable getting upstairs self,' Haffner said.

And so he was, and so he did, climbing slowly and stiffly but with dignity; with his wife a prudent step behind in case he fell, and in her pocket a prudent hanky in case he cried.

Chapter 4

RELEVANT TO A DETERMINATION

RAISON got in just before eleven. Haffner met him with the Mercedes and they cruised back to town. There was still time before the court hearing so they made for Haffner's office in the Sendlingerstrasse.

They didn't talk much. Raison couldn't tell if some dignified kind of offence was being taken at his presence here on such fiddling business, or whether Haffner was merely ill. He was certainly looking distinctly bushed. The face was grey and flaccid, the eyes behind their flashing lenses shadowed and lacklustre. Raison told him how well he was looking.

'Ah, you're kind. It's nothing but work. How is Rupert?'

Raison told him Rupert was fine, too. They ran over the Ludwig bridge in flashing sunshine, and picked their way through the hooting traffic of the Tal.

Behind his desk, Haffner seemed to liven up a bit. He said, 'Today of course provides no complications. It's purely procedural. But I've done you a memo outlining further action that must be considered. The only change – it affects nothing – is that Ansbach is going out today for a more exact date of death. The Swiss asked for it. They do sometimes. They don't like this blanket date of 8 May, 1945.'

'Is it possible to get a more exact date of death?'

'Of course not. But Ansbach will get it. The court always helps in these cases. If the Swiss want it, they give it.'

'I see,' Raison said. He didn't really, but he looked over the memo, and drank his coffee when it came. Haffner seemed to be drinking bicarbonate instead of coffee. Raison couldn't see much in the memo that called for immediate action, but he read it through carefully, and said, 'Well, I'll take instructions on this as soon as we're finished today. I suppose we'd have to know the name of the bank, wouldn't we?'

'We don't have to. We can approach the Swiss without knowing it. But we are certainly in a weaker position if the other side knows it and we don't.'

'Have we asked them for it?'

'Asked Ansbach?' Haffner said, smiling.

'I see.'

'Quite,' Haffner said, drily. 'Besides, he almost certainly doesn't know. The Israelis are very close. They'll have one set of lawyers here, another in Switzerland. It's for sure they won't have told Ansbach.'

'You don't think it would be proper to ask them, then – the Israelis?'

'My dear Mr Raison,' Haffner said. He came over to him and slipped an arm round his shoulder. 'How nice to be an Englishman. I don't know if it's proper. One forgets such niceties. Let us say merely that I think it would be the most rewarding of approaches.'

'I expect you know best.'

'I expect I do,' Haffner said. 'It's a pity you're not staying. There are many things I could tell you. But we ought to go now.'

They went in a taxi, and got out and left it in a traffic jam at the Stachus and continued on foot to the lawcourts at the corner of the Prielmayerstrasse. They were still quite early, but not as early as Dr Ansbach and his client. Haffner introduced Ansbach, and Ansbach introduced his client. Raison wasn't quite prepared for the client, or for his medieval-type rabbi's hat. He wasn't sure whether to shake the hand or kiss it, and Grunwald's perfunctory gesture in extending it gave little hint. Haffner found himself in no such difficulty. He pumped the hand with great warmth and expressed sincere pleasure in welcoming an Israeli colleague to Germany. He said he understood that Dr Grunwald had once practised before the bar at Frankfurt. Grunwald said huskily that this was quite correct. He had practised for fifteen years before the bar at Frankfurt. He had been banned from it in 1938. Then they went into court.

The business was indeed so purely procedural that Raison felt some embarrassment, sitting beside the lawyer who could have handled it standing on his head. Haffner showed great punctiliousness in explaining every point to him, but there was little enough to explain. As soon as the preliminaries were over, the restitution specialist Ansbach merely got up and read out appropriate sections from the statute, showing that the court had jurisdiction to do what he requested. His reedy voice and the words themselves seemed not unfamiliar to the judge who neither looked at him nor listened to them. He appeared to be going back and forward through his diary, filling it up.

'Section 176, subsection 1 . . . shall ascertain all facts relevant to the determination and take all the necessary evidence.

'Subsection 2. If owing to the position in which the claimant has been placed by NS terror acts any fact cannot be fully proved . . . may consider the fact as established in favour of the claimant.

'Section 180, subsection 1. Should a persecutee have had his last known abode in territories . . .'

Haffner said quietly, 'He's not to be judged on this kind of performance. He's really quite good.'

'He's certainly done this before!'

'Of course. He takes only the bigger cases. To his credit he doesn't work on a contingency basis. With him it is strictly fees.'

'. . . and should his whereabouts since May 1945 be unknown it shall be presumed that he died on 8 May, 1945, unless some other date of death has already been established under the law governing presumption of death . . .

'Subsection 2. Subject to the provisions of subsection 1 a date other than May 1945 may be declared to be the date of death if in the circumstances of any particular case and without further investigation being required another date of death appears to be probable. If it pleases the court!' Ansbach said, dropping the statute and hitching his gown. 'I ask for a declaration of death other than 8 May 1945, in the case of Helmut Wolfgang Bamberger deceased. The successors of the deceased Bamberger associate themselves with the application.'

The judge looked up for a moment. Haffner made a slow bob and said that this was so.

'Is there an existing declaration of death?' the judge said.

Ansbach said there was, and handed it in. The judge read it very carefully.

'What are the grounds for amending the declaration?'

Ansbach got up again, hitching his gown, and gave the grounds. He said that the deceased Helmut Wolfgang Bamberger, banker, had had his last known abode in Prague, Czechoslovakia, at the time of the establishment of the German Protectorate in March 1939. Since that date there had been no news of him. The rolls of Prominent Jews had been examined. (He explained parenthetically that the category of Prominent Jew had been officially introduced in 1942 to provide a reserve for exchange against prominent Germans interned abroad.)

The rolls of the exchange camps of Theresien-stadt and Belsen-Bergen had also been examined. Bamberger's name appeared on no known list of any camp, or any transport, or any other form of organized detention. He belonged to that numerous class of person, to be numbered by the hundred thousand, the manner and date of whose death had gone unrecorded.

What he would like the court to consider, Ansbach said, was that the banker Bamberger was not only locally prominent. He was widely known in financial circles in many countries. He was exactly the material to be held as an exchange Jew. If his name could not be found on the lists of 1942, the supposition must be that it was because he no longer existed in 1942. However, he was not asking for so early a date. As the court knew, the most notorious NS terror acts dated from 1943. He would be happy with a date of 31 December 1943.

The judge raised an eyebrow at Haffner. Haffner said that he would be happy with a date of 31 December 1943 too.

'Very well. The date of death of Helmut Wolfgang Bamberger is declared to be 31 December 1943.'

A couple of minutes later Ansbach and Haffner were discussing the probate certificate with the clerk of the court, and Raison was hovering in the doorway, wondering whether to stay in court or go into the ante-room. He decided on the ante-room.

'Excuse me.' He turned at the English words, huskily uttered. Grunwald still had his hat on. He had retained it throughout the proceedings. 'You're Mr Raison, the English attorney?'

'That's right.'

'I was confused. Your German is very good. I thought you were another . . .' He seemed to want to shake hands again. Raison obliged and found his hand wrung a good deal more warmly. 'So how is Mrs Wolff?' Grunwald said.

'Fine, I believe. I don't see much of her, you know,' Raison said.

'I think there's a good chance we can get this over with quickly. It's possible it can be agreed in Zurich today.'

'*Today?*'

'I hope so. I'm making a call in an hour to our attorneys there. They'll call me back to let me know if I should go right away with the new *Todeserklärung*.'

'I see,' Raison said, shaken.

'It's not convenient?'

'It's unexpected.'

'I organized it so I wouldn't have to stay away from home long. I'm an old man,' Grunwald said, grinning. It was not an unattractive grin. The husky voice, like that of some aged and confiding Rastus, was not without appeal either. He looked like a clever old ape under the enormous hat.

'What's the trouble – you want to make an application yourself at the same time?'

'Well, I don't know,' Raison said. 'You've caught me on the hop a bit. I'd better ring up and find out.'

'All right. I'll contact you. Where are you staying?'

'I'm not staying anywhere. I'm going back this afternoon.'

'Oh. That's a pity. It's a pity,' Grunwald said. 'What time do you go?'

'Just after three.'

'Is it possible to put it off an hour or two? Is it possible to wait, say, till five? I'll certainly have information by then.'

Raison thought about it. He thought about Hilda, and Haffner, and his memo, and Mrs Wolff.

'I wouldn't want to do anything without Mrs Wolff's knowledge,' the old man said. 'I wouldn't want to prejudice any claim she might have. Is there any way I can help?'

'I don't know,' Raison said. 'I'm not sure if we've actually got the name of the bank,' he said.

'The name of the bank? It's the Handelsbank Lindt.'

Raison looked at him. He got his diary out and wrote it down. 'Handelsbank Lindt,' he said. 'That's in Zurich, is it?'

'The Handelsbank Lindt of Zurich. Anything else?'

'There was a question whether it was paid into an investment or a deposit account.'

'An investment account.'

'Are you sure?'

'Of course I'm sure. I paid it in.'

'You did?'

'I did.'

'When?'

'In 1939.'

'I see,' Raison said. But he paused before writing it down.

'I went in February 1939 to Switzerland,' the old man said, nodding to the diary, 'and paid one million Swiss francs into an investment account in the Handelsbank Lindt on the instructions of Herr Bamberger. Then I went back to Germany.'

'Well, thanks. That's enough to be going on with,' Raison said.

'So if I can ask you a question. Did the matter of whether it was an investment or a deposit account arise in England or here?'

'It arose here.'

'So now I understand everything,' Grunwald said. 'Where can I contact you?'

'I expect I'll be with Dr Haffner.'

'Ah. So here you are,' Haffner said, coming briskly in at this moment, spectacles agleam. 'I think we should go to lunch. I am afraid, Dr Grunwald, we are in a very great hurry. Mr Raison is catching a plane at three o'clock.'

Raison brought him up to date.

Haffner took off his glasses and wiped them very quickly. He said, 'Of course we wish to help. Of course. But this is so sudden.'

'Yes,' Raison said.

'It's very sudden. I would say it's impossible.'

'I'd thought of calling Rupert.'

'Of course it's for you to say. But I would say it's impossible.'

'I'll have to let you know then,' Raison said to Grunwald.

'Good.'

'But in my opinion it's impossible,' Haffner said.

'Bon appetit,' Grunwald said.

Raison called Gunter from Haffner's office, and Gunter thought he ought to stay with it. 'If it's only till five,' Gunter said.

'That's what I thought.'

'Is the idea for you to go to Zurich, too?'

'I suppose it is.'

'Well, it isn't very far, is it?'

'No, not very far.'

'Is something on your mind, James? Is something worrying you?'

'I don't know, Rupert. We aren't disputing the codicil, are we?'

'What do you mean?'

'It seems the money was paid into an investment account and it's multiplied.'

'Oh.'

'Do we have a view about it?'

'I don't know,' Gunter said. 'What does Heinz think?'

'He thinks we ought to have a view.'

'I'll phone Mrs Wolff, then.'

'All right, I'll call you at five.'

He went and had lunch with Haffner. Haffner didn't eat much, but he expressed his view. Haffner's secretary altered Raison's flight.

Grunwald called before five. He said, 'Dr Amiron, our attorney in Zurich, thinks it might be best to wait until to-morrow.'

'What's the position now?'

'He has given them the new particulars of the *Todeserklärung* that I gave him on the phone. They want to look into certain items, the changed date and so forth. He doesn't expect any trouble.'

'Is that what you're going to do, then?'

'I don't know,' Grunwald said. 'For myself I don't travel on Saturday. I couldn't very well ask you to stay over till Monday, could I?'

'No,' Raison said.

'So perhaps I would travel on Saturday. In a case of emergency,' Grunwald said.

'Is it your idea I should travel with you?'

'It would be a great help if you were there to agree the settlement. Also, of course, it would expedite your own claim if you are making one. Are you?'

'I'm taking instructions on it from London. I'll be telephoning in a few minutes.'

'Good. Then let me know,' Grunwald said.

Raison telephoned London. Gunter said Mrs Wolff didn't have a view. She thought Raison was in a better position to have a view. She wanted consulting as soon as he'd formulated it. She also wanted him to stick close to the Israelis while the claim was being pressed, and she wanted her own claim pressing while the issue was warm. She didn't want anything done without her approval.

'Of course I pointed out to her that nothing was going to be done over the week-end,' Gunter said. 'It won't be, will it?'

'It might,' Raison said. 'The Swiss work on Saturday. So do the Israelis. In case of emergency.'

'Oh. What do you want to do, then?'

'I don't know,' Raison said, irritably. People seemed to be asking him that all day. What had started out as a straightforward chore had become suddenly one of wearing complications. It was Gunter's chore anyway. 'What would you do?' he said sharply.

'I suppose stay over, unless it's very inconvenient.'

'Hm.'

'Would you like me to phone Hilda?'

'She isn't at home today, Rupert.'

'If there's anything I *can* do, James.'

'I'll let you know, Rupert.'

He rang the nursing home. The operator didn't put him through to Hilda. She put him through to the doctor The doctor said, 'Ah, Mr Raison. I'm glad you called. We've been having a little bit of bother today. Has your wife been mentioning Skokholm lately?'

'Stockholm?'

'The island of Skokholm.'

'Oh. Yes,' Raison said. His heart sank.

'I'm afraid there was a little argument over her clothes this morning. She wanted to get dressed to go there. She said you knew about it and were meeting her. It was half past six this morning.'

'I see,' Raison said.

'She's under sedation now. She hasn't really been much on the surface of late.'

'How long are you keeping her sedated?'

'Oh, I think for a day or two,' the doctor said. 'I really think so. I think it would be a good thing if you telephoned before coming to see her.'

'All right,' Raison said.

He called Grunwald and told him he'd be staying.

'For instance, if I asked you what jewellery your mother had, would you be able to tell me?' Haffner said.

'Well, let me see,' Raison said. 'I'd have to think.'

'Think as long as you like. I can guarantee you wouldn't. Yet they can. Sworn statements, often with drawings, in the finest detail, stating weights, carats, niceties of design. . . . I assure you, it's a problem we have to live with. It's an attitude of mind. I'm not saying it's the Jewish people only. They have the most claims, naturally. But there are others. In the city of Danzig, for instance, there were claims for more property, for more dwellings even, than there had ever been in Danzig.'

'Please take cheese,' Frau Haffner said. 'I'm afraid it's been what you call pot luck.'

'It's been delicious,' Raison said. 'I'll just enjoy the cigar and brandy.' He was wondering when he could decently go. Old Heinz tended to swarm over one at close quarters. The pale-blue eyes behind the flashing lenses had been glittering at him for over three hours now; a lot of Heinz after a long day.

'Let me put it this way,' Haffner said. 'The machinery is here, the funds have been voted, *everybody wants to help*. But the law has another function. It must protect the people from the openhandedness of their legislators. It must see that people are not taken for a ride. Who likes to be taken for a ride? We see it every day in the courts.'

'Yes. I suppose it's natural enough for people who have

survived to feel they're owed something, though,' Raison said mildly.

'Of course. And we understand it. But here is something else. Who are the people who survive? It isn't always the nicest people who survive. There is a technique of survival. Crooks, cheats, frauds – these are the kind of people best able to survive. I don't say all! Of course, we're talking now quite frankly. I wouldn't talk in this way to everybody. And nobody was more anti-Nazi than I – it's a matter of record,' he said impatiently. 'But when I'm presented with a bill for damages I'm entitled to see that it adds up. I could tell you stories – '

'Mr Raison is tired of these stories,' his wife said. 'Isn't there anything pleasanter to talk about?'

'Just before we finish,' Haffner said. 'Don't think it's simply from our end. The Jewish restitution people are also very indignant. There is an enormous amount of unprofessionalism about. Amateurs involve themselves – crooks. I believe in Israel they even stop people in the streets – in the summer when they can see the concentration camp tattoos on bare arms. All kinds of fraudulent claims are fabricated, for property never owned, earnings never lost, even death benefits for people who never died.'

'How can you claim death benefit without a death?'

'How did Ansbach get his Todeserklärung today? What evidence is there that Bamberger ever died?' Haffner said gaily. 'Death has got to be presumed. There is a "probable causal nexus", in the words of the Act. The Nazis weren't so thorough. Thousands of names weren't recorded of people in camps or transports. When one of these amateurs finds one, it's a birthday! Maybe the person is a little deranged and has never claimed, maybe he's under-claimed. Maybe there's a son whose father died peacefully somewhere. Whatever it is, it's like striking oil. Death benefits, confiscation of capital, loss of breadwinner, loss of property. Or supposing a whole family perished, and you can falsely pin their identities on to others – it could be even better. For the "survivors", loss of education rights, loss of career, loss of economic advancement.

'. . . You see, it's a fantastic law, a beautiful piece of liberal and humane legislation, and any crook who puts his mind to it can milk it.'

'Heinz, please. No more now,' Frau Haffner said. 'Didn't you have enough last night?'

'I was up late,' Haffner said sheepishly. 'Working on the memo.'

'Ah, yes. Thanks,' Raison said. He didn't want to talk about the memo. Haffner had been a bit put out at the revelation with regard to the Handelsbank Lindt. He suspected a trick. Raison didn't want to talk about that, either. He was beginning to see what Mrs Wolff might have in mind about old Heinz. He said, 'I don't suppose there'll be any difficulty in getting a flight to Zurich tomorrow, will there?'

'No, no. There are frequent flights to Zurich.'

'Such a nice town,' Frau Haffner said.

They talked about Zurich till Raison was able to go. They'd asked him to stay, earlier, but he'd refused and Haffner had pulled strings to get him into the Ludwigshof; not easy with accommodation so hard to find in the crowded town.

He went at eleven, with a new toothbrush from Frau Haffner, and loaned pyjamas from her husband.

'I don't know why you wanted to talk in that way to him,' Frau Haffner said, when Heinz got back with the car. 'He'll think you are anti-Jewish.'

'Anti-Jewish? I?' Haffner said, astonished. 'What are you talking about? My principal client is Jewish.'

'Perhaps you ought to remember it. He represents her directly, remember. You've never talked to Rupert in this way.'

This was true, Haffner reflected. The occasion had never arisen. But there was something about Raison, a directness, an understanding honesty, a decency, that made him want to open his heart to him. They understood each other. He doubted if Klara would understand, so he merely poured himself a nightcap and shook his head. She understood nothing.

'You understand nothing,' he said. 'It was professional talk.'

'He was quick enough to change the conversation from the professional talk, anyway.'

61

'You're mad,' Haffner said.

But it made him angry, thinking about it. To accuse him of anti-semitism – him! – when she had been the one to run after the Nazi dignitaries, when he'd not even joined the Organization of Nazi Lawyers, at grave injury to his career. . . . It was typical of the Viennese, changeable as fashion, jumping on each new bandwagon. One had to look elsewhere for stability, decency.

But it was still on his mind in bed. Could it be said that he was anti-Jewish – *was* he anti-Jewish? It was preposterous. Of all people – he? It's honour, Uncle, he said to Uncle Albrecht. You know with me it's only a question of honour. In the latter days of nineteen eighteen he had had many discussions with Uncle Albrecht on the question of honour. Uncle Albrecht had been on leave from his defeated regiment, and at that grim period never nobler. The Bolshevik revolution had broken out in Munich, so Uncle Albrecht had taken them all to the cottage, his cottage. There in the woods they talked about honour, and Uncle Albrecht had given him his pistol. 'With your father sick, it's you I have to rely on, Heinzl,' Uncle Albrecht had said. 'Look after your mother, and if the swine come – see you take a few with you before attending to yourself and to her. This is the only guarantee of honour, Heinzl!' Uncle Albrecht had found his own field of honour in a small alley off the Theatinerstrasse in the course of a dispute with the soldiers' soviet, before the year's end. Haffner's mother had been left with the cottage, and Haffner himself with the Mauser. He had buried it, in a lead-lined box, and over the years had sometimes thought of it, on occasion with longing. But he'd never dug it up. It was still there, beneath the spice of cones. He thought of it now, and of the subject that had brought it to mind, and moved restlessly in the bed. 'You're mad,' he said with finality to his wife, and turned over.

Raison slept badly in his strange bed at the Ludwigshof, and was up early. He had arranged to telephone Grunwald at nine o'clock; the Israeli was staying with his lawyer, Ansbach. They hoped to be off by eleven. Raison had his breakfast and took a walk around the Max-Josef Platz, pleasurably sniffing the morning air. The square had been newly hosed down and was glittering in the early sun. He got back to the hotel in nice time, and was surprised to find Ansbach waiting at the desk.

He said, 'Good morning.'

'Good morning.'

'Is Dr Grunwald with you?'

'Dr Grunwald has gone to synagogue.'

'Ah.'

'I hope you slept well,' Ansbach said politely.

'Beautifully, thanks. Does that mean we won't be going this morning?' Raison said, registering.

'I don't know if there will be any need to go at all,' Ansbach said. 'I think we should go and sit down.'

Raison followed him, mystified.

'Tell me, Mr Raison,' Ansbach said, when they were seated in the lounge, 'how long ago was it that the claim for Herr Bamberger was settled here in Germany?'

'Oh, a long time ago, about nineteen fifty-eight. There were various subsidiary claims, of course. The whole thing was finally settled by nineteen sixty.'

'It must have been a large claim.'

'Enormous.'

'Property, investments, cash.'

'Yes. Very large. Why?'

'Yes,' Ansbach said. 'It's a problem. The Swiss say he isn't dead.'

PART TWO

Should the persecutee belong to a group of persons whom the N S German Government or the N S D A P intended to exclude in its entirety from the cultural or economic life of Germany, it shall be presumed that the loss of or damage to his property was occasioned by N S terror acts.

German Federal Indemnification Law
(*Bundesentschädigungsgesetz*)

Chapter 1

A PERFECTIBLE OLD SOUL

GRUNWALD was conscious, with a corner of his mind, of the curious glances as he walked slowly back from the synagogue through the Munich streets in the brilliant midday sunshine. He was wearing his round black hat and his long black sabbath coat with the silk-faced lapels. He would have liked to carry his tallith bag also, with its large embroidered shield of David, but he didn't carry anything on the sabbath.

Nothing changed here. He was mildly surprised at how little had changed, the same faces all around. Already, a number of the animals were weaving about on the pavements, the beer halls open. He remembered them. He remembered. But he was remembering with only a corner of his mind. A more recent impression was stamped there, the words of Isaiah that he had just recited from the lectern. He had been called up, as a visitor, to recite the prophetical portion for the week, and since it was the sabbath of the new moon, the portion had been that relevant one:

> And it shall come to pass,
> That from one new moon to another,
> And from one sabbath to another,
> Shall all flesh come to worship before me,
> Saith the Lord.

Grunwald's crippled voice had been less audible than ever as he recited the ancient words. He was deeply moved to be reciting at all in this place of desolation. But the words that remained most strongly were the further words of Isaiah. God, the ventriloquist, speaking through his prophet, had said:

> I will bring their fears upon them;
> Because when I called none did answer;
> When I spoke they did not hear,
> But they did that which was evil in mine eyes,
> And chose that in which I delighted not.

For years, the banker Bamberger had not heard, had not listened, had not wanted to know. The banker Bamberger was a German gentleman, only technically a Jew. He was an acquaintance even of 'Treue Heinrich', Faithful Harry, the whey-faced Himmler himself.

The Reichsführer SS had even given him a herbal remedy for his indigestion: he was one of his 'decent Jews'. So what had happened to this decent Jew, the German gentleman? What shameful things had he had to do to buy his life?

When he'd heard it from Amiron on the phone, the first thing in the morning, Grunwald had been shocked but not surprised, in the way that when electric terminals are held and a handle wound – and terminals had been held to Grunwald and a handle wound – one will receive a shock but no surprise. Too much had happened to Grunwald for him to be surprised by anything. But in the moment of hearing Amiron's voice on the telephone, he had had an instant picture of Bamberger as he had seen him last, in evening dress, impatient, striding briskly into the long rococo drawing-room above the offices in the Hauptwachstrasse in Bamberg; into the rococo room where Grunwald sat on the edge of the sofa. He'd come in sniffing. He'd said, 'What the devil?' And then, 'Come, Grunwald. You're always such a sad dog. I expected to find you swinging from the chandeliers. Did something go wrong?'

Nothing had gone wrong; Grunwald was merely very tired. But he saw he was addressing the confident German gentleman again; it had been a Jew last time, the only reason he had got the money. What had brought about the change in Bamberger, and why the evening dress? Was he going out to some function, a function to be graced by Nazi dignitaries? Had somebody told him he had nothing to worry about, that decent fellows like him would be looked after? Had Treue Heinrich given him another remedy, or some other token of his esteem? What?

Grunwald didn't know. He hadn't known then, and he didn't now; but he wondered just a little, seeing in his mind the man walking into the room of thirty years before. What had he done, Bamberger? What shameful things? He had heard stories before, of souls sick of themselves, of life. There was the man in Frankfurt, found there not so long ago, the janitor in the large residential block that he had owned. What had made this man bury himself so, shunning surviving relatives, shunning mankind? He had been found there, stoking the boiler, doing the most menial jobs in the large property he had once owned, a religious recluse, sick of his life, but frightened to take it. What shameful things was this man expiating? How many lives had gone to save his own, that was now so hateful to him?

There were stories, plenty of stories. Why not? The strain had been intolerable. Was it such a surprise that people should break under the strain? They were ordinary flesh and blood, not martyrs. God didn't expect all to be martyrs; had not made all to be martyrs. The soul was perfectible, and here, God knew, it had been given its chance; and for the more worldly, as ever, it had been more difficult. Nobody should point the finger. Here one should mourn, at another humiliation, another funeral of the human spirit. Thinking of this, Grunwald looked instinctively into the north-western corner of his mind, and saw the words standing black to the right of the line there, and knew again that there was reason for him, that was not invalidated by dust.

A drunken man with a peaked cap began to walk round him. The man had stopped in the street, gaping at him, and now began to circle him like a dog. Grunwald walked slowly on, paying no attention, but two students ran suddenly across the road and grasped the man, who fought them, swearing. A policeman standing on the corner came to the disturbance and Grunwald had to stop while it was investigated. He said nothing at all to any of them, until forced to, and then kept his answers brief. The policeman had been taking down the students' excited statement.

He said, 'Please come to the station, mein Herr, to charge the man.'

'No,' Grunwald said.

'But an example must be made,' the students urged him. 'Please do it.'

'No,' Grunwald said.

'He insulted you.'

'Not me,' Grunwald said. 'He didn't insult me,' and walked on, suddenly more cheerful. He had remembered a story. He had an urge, for some reason, to tell the story to the Englishman, Raison. So briefly encountered, why did he trust him?

'What is so remarkable,' he said, walking into the apartment and exchanging his hat for a skullcap, 'is the shortness of memory. How can you explain it?' Raison was there, he noticed without surprise, and he nodded to him. 'It's truly remarkable,' he said. Frau Ansbach helped him off with his coat and asked if he would have a glass of tea. He said he would have a glass of tea. 'You have a family,' he said, seating himself, 'that for some hundreds of years has been knocked down by ruffians. For some *hundreds* of years, by basically the same set of ruffians. What do they learn? What do they remember? I've been puzzling over it. I suppose I knew Bamberger reasonably well. It still puzzles me.'

Raison and Ansbach had been puzzling over more practical matters and looked at him glumly. Ansbach said, 'I've made an appointment at the Ministry of the Interior for Monday. They keep on file there all entries from the east, particularly Czechoslovakia. It seems that he came in between '45 and '47.'

'Why here?' Grunwald said. 'He could be anywhere. He could have gone any time.'

'He could have,' Ansbach said, 'but he didn't. I spoke further with Amiron. Bamberger worked the account from Prague up till 1945, and since 1947 from Germany.'

'So,' Grunwald said. He wasn't surprised. He, too, expected Bamberger to be in Germany, but he doubted if there would be anything in the Ministry of the Interior files. The man in Frankfurt had not been found under his own name. But the question held for him at the moment only marginal interest.

He said, 'Since the seventeenth century they were knocked about by these people, and yet they trusted them. They were surrounded as if by a pack of wolves, and yet they thought nothing would happen to them. It defeats all intelligence,' Grunwald said. He took his glass of tea and stirred it.

'They were the bankers,' he said to Raison, 'of the bishops of Bamberg – originally moneylenders, goldsmiths. They spread throughout the old empire, Vienna, Prague, Budapest. In every *one* of those towns they were plundered, murdered, in almost every generation. In the winter of 1920, I remember, his uncle and two cousins went to visit the Budapest office. In the Hungarian forest outside Kecsemet, the train was held up by a gang of patriots, quite a famous gang – Lieutenant Hejjas's Group, it was called. They took seventy-two Jews off the train, marched them through the snow into the trees and shot them, including the three Bambergers. Were there any arrests? Did the Bambergers make a fuss? Did they even close down the Budapest office? It defeats intelligence,' he repeated. He felt unaccountably gay. He remembered he had a story to tell Raison.

Before he could tell it, Raison, sandy eyelashes blinking slowly from one to the other, said, 'Why is everybody accepting that the man must be alive? Isn't it possible that somebody else is working his account?'

'No,' Grunwald said.

'Why isn't it possible?'

'It's a numbered account.'

'Numbers can be got for numbered accounts.'

'They can be got,' Grunwald said. 'It wouldn't do anybody any good. The number is only one aspect of a numbered account. The Handelsbank Lindt is a private family bank, with the most careful procedures. If they say he is alive, he is alive. There are financial and administrative reasons for this, which we can discuss when the sabbath is over. For the time being just accept that it's hard to believe the Handelsbank Lindt could be wrong.'

'It is easier to believe a man like Bamberger could simply hide himself away for twenty years?'

'There have been cases,' Grunwald said.

'Restitution cases?'

'No, no.'

'What?'

'Sometimes people did things that weren't so good.'

'Criminal things?'

71

Grunwald smiled. 'Between a sin and a crime there's a difference, and it's true a man will often try to conceal both. But from whom, ultimately, are you concealing a sin?'

'I'm not sure I understand,' Raison said.

'All the same, I've got hopes of you,' Grunwald told him cheerfully.

Raison stayed for lunch. Grunwald didn't eat any lunch. He ate grapes and drank water, and afterwards went to the synagogue again. Ansbach said, 'That's all he's done since he's been here – gone to the synagogue and eaten fruit. I'm afraid we don't keep a kosher household.'

'Isn't kosher food obtainable in Munich?'

'It's obtainable. But he wouldn't trust our pans or dishes. I doubt if he'd trust the kosher food, either,' Ansbach said, grinning.

'What about getting his own pots and pans?'

'Why not? But we can't suggest it, and he's too polite. We thought he would only stay overnight, at the most. It's a problem.'

Grunwald returned from the synagogue, and Raison went out for a walk with him. 'Tell me,' Grunwald said, 'how are they treating you in your hotel?'

'Fine.'

'We can take a walk in that direction.'

They walked to the Ludwigshof.

'Yes. I remember it,' Grunwald said, looking up at the hotel. 'What kind of a room have they given you?'

'Not bad.'

'I'd like to take a rest. Perhaps I can rest in your room for a while.'

'Of course.'

They went up to the room, and Grunwald examined it very carefully. 'So many cupboards,' he said. 'One could keep pots and pans in such cupboards.'

'I haven't any pots and pans to put in them.'

'All the same it's useful.'

After his rest he said, 'You know, I think I also will take a room here.'

'I don't think they've got a room.'

'We can see.'

They saw an assistant manager, who seemed hypnotized by Grunwald's sabbath dress. They saw the manager, who was just as hypnotized. It took the manager twenty minutes to work out if Grunwald could have a room. 'It will take a little shifting about,' he said, perspiring, and apologizing for the delay. 'But it will give us great pleasure to accommodate you, Herr Doktor. The room will be available tonight. It will be available next to Herr Raison.'

'You see,' Grunwald said, out in the street again, 'there's a fashion in Jews. Sometimes we're in, sometimes we're out. At the moment we're in. But the fashion can change. There's only one thing that doesn't change.'

'What's that?'

'At last,' Grunwald said, 'a subject suitable for the sabbath.'

He didn't move in till the sabbath was out, and it was late. Raison helped him unpack. 'I don't know if you saw this,' Grunwald said.

'What is it?'

It was a photostat of the codicil. It showed a copy of a crumpled sheet of paper, handwritten. It said, 'The investment made on 12 February 1939 into the below-mentioned account will become the property of the Hilfsverein der Juden in Süddeutschland in the event of the death of the account holder.'

There was no 'below-mentioned account'.

'The bottom's torn off,' Raison said.

'Yes. It's kept separately.'

'The top as well.'

'It showed the Bamberg Rider.'

'The what?'

'The bank's crest. It was on the notepaper. It identified Bamberger with the note so he tore if off.'

'What is the Bamberg Rider?'

Grunwald looked at him. 'It's a statue,' he said, 'the finest equestrian piece of the German Middle Ages. It stands in Bamberg Cathedral.'

'It's a knight, is it?

'Nobody knows – it's one of the mysteries of the Gothic past. If it's a knight, he carries no armour. If it's a prince – he wears a coronet – his clothes are poor. In my day a body of opinion thought he was Gawan – Knight Gawan of the legend.'

'Which legend?'

'Alas for German culture,' Grunwald said. 'Who knows about it except a few old leftovers from the concentration camps? It's a poem by Wolfram von Eschenback.' In a husky voice suitably modulated for medieval German poetry he began to recite:

> *'Ihn quält doch Schmerz,*
> *Seit Minn' ihm zwang sein Ritterherz.'*

'What does that mean?' Raison said.

'It's usually translated:

> "Tortured by pain,
> Love forced his knight's heart on again."'

'It's that kind of poem, is it?'

'Oh, yes. Very German. The hero does impossible things because he's told to. He doesn't ask questions. He does them and dies. He's the archetypal German hero, Gawan. I think we can say his propagandist is also the archetypal German propagandist. Where else would you find a poet so immediately calling attention to and demanding pity for the sufferings of the hero?

> "*Wen nicht bewegt sein Kummer gross,*
> *Der lass' es sein.*"
> "Who is not moved by his great grief,
> Let him be."

Perhaps you've heard the tone of voice before?'

'How did he come by his grief?'

'He was told to go into an impossible torrent. He went in and drowned.'

'Is that all?'

'What did you want him to do? Kill a dragon? Rescue a maiden? He did what he was told, which is even better. People get the folk heroes they want.'

74

'What about Bamberger?' Raison said, looking at the photostat.

But Grunwald didn't want to talk about Bamberger then. He was tired and he went to bed. The minute he was in bed he got on the train again. The same last night, at Ansbach's.

Chapter 2

WINTER JOURNEY

HE was tired when he got in it. He'd done a full day's work and had been up half the previous night. He didn't seem able to find enough time these days. He didn't seem able to stay away from trains. He fell asleep in his overcoat almost as soon as he was in it, columns of figures dancing before his eyes.

Somewhere about Erfurt he was woken up for his ticket. He panicked. He couldn't remember buying the ticket. He began to look through his pockets, in his coat, his jacket, his waistcoat, and then remembered the committee had got him the ticket, and it would be in his briefcase with the papers. He gave a quick mollifying smile to the inspector as he searched, but the fellow nodded calmingly; an old railway worker, a decent soul, thank God. He could have had his hat knocked off at the least by one of the other sort by now. He stayed awake after that.

It was snowing in Berlin. He looked for a taxi in the dirty dawn light. A couple of the drivers looked at his beard and told him to take his filth elsewhere. The third charged him double but dropped him at Schonfeld's. He had a schnapps with Schonfeld before his breakfast. The conversation at breakfast was not so cheering. Who expected it to be cheering? He was so exhausted he could have gone to sleep in his chair, but there was a tight schedule for this morning. By nine o'clock they were out again, on the way to Eppstein's office at the Vereinigung.

It was still snowing outside, and Eppstein gave them coffee when they arrived. He noticed a few of the familiar faces – Cohn, Meyer – and some not so familiar. The old Reichsvertretung, the National Association of Jewish Organizations, had been dissolved in the summer. (It had more or less had to be dissolved. Its whole object, to combat anti-semitism, was in conflict with official Party policy, and hence with the State.) The government had set up a new body, the Vereinigung. Most of the old people were still on it, but fresh blood had been brought in, and its object was now a State object: the *settlement* of Jewish affairs.

Grunwald knew this meeting of the emigration panel had been called to accommodate him. His appointment with the government man, Müller, was for eleven o'clock. He could hardly keep his eyes open all the same.

'So what's new in Frankfurt?' Eppstein asked as they drank their coffee.

'New reclamations!' Grunwald said. 'I've handled ninety this week so far.' (Never mind this week, he thought; what about the twenty-odd he'd done just last night? Last night? No, the one before, his timing out, as usual when travelling.) Whenever they pulled in a new bunch to the camps, it was a matter of negotiating the reclamation fees; 'fines'. With a little give and take on both sides, you could have a man out in a week. Lately there hadn't been too much give and take. Every time now there seemed to be somebody new to deal with, who hadn't the faintest knowledge of past agreements or of the factors that had to be taken into account, who was either simply amused by the whole negotiation or enraged by it.

'Well,' Eppstein said, 'you know what we have here.'

'It's no secret.'

It wasn't. The Nazi papers were full of it. Eleven weeks before there'd been, in the newspaper phrase, *Kristallnacht* – the night of the broken glass; the largest and most thorough pogrom that had ever taken place in Berlin. Every Jewish business had been broken open, every pane of glass smashed, every synagogue burnt down. To round the whole thing off, an extra twenty thousand Jews had been pulled in for corrective treatment. Yes, everybody had his little reclamation problems.

'So let's start,' Eppstein said.

They sat round the table and got out their pens and pads. Eppstein said, 'Before we begin,' and paused a moment, brushing the secretary's hand away from the minute book, '. . . it's best to say a few words about Herr Müller, a stranger, I believe, to Dr Grunwald?'

Grunwald nodded.

'To say the best first, he's businesslike, an admirer of Herr Eichmann, whom you've met, of course.'

'On the latest occasion only last week,' Grunwald said with a smile. 'In Vienna.'

'So it's unnecessary to state he approves of his methods. In fact I may say – we've not been officially informed yet, but it's reliable – Vienna is to be the model for the system here in Germany. Our problems with regard to *Vorzeigegeld* thus assume the first importance. But as regards Müller, remember that while he holds high S S rank – much higher than Eichmann – he has only recently been seconded to this office and is as yet by no means expert in the Jewish question. In dealings with him it would be unwise to assume the latitude that one finds with Eichmann.'

Grunwald smiled a little ironically to himself. There was not so much latitude in Eichmann either, these days. He'd seen him a week ago in his new headquarters, the Rothschild Palais. Eichmann had set up an enormous desk in the huge ground-floor room. He hadn't asked Grunwald to sit down. He'd kept him standing there. And when Grunwald had inadvertently addressed him as 'Untersturmführer' he thought the man would hit him. 'Hauptsturmführer!' he'd shouted, pointing to his chevrons. 'I do my homework, imbecile – see that you do yours!' The promotion that had come since Grunwald had seen him last had not brought further latitude.

Grunwald pulled himself together with a jerk. He was drifting off, eyes closing.

'. . . unlike Herr Eichmann, has a background as a senior police officer,' Eppstein was saying. 'From Bavaria. A shrewd and intelligent and, we think, a fair man. All the same, in matters touching on the *Vorzeigegeld* it would be wise to bear in mind . . .'

It was so hot in here, the central heating turned up in the freezing morning. The air was thick with cigar and cigarette smoke, electric light reflecting dully off bald heads. He could hardly keep his eyes open, but he forced himself to write on his pad the information it was necessary for him to know. He didn't mention Bamberger when Any Other Business came up. There was no need for them to know about Bamberger. He thought he'd got all the points he had to remember. If anything wasn't clear he could ask Schonfeld when he got outside.

It had stopped snowing outside, and the brisk wind livened him up a bit. It woke in him a sudden attack of nerves. It was always a bowel-loosening business going to the Prinz Albrecht-strasse. Who knew how long one would be there, or where one might find oneself by the evening? He lit himself a cigarette in Schonfeld's car, but his mouth was foul and he threw it away, half smoked, into the freezing street.

Schonfeld dropped him at the corner of the Prinz Albrecht-strasse, and pressed his hand in silent encouragement, and he got out and walked the rest of the way, stumbling on the ice-lumped pavement. He was there in good time, a quarter to eleven. He took a deep breath and approached the SS men stamping their feet outside. They examined his letter and motioned him in. In Eichmann's day he had been able to go right to the office, but now it was a matter of an escort on every floor. He remembered the exalted SS rank that Eppstein had mentioned. The heating was turned up and the institutional smell, of beeswax and ink, was strong as he walked, mouth dry and heart beating, along the corridors with his booted escort. The place shone. In every corner Party sweats spit-and-polished, turning to look sourly at him as he trudged in his crumpled clothes. His palms were damp.

'Wait here,' his escort said curtly, and left him, in an ante-room. He didn't sit down. One didn't sit down here, unless invited. He didn't move about, either. He'd taken his hat off on entering the building, and he felt furtively on his head and flattened the little skullcap that he kept pinned to his hair. A zealous SS man had knocked that off, too, one day when it had been too visible. He could hear voices from the inner room, and laughter.

A sudden terrifying thought struck him. How did one address Müller? He'd forgotten to ask. He was no longer in the police. He couldn't call him by his name. What was his official rank? Every thought flew out of his head. He stood there licking his lips, frantically trying to think what it could possibly be.

The inner door opened and two men came out, still laughing and shaking hands, one of them in uniform. Something about the other, the broken German, the cast of the lean tanned face, made him say quietly, '*Sholom Aleichem.*' If wrong, neither would notice. But he wasn't wrong. The man turned to him, smiling. '*Sholom Aleichem!*' he said warmly, wringing his hand. A Palestinian, a Zionist. They had been in and out of here even in Eichmann's day, not having to go through the Jewish committee, going direct and making their own arrangements with the regime. Eichmann had been very specific that they shouldn't go through the Jewish committee. Their business was concerned with getting Jews out of Germany and into Palestine, which meant hoodwinking the quota-governing British and smuggling them in. To go through the Jewish committee, even to have too close contact with it, was to risk a leakage to the British. The Palestinians were taken freely wherever they wanted to go, to whichever camp they wanted to go, to select their own material.

With only one thought in his head, Grunwald said in Hebrew, 'Tell me, how do you address him, what's his rank? – Don't mention his name.'

'His rank? God knows. I call him by his name and he calls me by mine.'

'What's he like?'

'What should he be like? He's a misbegotten fascist whore,' the Palestinian said, turning to smile warmly at the man, 'who should never know a moment's peace. But he wants Jews out of Germany, and so do I, *Chaver*. Keep your spirits up.'

A couple of minutes later, Grunwald was inside with Müller. He was a solid, square-looking man with a pair of watchful eyes. He didn't shake hands with Grunwald, but he nodded to a chair.

Grunwald sat, gratefully. The words 'Herr Direktor' immediately flashed into his mind. Of course! What could be wrong with that?

Müller was looking at a file card.

He said, 'Johanne Zadik Grunwald. What's the Zadik, Grunwald?'

'A family name, Herr Direktor. It means "righteous".'

'In Hebrew?'

'In Hebrew, Herr Direktor.'

'Born Frankfurt 1893. You've been a righteous Hebrew for forty-six years, Grunwald.'

Grunwald didn't know how to answer this, so he nodded.

'*Rabbi* Grunwald, I see. Also Doctor of Laws.'

'That is so, Herr Direktor.'

'Hm. Well, my predecessor seems to have had a high opinion of you. I hope you had as high an opinion of him.'

'The Herr Hauptsturmführer was always very helpful,' Grunwald said.

Müller's eyebrows went up and his eyes became somewhat more watchful and amused.

'You keep very much up to date in the matter of rank, Herr Rabbi.'

'I was with the Herr Hauptsturmführer in Vienna last week,' Grunwald said.

'For what reason?'

'They have been having some trouble with the reclamation procedure. It's essential for the new emigration methods that it should work smoothly, Herr Direktor.'

'Ah, yes. You had a chance to study the new methods, did you?'

'Yes, indeed, Herr Direktor.'

'And they won your approval?'

His approval! Eichmann had moved like the wind in Vienna. Since the Anschluss not quite a year ago his job had been to get Austria *judenrein* – Jew-clean; forced emigration of the whole community. It had been a major job. Under the Austrian officials, worse in many ways than the German, the emigration procedure had been senselessly difficult. Each one of the multitude of ministries that had to be visited, scattered all over the town, had issued a date-stamped clearance certificate valid for only a short period. Delays with legions of minor officials had meant that long before the last certificate could be obtained, the first had run out, and the whole procedure had to be started again. Eichmann's method had been to assemble officials from each of the ministries into one building, and to re-design the operation 'on the assembly-line principle'. An Austrian Jew would go in at one end, to emerge at the other a stateless one, fully certificated, but with all his property duly made over to the responsible authorities, apart from his *Vorzeigegeld* – the sum of money in dollars or sterling required by the immigration authorities of whichever country had agreed to allow him in.

'The system works efficiently,' Grunwald said neutrally.

'Good. Because we're going to have it here,' Müller said. 'Cast your eye over this.'

He opened a cardboard file and handed over a sheet of paper. It was a copy of a memo, with a ticked distribution list, signed with the scrawled initials 'R.H.' – Reynhardt Heydrich. Grunwald's eyes went confusedly over the words.

. . . problem not one of the rich Jews, but how we get rid of the Jewish mob. For this . . . necessary to investigate thoroughly the whole machinery of so-called *Vorzeigegeld*, in particular the fiddle they are carrying on among themselves with regard to the dollar rate . . . problem of foreign currency must be tackled with energy, and to this end radical and drastic . . . for your recommendations, which must reach me within seven days, by 16 February 1939. Heil Hitler!

'Everything clear?'

'Quite clear, Herr Direktor.'

'To business, then. What's the state of the float at the moment?'

Grunwald handed over Eppstein's report on the state of the dollar float. Müller read it briefly, and blankly. 'It's ridiculous,' he said. 'It's totally ridiculous. What the hell are you doing with the money?'

'Herr Direktor, our expenses are enormously increased –'

'It's to be applied solely for *Vorzeigegeld*.'

'We need money to operate. There's a constant drain on the funds, to pay reclamation, to pay –'

'Your rich brethren can pay their own reclamation.'

'Not all, Herr Direktor. Not all of them can. Those that can, do. In addition we charge them –'

'What's this funny rate for dollars? What's the rate at the moment?'

Grunwald looked over his figures. 'Fourteen fifty,' he said. The official rate was 4·20 Reichsmarks to the dollar. To enable poorer families to acquire their *Vorzeigegeld* cheaply, or at no cost, a premium had to be placed on it for the richer ones.

'Increase it.'

Grunwald cleared his throat. He said, 'Herr Direktor, if the problem of reclamation money could be eased in some way, it would be possible to pay more for *Vorzeigegeld*. As it is, with the continual drain –'

Müller grunted and made a note on his pad. He said, 'All right, let's get on. What new funds are coming?'

'With your permission, Herr Direktor, I am going now to Zurich, to the Joint.'

'To get how much?'

'I hope a quarter of a million dollars.'

Müller looked under his elbow, at a sheet of paper headed *American Joint Distribution Committee*. He said, 'It was only a quarter of a million last time.'

'It's a charitable institution, Herr Direktor. They can only hand over money in relation to –'

'I don't think you understand, Grunwald, "Radical" and "drastic" were the terms used. This needs a new effort, a totally different scale of thinking. When the Vienna system starts here, I am going to have to shift several thousand Jews a week. The Reich can't spare foreign currency for the problem. It's a Jewish problem, and the Jews themselves must take responsibility for it. What about Jewish bank accounts abroad?'

Grunwald didn't say anything.

'Jewish bank accounts abroad,' Müller said. He looked up.

Under the long overcoat, Grunwald could feel his knees begin to knock. He pressed the brim of his hat down on them. 'I don't know of any,' he said.

'I wasn't born yesterday, Grunwald.'

'No, Herr Direktor.'

'You know it's a hanging matter.'

'Everybody knows.'

'What if I offered an amnesty?'

'I don't know.'

Müller looked at him a moment longer. He said, 'Well, sound your people out. I expect word from them by tomorrow. Foreign currency has got to be raised! If they're frightened, I wouldn't need names. A procedure could be devised. It's a practical way for them to help each other. And I promise that all sums would be applied for *Vorzeigegeld.*'

'I'll put the proposal,' Grunwald said, with relief. He'd thought for a moment . . .

'The response must be positive. I expect a quite positive response,' Müller said. He picked up a pen and wrote. 'Very well, Grunwald. Take this down to the visa section. You can go. But I expect to see you immediately on your return. A solution must be found to the Jewish problem.'

'It must be,' Grunwald said.

A couple of hours later he was on the train again.

It was snowing the whole length of Germany. He changed trains. Sometimes the new carriage was heated, and sometimes it wasn't, so that he'd wake to find himself sweating or shivering. Outside, the blind country and the suffocated pines whirled away into greyness and blackness, and then to pallid grey again, steadying from time to time into steam-shrouded halts: Leipzig and Weissenfels, Eisenach and Bebra. He got out and he got in, suitcase and valise, and huddled down again. Fulda and Gemünden, Würzburg and Lauda . . . Osterburken and Heilbronn, Stuttgart and Horb . . .

He had lost so much sleep lately he could no longer re-member what it was like to stretch out between sheets in a bed. He was quite numb, and answered simple wants as they arose. When his mouth was specially foul he would go to the toilet and rinse it out at the tap. When he felt empty he had a sandwich. Frau Schonfeld had made him up a packet. In the last few months you couldn't rely on them letting you in the dining-car.

Some time before the frontier, his neck stiff from the chill air around the window, he thought he'd better straighten himself up. His feet had been perspiring in the last heated carriage, but were now merely damply cold. He took a pair of socks and his toilet bag out of his case and went to the toilet. He washed his feet with cold water in the icy swaying compart-ment and put on the fresh socks, and then gave his face a lick and brushed his teeth and felt better. But in his newly refreshed state he was able to sleep again, and he was asleep as they pulled in to the frontier. A blizzard was blowing there. He stood dazed and chilled in the draughty hall as they went through his luggage. They went through it with a fine-tooth-comb, despite his SS papers. But there was nothing there, nothing there shouldn't be. In half an hour he was on the train again, in Switzerland.

He was so stunned with fatigue he felt none of the familiar liberation. He got to Zurich at five in the morning and took a cab to the Bellerive. The Joint had booked him a room there. He got undressed and went to sleep. Sleep lay before him like an enormous unploughed field. He got three and a half hours in then. Lauterpacht called for him at nine. He had breakfast with Lauterpacht in his room, and then had a bath and went to the Joint. He stayed there all day. He had his lunch there. He fell asleep in the conference after lunch, so they adjourned for a while and he got another hour in. He'd asked Lauterpacht in the morning to get in touch with Löwe, Bamberger's agent, and when they resumed work again, somebody told him Löwe had turned up and was waiting for him in another room. When the session ended he went to see him.

Löwe was an old man, a garrulous old man, whom Grunwald knew. But he didn't waste time now. He said, 'I'm afraid I must tell you, Herr Grunwald, that things are now quite difficult. The banks are no longer dealing with third parties for German accounts.'

Grunwald's head was singing, but a certain ashen competence had set in; he was perfectly able to cope with facts; he felt he could limitlessly cope with them. But the facts had to be straight; they had to be capable of immediate interpretation, so that immediate decisions could be taken on them.

He said, 'We can do it, or we can't?'

'We can do it, but –'

'Have you arranged a bank?'

'The Handelsbank Lindt.'

'Can they explain the complications to me?'

'Of course.'

'Let's go.'

They used the Joint car and the driver ran around for a while on Löwe's instructions. 'We have to take precautions,' he said. 'There are people who know you're here.' Grunwald let him work it out himself. He sat with his eyes closed.

The Handelsbank Lindt had the advantage of being away from the Bahnhofstrasse, where the main banks were situated. It was small, even intimate. It was certainly somewhat grubby. It sat in what looked like a large private house, with only a small brass plate to show it was a bank at all. The two partners were elderly. Löwe introduced him to one of them, a Lindt, a plump and amiable little greyhead with sharp eyes, who after some minutes' conversation asked if Löwe would leave them together.

'It's not, of course, that I suspect Herr Löwe, an old and valued friend,' Lindt said in his sing-song Switzerdeutsch. 'On the other hand, there are rules now about these things. Our banking association in Zurich has had to bring in quite strict regulations. All interviews with Germans must be conducted on an individual basis, to avoid any possibility of pressure. I will explain the situation to you, Herr Grunwald.'

Grunwald set himself to absorb it. His neck was still stiff, and he held his head a little to one side as he listened. The economics branch of the SS had a very active staff at the moment in Zurich, the old man said. They had lists of German citizens suspected of having accounts there, and for some time they had been going about trying to deposit small sums in these accounts. Through inefficiency, or unwariness, or bribery, they had had some small success, and the money had been accepted for the accounts. Of course, very shortly afterwards the accounts had been liquidated. Some banks had then brought in a rule that only the depositor himself, and in person, could effect any movement with the account. But the SS had then taken to bringing the depositors from Germany and walking them into the banks. This placed the banks, naturally, in a very great difficulty. The depositor was obviously acting under pressure. For him, everything was up if the bank acted in accordance with his instructions: the mere operation of the account was a capital offence, and it was painful in the extreme for a bank thus to place one of its customers under the death sentence. But perhaps the customer had a wife and family in Germany, who were similarly under pressure, and it would go hard for them if the bank refused to act on instructions. Either way, the dilemma was impossible. So the association had now brought in the most strict regulations: no instructions could be taken unless the customer himself, and quite freely, advised the bank of his wishes. If he arrived in person he had to be interviewed alone; if his instructions came by some other means, the bank had to be quite certain they were voluntarily from him. Only in the most extreme cases could the bank deal with an intermediary, and in all cases confirmation had to come independently from the customer.

Grunwald listened very carefully. He said, 'Tell me, Herr Lindt, how you wish Herr Bamberger to confirm the instructions.'

'Ah, we go too fast, Herr Grunwald. There are other things first. There is the question of the money. What can you tell me about the money?'

'I can't tell you anything about it, Herr Lindt. It's Herr Bamberger's money.'

'The money's here in Switzerland, I understand.'

'It's here in the form of bills and drafts.'

'Is Herr Bamberger quite certain it can't be traced?'

'Herr Lindt – it's his head.'

'On the other hand, if the money is due to him or to his company, one would expect a record of it somewhere.'

'I'm no expert on these things, Herr Lindt. Herr Löwe is the expert.'

'On the other hand, it's you I am dealing with, and not Herr Löwe. It could be very painful if something went wrong. You see the difficulty?'

Grunwald didn't know what to say. He'd never been able to convince anybody – he didn't think he'd convinced the Joint. They saw inconvenience, unfairness, ill treatment. They couldn't tell what it was like. He said, 'We must assume Herr Bamberger knows the risk.'

The old man mused a moment.

He said, 'Is the intention to place the money on deposit, or for investment?'

'For investment.'

'On the other hand, we wouldn't be able to advise on the course of the investments.'

'Herr Bamberger relies on your judgement.'

'When would it be possible to see him?'

'I don't know,' Grunwald said. 'He can only travel to where he's given a visa. He won't be given a visa for Switzerland. That's why I'm here.'

'I'll tell you what we'll do, Herr Grunwald,' Lindt said. 'We'll ask you to sign documents. We will then give you a number, which will be the number of the account. You must give this number to Herr Bamberger, and he will send a copy of it back to us, written out fully in his own handwriting. The number will be his bank signature, and we'll accept it as confirmation. Alternatively, he can incorporate it into a normal business letter to Herr Löwe, or he can add it as a postscript. If Herr Löwe is not to know the number, then he can also add other numbers. But the number must appear whole, in words, in his own handwriting. Until we get it, the money will not be in account with us. If we don't hear by, say, three or four months, we'll return the money to Herr Löwe. How does this seem to you?'

Grunwald had been so busy stuffing the details in his mind that he hadn't bothered to evaluate them. He couldn't be bothered now. His head was singing. But he said they sounded feasible, and a few minutes later was back in the car.

'Tell me, Herr Grunwald,' Löwe said in a low voice, 'is the Joint able to provide the finance you require?'

'They do what they can. Enormous amounts are required.'

'It is scandalous. It's a monstrous illegality,' the old man said. 'A government expecting charitable organizations to provide foreign currency for its own citizens to go abroad. It's unbelievable.'

'Yes,' Grunwald said.

'It's hard to know what to accept these days. One hears such wild things. Tell me, is it true Jews can no longer go into the clubs?'

'Yes.'

'Or to the Bourse – can that be true?'

'Yes,' Grunwald said. Suddenly, on top of everything, he felt like weeping. It came on him from time to time, the feeling that he was among simple-minded idiots, who couldn't, or wouldn't understand. Clubs, bourses!

'People, of course, must cooperate with governments, but I'm surprised that officers and members of institutions allow such things,' the old man said. 'It is quite surprising. But Germans always do what they're told – if you will forgive me, Herr Grunwald.'

'I forgive you,' Grunwald said.

'You know, Herr Grunwald, I've lived a long time and I've seen many things,' Löwe said. 'Believe me, it isn't always good to do as one is told. Quiet resistance often works wonders. If these hotheads can take over your businesses cheaply and at the same time get you to provide foreign currency from organizations abroad, of course they want you to go. Don't work so hard at the foreign currency. Let them work at it. They would soon see the difficulties. They would soon blow themselves out.'

'Yes,' Grunwald said. He was sitting with his eyes closed. He knew he mustn't go to sleep now.

'After all, what can they do if you decide to stay – put you all in prison – you see?'

'Yes.'

'Cast a spell upon you – make you all disappear in a cloud of smoke? You see?'

'Yes.'

'They're after all human beings. There's a saying, "Nothing's so hot when you eat it as when it's being cooked." Everything in the end cools down, believe me. We're living now in a time of tremendous political excitement. Everywhere people are saying and doing things that they don't mean. Only the other night I was taking a walk when a party of young men rushed out of a meeting and nearly knocked me over. When I protested they said I should look where I was going. *I* should look! You see? We never had this before. It's infectious. But they grow out of it. We have to remember they're simply people, with mothers worrying about them, and with uncles and aunts and brothers and sisters. Yours is after all a great country, Herr Grunwald, of seventy million people, mostly good, like all others. It's not an island of savages. We have got to look beyond the newspapers and the speeches and remember that. Believe me, nothing very terrible will happen if you stay where you are.'

'What time will you call for me in the morning?' Grunwald said.

'It depends naturally on Herr Lindt and the documents.'

'I have to catch a train before noon,' Grunwald said. 'I have to see Herr Bamberger in the evening.' He didn't actually have to, but he was afraid that if a night intervened, if normal sleep intervened, he would forget the number. He knew he couldn't write the number down.

'Then I'd better let him know. Then I'd better go back now. I will tell them it's quite urgent. But as for you, Herr Grunwald,' Löwe said, 'if you don't mind my saying so, you are obviously quite tired. I think you should go right to bed.'

'Yes,' Grunwald said. The car stopped at the Bellerive and

he got out and went to bed. He got an hour in bed and then Lauterpacht came up with the transcript of the morning's proceedings, and everything started again. He had time for a meal in his room before they went to the Joint. He knew it was going to be a long evening, so he took a little brandy to fortify himself, and ate a couple of hard-boiled eggs and left the fruit. He was having trouble with his stomach and thought it wise to leave the fruit.

The first session started at half past eight and went on till half past ten. Then he got his feet up for an hour, and went into the next session at half past eleven. This session was with delegates from the Alliance Israélite Universelle, who had travelled by train from Geneva to confer with him. They'd wanted to confer the following morning, but he'd had to decline that.

'Why can't you stay over for another day?' Lauterpacht had asked.

He couldn't seem to explain to anybody. He couldn't seem to get through. *Because there isn't any time*, he wanted to scream. There was simply not enough time. From here he had to go to see Müller. He had to go to Berlin to see Müller. Then Bamberg. Then Frankfurt. Hours flying past, precious days and nights, while he trundled over the face of Europe. And every minute, work piling up for him in Frankfurt. Again the columns of figures swam into his mind, reclamation computations, reference numbers of past agreements, the faces of wives, hoarse commands across parade grounds. He should be there now. He should be attending to it this very minute.

'Because, let's say,' he'd said, 'it goes easier in continuous session.' And it went not too badly. He thought he could go on more or less indefinitely. But some time after two he had to go to the lavatory, and he fell asleep there. Lauterpacht came and got him out, and they decided to end the session then. The delegates said they could take it up first thing in the morning, and work on as long as was convenient to Grunwald. And first thing in the morning they did. Grunwald felt himself sharp as a needle after his five incredible hours of deathlike sleep. But his stomach was still uneasy. A doctor delegate gave him tablets and told him not to eat or drink. But the tablets seemed to make him both hungry and thirsty, and to cover the pangs he smoked more, soon regaining the foul mouth of the day before.

Löwe called for him at ten and he made his farewells and left immediately, with his bags. Twenty minutes later he was sitting with Lindt again.

Lindt explained everything to him very carefully, and he listened carefully.

'This is the number, Herr Grunwald. I've written the number down for you. It's a very simple number. It's a special number, so that you can remember it.'

Grunwald said the number aloud a couple of times, and repeated it mentally during the rest of the conversation. Then he signed the documents that he had to sign.

'That is everything, Herr Grunwald. I hope you have remembered the number.'

Grunwald told him the number.

'On the other hand, will you remember it tomorrow?' Lindt said, crinkling.

'I will give it to Herr Bamberger tonight. He can remember it himself tomorrow.'

'Until we meet again, then.'

'Until we meet again.'

But Grunwald never did meet him again.

Before noon he was rolling back to the frontier.

It was still snowing, and the pines still whirled whitely away in suffocation on either side. He drowsed on and off, stomach griping. He'd got a timetable at the station and he pored over it, in the carriage and in the toilet. He spent a lot of time in the toilet, overcoat clutched tight round his knees in the icy draught. He had a round ticket, Zurich–Berlin–Frankfurt. He worked out the various ways in which he could include Bamberg on his ticket. Via Munich seemed the best. It was less than five hours from Zurich to Munich, then just over three to Bamberg, and another nine to Berlin. There were lengthy waits at each change, of course. He ached at the very thought. He longed to go immediately to Frankfurt, to enter his own home, to climb into his own bed, to sleep, and sleep. He longed for some normality in his life. It had become entirely abnormal – for years, it seemed. It wasn't so much a life as a proxy one. He was a messenger of others' errands, a leaf blown by winds, a thing without significance in itself, to be abused, insulted. But suddenly, in the middle of a spasm, in the middle of the track between Lindau and Kempten-Hegge, he thought of a story his father had once told him, and with an icy draught blowing up the ill-fitting lavatory trap directly to his anus, found himself smiling. Nobody had insulted *him*! He suddenly wanted to tell somebody else the story. Who would most appreciate his father's story? But before he could think, he was possessed by another and even more compelling thought. He was happy. He was in fact, happy. Despite the physical unease, despite the fatigue and the humiliation. If he weren't doing this, what else would he be doing? If he were born to a time and a place where he could live out his days in normality, satisfying the smaller and larger appetites of the husk Grunwald and eating a track blindly like a worm through the hill of his days, would there be greater significance? And if he were a messenger, for whom ultimately was he a messenger?

On the track between Lindau and Kempten-Hegge and with his bowels moving freely, Grunwald had a revelation. He couldn't prevent the great equation of Judaism appearing suddenly in his mind: *Shema Yisrael Adonai Elohenu Adonai Achat*. 'Hear, O Israel, the Lord is God, the Lord is One,' it said. But it was an equation and it needed interpretation, and Grunwald interpreted it as the equation for the unity of matter. 'The message, Israel: everything is One.'

He mused on it the rest of the way to Munich.

He had two hours to wait in Munich. It was bitterly cold and he didn't know what to do. He hadn't eaten anything all day and he was light-headed. But he saw that he'd better not hang about the station. Police and uniformed Party men were circulating. A Jew could be picked up for almost anything here. Thinking of this, he repeated the number a few times to himself. He'd forgotten to repeat it for a while.

It would be best, he saw, if he could rid himself of his suitcase, so that he could keep on the move more easily. He went across to see what sort of official there was in the left luggage office. Sometimes they wouldn't take your luggage; sometimes they messed you about when you tried to get it back, so that the train went. He couldn't risk that. He didn't seem a bad sort of fellow. Grunwald put his suitcase in and carefully pocketed the ticket, and with only his valise to carry, walked out into the street.

It was misty and snowing in the Bahnhofplatz. He wandered about it for a while, empty and light-headed, wondering where he could go. He couldn't go to a museum or a gallery or a library; Jews weren't allowed. He thought he'd better go where there were plenty of people. He thought he'd take a look in the shop windows of the Neuhauserstrasse.

He wandered towards it down Prielmayerstrasse, but SS men were stamping about at the lawcourts on the corner, so he gave them a wide berth and crossed there. It wasn't so easy to cross; cars and lorries filled the square of the Stachus, moving nose to tail through the slush. The traffic had its headlamps on in the dirty leaden light. Here and there people edged their way across the slow-moving stream, but Grunwald stayed where he was, watching for the policeman's signal. He wasn't going to get himself run in for that.

It took him five minutes to get across and he'd no sooner made it than he heard above the traffic the faint sound of drums and fifes, and a moment later he saw them, a Party procession, banners and swastika standards bob-bobbing, just emerging through the stone arch of Neuhauserstrasse. He tried to get back again immediately. This was no place to be. But he couldn't get back. The police had stopped everything for the first files, just entering the Stachus. He melted into a doorway, coat collar up round his beard, and kept a weather eye open. The Neuhauserstrasse, he now saw, was full of them, a great river of marching platoons stretching the entire length of the street and blurring away at the bend of the road into the Marienplatz. Each platoon had an old army soup boiler and a cart stacked with logs. It was a ceremonial winter relief

93

parade. The files were turning left, right and centre, at the Stachus. Who knew where the devil they'd get to all over the town? The safest place, after all, was the railway station, and as soon as he could he went back there.

The alarm had brought on a touch of his now familiar trouble, and this was decidedly ticklish. He didn't know what the public lavatory situation was here. Did they let you use them or not? He found himself a seat on a public bench, and tried to control it, but waves of nausea left him weak, and he knew he wasn't going to make it. Suddenly he had a brainwave. He'd take a train ride. He'd buy a ticket for a suburban journey. They couldn't stop you using the toilet on a train. But the instant he was on his feet he knew he wasn't going to get as far as the ticket office. He saw the sign for the station lavatories and stumbled weakly towards them. There was nothing for it: he'd have to try.

The moment he entered he knew he'd picked a bad one. The attendant was a little ferret of a man with a wooden leg and a Party armband. But thank God, there was a place for Jews. He saw the door with the misshapen Shield of David on it. It was the semblance of a door, sawn off at top and bottom to provide only a narrow strip of wood. He managed to get to it.

'Hey. Shit-face! Pay first. It's a mark for Jews.'

Thank God he had a note in his coat pocket. A five-mark note. 'Keep it,' he said. 'Keep it.'

'Don't do me any favours, Shit-face. Wait for your change.'

The man stumped off to his cubicle, and with an effort, Grunwald gripped the top of the low door and managed to hold on. He saw over the door that there was no paper. He looked round and saw a table with a couple of toilet rolls on it, and took one, and with a sudden diabolical twinge knew he couldn't wait any longer and went in and dropped his trousers just in time. To his humiliation he was sick as well. He bent weakly and tore off paper and covered the patch of vomit, still loosely defecating, and was still doing it when the door swung violently open striking him on the head.

'Why, you cheeky bastard! Who said you could take paper? It's one piece of paper for Jews. Give it here, you – Why,

94

God's blood!' the man said, coughing as the stench came suddenly up. 'You filthy, rotten, stinking swine. Get out! Get out of here, Jew filth. Get out!' In a blind and choking rage, he had knocked Grunwald sideways, banging his head on the partition, and he kept on striking till Grunwald was off the seat, sprawled half on his knees and on his elbow on the toilet-paper-covered patch of vomit, still, to his misery, defecating.

'God's blood, you scum! You slimy filth! You'll get this clean, you bastard. You'll shine it up so you can eat off it.' He was prodding him in a fury with his wooden leg. 'And give that here. Germans have got to use that paper. You can use your coat. You can use your tongue. You're not going out of here till it's clean.'

Grunwald didn't go out till it was clean. He used his two handkerchiefs. He used two buckets of disinfectant and a mop. With the disinfectant and the mop he tried to do what he could about his trousers. It cost him an extra five marks for the disinfectant and the mop.

All this took time, of course, but he got his suitcase and caught the train to Bamberg.

It was half past eight when he arrived, and still snowing. There were two taxis at the station, but they wouldn't take him. He could hardly put one foot in front of the other, so he found a phone box and rang Bamberger, and in a few minutes Bamberger's chauffeur came round with the limousine to pick him up.

It was only a few minutes from the station to the Hauptwachstrasse, but he fell asleep in his overcoat in the back, and the chauffeur had to shake him awake. The man carried his luggage into the hall, and Grunwald made his own way upstairs, repeating the number to himself as he did so. Why forget it now, after everything?

Despite his wretchedness he hadn't meant to sit down in the magnificent rococo room, very conscious of the stench that accompanied him. But Bamberger kept him waiting and the room began to move up and down, so he looked about and found an illustrated magazine on a low marble table, and spread the paper on the sofa and sat down on it, on the very edge. He was sitting like that when Bamberger came briskly into the room, in evening dress. He came in sniffing. He said, 'What the devil?' And then, 'Come, Grunwald. You're always such a sad dog. I expected to find you swinging from the chandeliers. Did something go wrong?'

Chapter 3

A LITTLE NIGHT ENTERTAINMENT

'TAKE another potato.'

'No.'

'Take beans.'

'No.'

'I'll have a potato,' Haffner said, and took three. 'Of course, the implications are terrible,' he said. 'It's almost beyond belief. The mind reels at what has to be done. How old would he be?'

'Grunwald thought they were of an age – maybe Bamberger a year older.'

'What's that – seventy-five, seventy-six?'

'Grunwald's seventy-four.'

'Unbelievable.'

'Yes.'

'Unbelievable. I don't even know where we'd start.'

'We're starting on the files at the Ministry of the Interior in the morning.'

'Yes, but I meant –'

Raison knew what he meant. It was Sunday night, chez Haffner. In the interim he'd cast his eyes over Ansbach's copy of the *Bundesentschädigungsgesetz*, in particular over that section that spoke of 'refund of benefits already paid' in the event of a claim having been determined 'on the basis of incorrect statements'. He'd already frightened the life out of Gunter on the telephone by a recital of this section. But he wasn't interested in Haffner's comments. He was more interested in his daughter's. The girl had scarcely opened her mouth, so far, except to decline food.

'Take asparagus.'

'No.'

'Take another slice of goose.'

'No.'

'Take a *tiny* piece of *Torte*.'

'No.'

'With cream.'

'No.'

'You'll waste away. You are wasting away. You'll get haggard. You are getting haggard. I'm sure you don't sleep enough. How much are you sleeping?'

'It's true, I should have an early night,' the girl said, looking at her watch.

'Not yet. You've hardly come. We hardly see you. It's not polite to Herr Raison –'

'Could in any case be in South America,' Haffner said.

'Grunwald doesn't think so.'

'With an agent here to work the account for him.'

'Grunwald doesn't think so.'

'What reason has Grunwald to –'

'I don't know,' Raison said. 'I'm afraid this must be very boring for you, Fräulein Haffner.'

'No.'

'In any case the dates. I don't understand the dates. Is he supposed to have gone to Prague immediately afterwards?'

'I think so.'

'But he'd have complete freedom of movement, certainly in the February. The occupation didn't take place till March. What was to stop him going wherever he wanted, then? What was to stop him going to South America?'

'I don't know,' Raison said. 'I could ask. Do you do any work in Munich, Fräulein Haffner?'

'No.'

'Oh, Elke. She works hard. She works too hard. She studies at the College of Art. She is passionately interested in art.'

'In painting?'

'No.'

'Hm,' Raison said, almost, but not completely, sold out. The girl's negatives hadn't, however, been delivered flatly or crushingly; almost tentatively and with a lingering half smile as though, given half a chance, she'd amplify them. No amplification came, though. He looked into the remains of the half smile to see what he could see. She wasn't unlike her mother in some less focused and more tentative version; same long bones, same set of neck, same deep breasts; but with the mother's bright questing charm turned inwards, and the mother's almost violet eyes turned to indeterminate blue. She didn't seem entirely clean. The long fingers were grubby, and a cigarette had been in them for most of the meal. He said, 'I'm afraid this kind of talk must be dreary to an outsider.'

'No.'

'Very uninteresting for you, I'm sure.'

'Not uninteresting. Not dreary. Simple sordid.'

'Oh, Elke!'

'Sordid?' Raison said.

'What's past is past. The past is sordid.'

'Is it?'

'Our past is sordid.'

'You smoke too much. You don't know what you're talking about,' her father said. 'In your intellectual society, of course, everything is considered sordid. Perhaps rightly so,' he said darkly.

'We could have coffee now,' Frau Haffner said. 'We could have brandy. Herr Raison would like a brandy. Elke would like a brandy. Do you know, I still feel a little chilly in the evenings. We could have a bar on, I think, Heinz. Don't you think, Elke?'

They had a bar on, and they had coffee and brandy, but none of it warmed up the conversation very much, and at half past ten, Raison found himself suppressing yawns in time with the girl. Not long after, at the conclusion of some argey-bargey to do with his conveyance hotelwards, whether by taxi, Haffner, or his daughter, he found himself cruising through the streets of Bogenhausen beside the girl in a red E-type Jaguar.

'I'm sorry I wasn't better company.'

'Conversations between lawyers tend to be technical.'

'I always dry up with my parents, I don't know why. Perhaps it's Bogenhausen. Don't you hate Bogenhausen?'

'I'm not very good at places. It seems quite a nice place,' Raison said, looking out at it. 'What's wrong with Bogenhausen?'

'It's so well-fed. It's so awful.'

'Where do you live?'

'In Schwabing. Of course.'

'Don't they eat so well in Schwabing?'

'Come and see.'

'I'll do it some time.'

'Do it now. Buy me a drink. Unless you've got to get back.'

'All right.'

She'd been running him to the hotel, but she turned right up the Ludwigstrasse and bowled north, past the big triumphal arch of the Siegestor, to where the lights of the roof restaurant in the Herti skyscraper hung in the dark over Schwabing.

Deluded Ludwig's long straight road didn't change very much, but the scenery on both sides suddenly did, the classically faced buildings lining either side erupting into the bright lights of cafés, restaurants and open-air *boîtes*. It was alive with people and not unlike a fairground, little one-decker trams shuttling in tandem in and out of the surrounding darkness like mechanical moths round a light. A strong corduroy-jacketed element seemed to be a-stroll.

'Is this the haunt of your sordid intellectual society?'

'It's our Chelsea.'

'It doesn't seem underfed.'

'It's quite often overdrunk.'

She parked the Jaguar quite carefully by a No-Parking sign and they found a table in an adjacent café and ordered coffee and brandy.

'Here I can breathe,' she said.

There seemed to be just room.

99

'Whereabouts do you live?'

'Just across the road, in the Hohenzollernstrasse. It's convenient for the art school. I have a tiny apartment. I am financially independent,' she said.

Raison had long ago given up being surprised at this type of information being volunteered to him on slender acquaintance. But he remembered in the same moment something Gunter had told him, between South Kensington and Gloucester Road; something about money coming to the girl from her grandmother, and about a deformed Hungarian Jew, and for a moment, remembering more fully, shared Gunter's anxiety about the nature of the deformity.

He said, 'I forgot to mention, your godfather sends his love.'

'Oh, Uncle Rupert. He is very sweet. He thinks everything can be solved by reasonableness, doesn't he?'

'He thinks science usually has a cure.'

'I've lost my belief in science and reason.'

'Have you?'

'I've lost my belief in the reasonableness of people.'

'This will be to do with the sordidness of the past, I expect,' Raison said.

'The sordidness of the past underlying the sordidness of the present.'

'That seems to take in most things.'

'It takes in most things in Germany. It takes in most people over forty. They've begun to make me, I'm afraid, terribly sick. I can't respect them any more. If they are good now, why weren't they good then? If they are wise now, why weren't they wise then? I'm afraid they're morally bankrupt, all of them.'

'Perhaps they were both good and wise, and also powerless,' Raison suggested.

'Nobody is ultimately powerless. There is the power to protest.

'There's also the power to commit suicide.'

'Or to become a moral bankrupt. One has the choice.'

'I'm afraid not everybody is a hero.'

''Everybody is the hero of his own life.'

Raison looked into his glass, gloomily. A good deal more of this seemed to be on the way. But he'd asked for it, so he put the best face on it. He said, 'I think you prefer dead heroes to live cowards.'

'I prefer live cowards not to take up smug moral attitudes. I prefer them not to live so well or to be so sure of themselves.'

'I think artistic leanings incline you to the hair shirt.'

'Which is not in fashion now, is it?'

'Do you want another drink?'

'Have it with me, in my apartment, across the street. I promise not to be so serious,' she said, smiling.

Raison considered. Serious or no, there would be confidences, and very likely reminiscences. There had already been much in the way of confidence and reminiscence today. He was no longer at his freshest and best. 'Another night,' he said. But he took her telephone number before she ran him home.

He found Grunwald listening to the gramophone, in the dark. The window was open and only the light from the street showed where the old man was sitting. But it also showed one eloquent finger held up for silence. Raison sat down in a chair and smoked a cigarette till the Beethoven quartet was finished.

'Dr Ansbach kindly brought me it,' Grunwald said, switching on a table lamp, 'also the gramophone. He knows I like a little night entertainment. So how did your evening go?'

Raison told him.

'Very proper. Quite proper,' the old man said, nodding approval of the girl's opinions.

'I thought you'd agree.'

'Of course. But she's young, remember, she's German. There's plenty of time for her to learn better.'

'How do we stand on dead heroes as against live cowards?'

'It's an interesting point. Ecclesiastes, of course, tells us that it's better to be a live dog than a dead lion. On the other hand the great Hillel expressed the view that if man knew what was in store for him he would choose not to be born at all. For myself I've got to state a preference for life. It's better to be alive than dead. In principle,' Grunwald said. 'However, we can say that sometimes it's better for the living that they should have died. Perhaps we'll find one such tomorrow.'

Chapter 4

THE BIGGEST RABBIT HUNT OF ALL TIME

THEY were at the Bavarian Land Ministry of the Interior soon after nine o'clock, awaiting the pleasure of one Dr Fuss. Fuss came with a bow-tie, rimless spectacles and a special handshake for Ansbach 'We don't see so much of you these days, my dear Ansbach.'

'The cases requiring your assistance are falling off, Herr Assistant Director.'

'Yes. Time goes by. What can I do for you?'

'It's the Czechoslovakian section. The Sudetenland.'

'Sudeten,' Fuss said, and wrote it on a large sheet of paper. 'Name?'

'Bamberger. Helmut Wolfgang Bamberger.'

'Ethnic status?'

'German. Jewish.'

Fuss blinked. 'Which?' he said. 'That's to say,' he said, rapidly brushing non-existent specks from the paper, 'there's bound to be a classification – in the Sudeten section. Are you sure it's the Sudeten section you want?'

'The man was in Prague. If he came back, his records should be in your Sudeten section.'

'Yes,' Fuss said. 'All the same, it's a difficulty.' He worried at it. 'Is the suggestion that the Czechs held him in a camp with ethnic Germans?'

'I don't know.'

'The Czechs wouldn't have held him in a camp with ethnic Germans. They didn't place Jews together with ethnic Germans.'

'Not if they knew,' Ansbach said.

'Is the suggestion that they didn't know?'

'I don't know.'

'Well, it's a difficulty,' Fuss said. He blew out his cheeks. 'As a Jew the Czechs wouldn't have held him at all. As a Jew he didn't have to be an expellee. It's necessary that we should list the categories,' he said. 'Firstly, if he's an ethnic German, he is *a priori* an expellee. Secondly, if he's a returning Jew, he is a persecutee emigrant. Thirdly, if he's a German and a Jew and also an anti-fascist, then this is something else again. Under which category are we looking for him?'

'All I can tell you,' Ansbach said, 'is that the man returned some time between 1945 and 1947.'

' 1945!' Fuss said. 'It's more difficult yet. If he came in in 1945 he would have had to make an illegal exit and also an illegal entry. It's another category. What I'd better do,' he said, tearing up the paper and selecting a fresh sheet, 'is hand you over to Dr Tschadek in the Sudeten section. He is himself a Sudeten and the great expert on the question. It's Dr Dr Tschadek,' he said, writing it down for them.

'Dr Dr?' Raison said as they threaded the corridors.

'A part of your German education,' Grunwald said. 'If a man has a double doctorate, why bury it in initials after his name? There's no need for such modesty.'

Dr Dr Tschadek was a shambling and somewhat glowering man in an enormous suit of tweeds. He was of Slav build with luxuriant hair which hung low about his ears; but apart from this peccadillo, a tribute perhaps to one or other of his doctorates, set great store by tidiness and order. He arranged Ansbach, Grunwald and Raison in a semi-circle around his desk, and began to list the information offered to him into a series of columns annotated with an occasional question mark or asterisk. This took time, and it was after eleven before he was ready to initiate research.

Dr Tschadek's method was to give a brief introductory account of what he meant to do, and then to amplify it as he did it, his long questing finger moving from one section to another. His hollow, somewhat belling voice began to haunt Raison.

'I am now going to search the records of the transports from the camp at Budweis . . .

'The first transports from the camp at Budweis arrived at our transit camp at Furth-im-Wald on 25 January 1946. From this date, four trains daily with a total of some 3,800 persons, arrived until . . .'

At half past twelve they stopped for lunch, and at half past one arranged themselves again about Dr Tschadek.

'I am now going to search the records of anti-fascists who arrived by train . . .

'In the month of May 1946, eight trains, each with 300 anti-fascists, were received at Furth-im-Wald and Wiesau. From then until . . .'

'Would it be possible to smoke?' Raison said.

'It's not possible. There is a fire hazard. I myself suck mints. Do you suck mints?'

'Thank you,' Raison said.

'I am now going to search the records of anti-fascists who arrived by lorry. In the month of May 1946, a daily convoy of twelve lorry-loads of anti-fascists was received in . . .'

'So many anti-fascists,' Grunwald said with quiet wonder as they left at five. 'Who ever knew there were so many lorry-loads and trainsful of them . . .?'

But Bamberger's name wasn't among them. It wasn't among the ethnic Germans, either; or among the voluntary immigrants, legal or illegal.

Ansbach and Raison were flat and depressed after the day-long ordeal with Dr Tschadek. Grunwald strove to cheer them up. 'Because the name isn't listed among the living or the dead,' he said, 'does it mean he wasn't called into existence at all?'

'It might mean he's not in Germany,' Ansbach said.

'It might,' Grunwald agreed, 'and it might not.'

He began to tell them a long story about a man in Frankfurt who was the janitor of a block of flats.

'What does that mean?' Ansbach said.

'I don't know. But there's a meaning in everything. Only

sometimes it's known only to the true recorder of the living and the dead.'

Raison took a bottle of brandy back to the hotel with him and had a couple while he phoned Gunter.

Gunter said, 'I'm afraid Mrs Wolff is dreadfully pent about this, James.'

'Is she?'

'I'm afraid so. What's the latest information?'

Raison gave him the latest information.

'It might ease her a bit. It might,' Gunter said.

'Do you think so, Rupert?'

'From one point of view. After all, if the difficulties of tracing him are so. . . .Of course, she'd sooner have her father back than anything. Naturally.'

'Yes. She'd better steel herself to the fact that she might not be going to, though,' Raison said, sipping.

'She wants me to give her a note of the dates, James. Have you got the dates with you?'

Raison got his notebook out. The dates were in a neat column. It ran:

Grunwald returned from Switzerland and saw Bamberger	13 February 1939
Bamberger went to Prague	15 February
Bamberger sent confirmation from Prague to Zurich	18 February
Germans moved into Prague	10 March

'Are these the dates you want?' he said.

'Yes, why did he go to Prague, James, how did he go to Prague?'

'He went on a train,' Raison said. 'He had business there, he had a branch of his bank.'

'I have got here he couldn't travel anywhere.'

'He could to Prague. He saved up his confidential affairs to deal with there. Grunwald says he didn't deal with them in his own bank. He used the Escompte Bank in Prague. Apparently

Löwe, his agent in Switzerland, often got confidential stuff through the Escompte Bank in Prague.'

'Yes. You know, she always had the impression her father was executed in Prague. What was to prevent the Germans taking over his confidential papers when they marched in? What was to prevent them executing him and continuing the account?'

'Nothing. It's what you'd expect,' Raison said, having a drink. 'Only apparently they didn't. The point is he sent off his confirmation weeks before and the handwriting's been the same ever since. The Swiss have had graphologists on it. It hasn't changed at all, except for ageing, and it's aged in the right way. I'm afraid the implication is he got up to something disreputable in between.'

'Some sort of crime, you mean?'

'Between a sin and a crime there's a difference,' Raison said, 'only I can't tell you with precision what it is at the moment. I'd have to let you know about that, Rupert. It seems safest to assume that he's around, though.'

'What does Heinz think?'

'Heinz thinks he's in South America. He thinks he might have gone there before the Germans arrived in Prague.'

'What do the Israelis think?'

'They think he isn't. Grunwald says he couldn't have gone there from Prague. He says he always had to report twice a day to the German consul in Prague just to prevent him going elsewhere. Of course he could still have gone, but he couldn't have come back. Grunwald says it wasn't in the nature of the man to leave his business in that way. I'm inclined to agree.'

'What's your view then, James?'

Raison had a drink and considered. 'I haven't got one,' he said.

'So what is Grunwald expecting to find in Bamberg?'

'I'm not totally clear on that, Rupert. I can't say I've plumbed his mind on that one. Do you want me to stay?'

'Oh, you'll have to stay. We can't have people poking about in this by themselves, James. There are too many things involved. Mrs Wolff is very pent, James.'

'Yes.'

'Very pent. I should stay close to Grunwald. I should try to be discreet. Is there anything you want me to do? Is there anything you want me to tell Hilda?'

'I don't think she's at home today, Rupert.'

'Well, give her my love when you speak to her.'

'Thanks. I will.'

He put the phone down and had a drink and phoned Hilda.

'Ah, I'm glad you rang, Mr Raison. I'm afraid Mrs Raison has been a bit dicky of late.'

'What's the trouble?'

'The drug made her face swell. I'm afraid it came up rather a lot, and unevenly. It does in five per cent of cases.'

'Is she all right?'

'Perfectly all right, in herself. She's sleeping now. She's been sleeping for a couple of days. She has not been very much on the surface, you know, of late. We didn't know she had a mirror. She formed a stubborn impression that we were preparing her for another species, owing to her failure in this one. Almost certainly that will go. She'll have no recollection of it. She wasn't really on the surface when it happened. I thought it best to sedate her again immediately.'

'How is the face now?'

'Going down beautifully. But I'd let her sleep it out. I'd give it a few days. I wouldn't look in before telephoning first.'

'All right,' Raison said.

He put the phone down and walked over to the window and looked at the Volkswagens jockeying for position at the lights, and at Hilda wildly regarding the face of a new species in her mirror. She hadn't been much on the surface of late. He wasn't sure he'd been much on it himself. There wasn't anything very special about the surface. It was almost dark outside. From the next room he could hear a murmur, suggestive of Grunwald at his prayers. Appetite stirred briefly beneath the brandy. There was no eating with Grunwald. He didn't fancy Haffner again. He got out his notebook and went to the telephone.

'Hello.'

'Hello. It's James Raison. What about dinner at a sordid intellectual hangout?'

'Oh. I'm sorry. I would love it. I'm occupied tonight.'

'Never mind. Another night. How is art today?'

'Tomorrow night. Will you eat tomorrow night?'

'I'm not sure tomorrow night. I've got to go to Bamberg tomorrow. I might be late.'

'Tomorrow's Tuesday? Then have breakfast with me on Wednesday.'

'Breakfast?'

'I hate breakfast alone. Come and have breakfast. Do you eat a great breakfast?'

'I'm a coffee and cigarette man. I'm not at my social best at breakfast,' Raison said.

'Oh, I neither. I'm also a coffee and cigarette man. There's no incompatability there,' she said. She sounded excessively cheerful, and also slightly tight. He had some trouble reconciling the large and introverted smiler of memory with the cheerfully tight girl on the phone. He wondered who was with her, and the nature of his disability.

She said, 'Hello.'

He said, 'Hello.'

'It's a date for Wednesday?'

'Well, let's see,' Raison said. 'It's not a very formal engagement, is it?'

'Oh, it's terribly informal. We could have the most informal breakfast. You've got the address.'

'Yes, I've got it,' Raison said.

He had a wash and ate by himself, below.

'This is the Luitpoldstrasse. This is the Königstrasse. This is the Hauptwachstrasse,' Grunwald said. He was enjoying himself. It was very hot. The sun came blinding up off the water. 'This is the Maxplatz. This is the Rathaus. This is the Gruener Markt. This is the river. There is the Domberg. I always liked this place,' he said. 'It's medieval Franconia. It's in a sense the dark heartland of Germany, where blood flows and fairy tales spring. Princes are turned into frogs here, and back again.

They have a habit of overturning tombstones in the Jewish cemetery. You know where you are here. At the best of times you could look a long way before finding even a bicycle-load of anti-fascists.'

Raison loosened his tie. It was coming up to noon. The air was hot. Everything smelt hot. There was a vista of rose-red roofs and dormer windows. They'd walked from the station into the medieval and baroque town, and now it was suffocatingly all about them, steep roofs, leaning walls, towering steeples. Above the flash of glass and the glistening spires, the sky hung almost indigo. The place confused him. There seemed to be two rivers running through it.

'It isn't two rivers. It's the two arms of the Regnitz river. It splits the town in three. We're now on the island.'

'Can we get a drink anywhere?'

'First let's see where the bank should be.'

Turning this way and that, a finger on his lip, he worked out where it should be. It should be just about where they were. 'It's strange. There are changes here. What have they done with it?'

They'd put a new plate-glass window on it, and turned it into a branch of another bank. Grunwald paraded a little in front of the bank, his face buried in the mysteries of his large round hat in the noonday sun.

'Well, come, we'll have a drink, then, and work out what to do.'

They turned into a little entry which led to a beer garden, and sat under a tree with iced beer. The wall of a church rose sheer at the side of the garden. The air danced in the heat off the wall, and sitting there with his glass, Raison had a sharp impression suddenly of being seated in the very centre of a very old Europe, much land and forest on all sides, and no sea, in a settlement of people capable of anything.

'It's old,' he said.

'He had a lawyer hereabouts he used sometimes, he trusted him. We could see if we can find the lawyer.'

'What about the bank?'

'As I recall, the name was Nuschke or Puschke. In the Langestrasse,' he said. 'We could go and take a look there before the bank. It's only round the corner.'

They finished their beer and went round the corner into the blinding heat of the Langestrasse. Grunwald examined the plates on the doors. He found Nuschke.

'Herr Nuschke the elder,' he said in the reception room. 'He had a son,' he told Raison, 'a most earnest young antisemite. He had to be careful with that son about.'

Herr Nuschke the elder turned out to be the son.

'My father died in 1961,' he said.

'I'm sorry,' Grunwald said. 'He was a good man.'

'Yes,' Nuschke the elder said. He had a mat of neat black hair and dutiful eyes. They were turned raptly on Grunwald's hat.

'It was to do with Herr Bamberger. Of the bank,' Grunwald said.

'Yes?'

'Your father did one or two things for him.'

'Yes.'

'I wondered if you'd heard any further from him.'

'No,' Nuschke the elder said, his small mouth economical with words.

Grunwald sat easily in his chair, looking round the room. 'Well, it's nice to see nothing has changed here, at least,' he said.

'Things don't change here.'

'The front of the bank has changed.'

'The Americans bombed it.'

'Ah. It's a pity you've heard nothing further of Herr Bamberger.'

'There's no reason why we should,' Nuschke said, unwillingly. 'We were never his lawyers. We were the lawyers of his clerk. He came to us only because of a small transaction to do with the clerk, the lease of a house.'

'Pfefferkorn,' Grunwald said.

'Herr Pfefferkorn, exactly.'

'Pfefferkorn the hunchback. I remember him. He'll have been dead many years, of course.'

'On the contrary,' Nuschke said, permitting himself a small smile. 'Herr Pfefferkorn is in excellent health, although a man of ninety-three. We renegotiated the lease for him only last year, in behalf of his granddaughter. The house is the property of the bank.'

'He doesn't still work for the bank!'

'Naturally not. He's been retired twenty years,' Nuschke said. But he gave them Pfefferkorn's address, and they went out into the reeling street again, and found it.

An enormous Gretchen with beefy red arms and flaxen plaits answered the door. She said her grandfather was out fishing.

'Do you know when he'll be back?'

'Not till four. They took food,' the woman said, staring at Grunwald's hat.

'I'll call back. Kindly tell him Dr Grunwald called. Grunwald. From before the war. He'll remember,' Grunwald said.

'Pfefferkorn!' he said to himself as they left the house. 'Who would have believed it? Perhaps there's no need to look further.' But they looked further. They had lunch first. They found a restaurant under trees by the river, and Grunwald munched a little fruit while Raison ate. Then they had a look at the bank. 'The Bamber Rider used to hang here, above the street,' Grunwald said. 'Here was the big double door into the private apartment, and through there the door to the back and the garage. Bamberger used to stay here only during the week.'

The private apartment was now several private apartments as a cluster of bellpushes showed. They had a word with the manager. He was a young man and didn't know anything about Bamberger. He had a young staff, and they didn't, either. Grunwald asked to see the janitor. The janitor turned out to be an ex-serviceman of fifty with a wife and three children. Grunwald asked the janitor about the occupants of the apartments. The occupants of the apartments were all married couples with young children.

'So,' Grunwald said. 'There are other places.' There was the Heimatmuseum, and the Bibliotek, and the Observatory, and the Concert Hall, in all of which Bamberger had interested himself, and to all of which he had given munificently. Nobody in any of them had seen him back in town or even heard of him.

'Well, let this be a lesson,' Grunwald said, as they walked back into town. '*V'ana ta'azevu kevodechem.*'

'What does that mean?'

'It means *sic transit gloria mundi.*'

'I know what that means,' Raison said.

'He was a great man in this town,' Grunwald said, 'before the deluge. Maybe the police station has some record of him.'

But the police station hadn't; and it was now half past three.

In the heat Grunwald's face had become somewhat puffy, and he was walking slowly. But at each setback his gaiety seemed to have increased, as though the complete erasure of the great man and his works afforded some private satisfaction. He said, 'Well, we can take a rest now and leave things for Pfefferkorn.'

'Rest if you're tired,' Raison said. 'While I'm here I'll take a look at the cathedral.'

'Why not? I can renew acquaintance with the other forgotten eminence.'

They'd been passing and repassing the statue of Kunigunde the Good who had walked red-hot ploughshares to show her fidelity to her consort Heinrich the Holy, and now they passed her again on the Untere Brücke. Grunwald told her story again. Raison looked at him. He'd heard it once already. He'd also heard the story of how Hoffmann had written selected Tales here, and Hegel his *Phenomenology of the Spirit.* With some concern, he heard Grunwald begin to tell these stories again also.

'Are you all right?' he said.

'I'm fine,' Grunwald said, 'fine.'

'Maybe you'd like a rest. Maybe you'd like a pill.'

'Have I changed colour?'

'Just a little.'

'All right, I'll take a pill.'

They were mounting a small steep lane of the Domberg. They sat at the first café table and had a lemon tea. Grunwald had a pill with his tea.

'I don't feel unwell,' he said thoughtfully.

'It's the heat.'

'We walked slowly.'

'It's steep here.'

'You're like a son. How old are you, forty-one, forty-two?'

'Forty-two.'

'I had a son who would be your age. He also was very tall. He would be a tall man.'

'What was his name?'

'Otto.'

'Otto,' Raison said, and watched with some dismay as the old man took a bulky leather case out of his pocket. But there were no photographs in the case, only a bottle. Grunwald pointed to his throat and poured himself a spoonful from the bottle. As he did so, he wondered why he was telling Raison this, why he was speaking to him in this way, and in the same moment remembered he wanted to tell him something else, a story.

'Were there other children?' Raison said.

'A girl of seven, Ruth, and another boy, Benjamin, ten. He was the most intelligent, Benjamin. Otto was the oldest and the biggest but he was not the most intelligent. He had an ambition to go to Australia, Otto. He had an ambition to be an engineer, but he was not good at school. Of course he missed a lot of schooling, they all missed.'

'Did they?'

'Of course they missed. We had to get together our own schools in the neighbourhood, in people's houses. They missed their schooling, my children,' Grunwald said regretfully. 'Even when they let them in school, earlier, they missed. They couldn't concentrate. They were all the time abused, insulted. It reminds me of a story,' Grunwald said.

But the clocks all around chimed the quarter then and he checked with his watch.

'Stay and rest if you're tired,' Raison said. 'I'll go myself. I'll only be a few minutes.'

'I'll come with you.'

'There's no need in the heat.'

'I'm used to the heat. We can go slowly,' Grunwald said.

They went slowly. They went higher. They arrived at an enormous *pavé*-laid square, flanked by huge hushed buildings. The square was almost empty and very quiet in the sweltering heat. A few charabancs were lined up outside the cathedral. Grunwald took Raison's arm as they climbed the steps, and took off his hat and adjusted his skullcap.

It was an unlovely cathedral, gaunt and dark, an old stone penitential place from haunted Gothic ages. Grunwald looked for and found the effigy, familiar here as in other cathedrals of the Catholic south, of the pair of Gothic female figures representing Church and Synagogue. Synagogue was blindfolded. He nodded to her. 'Now whereabouts have they hidden the Rider?' he said. 'If memory serves, he's riding on a wall somewhere.'

Memory served. The Bamber Rider was riding his stone horse on a plinth some twelve feet up in the twilit murk of a pillar. A small group of people was peering up at him, directed by the hollow-voiced murmur of a guide.

'. . . in the ancient world better known even than Michelangelo's David, a wonder work of the sculptor's art . . . true expression of the German spirit and the role that . . . mission casts its shadow over the centuries . . . to notice that although the horse faces north, the Rider himself looks to the east – dare we say to the lost lands and Poland and even beyond . . . of who he is, who can say? . . . hypothesis that he is Stefan who was baptized here and married Gisela, sister of Kaiser Heinrich the Holy, while others again think . . .'

The party wandered away.

'Of course, my professor always took the view that it was Heinrich himself,' Grunwald said. 'He could cite much evidence, as for instance . . .'

He was still citing when a verger came up and asked him to keep his voice down. 'It's a holy place,' the verger said.

'Why keep voices down in a holy place? We should shout for joy in a holy place.'

'It's a holy place,' the verger said, 'also it's not Kaiser Heinrich the Holy. A representation of Kaiser Heinrich the Holy is

to be found in the south-east doorway, also of course above
his tomb in the central nave. Most probably we can say it's
Stefan, the brother-in-law of Kaiser Heinrich the Holy.'

'Personally I always thought it was Gawan.'

'Gawan?'

'Of the legend.'

'Which legend?' the verger said.

'Alas, alas,' Grunwald said, and began to recite:

> '" Ich kann hier nicht mehr weiter reiten.
> Wagt Ihr's, so mög' Euch Gott geleiten.
> Hier hilft kein Warten, hilft kein Zagen,
> Mit kühnem Sprunge müsst Ihr's wagen."
> So hielt sie selbst ihr Rösslein an,
> Doch weiter vorwärts ritt Gawan,
> Der unverzagte Held Gawan.'

'His lady is speaking to Gawan,' he said to Raison. 'It's
usually rendered:

> '"Here I can no further ride,
> Dare you, with only God to guide.
> No help to pause, no help to wait,
> But keenly leap towards your fate."
> And reined her steed, while in the van
> Still ever onwards rode Gawan,
> Undaunted brave Hero Gawan.'

'Undaunted brave Hero Gawan,' Raison said, looking up at
the cleft-chinned young Siegfried who stared sightlessly
towards lost lands.

'"Der unverzagte Held Gawan",' Grunwald amiably agreed.
'"Doch weiter vorwärts ritt Gawan." We can't say that he's ever
stopped for very long. So this is the hero of the Bamberger
family, and there he is.'

'Yes. It's very unlikely,' the verger said. 'It's more likely
Stefan, the consort of Gisela. If you could keep your voice
down,' he said, 'in a holy place.'

'We're going now.'

They went, into the blinding heat, down the Domberg,
Grunwald still musing as they descended. 'It's true it's a

strange and enigmatic figure, also true it shows the German virtues, determination, bravery, humility, purpose. The trouble is it shows them all at the same time.'

'Didn't Churchill point out they were at your throat or at your feet, but not at the same time?'

'They only deal with one thing at a time,' Grunwald said. 'It's a single-minded people. It's a people that lacks perspective, and hence a sense of shame. I suppose if you're single-minded and do as you're told there's no point in having a sense of shame. Many authorities have noticed it, including Schopenhauer. It was noticeable after the war, particularly, when the camps were opened up. They all knew what had gone on, but they weren't ashamed, only frightened of what would happen to them because of it. They felt that as a people they'd broken some rules and the people who had beaten them would punish them for it. And of course they were ready to put up with it. Everybody noticed how cowed they were, like a dog ready for a good hiding. And they would have put up with it. It's a people capable of enormous endurance, if they're told they have to endure. I know. I worked among them. When I came out of Dachau I was billeted in Munich, in charge of a work party – strangely enough in the ruins of the public lavatory in the railway station. But then the new policy became to Win the Heart and Mind of the German and turn him into a self-respecting democrat, which was a new order, so they set about carrying it out. They did it *incredibly* thoroughly. It was an order! Even the political parties, when they came about, were all democratic. There weren't any people but democrats any more. There were the Christian Democrats, the Social Democrats, the Free Democrats. Even the new fascists now, what do they call themselves? The *National* Democrats. This is the way they are. I witnessed it, almost overnight. It was the most incredible thing you ever saw. All of a sudden they were respectable again and the whole world was to blame for what happened, not them. They did a wonderful job of it.'

'Did they know what had gone on in the camps?'

'For some reason,' Grunwald said, 'it seems to have been my mission in life to bear witness to the obvious. People have short memories, or they don't want to remember, or they don't want to know. How could the enormous majority of the German people not know? If a man was a recluse or a madman or a cave-dweller, maybe he wouldn't know. Anybody who lived in communities of people knew. It wasn't happening only to Jews. It was happening to Poles, Russians. It was happening to people on an enormous scale all over Europe, wherever German armies were. They were armies full of ordinary people, who went home on leave. It was no secret what was happening. There were huge camps, work parties went out of the camps every day, people lived round the camps, businesses and industries supplied the camps. They knew and they didn't care. I'm not saying they supported it. It was nothing to do with them. It was none of their business. It was like killing rabbits. You remember a few years ago when millions of rabbits had to be killed off. Somebody took a decision, and experts worked at it, and they started killing off rabbits. But people are not rabbits. It's a special quality of the Germans that they could believe that people were rabbits. Even after the war when they could see that the survivors were not in fact rabbits but people, they still felt in their hearts that the dead ones had been rabbits. It was nothing more or less than the biggest rabbit hunt of all time, the sort of thing that authorities have to order for the health of the community, about which the citizen is not competent to express an opinion, and for which therefore he doesn't feel compelled to have conscientious qualms, then or now. Of course the idea had to be inculcated, and it went right through the community, young and old. I remember when I was brought down on a train transport to Dachau, a beautiful day, hot sun, summer. It was a public holiday of some sort. The train had to stop, and on the other track was another train, also stopped, full of children, on an outing, beautiful children in their little Youth Movement uniforms, hanging out of the windows. They could see us moving about in the cattle trucks, and they were singing and calling out to us, little rhymes about the putting-down of Jews. I can't remember the words now. All I remember is the charming little voices, like birds, all piping together as we pulled away again. They were calling after us, "*Juden in*

Katzet, Juden in Katzet". Katzet was KZ, the initials of "concentration camp". So we can say in answer to your question that certainly they knew; and with regard to your friend that she's wrong, at least over-dramatic, even melodramatic, about her countrymen. It wasn't a matter of heroes or cowards. They simply didn't care.'

'Surely some of them cared?'

'Some did. I'm no expert on the ones who cared. In any case they aren't to be taken as a yardstick to the German people. What we have to say about the German people is that most of the ones you see walking about over the age of forty knew what was going on and they didn't care. They thought it was happening to rabbits. Maybe in a few years someone will tell them that other people are rabbits – it's always a danger when you can't tell a person from a rabbit. From this, of course,' Grunwald said, 'I make exceptions. In particular, I except little Pfefferkorn. Now where is Pfefferkorn's street?'

Pfefferkorn was standing in it, a tiny brown-clad gnome of glistening eye, anxiously searching this way and that for them. He began to sob as he took Grunwald's hand. He sobbed over the hand and kissed it.

'Come, Pfefferkorn, what's this?'

'Ah, dear old friend, dear old friend!' the hunchback said.

'It's good to see you, Pfefferkorn.'

'Who sees a face from old times? There are no faces from those times. Ah, Herr Grunwald, I thought you were dead.'

'Not dead. Here before you. They didn't kill me, Pfefferkorn.'

'And your wife, Herr Grunwald? Your children?'

'They took them, Pfefferkorn, It's only me they left.'

'Ah. Ah,' Pfefferkorn said, the tears running down his hooked nose. They fell on Grunwald's hands, and he kissed the hands one after the other. 'It's all frightfulness that one hears. It's all horror that one hears,' Pfeffekorn said.

'But won't you invite us out of the sun, Pfefferkorn? Wont you take us into the house?'

'Yes, come in, come in,' his Gretchen-type granddaughter

called. She was standing anxiously at the door, and people were already looking round in the street.

'Of course,' Pfefferkorn said, shambling excitedly towards the house and drawing Grunwald by the hand. 'Your friend also. It's not every day one sees a face from those times,' he told Raison, letting go Grunwald's hand in the narrow hall. 'I've outlived them all. I've outlived them, I whom nature deceived,' he said, gesturing backwards to his hump. 'I've outlived my friends, my wife, my children.'

'You'll outlive your grandchildren, too, the way you're going,' the woman said, showing them into the front room. It was a small room with large furniture and an unused smell. 'Excuse him, he's a bit excited today. He caught a fish. He's a bit you know,' she said, tapping her head. 'You caught a fish, didn't you? I send my boy out to take him fishing now and again. He don't like catching them, really, but it gives him a bit of excitement. He wouldn't hurt a fly. You wouldn't, would you? What about the fish, then, Grandfather?'

'It's not a matter of fish!' the old man said. 'Sit down, sit down, Herr Grunwald. What can we give you to drink?'

'Please don't trouble –'

'I'll bring beer,' the woman said.

'So how have you been keeping, Pfefferkorn?'

'I live on. I live on. Nothing changes for me.'

'I see the bank has changed. The Rider's gone.'

'It's gone. Everything's gone. All's changed there.'

'Nuschke the lawyer told me where to find you.'

'Nuschke's gone. It's Nuschke's son. They've all gone. Everybody's gone from those days.'

'And Herr Bamberger? Did you ever see him again after my last visit?'

'Herr Bamberger?' Pfefferkorn said.

'Thunder weather, don't mention him,' the woman said, coming in with the beer. 'Don't let him start on that.'

'What with Herr Bamberger?' Pfefferkorn said.

'Nothing with Herr Bamberger. Here's a nice glass of beer. It's cold, don't gulp.' She was shaking her head at Grunwald over the small hunched back.

'You've seen Herr Bamberger?' Pfefferkorn said sharply.

'I was wondering if you had,' Grunwald said, apologetically.

'He sees him all the time,' the woman said, tapping her head. 'He can't accept things, you know. He was with them fifty years.'

'I was with them fifty years,' Pfefferkorn said.

'It grieves him, all that time, and not hearing anything. He can't accept he's dead.'

'Who's dead?' Pfefferkorn said.

'Nobody's dead. You drink your beer. *Zum wohl. Zum wohl.*'

'*Zum wohl,*' Grunwald said. He was looking at her. 'I don't want to –' he said. 'That is, he thinks he's seen him here?'

'Not here. Except up in his room, of course. He has arguments with him there.'

'There are no arguments!' Pfefferkorn said. 'There are absolutely no arguments. What are you talking about?'

'All right, no arguments,' the woman said.

'So where has he seen him?'

'Everywhere. Nuremberg, once. We took him to Nuremberg.'

'Not in Nuremberg. I told you I couldn't be sure in Nuremberg. I said that!' Pfefferkorn said furiously.

'All right, I'm sorry. It was Bayreuth, then. We gave him a treat in Bayreuth. You'll admit Bayreuth?' she said.

'Bayreuth, yes,' Pfefferkorn said, judicially.

'You saw Herr Bamberger in Bayreuth?' Grunwald said.

'As plainly as I see you.'

'And talked to him?'

'I was in the bus, he in the street. Through the window I saw him, and he me. He was wearing his new grey suit.'

'The one Grandfather ordered for him in 1938,' the woman said, winking.

'Of course I ordered. I ordered all his suits. That's to say the cloth. I ordered the cloths. This was the new grey.'

'Yes. I see,' Grunwald said. 'Well, Pfefferkorn, we mustn't tire you.'

'You're not tiring me. It's a great pleasure, my dear friend.'

'The gentleman means he's got something else to do,' the woman said.

'Ah. Of course. Well, of course,' Pfefferkorn said, getting up. 'So Herr Grunwald, when you get the chance, if you wouldn't mind mentioning,' he said, picking his words carefully, 'that just a line, or a word, would be appreciated. After fifty years of service,' Pfefferkorn said. 'When was it he came back?'

'It's hard to say, Pfefferkorn. It was a confused time after the war. There was much confusion then.'

'Yes, yes, I remember, all confusion. I used to read the newspapers. I still read them sometimes. I never saw his name.'

'Perhaps he changed the name, Pfefferkorn.'

'Perhaps, perhaps. I looked for both names, of course, for Boehme also. I read everything in those days. I read the personal columns. I thought he might be in trouble. I thought he might need help. I was his personal man, Herr Grunwald. I was his confidential man.'

'What name, Pfefferkorn? What other name?'

'The travel name. When he travelled, Herr Grunwald – a great deal, as I don't have to tell you. It was necessary sometimes that other business interests shouldn't know when he was in a certain town, Budapest, Vienna. In those days he became Herr Boehme. But who remembers them now? We're survivors, Herr Grunwald. They're lost days.'

'Boehme?' Grunwald said.

'Boehme. Hans Werner, H.W.B. The same initials. Because of the cases, naturally. I attended to all this, suitcases, razor case, pyjama case, writing case. All this was my preserve, Herr Grunwald.'

'And identity papers also in this name?'

'Certainly – all in my preserve. Who else could do it? I kept them in the confidential safe. I was the confidential man. Fifty years,' Pfefferkorn said, 'when next you see him. In no spirit of complaint,' he said.

They got the 5.30 train back.

'What do you think?' Grunwald said, in the train.

'God knows.'

'Yes. That's certain. Does he want us to know?'

'We'll have to see.'

'It's a job for detectives, Mr Raison. We're not detectives.'

'Yes,' Raison said. He closed his eyes. 'I'm not sure how keen Mrs Wolff would be on detectives,' he said.

Grunwald looked at him for a moment.

'It's distasteful to you,' he said. 'I can see it is becoming immensely distasteful.'

'It's nothing to do with me. I'm only the errand boy.'

'Yes, that's true. It's very true,' Grunwald said. 'I also.'

So he phoned Ansbach when he got back, and Ansbach phoned Fuss, and in the morning Fuss turned them over to Tschadek again.

Tschadek didn't take all day this time, and maybe God wanted them to know, for a mere hour and a half sufficed to turn up the name of Hans Werner Boehme. It turned up in Anti-fascist Section Number Two, for Herr Boehme was one of those anti-fascists who had arrived by lorry.

PART THREE

The persecutee shall have a claim to indemnification if at any time during the period from 30 January 1933 to 8 May 1945 he has lived underground in conditions unworthy of a human being, or has had to abandon chattels belonging to him because he emigrated, took to flight, or lived in illegality in order to elude N S terror acts.

German Federal Indemnification Law
(*Bundesentschädigungsgesetz*)

Chapter 1

A QUESTION OF STATUS
AND HELPING HANDS

THE early sun, streaming on to the newspaper, hurt his eyes. Jaws champing, he realized he'd been stuck on the same headline for a couple of sausages. REFORM DER KAPITAL-MÄRKTE DRINGEND ERFORDERLICH, and with an effort shifted his gaze. He'd been farther along than this. Yes. ... *Pensionsfonds, Versicherungen und Investmentsparen über Kapital-anlagegesellschaften dürften sich nach Ansicht der Konferenz als ...*

'More bacon?'

'Yes.'

'More sausages?'

'Yes.'

'Another egg?'

'Yes.'

... *und Investmentsparen über Kapitalanlagegesellschaften dürften sich nach ...*

'Coffee now?'

'Yes.'

'The peach preserve is fresh. Have some with another roll?'

'All right.'

... *und Investmentsparen über Kapitalanlagegesellschaften dürften sich ...*

'As it happens, her sister-in-law will be there for coffee this morning at Renate Heilbron's.'

... *und Investmentsparen über Kapitalanlagegesellschaften. ...*

'What?' he said.

'Magda's sister-in-law, Margrit. I'll be having coffee with her this morning at – '

'What are you talking about? What in God's name are you babbling at? I'll have some more preserve. I'm trying to read the paper,' he said, crackling it ... *und Investmentsparen über. ...*

'I told you not to mention Magda,' he said.

'Don't you think you're being a little ridiculous?'

'Yes,' he said. 'More coffee. Always ridiculous,' he said. 'As at the time of the soirées, and later. I don't ask you to try to understand this ridiculousness.'

'If there were some issue of principle involved.'

'Don't rack you brains with it,' he said. 'If you could just, for instance, see to it that the rolls are fresh.'

'Yes, I'm sorry. I don't know what's the matter with Hoffman lately. All his stuff's gone off.'

'It's perfectly simple what's the matter with Hoffman,' he said. 'He doesn't care any more. Hoffman is not alone.' It went right over her head, of course. It was no use being ironical with her. On top of everything, she looked beautiful. She looked as poised and fresh as a girl, as if she hadn't waited till all hours for him to go to bed. He felt crushed as an old boot himself... *und Investmentsparen über*.... 'And why are you seeing Margrit?' he said. 'You know very well I want you to stay away from the whole herd.'

'I'm not going out of my way to see her. Renate Heilbron asked her to coffee. Not everybody shares your elevated views as to who's untouchable and who isn't. Leave the roll, then. The cherry cake is fresh. It's quite good with the preserve. The flavours mix well.'

He grunted and tried a slice of cake with the preserve. It wasn't bad. It wasn't bad at all. He tried another slice. 'I don't ask you to try and reason it out,' he said. 'I don't want to overtax you in any way. I simply tell you how I expect you to behave. I don't mention such things as integrity. That it's a question of status should be enough.'

'If Magda's status is worrying you, don't let it. There's nothing wrong with her status, I can assure you, nor with the status of Princess Sibylla von Staffelberg or Princess Ulrike Schwanenburg Rappe. You're the only one who sees status problems there. Won't you ever understand how absurd it is always to be so fanatical, at the wrong time, for the wrong reason? Magda can help you. She's probably the only person who can help you, you've successfully alienated everybody else. Can *you* go to Stille Hilfe and Hilfende Hände? You'd soon get a dusty answer. You treated them disgracefully in the past.'

'I don't think we should talk of the past,' he said. 'I didn't know you were such a student of the past.'

'I don't harp on it. What's gone is gone. What I do say is that, even apart from other considerations, you have a duty to your clients, and you're letting personal matters stand in the way of it. You seem to be going out of your way to alienate them as well as everybody else. You don't suppose your friend Mr Raison won't run back to them with these charming stories of yours?'

'Try not to let my friend Mr Raison bother you so much,' he said. He noted pleasurably the two small spots of red that had come up on her cheeks. She was jealous. She was always extraordinarily acute about relationships. That antenna of hers had picked up right away the current between them, had known instantly that here he'd found someone he could talk to, unburden himself with, as he'd never been able to with her. It irked her.

'It doesn't bother me,' she said. 'It bothers me when you make a fool of yourself. You either talk too much or not enough. A single word now could regularize this stupid situation with Magda. Did your mother ask what politics the pair of you would favour before she bore you?'

'I won't talk about Magda. Magda has made her bed and she must lie on it,' he said with finality. But from nowhere the thought came: And how many with her? How long since Magda had lain in her bed alone? Rottenness. Rottenness. Suddenly, like a fissure in his heart, a new seam of speculation cracked open. Could the strain have come from his side of the family, the vein of rottenness in Elke? Could some ungovernable. . . . He had always had strong feelings, and his wife none, no passion whatever. Glutinous, nauseous memories stirred suddenly, like the taste of egg in his mouth, of lustful nights long ago, when the beast in him had wanted to do everything to her, had sometimes done everything, and she'd remained totally unmoved, unaffected, incurious even, immediately going to sleep while he'd lain detumescent, licking his lips and thinking of what he'd done. Nothing moved her. Nothing at all moved her. It suddenly drove him to the point of fury that an unmoved life had left her looking so fresh and beautiful.

'There'll be nothing more about Magda!' he said.

'If you'd let me make an approach, in no way involving you, a mere exploratory –'

'I absolutely forbid it!' he said. The taste of egg and of old nights was nauseous in his mouth. He couldn't eat the thickly-spread cake any more and flung it down, rising with his newspaper. 'You take my appetite away,' he said.

She said, alarmed, 'You can't go without eating!'

'I can't eat a bite in this house! You sicken me. I refuse to talk about Magda. I refuse to think about her.'

But in the Mercedes, as he sat in cold rage in one traffic jam after another, hooting the various swine who edged past and jumped the lights, he thought about her. What a bottomless piece of irony that Schonbach had gone to Magda. But much as he wanted to be there, much as it was necessary for him to breathe there, he wouldn't ask her. There'd been occasions in former times when she'd been in a position to help, and he'd not let her. Thank God he'd kept his hands clean of that swinishness. Why was it always his fate to be in a position where Magda could do something for him? Just a few years ago she'd been a social outcast, a pariah, and now here she was on top of the world again, hobnobbing with nobility and with Klara longing to resume relations. And yet Magda hadn't changed. She hadn't changed in any particular. What was the matter with everyone? Was he the only one to see the rottenness? Well, to the devil with them. Let the whole world fall in. In one soul at least decency would be preserved, even if nobody else cared. But he thought there was somebody else who cared. He rather thought there was somebody else. He wondered, as he turned into the Sendlingerstrasse, exactly what he was going to tell him this morning.

Raison had been having a rather ghastly sort of time in a world bounded by doctors. He longed with all his heart to go home, and he longed at the same time to tell Dr Ansbach,

Dr Grunwald, Dr Fuss and Dr Dr Tschadek to go to hell. He thought it would be a fine idea if Mrs Wolff went to hell, too. He'd had enough of her affairs, and of the affairs of her relations. Her relation Bamberger alias Boehme had consumed all of his mental and physical energy for all of the day, and he was sick of him. The day had started with some promise with Tschadek performing well at his files. But it had then turned out that all Tschadek was turning up was the headings to various items. The items themselves, with reference numbers, dates and other essentials, were elsewhere, in a series of other rooms, access by differently coloured permits.

To get these permits a collection of terrible old officials had to be visited in turn. It had meant running about the Ministry and there and back to Ansbach while filling in time between the officials, so that access to Room 48a, the last of the rooms, had come only three-quarters of an hour before closing time, and some of the items were still not checked.

'What is still not checked?' Ansbach said.

They were sitting on his old leather sofa in the late afternoon while he made an orderly list of the items culled during the day.

'There's a section F2,' Raison said dully, 'with information regarding transports from the reception centre to the rehabilitation centre. It didn't seem very exciting so we skipped it and got on to the next thing.'

He sat listening to the office clock, smoking, while Ansbach got on with it.

'One Pattern B blue Antifa Certificate of National Reliability, issued Prague,' Ansbach muttered as he wrote.

His list ran: One movement order, H. W. Boehme, for Antifa-approved anti-fascist convoy 487; one medical certificate Czech-type B–300/1990 showing when last D D T'd; one set German identity papers issued on arrival Furth-im-Wald 10 August 1946; one baggage check showing one small and two large suitcases monogrammed H.W.B.; one arrival certificate issued Würzburg rehabilitation centre 18 August 1946; one receipt for sixty marks advanced by Würzburg rehabilitation centre to H. W. Boehme 18 August 1946;

one Placement entry issued by Würzburg rehabilitation centre . . .

'What's this?' Ansbach said. 'I can't read the handwriting.'

Grunwald had a look at it. 'It's my handwriting,' he said. 'It's an exact copy of all that was there. "H.H. 180846".'

'H.H.?'

'It stands, apparently, for "Hilfende Hände".'

'Aha.'

'Exactly what is Hilfende Hände?' Raison said.

'A voluntary aid society,' Ansback said, writing. 'The number I presume, is the date – yes, same date as arrival, 18 August 1946. A voluntary aid society,' he said. 'Helping Hands. There were several others, "Stille Hilfe" – Silent Help. Also Mutual Assistance, Society of Late Homecomers, Christian Aid, and so on. They helped people who suffered in the war, more specifically Nazi people, war criminials and their families, people on the run, and so on. It became quite a social thing, with people like Princess Sibylla von Staffelberg, Princess Ulrike Schwanenburg Rappe, the odd cardinal. They got quite high-flown on the subject of German honour, and putting the right face on before the Occupation vulgarians. If Boehme signed himself out of the official rehabilitation scheme and on to the books of this voluntary body, we can say right away he's not likely to have the identity papers he was issued with. I don't think it's very promising,' he said.

'Apparently Hilfende Hände has further information,' Raison said.

'Of course.'

'You don't think there's much chance of getting it.'

'We can try. Try your friend Haffner.'

'Haffner? Won't he have prosecuted rather a lot of their clients?'

'Still try him. It intrigues me that anti-fascist Bamberger should go to Hilfende Hände,' Ansbach said.

'I don't understand what he wanted with anti-fascist papers at all,' Grunwald said.

'Boehme the ethnic German wanted them. Times were not so good for ethnic Germans. Evidently he had good reason for not turning himself back into Bamberger. There were various privileges for holders of an Antifa pass. For one thing they weren't subject to constant investigation.'

'Wouldn't it make him an object of curiosity in Germany?' Raison said.

Ansbach smiled. 'Plenty of well-connected fascists came in on an Antifa pass. It needed influence to get one, anyway. The thing could be conveniently dropped on arrival. Who would know about it here?'

'Students of Dr Tschadek's files?' Raison said.

'So how far did it get you?'

They fell silent for a while, brooding.

'The dates are puzzling,' Ansbach said.

'What dates?' Grunwald said.

'He arrives at Furth-im-Wald on 10 August but not till the 18th at the rehabilitation centre. That's a long time to stay at the camp of arrival. Trainloads of people were coming in every day. They had a rapid turnover in these places.'

Grunwald studied the list and shrugged. 'There's a certain perversity about the events connected with Bamberger,' he said to Raison. 'This is a matter to do with the transport, of course. You know where that will be?'

'F2, yellow permit,' Raison said.

'Exactly. The one that wasn't so interesting. Well, it can still be done,' he said wearily. 'I don't know what the relevance of the dates is,' he said.

'Maybe there isn't any,' Ansbach said. 'And again maybe there is. If he stopped off on the way somewhere it would account for the lapse of time. Where could he have stopped off? He could have stopped off in Bamberg. If so, there'll be something in the file. There's always something in the file, if you look. It's always worth looking. It's also worth asking your friend Haffner,' he said, 'if he can think of any way we can get information from Hilfende Hände.'

'All right,' Raison said, 'I will.'

And that evening on the phone he did; and that night Haffner paced his study, and in the morning could scarcely eat his breakfast.

Raison and Grunwald ate theirs together. Afterwards Grunwald went to the Land Ministry of the Interior for a yellow permit, and Raison to see Haffner.

'I am afraid it was meant to be hurtful.'

'Oh, I don't think – '

'Hurtful. In a devious way, of which unfortunately I have had experience in dealing with – in dealing with Dr Ansbach's people. It's a matter of innuendo, which naturally I wouldn't expect an Englishman to – '

'We were really just tossing it around, you know,' Raison said. 'We were thinking of all possible approaches and he merely thought, on the off chance, you might be able to help in some – '

'In some way. Exactly. Have a cigarette, James. I may call you James? He couldn't think of any specific way. Just *some* way. I am afraid, James, I have to explain to you a personal dilemma, a family – I may say a family grief.'

Raison drew thoughtfully on the mentholated cigarette that had been offered him and considered Haffner. There was no question the man had come to look habitually bushed of late. There seemed to be something about these days that stopped people growing old gracefully. The ageing people he knew seemed to be in a state of disturbance these days.

'I have a sister Magda,' Haffner said, 'who I am ashamed to say is a full Nazi. We have had a great deal of trouble with her for many many years.'

The lacklustre eyes were hanging sickly on his, so Raison nodded gravely. But in the same moment a vaguely unpleasant recollection came to him of having heard of this sister, of the sister being invoked in a context of unhappiness and embarrassment. He identified the recollection just as Haffner spoke again.

'Magda married a young man, while still at university, who became very prominent in the movement, a general in the SS. He was undoubtedly guilty of many crimes, and if he had come back it would have been a privilege to prosecute him. However he was killed, on the Russian front. Of course, his wife Magda had been very prominent, high positions in the Nazi social organizations, high friends and so on. This gave her possibilities to help me, which thank God I refused. As you know I never even became a member of the Nazi Lawyers' Organization, which was absolutely expected of every lawyer, everyone belonged, which I refused – at great risk, I may say. Of course, someone is sure to tell you there was no risk, that I had protection, which is absolutely not true, I always made my position perfectly plain and would have done whether my sister was Frau General Emmerich or not. And so after the collapse there was some trouble with Magda's pension, which she asked me to undertake, and which I did. She was after all legally entitled to it for her husband, whatever his crimes, and I was at this time having to support her myself. So this went on and then in some sections of the press some rottenness started about the prosecutor Haffner acting against the old Nazis to help his career and acting for them to help his pocket. I won't say how low some of them stooped, the bottomless swinishness I had to put up with. However. So things were made very difficult for me, and in the end I had to give up handling Magda's case, which led to various troubles between us, some bad scenes, she refused to take another pfennig, and so. So then my mother died and Magda got her money, a half of her money, my daughter Elke also had a half, and in the end her pension came through, and she lives her old life again. But of course, Magda is a person who doesn't change with the wind, one has to say it, and I am afraid she is still a full Nazi, with interests in every kind of Nazi thing, including these societies that helped the old Nazis, and an honorary position with Hilfende Hände among others, which is constantly making difficulties for me, we can still see in the press sometimes some paragraphs. So this is the story, and this is why Ansbach thinks I can help in some way. So now tell me, James, your opinion.'

He had been tapping his ash fairly freely during the recital, and now ground the cigarette out as he looked eagerly into Raison's face. Raison ground his own cigarette out, and wondered what his opinion was. There was something about the cigarette, as about Haffner's story, that was curiously deadening. One got a big mouthful of nothing, paralysing at once to both taste and judgement.

'It's difficult,' he said.

'It is. People refuse to see the difficulties. I knew you would see.'

'Hilfende Hände files are confidential, of course.'

'Of course.'

'Could she look at them?'

'Yes.'

'Mm.'

'I think,' Haffner said.

'Ah.'

'One must be honest,' Haffner said.

'Yes. Is she likely to tell you, though?'

'I don't know.'

'Depends how the questions are framed, I suppose.'

'I suppose,' Haffner said. But he was disappointed. 'If I may say, I don't think this is the question. I think the question is one of principles. Whether we can seek help from those we are opposed to, in the very area where we are opposed. It's a question of morality, don't you think?'

'Absolutely,' Raison said. 'Nothing else.'

The questions old Heinz was likely to put, he saw, were going to be funny ones, of doubtful productivity. The real question was how to take the framing of the questions out of Heinz's hands and into the hands of some keener question-framer.

'Even where the result one seeks,' Haffner said, still in moral orbit, 'is for a larger good. Which is still another question.'

'Same old thing, really, isn't it?' Raison said. He could see no clear need to define his own moral position in a context of Haffner's trials with his sister. 'Any other ways that we can get at it then?' he said.

'I knew you would understand, James,' Haffner said. 'I was certain of it. Have a cigarette, James.'

'I don't think I will at the moment.'

'I always keep up good relations with the defence lawyers in the prosecution cases. They knew things, of course. They had access to all sorts of things. Perhaps something can be done in that direction.'

'Good.'

'I never believed in bringing malice into these cases. There was never any point in malice. After all, it was a long time ago, a lifetime ago.'

'Yes.'

'When the world was different. So different, James.'

'Quite.'

'The times, the pressures, the people. Above all, the people. I sometimes think ... I see an old man in the dock and ask myself is this the same one, the same organism even, that did these things a generation ago?'

'Changed, of course,' Raison said. In Haffner's indrawn and somewhat lingering smile he suddenly saw a weird likeness to his daughter. At the same moment he remembered the breakfast he was supposed to have with her. When was it? Yesterday.

'Changed in many ways. Changed, perhaps, in all ways,' Haffner said softly.

'Yes,' Raison said. He looked at his watch. Ten fifteen. Late for breakfast. Was it late in all quarters?

Haffner caught the movement, and smiled somewhat sheepishly. 'Just a notion of mine. There are interesting philosophical, perhaps we may say metaphysical problems. ... Perhaps we'll talk of it again.'

'I'm sure we will,' Raison said, experience having made him quite sure of this. 'I want to think over this problem of yours.'

'Heinz,' Haffner said.

'Heinz. I want to think over it very seriously.'

'I know, James. I understand,' Haffner said. He had Raison's hand grasped warmly in both of his. 'Meanwhile I'll see what can be done in the other direction.'

'Good, then.'

'Wonderful.'

And all of a sudden everything was. As the door closed behind Raison, Haffner felt himself clear-headed again, amost young, almost hungry again. Definitely hungry. It occurred to him that he'd left his breakfast, and that in only half an hour it would be time for second breakfast, and that life had tang again, decency again. He lit himself a mentholated cigarette and drew in a mouthful of something that seemed to expand and creep through every nook and cranny of his cranium like some cool and unidentifiable marsh gas. It wasn't exactly like a cigarette. It was in some ways better than a cigarette. One was smoking and yet not smoking. One was having it, in a sense, both ways.

Chapter 2

ANOTHER PART OF THE FOREST

RAISON took a taxi to the Hohenzollernstrasse and sat in the back feeling liberated and at the same time deeply uneasy. He was getting used to the feeling of liberation on parting from Haffner. He was uneasy because he had been abroad now some days. He was always uneasy after being abroad some days. It was bad enough understanding them at the best of times, but abroad it was worse, and in Germany much worse. So much normality was all around here where so recently there had been so much abnormality. Depravity on a gigantic scale had been the order of the day here. Where was it? What had happened to all the depraved people? Where had they laid their depravity? What, here, was normal and what abnormal? These things bothered him.

He was bothered also by guilt feelings at what he was doing with Mrs Wolff's time. It was undoubtedly a funny way to be spending her time. He had put in a fair amount for her yesterday, of course. And her affairs were meanwhile going ahead. Grunwald was getting himself a yellow permit. Haffner was seeing what could be done without malice. All the same it was irregular to be paying a social call on Haffner's strange daughter in the middle of the working morning.

He could hardly remember what she looked like. He'd been trying to think what she looked like. In her father's lingering and indrawn smile he had caught a sudden glimpse, and he hung on to it now in the back of the taxi. It was a sketchy glimpse, a mere nebulous smile and under it the general rig of her breasts. The breasts were a good deal clearer than the smile which was now, indecently enough, Haffner's smile. All this made him more uneasy than ever, and as the taxi sped round the sunlit Oskar von Miller Ring and turned in to the broad straight of the Ludwigstrasse, he felt himself in a state of mild panic, identity rapidly crumbling. What he had got here, he realized, was nothing other than a touch of Gunter's trouble, but made worse, far worse, by the alienation effect of a foreign city and the attendant withdrawal into private fantasy. He had several quick fantasies with Elke Haffner in the Ludwigstrasse. He ran lightly upstairs, found her in bed wearing a lingering smile, and pausing only to throw his jacket off, got in and without words began making several months of bottled-up love. He found he had his trousers on. He ran lightly upstairs again, threw his trousers and his jacket off, threw everything off, and got back in. The girl was having a fine series of orgasms as they ran past the Siegestor, and he pulled himself together.

This was terrible, of course, quite awful, in the middle of the morning, unseemly. It was an absurdity, too. Some other aspects of her persona had returned to mind; a general impression of large seriousness and brooding concern. It was true the girl had had an affair – was it true? Gunter had said it was true – with a deformed Hungarian. But this didn't mean she was promiscuous. She seemed very far from promiscuous. What possible concern was it of his whether she was promiscuous or not, anyway? He couldn't be promiscuous. There was a very clear estoppel on that. He had to be constantly aware of that. Not to be aware of it was to risk dangerous deceleration and a falling-away into lunacy. All in all, after fantasies of this kind it was probably a lousy idea to be visiting the girl at all. He thought it was a lousy idea.

'Hohenzollernstrasse,' the driver said.

'Ah.'

'What number?'

A number of possibilities sprang to mind. He had lost the

number, or had been taken ill, or was meeting a friend on the corner, or merely engaged on a survey of the Hohenzollern-strasse.

'A hundred and seventy-six,' Raison said, 'I think.'

'You think?'

'I think a hundred and seventy-six.' It sounded wrong. He was almost sure it was wrong.

The man grunted and cruised down the street.

Number 176 was one of a terrace, raised in imperial times, and still doing useful service as the double row of buttons and the two-way speaker in the doorway indicated. Raison paid off the taxi and had a look at the names beside the buttons. He saw with panic that he wasn't wrong. Haffner, E., was on the third floor. A rhythmic cranking at his back told him that the taxi was still there.

'All right?' the man said.

'Yes, this is it,' Raison said, 'thanks,' and pressed the bell. Actions once started had to be finished. The tricky issue of standards was always present. Besides, she could very easily be out. There was every reason why she should be out, middle of the working morning.

'*Ja?*' Elke said from the speaker.

'It's James Raison. Good morning,' Raison said.

'Who? Oh. Yes.' The door had sprung electrically open. 'Don't bother. I'll come. I'll let you in. Yes.'

Raison went in, clearing his throat.

There was a large hall and a flight of stairs. He began to walk up the stairs. He had got to the second flight when he heard the girl running down.

'Mr Raison?'

'Yes.'

'It's strange, I was just talking about you. Hello, Mr Raison,' she said, rounding the bend. 'My mother was telephoning. Have you had breakfast?'

'I wondered if you had.'

'I'm afraid I've been lazy. I'm afraid I'm terribly lazy. Will you eat breakfast now?'

'Yes. I –'

'We could go across the street. There's a café, do you remember? Will you eat in the café?'

'All right. It's very nice out,' Raison said. 'You don't need a raincoat.'

'It's very light. I'm quite untidy underneath. I'm afraid I'm a quite untidy person.'

Her hair was somewhat tousled and she was doing something with it as she came down. Raison had to revise his ideas about brooding seriousness. The girl was fairly bubbling, far more like her mother than her father. The vaguely unfocused look he had noticed in the parental home was revealed in the light of day as nothing more than a slight unevenness in the set of the eyes. There was a top o' the morning air about her that was quite disconcerting after the steamy session in bed, and Raison found himself revising and unscrambling all round. This kept him silent as they went along the Hohenzollern-strasse and crossed the busy main road to the café.

They had coffee and rolls on the pavement while the busy world of Schwabing bustled by. Crowds of young men in corduroy jackets and girls in jeans seemed to be eating too.

'Isn't anyone working here today?' Raison said.

'It's like this every day. The university is just along the road. They've probably already done some work.'

'Haven't you got any work?'

'Oh, I have a project of my own just now.'

'You don't paint?'

'I do paint. I'm not interested in painting just now. I'm interested in propaganda. I think we have a huge need for propaganda, particularly here. You know?'

'Propaganda,' Raison said. The butter was melting in the sun. He was having a hard time with his knife.

'Simple messages, clearly put. The whole idea of communicating with people. It's very important. It's very interesting. I'm very interested in design, typography, layout.'

'It's printing, is it?'

'It's basically printing. But I'm interested in many other fields, film, the didactic theatre. I'm very interested in posters,' she said. 'Posters are so basic.'

'Yes,' Raison said. He used his teaspoon on the butter. 'I suppose they are,' he said.

'You're not laughing?'

'I'm not laughing. What messages do you put on the posters?'

'There's only one message. There's no room for more than one message on a poster. There's only one message, anyway.'

'What is it?'

'Men must love each other or they will die.'

'Aren't they going to do that anyway?'

'Not in that sense. But it's another reason. They are brothers sharing a common fate.'

'Do brothers love each other?'

'Why not? What else is there for them to do?'

'I don't know. It seems a very simple poster,' Raison said. 'You'll soon run out of posters.'

'But it can be applied to everything. Every issue can be judged by it. For instance – you're a Christian, I suppose.'

'No, I'm a lawyer,' Raison said.

'What does that mean?'

'I have to regulate matters between the brothers. I have to define what's legitimate and what's not legitimate for them to do. On behalf of the family as a whole,' Raison said.

'Can't you be a Christian and a lawyer?'

'Oh, no,' Raison said. 'No, you can't be a Christian and a lawyer. Not in a practical way. There's the law of damages, you see. There are several other laws. If a man takes my client's coat I couldn't advise him to give up his cloak, too. I'd have to advise him to sue for the return of the coat. Not that I'm against the general idea,' he said, 'or against your posters. They seem very beneficial posters.'

'Are you laughing?' the girl said. 'I don't think you're laughing. Maybe you're a cynic. I don't think you're a cynic.' She was looking at him with a good deal of interest through her uneven eyes. 'I think we'll have to talk about it much more, unless you don't like to talk about it.'

Raison didn't mind talking about it. It struck him as a much safer thing to be talking about than many others. And it had enabled him to unscramble completely on the subject of the girl. She was neither the unfocused brooder of Bogenhausen nor the erotic figment of fantasy. This was simply a girl who liked a rousing discussion. He felt secure. She had her light raincoat buttoned well up, too, which made him feel even more secure.

'Maybe my mother isn't so wrong. Maybe you should meet Magda,' she said.

'Magda,' Raison said.

'My aunt. She doesn't like me to call her aunt. She is rather a terrible person, but she says interesting things. She is a terrible Nazi. She was married to an S S general.'

'I think your father's spoken of her.'

'Oh, they don't speak. They haven't spoken for years. Don't speak of Magda to my father.'

'All right,' Raison said. 'Why does your mother think I ought to meet her?'

'I don't know. She gets these ideas. She's an awful scatter-brain. She just rang me up. Magda also says such provocative things,' she said, smiling. 'Do you want to meet her?'

'Yes,' Raison said.

'Oh. Well.' She seemed a bit taken aback at his ready accep-tance. 'We can do it. When do you want?'

'Now?' Raison said.

'Now? I don't know. She works in the morning. In the after-noon, perhaps. She has tea at the Luitpold Grill, she's there every day with her friends. You know it, the pavement café with umbrellas on the Briennerstrasse ...'

'I'll find it,' Raison said.

'Everybody knows it, it's very fashionable. Or if you want I can pick you up at, say, four, half past ...'

'I don't know where I'll be then,' Raison said. 'I'll meet you there. Well,' he said, writing it in his book, 'that's nice.'

'Is it? I don't know,' the girl said. She seemed a bit flustered. She was running her eyes over him. 'I'm afraid Magda is rather a terrible lady. I'm afraid she has something of a terrible reputa-tion.'

'Well, if you go about marrying S S generals,' Raison said.

'It's not the S S general. She's in her own right very – I don't know the word – provocative?'

'I like a provocative discussion.'

'It isn't the right word,' she said. 'I don't know the word. I don't know if you'll take to Magda.'

'Will she take to me?'

'Oh, yes,' she said. Her eyes seemed to have become very sharp as though she were newly looking at him. 'Oh, yes. Magda will take to you. I think.'

'Fine.'

'Yes,' she said dubiously. 'I wish I could think of the word. So how is your work going here?'

Raison told her how the work was going. He didn't tell her about Hilfende Hände. He told her about the Land Ministry of the Interior, and Dr Fuss and Dr Dr Tschadek. He told her about Grunwald.

Grunwald had found something out, but he didn't know what it was. He was walking very carefully from Section F2. He was trying to think how far it was from F2 to the main doorway. He remembered there were two flights of stairs and several corridors.

'Is something the matter, Herr Grunwald?'

'Nothing.'

'Do you want to sit down? A glass of water?'

'I want a chemist.'

'A chemist,' Tschadek said. 'Yes, there is a chemist. There is a chemist at two hundred metres. We can send to the chemist for you.'

'I'll go,' Grunwald said. No favours. Nothing. It was a matter of getting downstairs. He could rest downstairs. He remembered a bench there. He would rest on the bench and pace himself for the two hundred metres. He had slept very badly. It had happened before after he'd slept badly. He'd mistaken the signs. He'd thought it was exhaustion from all he'd done here. He'd done too much, Bamberg, the permits, this section, that section, on his feet, too much. He'd felt dazed at breakfast, a little out of sorts, restless, a desire to move, to alter his posture. It felt like wind. It felt like something fresh air would dissipate. He thought it might be the heat.

He'd left off his waistcoat because of the heat. The pills were in his waistcoat. Thank God he had the prescription. He had it in his wallet.

Tschadek hovered closely, observing, long hair dangling gravely about his ears. 'Take my arm, Herr Grunwald.'

'I have the banister.'

'We can rest on the next landing. There is a seat on the landing. Here is the seat.'

Grunwald went past the seat, groping for the next banister. There was a time element, he remembered. He would rest downstairs. There was no time to rest in both places. Slowly and doggedly, mentally controlling the uncertain thing in his chest that at any moment could lay him agonizingly on the floor with a sudden piledriver blow, he negotiated staircases and corridors. He came to the hall. He came to the bench. He sat himself on the bench and breathed through his mouth, looking out through the swing doors into the sunny street. He felt very ill.

Tschadek went away and came back. He had a glass of water. He held the glass to Grunwald's mouth.

'Leave it. Leave the water,' Grunwald said faintly.

'We can send to the chemist. There's no difficulty whatever in sending.'

'I'll be all right.'

'Do you want a taxi? We can get a taxi.'

He would have to climb into the taxi and out of it.

'I'll be all right,' he said.

Tschadek watched him while he rested. The porter watched him, and the receptionist, and some people waiting by the reception desk. They were murmuring with concern. Why so much concern now, Grunwald thought, for an old sick rabbit? Why now? Not then. Why now? They are culpable, he thought. Their sins are still upon them. If I should die here now, on the bench, on the floor below the bench, with my last thoughts I condemn them. Punish them. They have sinned against me, against the human order, against you.

They are still in sin. I don't recognize their concern. I am not a party to their concern.

'Herr Grunwald, I am very concerned about you,' Tschadek said. 'We must get you a doctor.'

Grunwald stood up. 'Which way to the chemist?' he said to Tschadek.

'Turn right. But you're not in a condition to –'

He leaned against the swing doors and went out to the street. It was so hot in the street. It hugged him all round. There was a brazen light in the street, the light of noonday. 'That ravageth at noonday,' he said. He found he was praying. It was the Prayer Before a Journey. 'Of the terror by night,' he said, 'or of the arrow that flieth by day . . . may fall at thy side, and ten thousand at thy right hand; it shall not come nigh unto thee . . .'

He saw the sign, 'Apotheke', and went in, into darkness. There were figures about, solid figures filling the shop, between him and the counter. But he made his way between them. There was a chair by the counter and he sat on it. He had his wallet out. He took the prescription and banknotes from the wallet. He felt so sick, so heavy suddenly, he could hardly lift his head. It's near, he thought.

'Bitte?'

He lifted his hand with the prescription and the money in it, and left it open on the counter. A hand took the prescription and went away and came back. Two men came back.

'We haven't got it,' one of them said. 'We can get it.'

'Something,' Grunwald said.

'Bitte?'

'Something else.'

'There are other preparations but here it's prescribed –'

'Quickly,' Grunwald said. 'Now.'

'I'll do what I can. Where is the doctor?'

'In Israel.'

'Then we must get another doctor. It's not possible to –'

'I am going to have a heart attack,' Grunwald said. He could feel himself slipping off the seat. He leaned against the counter. He said, 'I am going to have a heart attack in your shop.'

The man was swearing. Both men were swearing. Grunwald sat with his eyes closed.

'Take this. Open your mouth. Take it.'

In the dark he opened his mouth and bit into the capsule and leaned sideways waiting for it to work. It worked quickly. There was a twisting knife-like sensation like a bowel movement, and at the same time mist rose from his valley. He could feel his head against the counter, and sweat trickling. There was a crust of saliva in his mouth, gummy as his lips worked. 'And I shall be healed,' Grunwald said. 'Save me and I shall be saved . . . for that I am fearfully and wonderfully made: wonderful are thy works. Blessed art thou, the faithful Physician.' He didn't know he was praying. It came up in him as if through a wick, from channels. He leaned sideways absorbing the capsule and the prayer.

'If you're feeling better,' the man said.

'I'm feeling better.'

'Sign this. It's a serious matter. It's not my responsibility. It's your responsibility.'

'A man from these parts told me this once before. His name was Müller. It was in Berlin. But he was a policeman from these parts. One learns responsibility here,' Grunwald told him, signing.

'See, I've written it on this sheet of paper also. You should show it to your doctor. You should consult him as soon as possible.'

'I'm in constant consultation,' Grunwald said. 'How much?'

'There's no charge. I can't charge for this. It was on your responsibility,' the man said.

'All right,' Grunwald said. He got to his feet, and found he was all right there. 'You did well,' he said. 'You did better than expected.' But he put a note on the counter, all the same. Accept nothing.

He walked slowly to the corner and got a taxi. He felt overwhelmingly tired. He would have a sleep in the hotel, before anything. In the taxi, licking his lips, he thought over what he had found out. He still didn't know what it meant. When he was less confused he would know. Ansbach might know, or Raison.

*

'What does it mean?' Raison said.

'It's best to let him have his sleep. The figures obviously relate to the transport. The first one is 13 August and has a cross by it, the next 18 August with a tick. It looks as if Bamberger-Boehme missed one transport and caught another, which would allow for the missing time. But he missed it at the Furth-im-Wald end and not by stopping off on the way. What can that mean?'

'What's the scribble underneath?'

'What does it look like to you?'

'I don't know. Walsten. Is that something?'

'Waldstein is. It's a place.'

'And then "Town M. 13–17". What can that be?'

'He'll tell us when he wakes up. But 13 to 17 are the dates between 13 and 18 August when, presumably, he was waiting for the next transport.'

'In Town M.?'

'I don't know.'

'So what is Waldstein?'

'A village. Another part of the forest. When he wakes up he'll tell us. I've got to leave for an appointment in a few minutes,' Ansbach said, looking at his watch. 'Can you stay with him?'

Raison looked at his own watch. 'I've got one, too,' he said.

'So the floor waiter can look in on him from time to time. I think he'll be all right now. Can I drop you somewhere?'

'The Luitpold Grill,' Raison said.

She was already there, in sunglasses, when he arrived. Her bright red E-type was there, too, standing by the café's No-Parking sign.

'Tell me why it is,' he said, 'that you only leave your car where you aren't supposed to.'

'I'll move it if a policeman asks me. I long for a policeman to ask me. They never do. In this country the omniscience of authority is too easily accepted, don't you think it is so?'

'I expect so,' Raison said. It was hot and he felt a bit limp for this sort of talk. 'It sounds like a good subject for a poster,' he said. He sat down and called for an ice cream. 'Are we too early for your aunt?' he said.

'She isn't here. That's her table.'

A number of women were having tea at a near-by table, some in elaborate dirndls and looking like well got-up parlourmaids. He'd noticed large numbers of women in this outfit and at first had thought they were all parlourmaids. This crew were being girls together and having a fine time.

'I'm afraid,' the girl said, 'they all make me quite sick.'

'Have another ice cream.'

'The whole ambience here makes me sick. Women shouldn't dress themselves up to look like dolls. These ones are certainly not dolls.'

'You must learn to love them,' Raison said.

'I know it. It isn't them. It's what they represent. I don't have to love what they represent.'

'Ah. It's a dangerous argument. Isn't it getting a bit late?' Raison said.

'Yes. I'd better go and ask them,' the girl said, screwing up her face.

She was now, Raison saw, well enough dressed herself in what seemed like highly artistic sailcloth, and evidently not at all out of place in the ambience that bothered her so. She seemed known to the women at the table and was cheerfully greeted, and one or two of the sunglassed faces turned curiously towards him as they talked.

She was back after a while. 'She's away,' she said. 'I'm afraid we're out of luck. She is at her cottage for a few days. Lucky Magda.'

'Where is it?'

'At Schonbach, in the mountains. She sometimes asks me. There's skiing in the winter and the woods and the lake in summer. It was my grandmother's cottage. All the family used to go while she was alive. It's only an hour away by road.'

'Oh,' Raison said. He looked at his watch. 'What do you think?' he said.

The girl said hastily, 'Oh, I don't think now. She's there with a close friend.'

'Would she mind us meeting an old friend?'

'It isn't an old friend. It's apparently quite a new friend.' He was aware that more of the sunglassed faces were turning to peer curiously at him. 'Magda makes friends quite quickly,' the girl said briefly.

'Pity.'

'Yes. She'll be back on Monday. Will you be here then?'

'I don't know,' Raison said.

'You're married, aren't you?'

'Does it show?'

'What's your wife like?'

'Oh, quite mad,' Raison said.

'About anything in particular?' the girl said, amused.

'About islands, at the moment.'

'Islands. That's exclusive. There are obviously two sides to her character. Does she want to exclude people?'

'Yes,' Raison said.

'I'm not sure I altogether understand the English. Do you want to invite me to dinner tonight?'

'I'd love to. But it depends. I might be involved in a conference tonight.'

'Shall I leave it free?'

'Do. I'll call you,' Raison said.

But he wondered if he would. She hadn't got her raincoat on now, and she wasn't buttoned up. He thought he might have to watch himself here.

He found Grunwald having a glass of tea in bed. Ansbach was having a glass of tea with him. The old man was lying about in a striped nightie with his skullcap on. He looked a rather elegant, biblical old thing, and Raison told him so. 'How are you?' he said.

'It can't have been such a bad attack. I never move normally without the pills. I'm just tired.'

'Excitement brought it on,' Ansbach said. 'There's no question we have something here.' He seemed fairly excited himself. 'Boehme absented himself from the camp at Furth-im-Wald and went to Waldstein. Apparently he was picked up there without papers by the American military and sent back under escort with a charge sheet from the American Town Major – that is the "Town M."? He was placed on the next transport to Würzburg. All this has been sitting in the files there for twenty years!'

Raison adjusted his mind to the continuing complications of Mrs Wolff's relations. He said, 'Do we know why he went to Waldstein?'

'It seems we know Bamberger had a hunting lodge in the area, and some interests.'

'Timber interests,' Grunwald said. 'It's a logging area. The family had various interests, on both sides of the border, the whole of the Sudetenland. It arose from their finance house in Prague. With regard to the lodge I'm relying only on sketchy memory. It was something I heard many years ago.'

'Would Pfefferkorn know?'

'It doesn't need Pfefferkorn,' Ansbach said. 'The place is a little hole in the forest. Everybody will know everybody else's business. It's nearer even than Bamberg. You can be there in three hours.'

Raison sat down and lit a cigarette. He seemed to have been shuttling about a lot in the heat, and he had a headache. The thought of visiting this hole in the forest and inquiring into everybody's business made his headache very much worse. He said, 'Are we supposing that he is still there?'

Ansbach shrugged. 'It's the loneliest part of the country. It's an excellent place for a man to hide. But whether he is or he isn't, somebody will know why he went and perhaps where he is now.'

Raison looked at his cigarette and then at Ansbach. 'If we find him,' he said, 'what do we say?'

Ansbach looked back at him, and then at Grunwald. For a moment the three of them were looking at each other. Grunwald said simply, 'I will say to him, give me the money. It's rotting here in Europe. It wouldn't rot in Israel.'

'The money will come to you, anyway, in the long run.'

'How?' Grunwald said. 'If we don't know who he is or where he is, how will we know when he is dead?'

'Larger sums are involved than this sum,' Raison said. 'Larger issues than this issue. Don't you think he's entitled to the seclusion he seems to want?'

'I don't know what he's entitled to,' Grunwald said. 'I'm not his judge.'

Raison felt himself being driven slowly mad by the roar of traffic through the open window. He thought with sudden longing of the cool dim room in Stanhope Gardens and of himself sitting on the sofa in it with a whisky and soda.

He said, 'It's causing enormous unhappiness to Mrs Wolff, resurrecting this old tragedy.'

'I'm sorry,' Grunwald said. He sounded sorry. 'I understand,' he said.

'Raising hopes that he might be alive when he might not be.'

'I know. I know,' Grunwald said.

Ansbach had looked up sharply at this evocation of Mrs Wolff's sensibilities, and he cleared his throat. 'We didn't raise the hopes,' he said. 'The bank did. They would still have raised them, whoever put in the claim.'

'She is, I understand, very pent,' Raison said. 'She is highly strung. She's also naturally in doubt about her position. There's uncertainty about settlements already arrived at. It's quite understandable, I think,' he said.

He found the pair of them staring at him.

'You haven't taken fresh instructions?' Ansbach said shrewdly.

'No.'

'Haffner hasn't got cold feet about Hilfende Hände?'

'Not at all.'

'Then forget about settlements already arrived at. One thing's got nothing to do with another – so long as it's done with discretion. I hope Haffner agrees?'

'I haven't asked him.'

'H'm.'

A slight silence developed.

'I want to go to Waldstein tomorrow,' Grunwald said. 'I hope you will want to come with me.'

'I'll have to let you know. I'll have to lie down,' Raison said. He went and lay down. He closed the windows and drew the curtains, and in the hot semi-dark thought about things. There was a monumental triviality, after everything that had happened in this place, in smelling out a single squalid old sufferer who evidently didn't want to be found. A terrible waste of time; but it was Mrs Wolff's time. In the end all the splendid things of life like hotchpots, emblements and estoppels were for the purpose of settling the affairs of people like Mrs Wolff. He felt bored and depressed with the problems and he went to sleep.

It was seven when he woke. The headache had gone but the problems were about the same. He felt restless as well as bored and depressed. He got up and told Grunwald yes. Then he phoned Elke and told her yes.

Chapter 3

A SMALL PYRRHIC VICTORY

It was warm and noisy in the open-air restaurant, and flies and musicians harassed them. 'If you give him a small note he'll go away,' the girl said. The fiddler already had a sheaf of small notes, tucked into a notch on the end of his bow. Raison gave him a small note. The fiddler went away. 'They come in from Hungary,' the girl said. 'They're quite genuine Zigeuner. Everybody gives them money to go away. They make their fortunes here. You're not doing your duty,' she said. She was holding out her glass, and Raison gave her a refill from the jug. It was the second jug, and she'd already put away quite a lot of the first. She'd also sunk a few brandies before coming out to the garden to eat, but the only effect seemed to be a rather steadier flow of thoughts on life and a somewhat hectoring desire to bring his own into line. Raison was feeling a bit stoned himself.

'With regard to the Bavarian Forest,' she said, 'it's quite impossible. You can't go there. They've been intermarrying for centuries. They're all idiots. They sleep with their mothers. They'll probably kill you.'

'Do you think they will?'

'It's probable. It's all those trees. They were pagan for longer than almost anybody in Europe. Anyway, don't they go about killing hussars and everybody at this time of year?'

'Hussars?' Raison said.

'Haven't you heard of Trotz and his hussars? Baron Trotz came with his hussars, to fight either for or against them, I can't remember which, so every year now they kill Trotz, or Trotz kills them. Disagreeable things happen with pigs' bladders filled with blood. Or is that another village? They're all awful round there.'

'Aren't they a bit Sudeten?'

'A bit Sudeten. And quite awful. All people who live on borders are awful. Hitler was awful.'

'Yes,' Raison said. He'd done about as much as he could with the schnitzel. It was still hanging over the plate. There'd been too much of it. There was too much of everything here. 'I want black coffee,' he said.

'Not here. It's undrinkable.'

'I can't move anywhere else yet. Black coffee,' he said to the waiter.

'Anyway,' she said, 'you'd much better stay here and let somebody else go. Then I could show you Munich.'

'That would be very nice.'

'Must you go?'

'I'm afraid I must.'

'Then I must come and protect you, James. I can call you James?'

'Of course, Elke.' Why not? Most of the family seemed to be calling him James now. 'That's very gallant of you, Elke,' he said.

'You wouldn't understand the argot, anyway. You wouldn't

even know why they were killing you. Also you have to have a car.'

'We're hiring a car in the morning.'

'It isn't necessary. Don't. I'll come with you. I'll drive you.'

'Haven't you got any posters to get on with?'

'It's in the interests of my posters. I've been meaning to have another look at those awful people. What time do you leave?'

'Early. It's Friday tomorrow. We have to be back before dark. Grunwald won't travel on the sabbath. Apparently his sabbath begins tomorrow night.'

'I know. When the third star comes out. A friend of mine is a Jew.'

'A religious one?'

'In a strange way. He wrote poetry in abuse of God, but only in English. He refused to write in German.'

'Why?'

'He was Hungarian.'

'Ah,' Raison said. He didn't feel completely abreast of this conversation. He decided he must be more stoned than he thought, and greeted the coffee gladly.

'Would eight o'clock be early enough?'

'I think you mean it,' Raison said.

'I do mean it. Wouldn't it be a help?'

'Of course. If you can manage.'

'I can manage. Now I'll take you where they have better coffee,' she said.

The better coffee was in a jazz cellar, and wasn't all that much better. Raison leaped around a little with the girl between cups of it. The girl stuck to the brandy. It was after midnight as they reeled out.

'Do you want to go somewhere else?'

'No,' Raison said.

'Then finally I'm going to have to give you some real coffee. The blackest of all.'

They buzzed along to the Hohenzollernstrasse in the E-type, Raison somewhat tense. The night's heavy intake had left him bemused, but not too bemused to see that something could be shaping with this cheerfully tight girl. Earlier fantasies might be responsible for groundless fears, he thought, and certainly there'd been nothing in the joshing bonhomie of the evening to suggest any dramatic conclusions. All the same, he was nervous.

She fell over her feet a little as she let him in, cussing loudly, which calmed him. 'They're always going to do something about this light,' she said. 'They never do. Also about a lift. The stairs can paralyse you at this time of night.'

They nearly did paralyse Raison. He followed her up to the third floor, amost on his knees, and leaned against the wall while she opened the door. The door opened immediately into a bed-sitter. 'Sit down and recover,' she said, vanishing into the kitchen. 'I'll get the coffee.'

The main feature of the room was a divan bed, now a bed. Raison steered clear of it and sat in an armchair and studied the art work on the walls. A good deal of paper seemed to be about. The floor was littered with it, and a few sheets were stuffed between the seat and the arm of his chair. He picked one out and found a hand-drawn projection of a letter from a type face. Something was on the back and he turned it over. A scratchy pen had written irregular lines in English in Indian ink. His eyes were not focusing too well, but he pored over the words.

> And is it over, the entertainment of the ages,
> the perfect entertainment of the ages,
> that had so occupied the finest;
> is it over? One act at least.
> We couldn't sustain the fantasy
> of the invisible hero and his inaudible words
> and are left in saddest intermission.
> > And now what shall we say to thee?
> > And who can stand in place of thee?
> We can't go on with you now.
> Can't go on.

She said, 'It's quite awful. There isn't any coffee.'

Raison turned somewhat numbly to see her standing in the kitchen doorway.

'What?' he said.

'After my promise. No coffee.'

'Oh,' Raison said.

'Shall I see if there's tea?'

'All right.'

She went back in the kitchen. Raison knew he'd better go now. He had a rather awful feeling, as before an operation, that the moment had arrived. He could hear the heavy grind of blood in his ears. He didn't think there'd be any tea. He thought he'd better go. He stuffed the paper back in the chair, and saw another, and in distraction read it.

> If you're finished we must face it
> and we'll have to do without.
> We'll have to do without. We'll have to do.
> We couldn't live on in that way
> and we can't die here in this way
> and we don't yet know of ways excluding you.
> Having made you, we must make you, Gottenu.
> > It was evening, it was morning
> > and he saw that it was good.
> We must make anew the play now.
> Make anew.

She said, 'It's awful. There's only instant tea.'

'Oh,' Raison said.

'Do you particularly want instant tea?'

'No,' Raison said.

'No.' She came and sat on the arm of his chair and bent and leaned her head against his with one of her lingering smiles. 'I don't want instant tea,' she said.

Raison's eyes were at an angle that made it necessary for him to look immediately down her dress. Her breasts were hanging loose inside her dress. They hung free of the dress and the nipples were free. The breasts were the most beautiful things he had ever seen, and they were being offered plainly to him. He raised his hand and shoved the paper back in the chair. 'I'd better go now,' he said.

'Don't go.'

'It's late.'

'Don't go.'

He stood up, and she stood up with him and leaned against him.

'Stay.'

'There's a thing called an estoppel,' Raison said.

'What?'

'There are some things you can't go into if you've committed yourself to others. It's a legal thing. It's called an estoppel.'

'I don't understand.'

'There have to be rules,' Raison said.

'Rules change easier than people.'

'Yes. I know. That's the difficulty,' he said. 'You've got to try. Particularly here you've got to try.'

'You're a strange man, James,' she said. She touched his face.

'Good night,' Raison said.

'I'll run you back.'

'I'll get a taxi.'

'It's not easy at this time of night.'

'I'll get one.'

'You're very strange.'

'Good night,' Raison said.

She watched him over the banisters. 'There's no light,' she said as he got to the bottom.

'I know.'

'James,' she said as he opened the door.

'Yes?'

'Just James.'

'Yes.'

He walked almost to the Siegestor before picking up a taxi. He was sweating as he sat back in it. A victory of sorts had been won, he supposed. He didn't feel very victorious. He felt a bit of a fool, and a frustrated one, and a humiliated one. Victories like this didn't strengthen the resolve. They damaged it. It was a pyrrhic victory, and only a small pyrrhic victory. He didn't want to fight for another. He couldn't at the moment think what the point of the victory was, anyway. But he went back to the hotel, and to bed, and slept at last.

Chapter 4

THE SCENT OF BATTLE AND OTHER
SCENTS

'I HOPE you slept well.'

'I hope you slept well.'

'I've slept better.'

'Have some toast,' Raison said.

He hadn't expected her to turn up. He was unnerved at her turning up. He marvelled that he'd ever forgotten what she looked like. He couldn't think of anything now except what she looked like. He was sick with longing at the thought of her. He knew in some remote and irrelevant way that here was madness, that her mode wasn't his mode, that she was too long, too gawky, too barmy for him, and that she probably didn't wash enough. He simply lusted for her. He was crazed at sight of her. He longed to escape in lengthy dalliance, to examine every pore of her, to plumb her. He crunched stonily through his toast, curly toast, terrible toast, ashes in his mouth, hardly able to look at her, looking instead into the hall and to the red flash of the Jaguar standing in blinding sun beside the hotel's No-Parking sign.

She didn't seem to be quite looking at him. She said self-consciously, 'You said eight o'clock.'

'Grunwald didn't have a very good night.'

'It isn't off, is it?'

'No, it isn't off.'

He'd looked in on Grunwald at seven and found him in his phylacteries sitting weakly in a chair. He wasn't ill, but he'd been a bit ill. Raison had asked if he wanted to put it off, and he said he didn't.

'I didn't tell him about you,' he said.

'Will he mind?'

'I don't think so. I don't know.'

'What's he like?'

'Courteous. Obstinate. More durable than he looks.'

'Will he talk to me? To Germans?'

'Why not?'

'Some won't. I'd like to talk to him if he'll let me. I'd like to explain we're not all alike.'

'I don't know how interested he'd be. He's very Orthodox. There are Jews and there are Gentiles. As between the Gentiles, I don't think his expectations are high.'

'But he's lived in the world. He's a lawyer.'

'Oh, yes. Quite sharp. But it's only a trade.'

'What do you mean?'

'It's too complicated,' Raison said. He felt sick looking at her. 'I'll see how he's going,' he said.

He found Grunwald eating a couple of eggs in a glass. He had his hat on and was fully dressed, including his waistcoat. He was looking very brisk.

'How are you feeling now?'

'I've never felt better. You should pray. It's very efficacious.'

'Yes. Haffner's daughter is below. She's come to drive us. She has her own car.'

'That's very good of Haffner.'

'It's her own idea. I've told you about her.'

'Ah, the one who likes dead heroes. Well, it's meritorious. I hope it's a comfortable car.'

'It's a fast one,' Raison said. The strange image of Grunwald and his hat hurtling along in the tiny occasional seat of the red E-type suddenly struck him. 'You can sit in the front,' he said.

They wasted time at Regensburg, the metropolis of East Bavaria, looking for the Rathaus and making inquiries. Grunwald had an idea that it would be a good plan to consult a copy of the Land Register for the district of Waldstein on the subject of the hunting lodge. 'If there's been a transfer,' he said, 'then it might show us what new name he is going under.'

'Wouldn't it be easier to find out in Waldstein itself?' Raison said.

'It's never wise to make inquiry in the area itself in the matter of a former Jewish property. Who knows how the new owner got it – whom he paid, what he paid, how legal his title is? It's simple experience, and in forest areas they're clannish.'

But the officials didn't know in Regensburg, so they went on to Cham. They'd bought fruit and bread in Regensburg, and they stopped and ate it in the country. Grunwald had a Kirby-grip clipped firmly to his skullcap, and his beard was quite skittish from the eighty-mile-an-hour journey. He sat in the meadow breathing in the air.

'Ah, the smell of Bavaria,' he said, 'is there anything on earth like it?'

There wasn't. It was a peculiarly delicious smell that Raison had never smelt anywhere else. It was compounded of grass and blossom, and there seemed to be thyme and lilacs in it together with something more pervasive but unidentifiable, not quite of cattle breath but breathily succulent. It offered in abundance what other countrysides seemed merely to hint at, and the effect on Raison was terrible. It almost drove him out of his mind with hopeless longings. He'd sat in the back of the car watching the girl's neck and the small movements of her wrists on the wheel, and trembled. He sat in the meadow and trembled now, eating black bread and apricots. It was hot and silent in the meadow, the empty road shining in the sun. The country was hilly now, here and there upon it an isolated varnished wooden cottage with carvings and artistically arranged woodpile. All the villages they'd passed had been artistically arranged and ceremoniously prim; cuckoo-clock-type houses, fairy-tale-type inns, heavy about the eaves, mysterious about the windows. The villages had been getting increasingly woody as they neared the area of the forest, and now they could see it, a smudge of dense green, still some miles off, quivering in the sun.

'God has been good to this people,' Grunwald said.

'They've not been good in return,' the girl said.

'It's an orderly, hard-working people. They pay for their misdeeds, now or later. It's a mystery, all the same, why they are as they are,' he said. He was gnawing at his fruit, looking at the magnificent country. 'From places like this came the staunchest Nazis. From such cottages hard-working sons went out into the world and made horrors. It's no use asking why.'

'It was conservatism,' the girl said. 'They were in love with permanence. They wanted a thousand-year Reich, and everything to stay as it was for them for ever.'

'It's no use asking,' Grunwald said. 'With regard to individuals it's seldom possible to explain motive. With regard to nations, it's *im*possible. The most we can say is that the evil instinct is more easily roused here. That's all.'

Raison's own instinct, roused enough, kept him silent. He wasn't quite able to see the girl. She was keeping herself slightly away from him, on the other side of Grunwald, but he could see her long legs, shining in the sun, and her red toenails through her sandals. They got back in the car and pushed on towards the forest.

The Bavarian Forest is a series of densely afforested hills, some mountainous, cut across by the gorges of rivers from Bohemia. It is divided into areas, the Upper Palatinate, the 'Bavarian' Bavarian, the Bohemian: all comprising the most isolated and least known part of Germany, perhaps of central Europe. Until recent times it was an area a-flicker with mystery and folk-plays and with customs pre-dating the Christian era. In large sections of it there has never been any human settlement. A long slanting section, south-east to north-west, marks the boundary of the Sudetenland – a fuzzy boundary, for Czechs and Germans, forest people, have always lived and mingled on both sides of it. It was towards this section that the red Jaguar was buzzing, along minor roads, along the gorge of a little tributary of the Regen river, occasionally seen through trees far below, in a warm and spicy gloom.

They wasted a bit more time in Cham, where the officials didn't know about the Land Register either, and continued on to Furth-im-Wald, almost on the Czech border. The road, though minor, hadn't varied in width by a centimetre as it snaked and climbed through the forest; it was a new road, for even here the new German prosperity had reached. In the tiny farms, cut newly and rawly out of the forest, an occasional shiny tractor stood, and cigar smoke hung in the air. But central European custom kept the women working in the fields with the men, and their brown faces, kerchiefed, looked up and gazed after them as the red Jaguar climbed by.

They had heard thunder rumbling in the forest, and as they came out to the clearing of Furth-im-Wald, large single spots of rain were falling. They thought at first that it was the rain that had cleared the streets, for there was nobody about, but after cruising for a while and finding a likely-looking office and reading the notice on its closed door, they realized it was the time of *Mittagessen,* and that the population was at its victuals. They went in to a rather fusty old Gasthaus themselves, and had a drink.

They'd left Munich only four hours before, but already they were in a different world. Such road signs as there were no longer pointed to Munich and Nuremberg, but to Pilsen and Prague, and there were other subtler changes, a certain heaviness of old plush about the Gasthaus, a certain Slav stiffness of shoulder in the people who were about, and a tendency for some of the names above the shops to end in 'c' or 'k'. They'd noticed outside one shop a board with a list of tours, several of them to places in Czechoslovakia, and in the Gasthaus itself a little flyblown notice advertised a bus service to Pilsen and Prague at 27 marks, including visa.

They stayed till two, and then saw the village coming alive, and went out into the street.

They found the official opening up his office. He let them in, apologizing for the inadequacy of the place as he did so. 'They're very sleepy here, too Czechish, too much dumpling,' he said, holding his stomach. 'I myself am only temporary, from Regensburg. I am afraid it was too Czechish for my wife and family who have now returned to Regensburg. However.'

'Yes, I noticed various tours into Czechoslovakia,' Grunwald said. 'I didn't realize it was so easy to get in.'

'For the graveyards. A lot of them pay regular trips to tend their old family graves. Of course, at the same time they keep an eye on the old family property as well. That's all we hear of round here, the lost lands, the lost farms, how everything was taken from them. All the societies are concerned with it. Even the schoolboys have their own association. It's very uninteresting for a Regensburg man. In Regensburg, of course, there's much more interesting society.'

'Was everything taken from them?' the girl said.

'Everything. The whole parcel of them were kicked out, all the Sudeten Germans, two million of them, just bundled into trains with a suitcase or two and pushed over the frontier. They came pouring into here, into Furth. They had a camp down by the station, young, old, babes in arms. Still, it's all a long time ago, and they've had compensation from the government. In the end it will all be forgotten.'

'Will it?' Grunwald said.

'Hotheads try to keep memories alive, but people are basically reasonable and life goes on. They're very family-minded here, one can say that, and where you have families, with parents and children and uncles and aunts, things in the end work out reasonably. I attach the greatest importance to family life,' the grass widower from Regensburg said. 'Still, to be kicked out of lands where they'd lived for centuries – it's a tragedy, of course.'

'It's always a tragedy when people are kicked out of lands where they've lived for centuries,' Grunwald said.

'Yes. It's not within my competence, of course,' the man said, looking at him.

'We have to remember that the Sudetens caused great misery to the Czechs. They called in the Germans to make slaves of the Czechs.'

'I'm afraid I know very little about it,' the man from Regensburg said.

'So that the matter of the graves, though sad, has to be placed against this, and also against the record of Germany which left millions without any graves. We have to record it,' Grunwald said, 'though I don't know what good it does.'

'Was there something you wanted to know?' the man said.

Grunwald told him what he wanted to know.

'We don't keep a Land Register here for Waldstein. In Regensburg you'll find it.'

'They haven't got it in Regensburg.'

'In Munich, then. Or Waldstein itself – it's only eighteen kilometres away.'

'Is there some other way we can get at the information? It's a matter of checking the ownership of a property.'

'There's the rating return.'

'Have you got a Waldstein return here?'

The official had a Waldstein return. He unlocked a large wooden filing cabinet and got it.

'What's the address in Waldstein?'

'This is the difficulty,' Grunwald said. 'I don't even know if it's in Waldstein. It could be outside Waldstein, in the forest.'

'In the forest. What is it, a ski school, a logging camp?'

'A hunting lodge.'

'A hunting lodge. It shouldn't be so difficult. Let's see. Ski huts,' he said, skimming through, 'ski huts . . . cabin. . . . Here we are. . . . A hunting lodge. A hunting lodge two kilometres north of Waldstein, beyond the river. Very high rates payable, evidently a big place. Haus Adler,' he said. 'Can this be the one?'

'Haus Adler,' Grunwald said, curiously. 'What others are there?'

The man went methodically through. There weren't any others.

'Haus Adler,' Grunwald said again. 'Who owns it?'

The man consulted the list. 'Alfried Hans Adler,' he said. 'Which no doubt accounts for the name. He seems also to own some other property, the Gasthof Goldener Adler in Waldstein, also some timber. Yes, he sounds the most likely owner for such a place. Very high rates payable,' he said, checking with the list again.

'Is there any way of telling how long he's owned it, or what it was called before he owned it?'

'Only with the Land Register. I'm very much surprised they didn't have it in Regensburg. You're quite sure it was Regensburg you tried?'

'We have just come from there.'

'It's the principal city of East Bavaria, Regensburg.'

'It's a fine city,' Grunwald said. 'But it didn't have the Waldstein register.'

'Strange.'

'Yes. You wouldn't, as a matter of interest, have heard of a Herr Bamberger? A Herr Bamberger or a Herr Boehme?'

'Furth men?'

'Waldstein, rather. But in the area generally.'

'To tell the truth I mix very little locally. As a Regensburg man,' the temporary town clerk said.

'Well, thank you anyway. You've been a great help.'

'Any time,' the town clerk said. 'We could talk again a little of Regensburg.'

They got back in the car for the last eighteen kilometres.

It was grey now, no sun, dark in the forest, the air steamy and thunderous. They lost the way in a thicket of unmarked roads and pulled up to have a look at the map. The girl took the opportunity to put the hood up while Raison looked at the map. They heard an engine starting while he looked at it, and a little jeep came slowly out of the trees and circled them. A couple of green-uniformed men with binoculars and automatic guns were in the jeep. They didn't say anything.

'Waldstein?' the girl said.

'You're off the road. Go back.'

'Can you direct us?'

'Take the first left fork. Keep going.'

'Are we near the frontier, what?' Grunwald said, looking curiously out.

'Can't you see?' The man nodded down the avenue of cleared trees into which the road degenerated. The clearance ran quite straight, as though cut with a razor, into a valley and up the steep afforested hill at the other side. Capping the hill and looking down into the cut corridor stood a stilt-like pylon, black against the grey sky. 'They're watching. Move.'

They turned the car in silence and went. It was steamier than ever with the hood up. 'Sorry,' Raison said. He'd been navigating.

'It's dark. It's badly signposted,' Grunwald said.

'Yes,' Raison said. But that had not been the reason. He'd hardly been able to concentrate on the map. He could hardly concentrate on it now. He'd stood behind the girl in the office at Furth-im-Wald, and he'd not been conscious of anything else: long legs, the warmth of her body beneath her dress. The dress was a little creased at the waist, and he'd put out one finger and touched the crease, not able to prevent himself, touched very lightly, in a way that she couldn't have felt, and her own hand had come instantly around and caught his. She had held the finger, pressing her long thumbnail beneath the nail of the finger. The finger still seemed irradiated. The knowledge that she was as electrically aware of him as he of her, and every moment of the time, had gone off like a bomb-burst in his mind, scrambling him for everything else, sensitizing him most acutely for her. He had begun to notice small things that he'd not been aware of before, her gums, her eyebrows, a certain way that her lips formed in the corners of her mouth. In some mad and adolescent way, in some way between last night and now, he had fallen suddenly and hopelessly and horribly in love. He didn't know how it could have happened. It hadn't happened in the morning. He had lusted for her, no doubt about it, in the morning. It hadn't happened in the meadow. It had been different in the morning and in the meadow. It had already happened when he walked in behind her to the office at Furth-im-Wald. And it had possession of him now, had taken him over so completely that he sat in a kind of stupor, aware in an unlocalized and post-operative way that the thing had happened and that horrible upsets were bound to follow, and that he had to get away from it before it went any further.

It began to thunder again in the forest, and the light suddenly went so that they had to drive with headlamps. It was raining up above; they could hear it swishing and lashing, but no rain fell beneath the umbrella of trees, except that mysteriously, and as if from the ground itself, pools formed around the base of the trunks. In thunder-clapping darkness, alone on the road, they presently found the signpost for Waldstein, and in a few minutes were there.

They came out of the dark forest into a baleful gunmetal gloom rent by lightning flashes. There was an uproar of muffled kettledrums as rain lashed fantastically down on the fabric hood. The muddy streets were awash with water and not a soul was in sight. They cruised with their headlights on into a square, passed an onion-domed church and a few empty cars and cruised out of it again into a steep lane down which muddy rainwater was pouring. It was almost impossible to hear anything above the drumroll on the roof. 'What shall I do?' the girl shouted.

'The Goldener Adler,' Grunwald said in her ear. 'Go slowly. We'll find it.'

They nosed slowly in and out of the small lanes that ran off the square, and found the Goldener Adler on the corner of one of them, a tall graceful building, steeply roofed, hanging eaves, wings trailing round each corner, not unlike some large bird facing the storm. A gilt eagle, the *goldener Adler* of the name, was painted above the door. They scrambled out and up the steps into a small dark hall. Through a glass door they could see a couple of candles burning, and they pushed the door and went in. It was a large pillared room, almost in complete darkness except for the candles, with trestled drinking tables and benches. The candles were standing on the bar.

They rapped on the bar, and got no response, and waited for a while listening to the gigantic thunderclaps outside and the rain hosing down. A cowbell hung on a beam above the bar, with a cord hanging from the clapper. Grunwald pulled it, and the dull clonk presently caused a door to open and a crone to appear behind the bar.

'Not closed, I hope?' Grunwald said.

'No, no. It's the electricity. It's the storm.'

'Can we have coffee?'

'There's no hot water. The electricity.'

'Beer, then.'

The crone pulled them beer and lit more candles, watching the visitors carefully with old-cat eyes.

'It's a storm!' Grunwald said.

'We're used to them. It's the forest. It does something to the air. In some places they have batteries for the electricity. Herr Adler won't have the batteries.'

'Herr Adler,' Grunwald said. 'Is Herr Adler about?'

'Not at the moment. Did you want him?' she said, peering at him.

'Just a word while we're here.'

'He won't be back till the evening. Was there anything else?' she said.

'Till the evening?' Grunwald looked at Raison. 'So what is to do?'

Raison opened his mouth to say they'd go back right away, but as he did so a livid flash lit up the room, followed by a ripping, razing uproar as if the roof had been torn off, and a heavy explosion as if a thunderbolt had gone through it. They ducked. The crone didn't turn a hair. 'Was it rooms?' she said.

'Have you got rooms?' Grunwald said.

'Two rooms or three?'

'Three rooms.'

'I'll show you.'

She turned and took keys from a nailed board, and with a candle led them through the room to a door at the far end. There was a smell of bacon and sauerkraut on the staircase. They followed her to a first-floor landing in flickering darkness. She opened three adjacent doors. The rooms were identical, wooden walled, a Christ on the Cross on each wall, blood spurting from the Christ's nailed hands and feet, and from his side, and from his crown of thorns.

'Is it all right?' she said.

Grunwald looked at the Christ. 'It's all right,' he said.

She lit a candle in each room. 'You can sign later,' she said.

They gathered somewhat dispiritedly in Grunwald's room. It was hot in the room and strangely wearying in the flickering candlelight. Grunwald sat on the bed. His briskness had gone. He looked a little like a dishevelled crow. He said, 'It's difficult. We haven't any sleeping things or a toothbrush.' But he wasn't thinking of his sleeping things or his toothbrush. He was thinking of the smell of pig on the stairs, and of the Christ bleeding on the wall. He didn't want to spend the sabbath here. He felt immensely depressed. He said, 'I don't know. I think I'll take a rest.'

They left him and went into the next room. It didn't seem to matter which of the anonymous rooms they had. Grunwald had taken the first, and Raison suddenly saw he shouldn't have let him. Grunwald should have had the middle room, between them.

The electricity in the air, the electricity between them, made it impossible for him to stay in one room with her. He felt himself blundering like a moth about the dark, humid place, banging into the bed, the wardrobe. He said, 'I think I'll go and have a rest myself.'

'You can't rest in this awful noise.'

'I'll go and have a rest.'

'James.'

'I'll see you later,' he said.

He got out of the room as if it were on fire, and went into the next. He seemed to be shuttling from one to another of the dark anonymous boxes. He lay on the bed and watched Christ in the candlelight. It was going to be difficult. It was going to be desolating. He didn't know why he was doing it. One didn't in the middle of the battle. In the middle of the battle one fought to survive. Perhaps he was fighting for survival now. But the objectives of his battle were complex. They were nebulous. He wasn't sure what they were. He tried to clear his mind, and looked instinctively for help to the agonized Christ, but the arcane prescriber of old Judea had nothing on this occasion for him. What was wanted were reasons for maintaining private codes in this world, other than for facilitated entry to the next. What reasons? For whose benefit? Who would know? He thought he'd better have a drink.

He took his candle and went down to the bar, and found the girl having a drink, too. She'd got herself a bottle of brandy, and was staring moodily at it in the light of four grouped candles.

She said, 'Hello. I got a bottle. It seemed safest to get a bottle.'

'Yes. It might be a long storm.'

'Why are you keeping away from me?'

'I'll have a drink,' Raison said.

'Why are you doing it?'

'Bottoms up,' Raison said.

'James, there's nothing wrong with love.'

'There is,' Raison said. 'There's plenty wrong with it. It's a silly word for so many different things.'

'It's a beautiful thing. It's the most marvellous thing that can happen to people. There's nothing to do when it's happened except be very glad and accept it.'

'It isn't such a marvellous thing,' Raison said, 'if it happens at the wrong time. It can ruin all sorts of other things.'

'How ruin? It's entirely private. It's got nothing to do with others.'

'When one's married.'

'That's only part of your life. It isn't the whole of your life. You've only got one life, James.'

'I know,' Raison said. 'That's the reason. It's a pity. Thank God,' he said.

'I don't understand you.'

'Have another drink.'

They had a few more before the storm rolled over. They weren't aware it was over till powerful shafts of sunlight invaded the room. It seemed to be half past four. The girl went and had a look out of the window. The street was steaming in the sun.

'Shall we walk a little?'

'All right,' Raison said. He felt a bit tight. But the sensation of upholding the moral pillars of the universe had dispersed. He wondered if, having stated and discussed it, the worst was over for him now. They picked their way through steaming puddles under a sky of pale blue and grey-black.

'It isn't really over yet,' the girl said, looking up.

Looking at her, Raison didn't think it really was, either.

'We'd better not go too far,' he said.

They went down the lane, into the forest. It was damp underfoot even in the forest. The ground was spongy and brown and built up of generations of twigs. There was a faint sensation of columns of vapour rising from it. It was cooler and a sharp scent of resin was in the air. Cones were littered about, and in the misty aquarium light, the dizzying ranks of trees stood like cathedral pillars. A lane of trees had been felled and every fifty yards or so the pole-like trunks stacked. They walked slowly along the line of stumps, not speaking for a time. Birds were singing, after the rain, but distantly, in the tree-tops.

'It's terribly wrong-headed, James.' She took his hand. 'You've got such a mixed-up view. It's so narrow. It goes against everything I believe.'

'I know. I'm sorry. I wish there'd been a bit more for you in the poster line.'

'Don't joke.'

'No joke,' Raison said.

It began to rain again. The rain lashed the tree-tops and thunder growled, silencing the bird-song. They turned and went back.

A dreary scene met them at the edge of the forest. There was little lightning, but rain beat ferociously down, splashing up in a muddy mist from the ground. They waited under the trees for it to stop, watching the grey sky and the dismal backs of wet houses. The girl leaned against him as they waited.

'What are you going to do, then?' she said.

'I'll leave on Sunday or Monday, as soon as I can.'

'Oh, James.'

'It's best,' he said.

She kissed him. He found suddenly that his hand was on her breast, and that she had put it there and that he couldn't take it away. He felt slightly demented. She put the hand inside her dress.

'No,' Raison said, shaking his mouth against hers.

'I love you.'

'No,' Raison said. He pulled away from her. He walked away, in the rain. He found she was walking beside him.

She said, 'It's so ridiculous, so stupid.'

'It isn't,' he said. But he saw that it was. He felt he was being put in the position of an outraged spinster, and he felt stone cold sober suddenly.

'Let's run at least,' she said.

They ran. They were soaked to the skin when they got to the Gasthof, and steaming gently. Nothing had changed in the bar. The bottle was where they had left it in the ring of candles. They took a candle each and went upstairs.

She said, 'I don't know what we're going to do. We haven't any clothes. We'd better have a bath.'

There was only one bathroom and the girl took it first. Raison went to his room and undressed and put on a towel and walked up and down in the warm gloom, smoking. In a few minutes she was banging on the door.

'I'm finished.'

'All right.'

'Can I come in?'

'No.'

He waited till she was in her own room and then went and had a bath himself. His clothes were still damp when he got back, but he put them on and went down to the bar. People had come into the bar. Four men were sitting at a table with their beer playing dominoes. The crone was behind the bar.

'I want to telephone,' Raison said.

'There's only this telephone.'

'I want to call London.'

'I don't know about London. Herr Adler isn't here.'

'I'll find out what it costs. I'll ask them. I'll have a brandy,' he said.

He had a couple before the call came through, sitting watching the domino players and listening to the rain. More domino players arrived, shaking their waterproofs and sitting down to play among the beer mugs. The crone went silently back and forth in the candlelight, supplying them. The call came at a quarter to six. Gunter said, 'James! I've been worrying about you. What's happening exactly?'

Raison told him, but not too exactly. He said, 'Rupert, I'd

171

like to come home now. I'd like to leave tomorrow, if that's okay.'

'Leave tomorrow? But what's the trouble, what is it?'

'It's personal, Rupert.'

'But somebody's got to be there. Somebody will have to take over. Do you mean you want me to take over?'

'I suppose that's what I mean, Rupert.'

'But what is it, James? What's worrying you? If your work here is worrying you . . .'

'The work and other things, Rupert.'

'The work's going well. All's under control here. Wilkinson is under control. I've been looking into Wilkinson. I don't think you need worry further about the nullity suit, James.'

'Don't you?'

'There's definitely malformation. It seems to be a matter of size, James, among other things. It seems to be a bit small. He wouldn't get far with that, James.'

'Wouldn't he?'

'In a court of law. I'm advising him to drop it. I knew there was something funny there. Poor Wilkinson,' Gunter said. He didn't seem too depressed about Wilkinson. He seemed rather cheered by Wilkinson. 'He's to be pitied, of course,' he said.

'Yes,' Raison said. He wasn't so sure. 'It isn't only that, Rupert. It's personal. I can't personally stay on. It's a personal thing.'

'No trouble with Heinz, I hope?'

'Not Heinz,' Raison said.

'Family not being cool to you, I hope?'

'Not cool,' Raison said. 'No, not cool.'

'Well, what is it – Hilda? Do you want me to ring Hilda?'

'I don't think she's at home today, Rupert.'

'Well, sleep on it. Let's have a word when you've considered. I'll see what I can do meanwhile. I'll see if I can't alter my arrangements.'

'All right,' Raison said.

'Did you get the price?' the crone said.

'They're ringing back with the price.'

He had another brandy while waiting for them to ring back. When they rang back, he put a call through to Hilda. Hilda's call came through quite quickly. She said, 'James, I was just thinking of you. You're ringing early. What are you doing?'

'I'm having a drink,' Raison said. 'I thought I'd ring you.'

'I got your card from Munich. It sounded lovely in Munich. Was it lovely there?'

'Fairly lovely,' Raison said. 'How are you?'

'Much better, but sleepy. I've been sleeping a lot lately. I'm only just awake now. I'll be going off again at half past seven. It's doing me a world of good.'

'I'm so glad, Hilda. I'm really glad.' Raison said.

'So unless you can get here by half past seven I wouldn't really bother coming tonight.'

'All right,' Raison said.

'They're doing it for another few days. I think they're doing it till about Wednesday. I'm sure it's doing me the world of good. I'm almost back to normal now.'

'Oh, that's marvellous. That's really good news.'

'And James. I'd like to come out next week-end.'

'Terrific.'

'A bit of a drive would set me up, I'm sure.'

'Do you want a bit of a drive?'

Elke came into the bar. She came and stood beside him.

'It's only five or six hours,' Hilda said. 'It isn't all that far.'

'Where to?' Raison said. But he already knew. The girl took his hand and he didn't withdraw it.

'Through Haverfordwest,' Hilda was saying. 'Not as far down as Pembroke. You get a boat from the coast – I'm not quite sure at which point.'

'I see,' Raison said. 'Yes. I see.'

'I'll work it out. I'll do that, James. It's marvellous feeling on top of things again.'

'Well, keep it up,' Raison said. 'Have a good night, Hilda.'

'Did you get the price?' the crone said.

'They're ringing back with the price.'

'Was that your wife?' the girl said.

'Yes.'

'How is she?'

'Mad as ever,' Raison said. 'But on top of things. She wants me to go and look at an island with her.'

'Oh, the island. It isn't any good trying to exclude people, James.'

'It is,' Raison said. 'It's marvellous. It's the best thing going.'

He wondered how he was going to get through till morning.

They ate at a trestle table in the bar. Grunwald didn't eat much. He nibbled at some bread and fruit. The electricity was not back on and when coffee came up he had black coffee.

He saw that the forty or fifty people in the bar were glancing constantly at him. It had always been so here. They'd rarely seen a Jew but hatred of the Jew was in the bone, in the mother's milk. The faces all around him were faces he had seen in dreams, faces carved on church doors. All around he could feel the hostility. It wasn't the hostility of Bamberg, or Frankfurt, or Munich, not the hostility of towns at all; something more primal and longer-lasting, an ingredient of soil or blood. It tired him. But one thing, he thought, there was no dissimulation here. A Jew was a Jew here, which was best.

'You would still,' he said aloud, 'in such places find believers in the blood libel.'

'The what?' Raison said.

'The Jew needing the blood of a Christian child to celebrate the passover.'

'Only among the old ones,' the girl said. 'I'm sure not the younger, not the ones with schooling.'

'Is it a matter of knowledge, intelligence?'

'Did anybody actually believe that?' Raison said.

'And a great many other things,' the girl said. 'I have a collection of the Nazi posters. They had special ones for special areas. There was the crucifix one – Jews breaking crucifixes and collecting them to burn. Jews killing young trees – gouging the Star of David in them . . .'

'So where is Adler?' Grunwald said heavily.

Two extra waitresses were on duty to cope with the evening

business and Raison caught the arm of one of them. 'Herr Adler?' he said.

'Herr Adler? He's behind you.'

A big man with a melancholy face and a somewhat hawk-like nose turned as his name was mentioned. He got up. He'd been sitting almost back to back with Grunwald. 'I thought I'd let you finish your meal. It rejoices me,' he said. He shook hands all round. Grunwald, after a long look, shook hands sadly. He hadn't really expected Bamberger, the bleeding Christs, not even Bamberger.

Adler was wearing a Bavarian tunic, a grey collarless jacket, piped and cuffed in green, and in the vertical was a somewhat hunched and desiccated figure. He said to Raison, 'You are American, I understand?'

'No, English.'

'Ah, English. The woman hadn't a very good ear. Shall I sit with you?'

'Please.'

'How can I help?'

'We were making inquiries about a Herr Bamberger,' Grunwald said. 'He had interests round here. He had timber.'

'Bamberger? Bamberger?'

'He had a hunting lodge here.'

'Ah, Bamberger. Before the war.'

'He came back after the war.'

'Did he, indeed? Did he? I didn't know. Take a brandy with me, gentlemen. You'll have a brandy, Fräulein?'

'Thank you,' Elke said.

'Yes, I remember Bamberger,' Adler said. 'A banker, if I'm not mistaken. With timber.'

'Also a hunting lodge,' Grunwald said.

'Also a hunting lodge.'

'I wonder what happened to the hunting lodge,' Grunwald said.

'*Zum wohl, zum wohl,*' Adler said.

Grunwald was in two minds with regard to the brandy. He needed the brandy. He didn't like to accept the brandy. He didn't like to say the blessing over this brandy. On the other hand, Adler was not the source of the brandy. There was only one source for brandy. He temporized by looking at the ceiling and allowing the words, 'who hast created the fruit of the vine', to appear in his mind.

'As a matter of fact,' Adler said, setting down his brandy, 'I have the hunting lodge. That is to say, a school has it. I am the responsible landlord for it. It had to be put up for sale by the municipality some years ago. It was in a bad state of repair and nobody wanted such a big place. I took it off their hands.'

'It belonged to the municipality, did it?'

'No taxes had been paid for years. The municipality wanted to see some taxes coming from it.'

'The municipality could have got in touch with the estate of Herr Bamberger with regard to the taxes.'

Adler looked at him. His thin neck sticking out of the collarless jacket turned a little pink. He said, 'Of course, we're somewhat remote here. . . . May I ask your interest in the lodge?'

'I have no interest in it,' Grunwald said wearily. He'd meant to dissemble but he didn't want to dissemble now. Simply to breathe in this place was a desecration. He felt among pigs, among abomination. 'My colleague is perhaps interested. I'm interested in Bamberger. He came back here.'

'You are a lawyer, are you?'

'We are both lawyers – Mr Raison for the Bamberger estate. We have information that Bamberger was alive after he was presumed to be dead.'

'Have another brandy.'

Grunwald needed another brandy. 'I will pay for the brandy,' he said.

'As you wish.'

The second brandy came up immediately. Raison had already drunk a lot, but the brandy was no longer affecting him. He wished that it would. He would have liked to knock himself out. Elke's hand was on his thigh under the table. He heard with somewhat sluggish dismay Grunwald involving the estate in this inquiry that had to be kept discreet, and knew that it was his business to put a stop to it. He put his hand on Elke's thigh instead. The hand began to burn right away.

His whole body burned. He wanted to go to bed with her, now. A battle wasn't a war. It was sometimes necessary to lose a battle to win a war.

'When did he come back?' Adler said.

'In August 1946. He was here for three or four days. He was picked up by the American military authorities and taken back to the camp at Furth-im-Wald. Their certificate is in the Land Ministry files in Munich. He was going under the name of Boehme.' His voice was flat and depressed and he wasn't looking at Adler but at the scrubbed table. 'There's further information with some specialized agencies, and if we don't find what we want here we'll have to go to them. We thought somebody here would have seen him when he came back – at least it's probable.'

'More than probable,' Adler said. 'A near certainty. Nothing happens here that people don't know about. Do you want me to make inquiries for you?'

'Thank you.'

'Our locals don't talk easily to strangers. But I must say I heard nothing of it. In 1946, you said?'

'13 to 17 August.'

'With regard to the hunting lodge, I paid little for it. It's let at a purely nominal rent – if there's any interest in it.'

'There's no interest,' Grunwald said. 'I'm not interested. Are you interested?' he said to Raison.

'No,' Raison said. He stroked Elke's thigh.

'What exactly is the information you wish?'

'Why he came here. If he gave any indication of his plans. And where he might be now.'

'Where he is now?' Adler said. 'Isn't he dead?'

'No.'

'Then what is this about the estate? I thought you mentioned there was an estate.'

'It's a complication we don't have to go into,' Grunwald said.

'Also the camp. Wasn't the camp at Furth-im-Wald purely for ethnic Germans? Herr Bamberger, forgive me, wasn't an ethnic German.'

'He was a Jew,' Grunwald said. 'Which is another complication. He came back as an ethnic German.'

Adler had been writing on the back of an envelope, but he gave up then. He looked at Grunwald a bit blankly. 'Perhaps another brandy,' he said.

Elke said in Raison's ear, 'Don't drink any more.'

'I'll have one more.'

'I'll go up now,' she said, pressing his thigh.

He watched her go, and had one more, listening to the flat depressed voice of Grunwald spelling out the information they had so laboriously gained.

'Well, if it's all established there must be something in it,' Adler said. 'If it's established. One's read of these things. It's strange.'

'Yes.'

'I'll inquire. But with regard to the hunting lodge, it brings in next to nothing.'

'All right.'

'One more brandy!' Grunwald said, when they sat alone. The brandy had made him sleepy, but not sleepy enough. He didn't want to lie awake in this place.

'One more,' Raison said.

'How do we stand on temptation?' he said, when the brandy came up.

'On what?'

'Temptation.'

'On temptation. It's an interesting question. The Baal Shem Tov – he was the founder of a Jewish sect, the Hassid movement – the Baal Shem Tov had a story about temptation. A weak man sat in his house and heard a burglar trying to get in. He cried out and the burglar ran away and was free to try again. He tried again in the house of a strong man. The strong man also heard the burglar trying to get in. He quietly waited for him and grappled with him and overcame him and had him locked up so that the burglar was no longer a danger to him. What is your temptation?'

'Temptation is everywhere,' Raison said.

'At my age, not,' Grunwald said. 'It's one of the few

compensations. Well, I'm ready for bed. Are you ready for bed?'

'Yes,' Raison said.

They went up together. Raison went to his room and undressed. He locked the door and got into bed and pulled the bedclothes up so that he shouldn't hear. He heard her, all the same. He heard her tapping at the wall, and later on, at the door. He didn't answer. He didn't cry out. He doubted if the Baal Shem Tov would have approved all the same. He wasn't feeling like the weak man tonight, and still less the strong. The brandy had finally caught up with him and he was feeling like the man who'd had one too many. If battle had to be joined, and he thought it might, and if he had to lose, and he thought it was a possibility, he'd like it done with a certain style. Actions, once started, had to be finished. He couldn't absolutely guarantee the style tonight, or a finish.

Chapter 5

THE SON OF MAN AND OTHER SONS

GRUNWALD came to with a gasp and said, 'What?' Someone was standing over him. He saw with relief that at least it wasn't dark any more. 'What time is it?' he said.

'It's half past nine,' Raison said. 'It's a fine morning. We're going out for a walk. How did you sleep?'

'I don't know. I don't think so well. Half past nine,' he said. At exactly the same moment he remembered he had a story to tell Raison.

'Stay in bed. You won't be doing anything today. It's Saturday. Do you want your breakfast up here?'

'I'll see. I don't know. Saturday,' he said. No synagogue, no congregation, no book. Still. A man could pray wherever he was. 'Is there any water here?' he said.

'A jug and a bowl. It's cold.'

'All right. I'll see you when you get back.'

'Sure you're all right?'

'I'm fine, fine,' he said. What was the story?

He stayed in bed a few minutes after Raison left, and remembered the story. He leaned over and looked through the curtain. Yes, it was a fine day. He got up and washed and dressed, sitting on the bed. He felt dizzy. Well, a disturbed night was nothing new. He'd been thinking of everything in the dark hours. He'd been thinking of his wife. He hadn't heard from her. He'd written to her a couple of times. He'd asked Landsberg to ring her up.

He hoped with all his heart that Landsberg's son-in-law had found nothing. Not only the thing itself – that naturally – but that she shouldn't come here. Why should she want to come here? For himself, even if at death's door, he wouldn't want to. He couldn't understand how any Jew would want to. Yet some did. A peculiar people. In many ways an impossible people. If they hadn't been such an impossible people would they have needed the prophets to chide them?

He tied his shoelaces and washed his hands again and opened the curtains and looked for the sun. He couldn't see the sun. He could tell where it was. He worked out the direction of Jerusalem, and then worked it out in the room. The Christ on the Cross was in the direction of Jerusalem. This was worrying, and he thought about it, a hand on his lip. He couldn't pray towards the idol. What was to be done about the idol? It was quite large, half a metre, carved in wood and brightly painted. He couldn't think of anything to put over it. The pillow-case, maybe? It was a bolster. He took the case off the bolster and stood on a chair to drape it. The crucifix hung on quite a small nail with little in the way of a head to support the cloth. If he pulled the idol away from the wall and wrapped it round with the cloth, its own weight would keep everything in position. He didn't like touching the idol. He didn't even like the smell of it. He turned his head away and held his breath and grasped it with the starched bolster case. The thing fell off. The weight of it surprised him. It slipped through the shiny linen, slipped right through his hands to fall with a crash on the floor. It broke in two.

He stood on the chair looking down at it in consternation.

The first thing that occurred to him was that he had broken something on the sabbath, and the second that even if it weren't the sabbath he couldn't put it together again, even if he had the means. Restore an idol?

But something had to be done.

He got down off the chair and looked at it. The broken Christ looked back at him. It had split neatly in two pieces at the navel. He wondered if it would be possible for him to hang back a part of it, the top part of it. He tried for a confused moment to think of any similar case relating to the repositioning of idols inadvertently misplaced. He couldn't think of any. The Talmud tractate *Abodah Zarah* dealt, he knew, fairly thoroughly, with found fragments of unidentifiable idols, as it might be pieces of stone, masonry, but in a context regarding the use of such fragments in house and road building. The *replacing* of idols, even the picking up of idols, identifiable idols, was surely something entirely different. *Abodah Zarah* must have a word on it. One of the tractates would have a word. He had an urge to run through right away to see, to run through to his front room overlooking Independence Park and the Sheraton Hotel, to the shelf where he kept his thirty-four uniform volumes of the Talmud; and in the moment of confusion actually turned to do so. But through the window he saw not the light and sparkle of Tel Aviv but the timber-clad gloom of Waldstein, and the forest of Germany.

It wasn't till that moment that any other aspect of the matter struck him at all. Then he realized the special nature of the predicament. He bent slowly and with the bolster case picked up the two pieces and looked at them. He was doing this when the door opened and the cat-eyed old woman of the bar said, 'I heard a crash –' and stopped.

She stood quite still, holding her breath, seeing the Jew holding the smashed crucifix between his hands in the bolster case. Then she took the key from his side of the door and placed it in the other side, and slammed the door shut and locked it, and ran, shuffling, down the corridor.

'The river,' Raison said. There was a little road bridge, and they crossed the river. They were keeping to the road. The tracks through the forest looked vague on the map. They'd looked in to the tourist bureau to get the map. He hadn't remembered much of what the official in Furth-im-Wald had told them about the hunting lodge, but Elke had remembered one had to cross a river. It wasn't far. It was only a couple of kilometres. They walked there, holding hands.

He'd woken up surprisingly cheerful, with an obscure feeling that a point had been won. He felt whole, buoyant, a tamer of beasts, a keeper, however fortuitously, of codes, and a bit of a broth of a boy, to boot. Elke had been sunny, too, which he hadn't expected. She said, 'Didn't you hear me, last night? I called.'

'I was a bit drunk, I think.'

'It's not a good place, this, I think.'

'It's a bad place.'

'Schwabing is all right, as a place?'

'Schwabing is better.'

'Yes. Oh, yes.'

They sang a bit, and whistled. He was full of admiration for her this morning. She was rangey this morning. She was full of lore.

'It's almost answering you,' Raison said.

'It is answering me. I'll do it again.'

'It's answering you.'

'I told you it was answering me.'

'Where did you learn that?'

'My father. He's keen on birds.'

'Can he do that?'

'He does it with instruments. He has reeds and warblers. It's the great passion of his life. He doesn't tell anybody.'

'Why not?'

'I don't know. He's sung with the birds since a boy. He knows all of them at Schonbach, where Magda has her cottage. I think he has the feeling nothing's gone right for him since he's been away from those birds.'

Raison couldn't imagine Haffner singing with the birds. He couldn't see him at it. They came to a finger-post, red, yellow and black, pointing into the forest. There were no words on the post, and not much of a track, a few tyre marks.

'Is it an army sign?'

'It's the national colours,' the girl said.

'We aren't on the frontier are we?' He looked at the map. They weren't on the frontier. 'Let's have a look. If it's an army camp, they might know where the lodge is.'

They followed the sign between the trees. There was presently a clearing. A tall reeded fence surrounded the clearing. They could see the tops of buildings beyond the fence. They walked round it and found a door set into the fence, and pushed it, and went in. A number of young men in shorts were wrestling, bare to the waist, in brilliant sunlight, on a rough lawn in front of the buildings. There was a largish single-storey building, log-faced, with several outhouses. Two cars and a truck were standing beside the house, and at the other side of the lawn, farthest from the house, a group of other young men, also in shorts and without shirts, were sitting in the sun on the grass while a man straddling a chair addressed them.

One of the wrestlers spotted them right away and came across, breathing heavily. He said, 'Yes?'

'We were looking for Haus Adler.'

'Yes, this it it. What do you want?'

'I was talking to Herr Adler. We walked across to see the house.'

'Herr Adler isn't here.'

'I don't want to see him. I want to see the house.'

'It's private property.'

'It's a school, is it?' Raison said.

'A school. Who let you in?'

'The door was open.'

'Well, it's private property.'

'Can we have a look round? The grounds?' Raison said.

'There aren't any grounds. There's just this. There's nothing to see. It's private,' the man said.

'All right.'

'Where was it you've come from – Waldstein?'

'That's right.'

'All right. Good-bye.'

He'd taken them to the door, and he closed and locked it after them.

'They're fascists,' the girl said.

'Hm.'

'Fascists. I know it. That awful Adler, letting the property of that poor old Jew out to people like that.'

Raison hadn't told her the complications there might be in the background of this particular poor old Jew. He thought about it as they made their way back to the fingerpost with its national colours, and turned on to the road. After a few minutes a car approached down the road and stopped beside them.

'Good morning,' Adler said.

'Good morning. We took a walk down to the lodge.'

'Yes. They telephoned me. I was in the council offices. I am on the council. Let me give you a lift back.'

'Not if it's taking you out of your way,' Raison said. The car seemed to have just come from Waldstein.

'I came for you. Sit in the back, Fräulein.' They got in the car and he reversed it. 'I wish you'd had a word with me before you went to the school,' he said. 'They were very alarmed. They thought I was thinking of letting the place over their heads.'

'Ah.'

'People get flustered with strangers here. They're not used to strangers – only hikers and skiers. I wish you'd had a word with me,' he said. His neck was pink in the collarless jacket. 'One has to find tenants where one can. One can't have places standing empty. One shouldn't antagonize tenants however little they pay. There are ways of doing things,' he said.

'I'm sorry. We were only wandering about.'

'I have some information for you.' His neck was wriggling inside the jacket. 'It puts me in the most damnable fix – excuse me, Fräulein. It's perfectly true your man came back. What I shall do now, I don't know. I shall have to see my own lawyer.'

'What do you mean?' Raison said. 'You've found someone who saw Bamberger?'

'Yes. I knew nothing about it, nothing whatever.'

'Does he know why Bamberger came here?'

'He came to see him. To make some arrangements.'

'What arrangements?'

'Naturally, I didn't ask. He wouldn't have told me. He's a respectable man, a trustworthy man.'

'Can I see him?'

'No. He still makes the arrangements.'

'What do you mean – for Bamberger? He sees him?'

'He deals with somebody else who sees him.'

'Here?'

'In Prague.'

'Somebody sends him instructions from Prague?'

'He goes there. It's quite simple. He goes on the bus. Anybody can.'

'Is Bamberger there?'

'That's not his affair. It seems likely, doesn't it? I wish I'd never started with the damnable place, devil take it. Excuse me, Fräulein.'

'Why should he have gone back to Prague?'

'Who knows? They're always troublesome – Excuse me, you're not a Jew?'

'No. Can I get in touch with Bamberger?'

'You can pay the man and he'll take a letter. It's not to say you'd get an answer.'

'When can he take it?'

'There's a bus on Monday. I don't know if it's convenient for him. He has arrangements to make. I wasn't looking for property. The lodge was offered to me. It's placed me in an impossible position.'

'There's no problem with the lodge,' Raison said.

'I'm on the council here. We're an old family here. I can't risk any nonsense of defrauding Jews. Can't you imagine the howl that would go up in the press?'

'Forget it,' Raison said.

'If you send a letter, I'll send one also. At least, it will be something to show if there's trouble. There's always trouble with them,' he said. He was slowing down as they approached the Gasthof. 'Why it is, I don't know. Of course, I've got nothing against them myself . . .'

'Can you see this man again and ask if he can go on Monday?' Raison said.

'Very well. I suppose the sooner the better. I don't know what I'm going to do. It's a talent for making trouble,' he said. 'The minute you turn your back they make trouble.'

Rather a lot of shouting seemed to be going on from inside the Gasthof as they got out of the car.

'It's all right,' Raison said. 'It's all over now. The whole thing is finished.'

'I'm not staying.'

'Where can you go? We can't sign into another hotel just for a few hours. They've all said they're sorry.'

'They sent people up from the kitchen even to swear at me. A man, a kitchen hand, took my pills from me. He threw them out of the window when I needed one. He said the concentration camps hadn't been thorough enough. If you want, stay. I'll go and sit in the square. I'll sit in the forest. I'm not staying here.'

'All right,' Raison said. 'If that's what you want. But it's hot out there. The sun is scorching.'

'My hat will protect me from the sun.'

It did that. The enormous thing threw a shadow like an umbrella. It didn't protect them from the Saturday morning eyes of Waldstein. For the first time Raison was aware of anti-semitism as an almost palpable current in the air, the particular anti-semitism, the partly religious anti-semitism of central Europe. He and Elke sat on either side of Grunwald and felt it, and Grunwald sat between them and felt it; but he knew about it, and he snoozed a little under his hat, because it always had made him tired.

Grunwald didn't eat in Waldstein after that. About one they went over to a restaurant and ate, but Grunwald only watched. In the afternoon when it was hotter they sat in the forest, and at five when it was cooler they went back to the village. Adler found them having a beer in the late afternoon.

He said, 'He'll go on Monday. He'll charge you one hundred and ten marks, including the fare. It's reasonable, I think.'

'All right,' Raison said.

'Also something else. You were asking why a certain person went back. He went back because he's married there. He has children there.'

'Oh.'

'I don't know how it affects the "estate",' Adler said. He seemed much perkier.

'Male children?' Raison said.

'One,' Adler said.

'Ah.'

'Yes. Write the letter now, if you want. Mark it confidential and leave it for me at the Gasthof. You don't have to wait.'

But they couldn't write the letter then. Grunwald had to wait till the sabbath was over. He wrote it when the third star came out, and then they left Waldstein and went back to Munich.

It was late when they got in, after midnight. They'd hung about too much together, had wasted too much time together. 'Good night,' they said on the pavement. Raison went up with Grunwald to the second floor. 'Good night,' they said in the corridor.

Raison went to his room and looked around it. It had the hushed weary look of any other hotel room at night. It seemed more than two days he'd been away. He felt as if he didn't live anywhere, as if he were hovering somewhere above the surface, or hibernating somewhere below it, with everything above or below in constant motion, and all the points of reference changing. What with one thing and another, there was a lot to think about here. But he was too tired to think any more. He got into bed, and fell into heavy sleep, mouth open, the lights of the room still burning, forgotten.

He saw her early, at eleven. They drank coffee somewhere outside. Organs were booming and choirs were singing in Munich. They looked in shop windows and walked through

187

squares and gardens. They went into a church. The organ was playing Bach in the church and sunlight streamed through the windows. It was a large church, baroque, richly decorated, serene in the warm light. All about it, between the pews and in the wide spaces, people knelt, some on one knee, others walking to and fro with hands clasped in prayer before them, to the place where a young priest, like a conjurer, united them with God, raising a large silver beaker with both hands and draining it, and wiping it out with a cloth, and upturning it, to place other cloths on it, and laying wafers on tongues. All over Munich, as they walked about, the supernatural exercises were being held, unions made, sins forgiven. They walked till two, not talking much, not even hungry, till they found themselves beside a particular restaurant in the Maximilianstrasse where the girl said it would be a good idea to eat gulls' eggs and radishes, because it was the time for them. They sat and ate them outside under an umbrella, with salt, and a jug of Bernkasteler.

'It's quite over with the Hungarian?' Raison said. He'd been brooding over it.

'Quite over.'

'All finished?'

'A long time ago.'

They finished off the Bernkasteler and went back to the Hohenzollernstrasse and to bed.

They went out again later and ate. It was still warm and they ate outside in the Englischer Garten. Then they went to bed again.

'James, James, James,' the girl said as they united. Raison said some things, too. He felt a bit lost and a bit found. He thought there had to be exceptions to the rules, genuine ones, true ones. He thought this was a true one, unlooked for, quite genuine, for both.

They were smoking a cigarette when the buzzer went in the morning. It was the downstairs microphone buzzer, and Elke got out of bed with her cigarette and answered it. A man's voice said in the little loudspeaker, 'I haven't got my key. It's Franz. Where have you been?' She said quickly, looking at

Raison, 'Don't come up. I'm coming down,' and looked swiftly round for her raincoat, and put it on.

Raison watched her, on one elbow. He said, 'It's true. You really are quite untidy underneath.'

She said, 'It isn't anything. Honestly. I'll be only a few minutes. Make coffee.'

But on the way downstairs she suddenly remembered there wasn't any coffee, only instant tea.

Raison remembered it, too. He still didn't think he wanted instant tea. He didn't think he wanted instant anything. He remained on one elbow, smoking his cigarette, blinking slowly at the door. Then he got up and dressed and went.

PART FOUR

The persecutee shall have a claim if at any time
during the period he has been deprived of his liberty.
This shall be deemed to include in particular arrest
and detention by the police or by military personnel,
arrest by the NSDAP, preventive custody, penal
imprisonment, detention in a concentration camp
and forced stay in a ghetto.

German Federal Indemnification Law
(*Bundesentschädigungsgesetz*)

Chapter 1

A FEW FLOWERS FOR REMEMBRANCE

IT was quite astonishing the way the weather was keeping up.
It was quite incredible. Normally you couldn't count on a
run of good weather here, but now day after day it went on.
Beautiful. Heartening. He heard a couple of chaffinches in the
Tal. Charming. Cars were streaming past him, fellows giving
themselves coronaries. Let them. At a certain time of life you
knew better than to hurry. At a certain time you knew there
was no need. Events materialized in their own way without the
necessity to run like a chicken in six directions. He let the
Mercedes amble sweetly along. He had had a very nice piece
of information this morning.

Wasserman had telephoned him with it personally at home.
This was a reciprocal act of courtesy. He had telephoned
Wasserman with the original inquiry to *his* home. It was by
initiating such an atmosphere of courtesy that the individual
was able to exert an influence on his own times. Nobody could
have said that Wasserman had been particularly courteous in
former times. There had been some funny stories about Wasserman in the Judge Advocate's office in former times. But
then, in former times had lived a former Wasserman: that was
the thing, a wonderful thing. Already the new philosophy had
exerted a tremendous influence on his life. Former times,
former people. The identity was new, endlessly new, endlessly
evolving. Wonderful.

A very nice piece of information.

Wasserman had told him that the Hilfende Hände file room
had burned down.

It had burned down, Wasserman said, shortly after the last
elections when the NPD had done so well, and all the files had
burnt with it. It had been kept quite quiet, Wasserman said.
There were always people around with bad minds who looked
for sinister political motives. Wasserman didn't think there was

anything political in it. Wasserman had been so courteous that he didn't argue with him. Anyway, he didn't care. It had burnt down. There was nothing to look into, nothing for Magda to do, nothing for anybody to do. They could all go home now. They'd find nothing here.

He'd hardly dared to hope for such a simple solution to the problem. He'd hardly been able to see any solution. Yet change one tiny part of the pattern, and everything changed. The problem didn't exist any more. It was all in the mind.

He pulled up at the traffic lights and looked up through the open sun roof directly at a little robin sitting on a lamp standard. The robin looked back at him. 'Diduli,' Haffner said. 'Diduli,' the robin said. It couldn't have heard him, of course, above the idling motors, and yet it cheered him enormously. There the little creature sat, taking in it's bird's eye view of the world, not trying to make sense of any of it, perfectly free. Ah!

Cars began hooting him, and he moved. It was in the mind. Change the point of view and everything changed. As he drove he looked around at the elegant new shops overflowing with the best of the world's goods, at the chic of the men and women in the streets, at the gleaming new cars on every side. Search Europe and you wouldn't find such tasteful prosperity. And yet to think – how few years ago? – of the shattered city and the broken people. Who could have thought that this hopeless generation would ever recover? They'd queued here, waited there, run wherever they were told, barely existing in their cellar hovels, seeing themselves as criminals awaiting justice. It had only needed another point of view – how could a whole nation be criminal, so many people accomplices? – to show the absurdity of the first. They were victims, like everybody else. As victims, they had the same rights as everybody else, democratic rights. And what a job they'd done with them. Who would show as thriving and successful a society as this one? It was all in the mind. It was all according to the point of view. There was no objective reality, only the human identity constantly reorientating, endlessly changing.

He bustled into the office to see what changes there were this morning. His secretary had changed this morning. The young girls rarely stayed long, too many jobs available. A woman from the outer office was standing in this week. They were older women in the outer office. He didn't like the older ones so closely about him; preferred fresher young things. He didn't mind this one. She was a widow, in her forties, quite fresh, quite trim. He surprised her bending over his desk, and because he was feeling in such a good mood gave her a playful pat on the bottom. '*Grüss Gott*, Gerda!' To his surprise his cupped hand encountered softness, no stiffness of belt or buckle, and for a fraction of a second stayed there.

'Oh! *Grüss Gott*, Herr Direktor!'

As she turned, startled, he saw she'd been arranging a little posy of alpine flowers for him, and moreover that she was blushing. He liked blushing in a woman.

'But how beautiful, how kind,' he said. 'Where did you get them?'

'From the country. From my little cottage, Herr Direktor.'

'Indeed. Where is the cottage?'

'At Schliersee, Herr Direktor. It isn't anything much.'

'Schliersee. By the lake?'

'By the woods, Herr Direktor. It's so beautiful now. The flowers, the birds. The birds are wonderful, Herr Direktor.'

'Indeed,' Haffner said. 'Indeed. Very kind,' he said.

He looked frequently at the little posy of flowers for much of the morning, and thought of the woods above Schliersee. Strange. The woman had worked in the office for five or six years. Surprising that he'd never particularly noticed her. He should take more of an interest in the staff. A certain softness remained in his hand, no belt or buckle. But it was a busy morning, a very active one. He tore into his work like a youngster, phoning, conferring, dictating, through all interruptions. He was dictating when Raison arrived. Raison was looking weary. He'd had a wild goose chase to the Bavarian Forest, of course. Haffner could have told him it was a waste of time but he listened tolerantly. It seemed they'd made general inquiries, had left word with one of the half-witted innkeepers there to get in touch if anybody should hear anything; nothing. As he could have foretold!

So he told Raison his own very nice piece of information. 'And to speak the truth, James,' he said, 'I'm really glad. Who knows where it might have ended? It's never wise to stir things up. As it is, the Israelis will have to wait. Death must be presumed some time. *We* can wait. Let them wait!'

Raison didn't stay long, and Haffner was glad of it. He always liked to see Raison, of course, but after all a lot of time had been devoted to this business and other matters demanded attention. But the Englishman took himself off so wearily, he felt bound to advise him, 'James, you've been pushing yourself too much lately, I can tell. Take it easy. Don't overdo things, give yourself a rest.'

Then he could dive back into his work again, but again for only a few minutes before the next interruption came. Surprisingly, it was Elke. He couldn't remember when Elke had last phoned him at the office. Elke was asking if he knew where Raison was, and this surprised him, too. He hadn't realized they knew each other all that well. 'He was here, but he's gone,' he said. 'About ten minutes ago. He was meeting somebody, an Israeli lawyer. No, I don't know where, I am very busy, my dear.' He sniffed the little posy of alpine flowers as he put the phone down.

The street was full of flowers. There were flower-sellers everywhere. They were sprinkling the flowers from their water bottles in the reeling heat. It wasn't far from town, fourteen kilometres on the suburban train. They came out into the bustling street with its supermarkets and its sun-flashing cars, and Grunwald looked about him for a while, trying to place everything. He found he couldn't place anything; all new here. They tried asking a few people, and got nowhere. So they found a policeman and asked him. It was a young policeman, and he got his book out and had a good look through it, but there was nothing there, either. He said, 'It sounds to me like something the Americans will know about, perhaps it's on their base. It's quite a long way, some kilometres, you should take a taxi.'

'The Americans? Why the Americans?' Grunwald said.

'Isn't it military? It sounds military. There's no other sort of detention centre here. You're quite sure it's *in* Dachau?'

'The *concentration camp*. The *concentration camp*,' Grunwald said. It was the first time Raison had seen him nearly speechless. 'Surely . . .' he said.

'Just a minute,' the policeman said, and went to talk to a taxi-driver. 'Go with him,' he said, coming back to them, 'in his taxi. If there's something like it, he'll find it.'

They went in the taxi, the driver muttering various possibilities to himself. He stopped suddenly, a short way out of town, and flagged down a little M.G. going the other way. An American airman was at the wheel of the M.G. The taxi-driver didn't seem to be getting far with him so Raison got out. The airman's German was terrible and he gladly lapsed into English.

'We haven't any sort of place like that,' he said. 'What kind of place is it you want?'

'The concentration camp,' Raison said.

'Oh, *that*. They call it something else. I forget what they call it. Could it be crematory, could it be memorial site?'

'*Das Krematorium?*' Raison said to the driver.

'*Welches Krematorium?*' the driver said.

'*Die Denkmalstätte?*'

'*Aha!*'

'*Kennen Sie die?*'

'*Jawohl, natürlich! Das Krematorium der Denkmalstätte. Oh, ja. Danke schön,*' he said to the American. '*Das Krematorium, yoh yoh!*'

They got back in the taxi and in the highest good humour the driver drove them to the Krematorium, explaining on the way how the confusion had arisen. 'We were looking, I thought, for a prison! There was talk of a prison. It isn't in any way a prison. It's a memorial – to the fallen in the war. Thousands had to be cremated on the site because of disease, typhus. Terrible to think of it. I don't like to go to such places myself. Still, I understand they've made a beautiful memorial of it, beautiful gardens and so, everything very reverent. Here we are.'

He dropped them at the entrance and they went on to the site where thousands had had to be cremated.

The entrance led to a group of buildings, the first of which turned out to be a museum. There were pillars in the museum, inscribed with the names of various countries; and there were photographs and documents and exhibits of clothing and instruments of torture. Looking about, Raison heard a dry chuckle and saw that Grunwald was examining some figures showing the tentative numbers of those who had passed into the care of the memorial site. The numbers went to over 200,000, but as a small text explained some of the numbers had been used again, and the thousands killed on arrival hadn't needed numbers, and the thousands already dead on arrival hadn't needed them, either.

Grunwald nosed quietly around by himself. 'Do you see something from the German government?' he said. 'I'd like to see in what terms the regret is expressed.'

Raison had a look. There were all kinds of things in the museum, which was a model of its sort. Every kind of fact and figure about the phenomenon of National Socialism had been assembled; which was only fitting, for the phenomenon had sprung to life only fourteen kilometres away, with the memorial site as its first practical expression. There were photographs of the cutting of the sod, the celebratory announcements in the local Munich press on opening day, and all the activities in between till the even more celebrated closing day. There was even, here and there, some strong ecclesiastical denunciation of the activities; meaty stuff with no punches pulled. But the denunciation tended to be general in tone, showing what men could come to when God was left out of the reckoning, with no particular men, except Godless ones, specified. In this context it was unnecessary, and probably unseemly, for any particular government to take on its shoulders the crimes of Godless humanity. So far as Raison could see, the German government hadn't. 'No,' he said.

'A pity,' Grunwald said. 'I'd like to have seen it.'

But it was quite an old phenomenon now, and it was hot in the museum, and there was nobody else in it. They wandered through the empty rooms and went out at the other end. A blast, as if of reality, and as if from a furnace, hit them at the other end. The heat rose from an enormous parade ground. The expanse of hot grit, white in the sun, stretched nearly half a mile in length and nearly a quarter wide. It was quite regular, surrounded by concrete walls topped by wire, and overlooked at intervals by observation towers. A few hundred yards away the blinding emptiness was broken by a double line of what looked like the foundations of large rectangular buildings; there were some dozens of them, a brick or two high, topped with gravel, like graves. The shock of coming so suddenly upon it, of finding it lying so barefaced in the sun, the concentration camp of imagination, was at once so banal and so shattering that Raison felt his back hairs rise at the same time that his facial muscles tightened to suppress a smile. The mementoes of old evil like the mementoes of old carnality were so obvious in purpose, so guileless. A vengeful child could have dreamed it, a vengeful child lovingly have organized the construction. With a shock of horror and amusement the nature of the beast's living dreams was perceived. Here the bully boys had got those they didn't like, and here they had done with them as they pleased, not overlooked, ingenuity the only limit.

Grunwald began to walk across the parade ground. Raison walked with him. The heat, as tangible as cotton wool, flowed up his trouser legs and sought out the skin beneath his clothes. Almost at once his shirt was damp. They walked for several minutes. They came to the wide aisle between the double line of foundations, and they walked along it. They walked past several of the foundations, and then Grunwald stopped, and looked at one of them, and walked a little around it, and sat down on the hot gravel. Close up, the foundations were large, a hundred yards or so in length, perhaps ten wide. Raison went and sat next to him.

'Home sweet home,' Grunwald said.

'Is this where you were?'

'This is it.'

'How many of you?'

'The barracks were built to accommodate a hundred and eighty each. In this particular one there were eleven hundred at the end. Including three hundred and twenty dead,' Grunwald said. He didn't sound distressed, or specially commemorative. He sounded chatty. 'They'd stopped dealing with the dead,' he said. 'There was no way any longer to deal with them. We had an epidemic. They were lying in mounds outside. They were stuffed to the roof in the crematory, and tumbling out of the doors. There were trucks and wagons filled with them. If you've not seen such things, it's impossible to imagine. It's hard even to remember. I can't really believe it happened,' he said.

'Shall we get in the shade?' Raison said. The nearest shade was a long way away, but he had a feeling he was frying. He'd taken off his jacket and tie, but was not sure it was better with his jacket off. The radiating surface of the concentration camp was like a grill.

Grunwald got up and they walked to the shade. 'The heat I can remember,' he said. 'When it was hot it was always like this. When it was cold it was very cold. The place is built on a somewhat unhealthy moor which gets the worst of everything. When it rained or snowed here, we got very wet. We were out in it all day – in the summer from three in the morning, in the winter from five. We wore clogs and we ran. We ran everywhere. We ran to the gravel pits and we ran back, in companies. We pulled large wagons about, railway wagons with special wheels – the Moorland Express, it was called – all about this ground. When the weather was wet there was no way to get dry. The clothes were wet in the morning. For some reason,' he said, 'the human spirit never gets used to misery. The body sleeps and wakes up and is ready for more misery; it has an endless capacity for it.'

'Yes.'

'It's hard to believe. . . . They were hitting people all the time. I myself – not a day passed, a blow, a kick, a lash. Unbelievable. And all the time we ran. They called "Tempo,

Tempo". The loudspeakers called "Tempo". People dropped with exhaustion, sometimes dropped dead, pulling at the wagons. There was death all around, shooting, hanging, flogging. Bodies were being burnt all the time. The smoke from the crematory hung in the air. There were people with terrible injuries, crushed organs, broken limbs, noses, eyes, unbelievable horrors, who if they were actually still alive, or even if they were dead and hadn't yet been booked as dead, had to be produced at roll call. The numbers from the last roll call had to tally! The dead and the crippled we wheeled out in barrows. We sometimes stood all night if there was a discrepancy. There was an infirmary – but only for those who wanted a quick way out. If a case needed treatment in the infirmary, there was right away an injection. Why go there otherwise? To get better? For what? There was only one end here. It was punishment to death. It was all a matter of what the bodies could stand. The doctors were in a way, every now and again, interested. It wasn't Jews only. We had Russians, Poles. But with the Jews there was the difference that we were here only for death. It didn't matter who finished us, how, for what reason – only book-keeping. Transports went out to be gassed – there was no gassing here – I don't know on what basis. I don't know if there was any basis, except the numbers the gassing places could cope with. I don't know why I didn't go. I don't know why I survived. I don't know what in the end it was that did in fact survive. There was no longer any identity, no other life beyond this place, just a biological unit of a Jewish corpus that survived. Yet it survived, and life revives. . . . After all, the thing's a gift! It's not to be spurned, whatever you feel. There's a duty on the living to maintain the idea of it. In the end, there's always meaning. . . . I'm not sure if it's possible for you to understand this.'

'Nor am I,' Raison said.

'Well. . . . This was the worst, the worst that happened to the human species in the history of the planet. It happened in the twentieth century, in the middle of the enlightened continent, at the hands of the advanced people. It was a demonstration that the animal is just below. In the end, if man's to survive here he has to be judged on his ethical standards, not his intellectual achievements.'

'I hope the SS got the message,' Raison said.

'The SS – there's more than the SS on the planet. It was a message for all. It wouldn't be the first time we've served as an illustration.'

'Do you think God used you as an illustration?'

'Who can say that?'

'Some would say it's blasphemous.'

'One's ideas of blasphemy naturally depend on one's idea of God. To say we served as an illustration, which is irrefutable, isn't to say that God willed it. Perhaps, by existing, *we* willed it. Did we have to continue, as Jews? Did it have to be us?'

'Did it have to be anybody? Did it have to happen at all?'

'Ah, was it an accident? Were six million people murdered, over some years, with the world looking on, many of them helping, as part of some accident? Perhaps. Perhaps everything is an accident. Perhaps, God forbid, God doesn't exist. Perhaps he exists and he's tired of his work. Even if it were so, what would it mean? Only that we would have to do the work for him. If he didn't exist we would have to act as if he did exist. We would have to act as if carrying out the original purpose, and if there were no purpose, we would have to make a purpose. The world, at least, exists! It's a going concern! There has got to be some sanction for the activities in it. But I believe he does exist, and I believe the creation didn't end on the sixth day, or whichever period you prefer, and that we have a role, and that there's meaning here.'

'Here?' Raison said.

'Here,' Grunwald said. 'Yes.'

'Okay,' Raison said. He didn't know why he was challenging this man's beliefs, in this place. He felt sick suddenly. They'd reached the shade. They walked in the shade beyond the area of the parade ground, into green places. They passed a grassy knoll with its mass dead, and then another, and then an execution place, and its blood trench; gardens of remembrance now, all, with inscriptions, with records. They were making, along shady paths, towards a stark memorial chapel dominated by a cross, when they caught a passing glimpse of another memorial garden, and they turned and went to it. It was a small garden, screened by hedges, with a narrow entrance; a private place, very quiet in the heat of the afternoon. A few begonias grew in a circular bed in the middle of it. A candelabrum of granite stood on a granite Shield of David which in turn stood on a single tombstone. There were no records and no explanations. A single line of lettering cut in the stone carried a simple message. *Vergiss Nicht,* it said in German, *Loh Tishkach,* it said in Hebrew, *Do Not Forget,* it said in English.

Raison heard a creaking, like the creaking of leather harness, and couldn't place it, and after some moments looked about him and placed it. What the museum and home sweet home and the mass graves hadn't been able to do, the single line of lettering in the stone had done. Arms down at his sides, Grunwald was crying. His face seemed to have collapsed in on itself and some broken words were issuing from his straining larynx. '*Av Harachamim,*' Grunwald said. 'Father of Mercy,' he said. Raison heard some names tumbling out, a Hannaliese and an Otto and a Benjamin and a Ruth, and he walked out of the garden and found a seat under a tree and lit himself a cigarette.

Grunwald didn't take long. He was out presently, blowing his nose.

'So,' he said.

'Yes.'

'We can go now.'

They walked along the path. Grunwald blew his nose a few times more, but he didn't say anything till they were approaching the exit. Then he said, 'You didn't tell Haffner what we found there?'

'No.'

'No . . .'

'You see,' he said a moment later, 'repentance needs guilt – and they feel no guilt. For this generation there can't be any *Wiedergutmachung.* How is it possible for them to make good again? The dead they can't repay. The dead family without an heir they can't repay. If they'd managed to kill every member of every family they'd have nothing to repay. It's actions for damages on behalf of ruined survivors that we bring against them, and even these . . .'

He stopped, for Raison had stopped, too, and he looked where Raison was looking. An enormous advertisement, apparently of recent erection, stood beside the exit. FOR GAS INSTALLATIONS, it said, CALL DACHAU 3904, BURG-FRIEDENSTRASSE 7. The advertisement stood on stilts on the spot beaten down by the clogs of the many thousands who had double-marched to earlier gas installations.

'How else can you describe it,' Grunwald said, shaking his head slowly as they walked on again, 'except as a sort of colour-blindness? It's a national disease. Something is simply missing.'

It was late when they got back, after three, and Raison felt exhausted and depressed. Three messages awaited him at the reception desk. Fräulein Haffner had telephoned at one o'clock and at two o'clock, and at three o'clock. She was going to telephone again at four o'clock.

'I won't be in,' Raison said, and went up to his room.

Chapter 2

RHYME AND REASON

HE'D meant to phone Gunter, but he fell asleep. He was asleep when the door went. He said wildly, from out of a dream, 'Yes?'

'Ah. You're in. I thought so,' Grunwald said.

'Come in, come in.'

Grunwald's head was already fractionally in. 'It's nothing – a call for you on my phone, Haffner's daughter. They told her you were out. I can tell them to put it through.'

'All right,' Raison said. He still wasn't awake, but even not awake he saw it was easier to take the call than to explain.

'James, I'm below,' she said in his ear.

'I'm busy, Elke.'

'James, there's Magda. She's expecting you.'

'We can forget Magda.'

'James, you must let me say a word. It's not fair. I'll come up.'

'I'll come down,' he said. He couldn't have her banging on the door, banging on Grunwald's door; explanations.

He had a wash and went down.

'James, why did you go away, why didn't you let me explain?' She was looking tall and tired and beseeching.

'There's nothing to explain.'

'He's young and mixed up and very poor. He drinks his money. When he has nowhere to stay I let him stay there. He's an artist. He has to be able to work.'

'We all have,' Raison said, looking at his watch. 'I'm afraid I can't manage Magda just now.'

'But she's expecting you. She's putting herself out to meet you. I've been trying to get you all day.'

Raison looked at her. It was no use explaining the matter of the Hilfende Hände file room and pointing out that Magda was no longer needed. She didn't know about any of this, anyway. And she'd certainly been running about on his account all day. He looked distractedly at his watch again.

'It's five o'clock – we're half an hour late already. I've got the car outside.'

'All right,' Raison said.

'Thank you, James. I'll make you understand. I *will*,' she said.

She didn't try in the car, concentrating grimly on getting it in the shortest possible time to the Briennerstrasse. They screamed to a halt beside the familiar No-Parking sign, several dirndl-clad patrons turning to observe the commotion. One of them stood up and came across, accompanied by a couple of disinterested Afghan hounds.

'*You're* a fine one. I was just going,' she said.

'Magda, I'm so sorry. We got held up. Magda, it's James Raison. James, it's Magda Emmerich.'

'It rejoices me,' Magda Emmerich said.

'Yes,' Raison said. Her hand was held up high under his

nose, and he kissed it. He felt a bit of a fool, and temporarily out of German.

'Let's at least have a quick drink,' Elke said.

'All right. Very quick. Charles and Abdel have to get to the kennels before it closes. I'm going to Madrid on Wednesday,' she said to Raison. 'All tomorrow is a rush.'

'Madrid,' Raison said. Magda was something of a surprise. He'd been expecting a model on Haffner lines with possible Wagnerian overtones. No trace of Haffner or Wagner showed here. The terrible SS widow was petite, with amusing and well-formed features. Her dark gamine hair style featured a fashionable streak of white, and her eyes, revealed on removal of the sunglasses, were lively, not to say sunny. Apart from the attendant hounds there was nothing of the female heavy here. He found himself boggling, and was still mentally boggling as they sat at a table receiving their drinks. He received his very gladly. He seemed to be just awake. It had been a day of disturbances. He felt himself churned up, a battle mire of drifting gases with pockets of poisoned memories: girls in raincoats with multiple lives, old men with broken soundboxes straining to sound grief, flower-filled streets where all was forgotten, and the concrete obscenity of the concentration camp. Looking at the birdlike creature chattering with such vivacity he remembered too the celebratory announcements on opening day, and tried to find in the face something that was necessarily and inescapably evil. Her husband hadn't, after all, sprung to life a full general: he'd been in at the rowdy start, a young militant, a political activist, with his girl friend's enthusiastic support. Had she been there on opening day at the unambiguous place? Had she celebrated with the others at this first purposeful expression of ideology? Something of the viciousness must show in the face. But it didn't; any more than in the faces of those across his desk in Lincoln's Inn. There was no plumbing any of them, Raison thought, and that was the fact.

In a mindless way he'd been contributing to the conversation himself in ways apparently not unpleasing to Magda. As Elke had foretold, she seemed to have taken to him. He was aware of her eyes turning constantly to his, and of her hand needlessly steadying his as he lit her cigarette.

'Tell me, how do you get on with that legal brain, my brother?'

'Fine.'

'An honest opinion – is he any good?'

'Well, I . . .'

'Magda, really!'

'I mean it. If he's going to get involved in my affairs again –'

'Is he?'

'Your mother seems to want it. Anyway, he cares more for Schonbach than I do. You'll have gathered,' she said to Raison, 'that I haven't invariably seen eye to eye with my brother. He's bound to have told you in one of his confessional moments.'

'What about Schonbach?' Elke said.

Magda cocked an amused eye at her. 'If you don't know, you probably don't need to,' she said. 'It's a bore, anyway. But tell your mother, if you want, that it's all right with me – she'll understand. Not that it will make any difference. In my opinion,' she said to Raison, 'your colleague's a born loser. Some people are – soft at the centre, impotent.'

'Magda!'

'Oh, not necessarily in that way. Which wouldn't, however, surprise me. It's a natural deficiency – jelly where the backbone ought to be. Every now and then it will stiffen – long after it means to or long before it needs to, because it's after all not backbone and there's no certainty of response. Either way the timing's always wrong. It induces a general paralysis of the will, which leads to a desire to accommodate, and ultimately an inability to do what's required at the proper time – in a word, impotence.'

Elke had been looking back and forth to see the effect of this example of her aunt's trenchancy on Raison, but she said, 'Is *that* what the architect from Stuttgart was doing at Schonbach?'

'Who told you about the architect from Stuttgart?'

'I heard you had an expert of some kind down for the week-end.'

'Yes. He wasn't so very expert,' Magda said drily. 'I brought him back today.'

'Can you tell me about National Socialism?' Raison said.

He was aware that it came out a bit lumpenly, and also that he was staring at Magda. So soon after the memorial site, the female fascist fascinated him. He had an enormous desire suddenly to try and understand her, to try and understand *it*.

'National Socialism?' Magda's eyes were amused but interested. 'What about it?'

'What was it? What was the idea?'

'What else but what we've been discussing? It's about backbone. About the desire and the capacity to act.'

'But its aims, its objects?'

'Aims and objects,' Magda said, 'are something larger, and at the same time something smaller. Movements aren't political parties. It's an idea, a way of thinking. I think you'd understand,' she said, looking at him. 'I really think you would. Unfortunately, I haven't a minute now, and I don't know – Abdel! Charles! – unless – What are you doing tomorrow?'

'I thought you were busy tomorrow,' Elke said.

'I'm running down to Schonbach in the afternoon. I came away in a hurry and left things there. If you care to come for the ride?' she said to Raison.

'All right.'

'I'll come with you,' Elke said.

'There's no room. I'm running the two-seater.'

'There's my own car.'

'There's no *point*. I'm only popping in and out, *Liebchen*. I've got a dinner date back here in the evening. If you don't mind merely talking on the way there and back,' she said to Raison.

'All right.'

'Where are you staying?'

'The Ludwigshof.'

'I'll pick you up, then – between four and five. Don't keep me waiting.'

'That's Magda,' Elke said, smiling after her.

'Yes. I'll be going now, then,' Raison said.

'James.'

'I have some work.'

'Please stop it. Talk.'

'Some other time,' Raison said.

'James, he means nothing to me. Less than nothing. I didn't lie to you.'

'Didn't you?'

'You asked about Tibor, the Hungarian.'

'Well,' Raison said, after a beat, 'I didn't have the list.'

'Am I supposed to slap your face? It's too infantile. Do you want me to tell you or not?'

'No.'

'Then I will. It isn't *anything*. It's absolutely nothing. If anything I feel maternal, he drifts, he has nothing. It's just affection, warmth for a waif . . .'

'Don't bother coming,' Raison said. 'I'll get a taxi.'

'I love you.'

'You love everybody. You're a living poster,' Raison said. But he saw as he stood that she was crying, and something stirred. He said, 'I'm sorry, Elke. We're simply different. It's my fault.'

'It isn't anybody's fault. What fault?' she said. She was snuffling irritably into her handbag, apparently in search of a hanky. She didn't seem to have a hanky. Raison gave her his.

'Go if you want, then,' she said.

Raison sat down.

'Why have there got to be any faults? I'll send you the handkerchief back,' she said, blowing into it again. 'I think you're mad with faults,' she said.

'I can't leave you like this. Where do you want to go?'

'I'm not going anywhere. Come home with me, then.'

'I can't.'

'Then go away. Do you think I'm going to attack you? I think you're mad.'

'All right, we'll go, then.'

'Don't bother.'

But they went, to the Hohenzollernstrasse, and she didn't

attack him. Nobody attacked anybody. They played the gramophone and talked. 'Why always faults?' she said. 'We're here to amuse ourselves, to love each other, what else? There's no other purpose. Why is everyone always looking for purposes? We're all going to die. We could all love each other. We're predisposed to love each other.'

Raison didn't argue with her. He had a drink and presently she made dinner. While she was making it he found another verse in the armchair. It said:

We need a stand-in for the true one, for the alien unknown
that has made what it has made as it has made.
(The Milky Way and battery hens,
the dinosaur, carcinogens.)
No dialogue with that one – how with that?
But we couldn't do without one so the Teacher dreamed us Du
and he made you in our image and he wrote the play for you.
                 (A tree of life to them that grasp it,
                   endless life for them that grasp it!)
But you fluffed your lines and faded,
oh you faded Gottenu.

Later they played the gramophone again, and he left at ten.

The strains of music were issuing from the next room when he got back so he looked in. Grunwald was also at his gramophone.

'Are we predisposed to love each other?' Raison said.

Grunwald let Beethoven finish. Then he said mildly, 'Perhaps I'm not the one to ask. But it puts me in mind of the morality machine.'

'The morality machine?'

'A certain organization had a machine and invited passers-by off the street to try it. Anyone who wished could press a button and in the same moment an unknown man in the heart of China would instantly die and the machine would reward the presser with a dollar.'

'What happened?' Raison said.

Grunwald told him.

*

There wasn't enough gravy. There was never enough gravy. There ought to be less twittering and more gravy. What was she twittering about?

'The hammock's so shabby now I don't think there's any point in cleaning it.'

'What?'

'The hammock. I was thinking –'

'Why do you make so little gravy? There's never enough gravy.'

'I'm sorry. I misjudged. There's nice bottled sauce in the kitchen, shall I get it?'

'All right. And bread. It isn't still Hoffman's, is it?'

'I forgot. I'll change tomorrow.'

He grunted. To mention a thing here was to ensure it disappeared from the table. The strain of trying to remember seemed to set up a block in her mind. Too little to do, of course; an aimless butterfly life; never any rhyme or reason in it. Hammocks, now. What did she want with hammocks? Did she spend any time in the garden? Did she pick a bunch of flowers, even, a posy of flowers . . . ? He had a sudden restless sensation and an itching in his hand, and at the same time his appetite went. Waiting for food, of course. She knew he hated waiting. But he'd asked for it so he had to eat it when it came. A maddening brainless creature. No sensitivity at bottom . . .

'What?' he said. 'What?'

'I said I saw Ursula Lohr also looking at hammocks. They've taken a cottage –'

'I won't want cheese. I'll just want coffee. Is the coffee ready?'

'It's on. What's the matter with you? Can't you talk a little at dinner?'

'If anything interesting was said. What possible interest can there be in a hammock as a subject? If you want one, get one – your unknown friend also.'

'Of course you know them. Lohr the engineer, the electrical engineer.' The two little red points had come up again on her cheekbones and he watched them curiously. They came up when she was angry or pursuing some ulterior motive. There was nothing ulterior in this twittering, and he hadn't meant to make her angry. He was restless and on edge, he didn't know why; strange after his high spirits of the morning, strange. But he saw he'd better make an effort, so he said heavily, 'So Lohr is buying himself a new hammock, is he? Well, then. H'm.'

'For their new cottage. At Schliersee. It will be more convenient for them than running in and out of town.'

'Schliersee.' There was something about Schliersee. What was it now? 'What is so convenient for Lohr at Schliersee?' he said.

She seemed to take a breath. She said, 'It's a new power station. His firm tendered for a sub-contract. Of course, they're expecting –'

'A power station at Schliersee!' he said. He'd suddenly remembered about Schliersee. The woods above Schliersee. A cottage in the woods. Terrible. It mustn't be allowed. Something leapt in his heart and died again immediately. There was no stopping these juggernauts, of course. A desecration. He said mournfully, 'It shouldn't be allowed.'

'Naturally, they're expecting protests. It's worrying for Ursula. Local residents will be paid off handsomely, of course, but in a matter like this, with regard to a beauty spot, anyone can protest. They're going ahead with the cottage, but –'

'Whereabouts in Schliersee, the power station?' he said.

'It isn't exactly in Schliersee. It's a few kilometres out, seven or eight. They had to have a section of level ground in the hills with water. Of course –'

'Seven or eight kilometres from Schliersee?' he said, looking in his mind at all of the well-loved area. What idiot's talk had she picked up now? There wasn't any level ground in the hills seven or eight kilometres from Schliersee. There wasn't any level ground till . . .

His stomach knotted suddenly in a single paralysing spasm that brought a red mist to his eyes and the sound of the sea to his ears. Hills, level ground, water . . .

Not possible. Not thinkable. The one unblemished area of existence, all purity, all serenity, the spice of cones.

'No,' he said.

'What?'

'No!'

'Heinz, what is it? What's the matter?'

Surprising obscenities were coming out of him. His face had turned a dark mahogany colour. His eyes glittered. He looked a little mad, a little terrifying – potent, even. Long forgotten, a small *frisson* went through her, quite pleasurably.

'They won't,' he said. 'They shan't.'

'Heinz – the coffee.'

But he'd already lumbered away from the table, shaking.

'What is the whore's number?' he said thickly.

Chapter 3

A TOUCH OF THE WANDERVOGEL

THEY had a fast run down on the autobahn and turned off it at Weyarn. She drove at speed along the twisting minor roads, and at Schliersee turned off again, with no reduction of speed, to a still more minor road. *Schonbach, 8km*, the sign read as they flashed past. Raison cautiously released one hand and threw his cigarette out. Peaks were all about, and steep buttercup slopes and occasional puzzled-looking cows. They were in alpine country. Fields, where cultivable, were lush, the ground rich, sky blue, the whole field of vision suggestive of wholesome Swiss chocolate.

The promised talk hadn't yet come about, and Raison was glad of it. She was a dangerous driver. Her occasional sideways comments to him had already produced two near disasters, with a farm cart and a hearse, together with a rich flow of language. The language continued, as an occasional beast or vehicle was encountered, as they swung and lurched the last few perilous kilometres. It was still early. Despite the rush of wind in the open convertible, Raison could feel the sun hot on his head. She'd surprised him by reporting before time, at a few minutes to four. 'If we don't get a chance to talk properly on the way, it will give us a little time there. So long as I'm back before seven,' she said.

From Schliersee the road snaked steadily upwards between rock walls, but as they rounded a bend Raison saw the peaks opening out and espied across a small gulf a stretch of level ground with a fuzz of trees and a village. They zeroed rapidly in to it, stopping abruptly at what seemed to be a grocer's. 'I'll get something to drink,' she said.

She was out in a brace of shakes with a bottle, swearing hard. 'The disgusting swine is supposed to keep it in his cellar for me. Never mind. We can cool it in the stream.'

The cottage was a little out of the village, approached by a dirt road and a wooden bridge over a stream. They shot across the bridge with a rumble of logs, and halted at the other side. A little lawn, dusted with daisies, ran down to the stream. The cottage, a largish log structure, was at the other side of the lawn.

'Here. Go and cool it. You'll find a holder,' she said, and without further explanation went into the house. Raison remained where he was for a moment, allowing the scenery to get back in place. It was certainly an idyllic spot. There was a heady feeling of altitude and remoteness on the warm mountain side. In the still of the afternoon the only sound was of water over rock.

He got out and went to the stream. The banks were steep with overhanging trees and shrubs, and he climbed down. He wasn't too sure what he was looking for, but presently found a stake to which was chained a wire basket. He inserted the bottle in it and lowered it into the water. Then he climbed back and resumed his survey of the locality.

The house sat with its back to the woods, on the very edge of the trees. A pile of logs leaned against the side of it. At either side of the front door was a wooden bench and a rough table.

'Come in when you're ready!' Her head was poking out of a fanlight in the roof. 'There are glasses in the kitchen.'

He went in. The windows were small and it was dark inside, with much rush matting and rustic furniture. A wide pine staircase – open-slatted and rope-banistered – slanted directly from the front room to an open trapdoor above. He could hear her moving overhead. All the interior doors of the ground floor had been removed at some stage, and the small rooms wandered somewhat mystifyingly one into another. But he found the kitchen, and the remains of a meal, and several used dishes. He also found a couple of clean glasses and a corkscrew and took them outside to one of the tables. He lit himself a cigarette and looked around again.

'Come up, if you want. I'm only tidying.'

He went in and up the ladder. The upper floor was a single room, thirty feet or so in length, the full extent of the house. Its roof sloped steeply from a central apex. Several windows were cut in the roof and everywhere sunlight shone genially on rich colours—varnished pine, Spanish rugs, divans, cushions. Central heating pipes ran round the room.

'Very snug,' Raison said.

'Yes.' She was straightening one of the divans, made up as a bed. 'But dark in winter. The snow,' she said, pointing at the windows in the roof.

'What happens here in winter?'

'Skiing. House parties. It's very good in winter.'

'This is a sort of lounge-bedroom, is it?'

The phrase seemed to tickle her. 'Exactly. A lounge-bedroom. There's another couple of bedrooms below. But this is the one to lounge in,' she said. She picked up a packed bag. 'We can go down now.' She pointed out a hefty bolt on the inside of the trapdoor, as they did so. 'For extra snugness,' she said. 'It can be quite secluded here.'

'It seems secluded enough without the bolt.'

She said vaguely, 'Well, if there's a party below and one needs the privacy for any reason . . .'

She had a look at her watch when they were down. 'Very good. Not five. We have over an hour. Do you want to see the woods while the wine cools?'

'All right.'

They walked round the side of the house and into the woods. It was dark in the woods and cones were thick underfoot. The scent of spice was very strong. A lot of birds seemed to be about. They were going *Didloi didloi didloi tüttüttü-wiiui diduli diduli diduli lululu-u dwüid dwüid dwüid pii-iiüu-ui.*

'Very pretty,' Raison said.

'Yes. Your colleague my brother has a particular attachment to this place. He's quite mystical about it. For me, too, it's sad to say good-bye.'

'How long will you be gone?'

'How long?'

'To Madrid?'

'Oh. Not so long. About a month.'

'Isn't that what you meant?'

She said obliquely, 'Things have to keep moving. Nothing stands still. There's a touch of the *Wandervogel,* the bird of passage, about all of us. It's a law of life. Get the wine and I'll tell you.'

Raison got the wine and they sat on a bench with their feet on the table. She said, 'I know you're one of those who can understand. It's in your face. There's directness and virility. It's the important quality for a man. You've fought, haven't you?'

'Like a lion,' Raison said.

'Us?'

'Fleetingly.'

'I know the tone. It's proper. I'd have known anyway. I'm a fighter also. There's an urge to exert oneself in proper people. In the better animals, even. Which after all we are, in our own jungle. The good ones have to want to tame it. For the rest they're shit, if the language doesn't offend.'

'Not as between old fighters,' Raison said.

'I talk the way I think. Life's too short. It's an affair of back-bone, an adventure. One goes out for goals – in the higher regions with like-minded people. But the goals aren't as important as the will to go for them.'

'Burglars have goals,' Raison said, sipping his wine. 'Burglars have wills.'

'I'm talking socially, not of low elements. But even with them you can find something – individuality, audacity. With the right people, of course, the goals *are* important. Creating order in the jungle is important.'

216

Raison began to get a bit bored with Magda. He couldn't think now what it was he had wanted to know about her. He thought it must have been the sudden reality of the concentration camp, and the difficulty of reconciling the naked savagery of the place with the normal enough female who'd sat opposite him at the Luitpold Grill. But already the reality of the concentration camp was fading from his mind, and he saw how much quicker it could fade from Magda's. Reality faded fast: the committed mind imposed its own. So he drank his wine and admired a handsome mountain opposite, reflecting on the humble springs of her ideology: the urge to secure more of the planet's amenities at the expense of others, and he saw more than ever that they needed keeping in order and that rules were the thing, to be read out in their entirety at least once a year, after the manner of the Jews.

A couple of glasses had set Magda off. '. . . Roman order a thousand years . . . totally new order . . . break up rotten decaying . . . incontestable that some races . . . the great Darwin even . . . face facts and solemnly decide . . . dedicated ruthlessness . . . not a task for weaklings . . . virility . . . backbone . . . will . . .'

'There isn't any wine left,' Raison said.

'It's all right. There's schnapps inside.'

'Is there? Only it's getting on a bit,' he said, looking anxiously at his watch. It wasn't getting on all that much, but half a bottle had brought out a tendency in Magda to throw herself about, and he was recalling the farm cart and the hearse.

'A schnapps or two won't make much difference. It's just good to talk to somebody who responds to ideas.'

Raison hadn't made any response whatever, by thought or gesture, but he realized his traitor's face must have kept the watch, so he drummed his fingers uneasily as Magda lumbered away and returned with the schnapps.

'Still, to say all this,' she said, clinking glasses old-fighter style, 'isn't to give an idea of what we had here while all this was bubbling. It was simply fun.'

'Fun?' Raison said.

'Incredible fun. Unbelievable fun. Of course, there's a good deal of swinishness about now and people try to forget. But how can they forget? It was the best time of their lives. They were twice as tall. Something was happening every few *weeks*. Re-arming, marching into the Rhineland, Austria, the Sudetenland, Memel, Czechoslovakia – all without war, with the rest of the herd scuttling aside and respecting us for it. All of a sudden boldness and audacity were the things in demand, and men began to feel like men again. Take my husband, Kurt. He'd studied economics and banking, for what – a stinking little job as a bank clerk? In no time he'd taken *over* a bank! Marvellous days. Have another.'

'No, thanks,' Raison said, looking at his watch again. 'Aren't you going to have to leave time to change when you get back?' he said.

'Change? Don't you like my dress?'

He didn't have any views on it. It was another dirndl. The pinny-type garment came with a fluffed-up lace apron upon which at the moment she was jiggling her schnapps glass, legs comfortably on the table.

'I thought for a dinner party –'

'We often wear dirndls for dinner parties. Invitation cards frequently say "Dirndl". It's considered very becoming,' she said, looking down at her own. She took off the apron and breathed her waist in. 'Don't you think it's becoming?' she said.

'Very becoming.'

'Then pass the schnapps.'

Raison passed it, gloomily.

'Marvellous days,' she said, taking it. 'When else would a boy of twenty-four take over a huge bank on his own? That's all he was, twenty-four. Are you going to join me?'

'No, thanks,' Raison said.

'With the Czechs and the Jews sitting there gloating over it and counting their money. It was after all one of the great banks of Europe, the Escompte.'

'The what?' Raison said.

'The Escompte. Sure you won't have one?'

'I will have one,' Raison said.

Magda breathed her waist in again. 'I see you're feeling better about the dirndl.'

'It's a fine dirndl. I've got nothing against the dirndl. The Escompte Bank of Prague, did you say?' Raison said.

'It was the apron you didn't like without knowing it. I also don't like it, but that's the way it comes.'

'There's nothing wrong with the apron, either. It's a wonderful apron,' Raison said, gritting his teeth. 'Was it in Prague, this bank?'

'Prague. Only a minute ago you were in such a –'

'I was thinking of your dinner party.'

'Well, you know what I think?' Magda said. 'I think it's going to be a bore, that dinner party. I think I am going to skip that dinner party, and join them just for coffee. What do you think about that?'

'Fine,' Raison said.

'Dandy,' Magda said. 'And you know something else? We can have our own dinner party. And our dinner party could be a hell of a sight more interesting than their dinner party. What have you got to say to that?'

'Without knowing of their dinner party,' Raison said, 'I would nevertheless say the same.'

'Oh, you would, nevertheless?' Magda said. 'In that case, I'm even going to tell you something else. I've never been, if you know what I mean, on any particular sort of terms with an Englishman. Which is not to say that I never will be. Also, our dinner is going to have to come out of cans, which is not to say that it won't nevertheless be very good. Whenever you're hungry. Old chap,' she said.

'All right.'

'I'd only ask you to stay a little hungry.'

Raison heard his teeth grinding quite audibly. The wine and a few schnapps had brought an ogle out of Magda. Magda with an ogle was nothing but a terrible pain in the neck. But he persevered.

'That was a remarkable thing for a young man of twenty-four to do,' he said. 'When did he do it?'

'It wasn't only him. Young men were grasping their

opportunities everywhere. The movement released fantastic energies. It's what I'm telling you. All manner of people suddenly found their manliness. Take Kurt's assistant, a piddling little waiter, with even more piddling hobbies – folk lore, rural dancing, arts and crafts, a country boy. But came the entry into the Sudetenland, and my God – a tower of strength, an organizational genius with all his knowledge of their little ways.'

'Yes. When actually –'

'Which isn't to say they were on the *make*. They were given tasks, and did them, as part of the adventure, an amusing adventure. Their minds were on higher goals. They were our young lions, our soldiers. When the call came to fight, they fought. Their courage was never in doubt. I'll tell you about their courage. I'll have another schnapps,' Magda said.

They had several more, while the sun shifted off the lawn, and the peaks went pink and then bronze. Magda went into the SS lions' courage in some boring depth.

'Then they had,' she said, apparently winding up, to Raison's relief, 'the grenade test. Have you heard of the grenade test? All the SS leadership cadres had to pass out with the grenade test. Each man had to go out alone on the parade ground, in full kit with steel helmet, and arm a grenade and stand it on his helmet. He had just four seconds before the grenade went off. If he wasn't controlled in his movements, or if he trembled, or even if he wasn't so good at balancing grenades on his head, the grenade would fall off and blow it in half. One or two heads did get blown in half,' Magda said. 'Not Kurt's, though. Not any of his friends', though.' Magda was beginning to look a bit the worse for wear. 'We could go in and eat now if you're hungry,' she said.

'All right.'

'But stay a little hungry. Nevertheless.'

They went in and ate a tin of turkey and a tin of vegetables and a tin of brandied peaches, with further schnapps. It got dark as they ate, and Magda lit an oil lamp. She said, 'Why, for God's sake,' looking at him in its innocent glow, 'you're nothing but a big fresh baby. How old are you?'

'Forty-two.'

'I'd never believe it. What do you think I am?'

What Magda was, and no doubt about it, Raison saw after a cursory survey, was thoroughly drunk. He felt drunk himself, but he collected his scattered wits and considered the question. So long as she didn't lie it seemed a good one for getting to the nub of the matter. He still hadn't found out when Kurt had taken over the Escompte Bank. But he'd been twenty-four when he'd done it. And Magda had told him, at some stage, that she was four years younger.

'Well, let's see,' he said.

'Don't be fooled by the hair,' Magda said. 'Where there's winter in the hair, there can be summer in the heart.'

'I'm sure of it.'

'And more important, spring in the backbone. And plenty of it,' Magda said. 'Which I can promise.'

'H'm.' The schnapps seemed to have dowsed that part of the brain that did the computing for him, but he said gallantly, 'Forty?' dimly aware even as he did so that she'd told him she'd married in 1938, which would have had her a bride of eleven.

Magda wasn't displeased. A smile divided her face, as though by grenade. 'Try again,' she said.

He tried again, but there were so many things for the computer to compute, relative to banks and husbands, that though he listened very hard he couldn't hear himself say a word.

Magda got a bit bored after a while. 'I'm forty-eight,' she said, terminating the matter. 'Which is no occasion to linger. Shall we lounge with our coffee in the lounge-bedroom? It's more comfortable.'

Raison tried a few more sums as he went up the ladder. Computed in any way allowed by the schnapps, Kurt seemed to have taken over the bank in 1939. There didn't seem to be anything wrong with that. The Germans had moved into Prague in 1939; in March 1939. He had a funny feeling there was something wrong with it, though. There might even, for God's sake, he thought indignantly, be something significantly wrong. He was damned if he was going to be robbed of anything significant after putting up with so much of Magda's old nonsense. He thought it was time to stop this flumming around and pin her down, if necessary to the floor, till she answered. She was older, but he was bigger. He felt a lot bigger, suddenly so much bigger, like some extravagant beast that had overreached itself in the evolutionary process, that he could hardly articulate his limbs. Small Spanish rugs skidded beneath him, portions of furniture and appurtenances were not where understood to be; beams were not where understood to be. One struck him cruelly and he fell on the floor.

'The sofas are quite comfortable,' Magda said, coming up with the coffee at that moment, 'and quite full length, you'll find. Also the divans. Only I forgot the frigging schnapps. Do you want to go down for the schnapps? You're fresher. I hope,' she said.

'Never mind the schnapps,' Raison said, one thing at a time. 'When did Kurt take over that bank?'

'What's the matter with you and that bank? Why don't you take your mind off the bank?'

'You said he was a soldier in the war,' Raison taunted.

'Of course a soldier. He left the economics branch as soon as he could, it wasn't so easy, he was brilliant there, he had a brilliant record, by no means so easy,' she said. 'But he did it because a brave man gets what he wants. So forget all this frigging banking and come and sit over here,' she said, kicking her shoes off.

'I suppose he was so brilliant,' Raison taunted, 'that after the Protectorate they just gave him the bank. To be brilliant with,' he said.

'Nobody gave Kurt anything,' she said. 'What's the matter with you? Kurt took what he wanted. He took the bank before the Protectorate. Are you jealous of him or something, are you crazy or something, what is it?'

'All right,' Raison said. 'I'm jealous of him. I just don't believe a boy of twenty-four could walk in and –'

'*Süsser*, don't be jealous,' Magda said, delighted. 'It's insane

222

to be jealous of a man dead twenty-three years. Live men are more useful than dead ones. What can a dead man –'

'He can diminish me. That's what,' Raison said. 'He diminishes me,' he said owlishly. He picked himself up off the floor and went directly towards her, a bit quicker than expected at the end, by way of a Spanish rug. But he managed to seat himself with some gravity beside her. 'What we have got to do,' he said, 'is get this out of the way. I can't understand how anybody could be that brilliant. And brave,' he said. 'So you just get the whole thing off your chest and then we'll be diminished with it. De-finished with it,' he said. 'Okay?'

'Okay,' Magda said. 'If you think you can follow. But I still think you're crazy. It was something he'd tried a year before with the Wittkowitzer Coal and Steel Foundry. They called it aggressive economics. Later on in England you called it takeover bidding – I read about it. He got the idea of looking through the shareholders' list of any big firm or industry the Party was interested in, and quietly getting a majority of the shares. When he went to Vienna after the Anschluss he found a lot of Jews there had shares in the Wittkowitzer plant in Czechoslovakia. Many wanted to scuttle from the country so he did a few deals and he got a lot of shares. But he couldn't get a majority because the Rothschilds had them and there was international banking pressure to stop him. So he got the idea of trying a bank instead – a bank which itself controlled shares in many industries. It was a short cut and less obvious. So he looked around for something suitable, and then the Sudeten business blew up and the Escompte Bank came along like a dream, and that's all there is to it.'

'What do you mean all there is to it?' Raison said. He'd been hanging practically in her mouth, to pick up the words as they fell. He didn't think he'd missed any words. Magda must have missed some. 'What dream? How came about? What are you talking about?'

'The Escompte Bank,' she said. 'One way or another it was the biggest shareholder in about twenty-five per cent of Czech industry. All kinds of people had shares in the bank. They were widely spread, the shares, for the security of the bank – that was the Czech idea, so that no single investor could ever get control. They thought they were very clever with their bank, they thought it was the safest thing going. A whole lot of the big crooks in German-controlled territory used to keep safe deposits there because it was so safe. Kurt picked up all kinds of their safe shit when he took it over, if you don't mind the word.'

'I don't mind the word. Get down to business,' Raison said.

'What business? It's the most boring bloody business. Why don't you just give me a kiss?'

Raison gritted his teeth and gave her a kiss, and found his mouth immediately prised open to accommodate a considerable mileage of Magda's tongue. She left it in for a while. She took it out only to say softly in his ear, 'Brave men take what they want without asking. It's better that way.'

Raison found her ear and whispered in it, 'Why don't you just tell me how he took it, then?'

'Honest to God,' Magda said, 'I think you're out of your mind.' She squinted at him in some perplexity. 'I don't know what's got into everybody these days. I'm pretty sure it isn't me. I'm almost sure it isn't me. What's the trouble?'

'It's me,' Raison said. 'I'm complicated. I have to get this out of the way. Nothing wrong with you,' he said kindly.

Magda sighed gustily. 'There's a hell of a lot too much talking,' she said. 'If we're going to sit around and talk, you'd better run off and get the schnapps. I need one.'

'No, you don't,' Raison said, studying her face. The face was distinctly cross-eyed. He calculated that one more would lay her out, which would be a useful and humanitarian thing to do when the moment was right. It wasn't right yet. 'Not yet,' he said.

'Maybe I'll have to get married,' Magda said. 'I swore I wouldn't till I positively had to. A woman should only have one master. I believe in the principle. He was a wonderful master. I try to keep his memory green,' she said, weeping a little.

Raison forbore to point out the golden opportunity that was here, in deference to her tears, but as soon as was seemly briskly did so. 'It's good to recall the actions of loved ones. We ought to praise famous men,' he said.

'It's true. It's true. We ought to.'

'Of course we ought to.'

'It isn't that I forget. I don't forget anything.'

'It just needs a little effort, that's all,' Raison encouraged her.

'Both the good times and the bad.'

'Rough and the smooth, eh?'

'All of it.'

'Righto. Shoot.'

'Shoot?'

'The shit,' Raison said, talking like an old fighter. 'As found by Kurt when he took over the Escompte Bank.'

Magda drank her coffee, focusing on him over the rim of the cup. 'I've never been on any particular terms with an Englishman,' she said, as it seemed to Raison almost to herself and in exoneration. 'You're not a homosexual or anything?' she said.

'Nothing like that.'

'Not impotent or anything?'

'Absolutely not. Quite up to scratch.'

'All right,' Magda said. 'Give me a cigarette.'

Raison gave her one and lit it. Magda gave him a leg. She slung it casually on his lap and hitched her dirndl comfortably up to her navel. 'Let's have a nice long fascinating talk about banking,' she said.

The leg, as legs go, was very presentable, and had grown to its full proportions in forty-eight years. It went all the way up, as Raison was in a position to observe, and Magda put his hand companionably on it, in a fairly northerly aspect, as she made her proposal.

Raison remained attentive. 'When actually *did* he take it?' he said.

'Before we moved in there,' Magda said, tightening her lip a little but stroking his hand firmly. 'Before we went in in full strength and did whatever else we wanted, *Süsser*.'

'Before the Protectorate, in March?' Raison said.

'Of course before. In January or February, I can't remember

which. It was a little softening-up process,' she said, stroking his hand. 'That's why they knew what was coming. That's why they didn't resist when we marched in. It was quite well understood what would follow, *Süsser*,' she said.

'You mean they let him take it over, knowing what would happen?'

'Who had to *let* him?' Magda said, exasperation breaking through. 'They didn't even know about it. The shares were too widely spread. He went about picking them up half the winter. He was in the Sudetenland. He set up an office in Pilsen as soon as we took over the Sudetenland the previous October. That was after the Munich agreement, you remember? We'd just got married, and I went with him. He had his assistant, a Sudeten, who knew the whole area like the back of his hand. There was a tremendous lot of private industry there. We travelled all over looking at it. Of course the rich swine in Pilsen and Prague and Brno who owned it were terrified it would be nationalized. But Kurt had gone through the list of shareholders of the Escompte Bank, and any of them who owned property in the Sudetenland he went to see. He promised there'd be no interference with their concerns, that Germany was interested in industrial growth, and moreover that his office would make it a special concern in the confusion of the moment – the Sudetens had various cockeyed committees drafting plans every ten minutes on capital and labour – to keep their organizations in being. Of course this was going to need extra staff and expense, and some quid pro quo was required. Et cetera,' Magda said.

'You mean they gave him their Escompte Bank shares just so that he'd look after their other interests?'

'He only went to the ones who had them. Nine times out of ten they made the offer themselves. What else could they offer? The Czech crown was in a pretty shaky way. It wasn't currency in the Sudetenland, anyway – we introduced German paper currency immediately and collected all the Czech crowns and presented them at Prague for redemption in gold – it was incredible the ideas the economics branch got up to in those days! Also the owners of these businesses couldn't *sell* them. Who was going to buy at that time? The Escompte Bank shares at least had an international quotation. Anyway, that's what happened.'

'But didn't the Bank find out? Didn't anybody at all realize what was happening?'

'The essence of successful rape, *Liebchen*,' Magda said, rapidly tiring of this technical lore, 'is boldness. The thing was quick. Kurt didn't hang about in ways that could drive a person demented. Also it was done with a variety of names. I doubt if the whole affair from start to finish took longer than six weeks. Then he was in. Which come to think of it,' she said, 'was anyway quite a rape.'

Magda had grown livelier since offering him her leg. She'd also taken to puffing smoke at him and throwing him a look to underline various of her meanings. She threw him one now and Raison focused on it through the smoke. He said, 'You mean when he'd got a majority he simply moved himself into the Bank?'

'Of course he moved in,' Magda said. 'What did you expect him to do? It was his. It was lying wide open and waiting for him. What else would any man do?' Smoke was issuing from her nostrils as from an excited racehorse and her hand was calling him insistently to northwards.

'You mean he actually installed himself physically?' Raison said, panting a little with the effort of clawing south.

'What the hell else could I possibly mean?' Magda said. 'It's a physical world, isn't it? Physical things happen in it. Are you a bit weak in the upper storey or something? Have you gone to sleep in every storey? Wake up!'

'Now, Magda,' Raison said. Something of a tug-of-war had commenced with his hand. 'Any moment now you're going to need that drink, Magda.'

'Of course I need a drink. But I need something else first. What are you fighting me for? What's the matter with you? Don't you like me or something?'

'Of course I like you, Magda. I think you're fine, Magda,' Raison said. A fine perspiration was standing out on his head. 'Only we had a little agreement, remember? We were going to get all this out of the way first, all this about the Bank,' Raison said.

'Jesus Christ, I swear to God you'll drive me mad,' Magda said. 'All I want is whatever you want. All I want is to please you, you red brute, you fresh lump, you bull you.' She was inflaming herself with her words, and at the last threw her cigarette away and lunged at him. Without breaking a leg she couldn't get herself in an effective lunging position, and by grasping both wrists Raison easily held her off. He said into her face, 'Now, Magda. A deal's a deal. I can't help it if I've got a block.'

'You've got a what?' she said, goggling at him.

'This block. About your husband. Get all this out of the way and then we can relax.'

'We can?'

'Absolutely.'

'Then for Christ's sake, get on with it. What is it you want? What do you *want*?' Magda said bemusedly.

In the sudden emergency Raison had forgotten what he wanted.

'If it bothers you, he didn't go in the Bank himself,' Magda said rapidly, anxious to help. 'He put his assistant there.'

'The waiter?'

'In the headquarters branch as chairman of the shareholders' committee. Kurt couldn't speak Czech, anyway, and the assistant, as a Sudeten, could. The Directors they took into custody with a few other people and put fresh ones in. Hardly anybody knew what had happened in the first few days, and those that did saw it was healthier to keep quiet. They were going round the safe deposit boxes every night and picking people up as they came to open them during the day. There really wasn't anything to it. Anybody who looked a bit sideways, *ein, zwei, drei* – eliminated. The committee decided everything in the Bank.'

'This waiter's committee did?'

'He wasn't just a waiter. He had all kinds of interests, I told you. He was at university with Kurt. He was learning the hotel business in Munich. He was an innkeeper's son, a Sudeten, from our side of the border. Anyway, Kurt was giving him his orders, from an office he took in Prague. And he was getting *his* orders from Berlin. So you can *see* there wasn't anything in it,' Magda said desperately. 'It didn't need bravery or brilliance. All it needed was a man. Who the hell doesn't?' she said, removing her leg.

'Just a minute,' Raison said, revelation breaking in on him suddenly. 'That raises a couple of other difficulties –'

'So they can be solved,' Magda said unsteadily. 'But now, oh Jesus, I'm going to solve one of mine.' She stood up and took her dirndl off. Underneath it she had a brassiere and a pair of pants. She took these off also. 'You bull,' she said between her teeth. 'You rampant steaming bull.'

'Eh? Eh?' Raison heard his own stunned voice.

'Take me, you red bull. Take me quick.'

'You put all that back on,' Raison said.

'Undress me another time. There's no time now. Oh, Christ, strip!' she said, running amok almost in her desire to assist.

In a panic Raison felt his jacket torn off. It didn't seem to be the moment to explain to Magda about his estoppel. He said, 'I need a drink!'

'You don't need a drink. You'll have a drink later. Oh God, it'll never be better!'

'It'll be better with a drink,' Raison said. 'Much better. Fantastically better.'

'It will?' Magda said, and swarmed for the ladder. Raison swarmed after her. The sound of her pounding feet had scarcely died away before he had the trapdoor shut. He shot the bolt, and to be on the safe side lay on it as well. He lay almost without breathing till a solid thump some inches below his midriff suggested that Magda might have come up without noticing the trapdoor, and another, a second later, combined with the tinkle of glass, that she might have gone down again rather faster.

He waited a while, listening for sounds below. There weren't any sounds below. He cautiously drew the bolt and raised the trapdoor. Magda was lying on her back with her mouth wide open, one leg still on the ladder. He went unsteadily down the ladder and took her leg off it and examined her. No breath came out of the open mouth; no rise and fall from the breast. 'Oh, my God,' Raison said, in a low monotone, and went round and about, wringing his hands. The situation was so absurdly horrible he couldn't think what to do. The police? Haffner? Not Haffner, for God's sake. A doctor, then? He paused and took a long panic-stricken look at Magda. Magda didn't look as if she needed a doctor. She didn't look as if she would need one ever again. The neck was at a strange angle. 'Oh, my God,' Raison said again.

A faint hiss came from the open mouth as he spoke and he bent instantly and put his ear to it. Another hiss came. Raison drew back and examined her intently. No trace of movement was visible in Magda. But breath was evidently around in her somewhere. With shambling haste, not pausing to consider whether the therapy was beneficial in the case of a broken neck, Raison straddled the old fighter, placed both hands firmly on her breasts and pressed. Magda responded instantly with a long sigh and something like a smile, as though, even in her coma, recognizing the small pleasures of every day. At the same time she eased her head more comfortably, opened her legs and said quite clearly, *'Du Süsser,'* before relapsing into a snore.

Raison got shakily off her and wiped the sweat out of his eyes. The fracas had pulled him sharply together, but only to a realization of how drunk he was. He looked at Magda. She couldn't lie around on the floor all night. Equally he couldn't carry her up the ladder, even if he wanted to, which he didn't. He lurched off after a moment on an investigation of the down-stairs bedrooms. One was suitably near and suitably equipped and he reeled back and picked her up. The bottle had broken underneath her and her bottom was awash in schnapps; usefully enough at the moment, because she'd cut it. It was not a big cut, but it would be a trying one when she came to. It certainly wasn't bothering her now. From her coma she murmured a few words of encouragement to him as he hauled her into the room, and even gamely tried to open her legs again as he fell on the bed with her. But he stuffed her in as well as he could and pulled the covers up to her chin, and in a well-thought-out series of operations, staggered up the ladder, staggered down again with her clothing, staggered back up, shot the trapdoor bolt, and took himself to bed, seriously drunk.

He heard Magda in the night. He heard her banging on the trapdoor. 'Are you there?' she said.

He didn't say anything.

'I know you're there,' Magda said. 'You must be there.' She still sounded drunk. 'The trapdoor couldn't be locked if you weren't there.'

He still didn't say anything.

'*Süsser*,' Magda said. 'I want you.'

Silence.

'I know you're not asleep,' she said. 'Wake up! I'll bloody well wake you up!' she said.

She went away and came back and started throwing things at the trapdoor. Some of the things sounded like grenades.

There was silence after a while. Magda said plaintively, '*Süsser*, what's the sense in you being there and me here? It's night-time, *Süsser*. I want to be with someone. *Let* me in, *Süsser*,' she said.

Raison didn't say anything.

'You bloody bastard, *Süsser*!' she said. 'You bloody useless something,' she said. 'You something bloody eunuch,' she said.

He heard her furiously shifting furniture about. There was something he wanted to ask her but he couldn't remember what it was. He didn't think it was a very useful time to ask her things, anyway, so he went to sleep.

He opened his eyes to an H-bomb explosion and closed them again. He shielded them next time, but still got a threshold dose. Something terrible, of a radiational nature, was going on. He identified it presently as the sun peeping cheerily through the roof lights. The whole room was an agonizing mass of colour. He lay for a while with his eyes closed getting acquainted with the fact that he'd never felt lousier in his life.

His eyeballs seemed paralysed, but in a special way that still allowed them to hurt. They hurt all over, both the parts that did the seeing in the front and the out-of-the-way parts that normally remained quietly in sockets at the rear. His whole head hurt. He felt at the same time dizzy, with a form of swooping vertigo, and also sick as though from some special stomach-removing poison. At every minor movement, as it might be to take a breath or let one out, the whole thing got that little bit worse. This kept him from crying out. It kept him almost incredulously still.

But he sat up after a while, in stages, wondering what it was that stopped him from fainting away, and got his legs out of bed. He noticed immediately that his socks were on one end of them and his pants on the other. He sat on the bed, one hand to his head, and thought about this. He remembered, in fragmentary and unpleasant snatches. All seemed quiet below. He couldn't hear very well through the surge of blood in his head, so he got up and walked quite slowly to the trapdoor and carefully folded himself up so that he was kneeling and put his ear to it. The wood seemed very loud. There was a lot of resonance this morning.

He thought, while listening, that if she'd heard him moving about and was waiting with something to throw at the trapdoor the impact would certainly kill him. But nothing landed on the trapdoor. It merely went on resonating. The resonance was strangely harmonious, in tune with what was going on in his head. But he took his ear away after a while. He remembered that she was flying away like a *Wandervogel* to Spain at midday. It wasn't right to let her lie about sleeping it off, whatever had passed. What time was it?

He had some difficulty in finding the time on his watch, but presently read it as ten o'clock, or perhaps eleven o'clock. It certainly wasn't nine or twelve. H'm. He withdrew the bolt, and after gathering strength raised the trapdoor. One of the first things that he noticed was that the ladder was no longer there, and among the second that some conscientious hand had set to rights the shambles of the night before. He could see the table from where he was, and the clutter of tins and plates had been removed. There was also no sign of the broken bottle.

He called huskily, 'Magda!'

There was no response.

'Magda,' Raison said into the hole.

He couldn't hear her snoring. It was rather quiet below. H'm, Raison thought. He didn't see how he was going to get down from the lounge-bedroom without the ladder. It was quite a long way down. He recalled that Magda had gone down the previous night without getting the benefit of the ladder, and had knocked herself out. He didn't see how he could be expected to wake her up with the ladder removed.

His brain wasn't working very quickly this morning, and it wasn't till he was lying on the bed again that he realized who might have removed the ladder. The same authority might be responsible for the restorations below, and also for the preternatural silence that reigned there.

He got up again, a bit quicker, and stuck his head well down in the hole.

He said, 'Magda!' . . .

'Are you there, Magda?' Raison said.

He said it a few times more, and removed his head from the hole, and rubbed his chin. H'm. He picked himself carefully up and put his clothes on. There wasn't any water up here. His mouth felt fouler than he'd have believed possible, glued, the tongue for long stretches integral with the roof. He went and had a look down the hole again. Quite a long way down. The top of his head seemed to rock forward as he bent it. He couldn't see himself jumping down the hole. It would be suicide. There must be something one could do with sheets. What was it one did with sheets?

'Magda?' he said faintly into the hole. 'Are you there, Magda?'

He decided to skip the sheets. He thought he would *lower* himself into the hole. It couldn't be as far as it looked. It looked a little over a hundred and fifty feet. Faith suggested that it could not be more than ten. He must be about six himself, and then there were his arms. His arms felt heavy this morning and rather longer than usual, perhaps a yard or two longer. H'm.

Raison began to lower himself into the hole. It was difficult knowing where to start. He started by sitting on the edge and lowering his feet, and sat there for some minutes wondering how to employ his arms. There was nothing for his arms to do. By inserting more of his body into the hole his arms would merely unfurl behind him, ultimately breaking off without benefiting him in any particular way. Obviously his arms must be in front of and not behind him. This meant either reversing his position and going down backwards while clutching on to the edge or – he came on the thought after some reflection – not reversing his position but simply reaching forward to the opposite edge. He reached across to the opposite edge and put his weight there and lowered himself. His arms, though long, were strangely nerveless, and he immediately fell, landing in the room below with an impact so shattering that pain alone convinced him he hadn't killed himself. He lay for a while with his head on the floor and his hands on his head, crooning a little. Then he slowly picked himself up, and still supporting his head went to the room where he'd deposited Magda, to convince himself of something else. After that he went outside to look for the car to settle the matter finally. When he'd done that, he came back in and pushed the ladder back in place and washed and rinsed his mouth out and made himself a cup of coffee and left.

The grocer in the village said he'd heard Frau General Emmerich's car shoot past at seven o'clock. It was half past ten now. The grocer was also the taxi-driver and he ran Raison to Schliersee. He got the bus from Schliersee. On the journey, between waves of pain as the thing lurched and juddered, he remembered what he'd wanted to ask Magda. He'd wanted to ask her the name of the innkeeper's son from the Bavarian Forest who'd become the chairman of the shareholders' committee of the Escompte Bank.

He thought he knew it, anyway.

There wasn't anything that anybody could tell him that he wouldn't have believed just then. Everything struck him as about equally believable. He could believe that a fiddling nervy hotel apprentice could become a hero of the economics branch of the SS during its heroic period. He could even, by a stretch, see him balancing a grenade on his head. Perhaps he hadn't had to balance a grenade. Perhaps he wasn't leadership material, merely a useful lieutenant with plenty of local lore.

But he could see him as chairman of the shareholders' committee. Through flashes of pain he could see Bamberger also, a large man, brisk of tread, with a sniff, clothed in a good grey suit and with a face like Mrs Wolff's, arriving at the Escompte Bank to deposit his private documents in his safe deposit box. He saw him being invited to another room for a word with the chairman of the shareholders' committee.

And then? Bamberger looking a bit sideways? Bamberger *ein zwei drei*? The chairman of the shareholders' committee himself sending through the confirmation to the Handelsbank Lindt in Zurich? The confirmation had only been the number of the account, written out in full; a method that couldn't have been news to a member of the SS economics branch, even if Bamberger hadn't been prevailed upon to reveal it. So the signature from the start would have been that of the chairman of the shareholders' committee; and the chairman's signature would have continued; the same signature throughout, ageing properly, as the wisest graphologists in the world, meeting in conference, would have no difficulty in deciding.

When he tried to think of it in real terms, with real people, instead of as a hangover hypothesis, the thing struck him as so mad that he stopped.

But before he got to Munich he thought of other mad things. He thought of Dachau, and of the bustling camps where entire trainloads of people, grandmothers and babies and middle-aged men of affairs, had got off the trains to queue up to be gassed, under the supervision of young lions whose wills didn't flinch from bold solutions. Everybody had felt twice as tall in those days because fate was being mastered and the jungle tamed; after a pattern to meet the desires and aspirations of a hardworking people whose instincts, evil or otherwise, were easily aroused and whose imagination allowed princes to turn into frogs and back again.

Nothing impossible. Capable of anything, Raison thought.

He looked at the back of the driver's neck, and at the decent people who got on and off the bus, greeting each other with kindly *'Grüss Gotts'* in the beautiful morning, and he thought he wouldn't think about it any more just now.

He thought what he'd do, he'd go back, and have a short word with Grunwald, and then he'd get his head down. He'd get it down for about three hours. Then he'd have a pot of black coffee. The perspective was a little bit peculiar now. Three hours and a pot of black coffee ought to fix it up.

He got back at about a quarter past twelve and found there'd been a few calls for him while he'd been away. Gunter had called from London, and Elke, and Ansbach. He was puzzled about Ansbach.

'Is Dr Grunwald in?' he said.

Dr Grunwald wasn't. But he'd left him a note. Raison opened the note. It said, *'Come urgently to Dr Ansbach's. Adler has telephoned from Waldstein. He has arranged a meeting with Bamberger for Thursday.'*

'Has he?' Raison said. 'It's bloody effrontery. It's a piece of impertinence,' he said. 'What day is it?' he said to the receptionist.

The man looked at him. 'What day it is? It's Wednesday.'

'Wednesday, eh? Wednesday, is it? I'll have a sleep, then. I'll have a pot of black coffee. At half past three. See I'm not disturbed, eh?'

'Yes, sir. Not disturbed. A pot of black coffee. At half past three,' the man said, writing it down. He watched Raison all the way to the lift.

Raison rode up the two flights feeling distinctly scrambled. He was so indignant he was almost laughing. The effrontery of it. The bloody effrontery! Still: the old fighter spirit.

He wondered if the other old fighter had got off yet, and if she was sitting comfortably.

PART FIVE

Delivery up to looting shall be deemed to have occurred if (i) chattels belonging to the persecutee were misappropriated or distributed among a rabble by persons who exercised or usurped powers of authority, (ii) the persecutee was deprived of his liberty in circumstances leaving his chattels without supervision by anyone safeguarding his interests.

German Federal Indemnification Law
(*Bundesentschädigungsgesetz*)

Chapter 1

THAT POSTER INSTINCT

'After all, what need have they of lawyers? There are plenty of lawyers. It's not as if I'm ready to retire,' Ansbach said.

'With your experience? It would be a crime.'

'Exactly. I'm of more use here, working. Restitution practice changes. People don't realize. It isn't just a matter of decisions handed down from Karlsruhe. There are all kinds of minor court decisions. There's the Bundestag, the Länder, legal opinion. It's necessary to keep an eye on these things. How could I do it there? I couldn't do it there.'

'Listen,' Grunwald said, 'if everybody who wanted went, it would be standing room only. There's no question of everyone going. The place is the size of a pocket handkerchief, after all, what's the use of talking.'

They were talking about Israel. Ansbach had wanted to for some time. He said regretfully, 'It's true, I know, it's true. But still. There was a place we went to see north of Tel Aviv near Herzlia, a nice house, very nice. It needed to have air conditioning put in, the heat, neither Helga nor I can stand the heat, but that was all, no special difficulties. But for one thing the rascal was asking an incredible price, outrageous, and for another we thought when are we going to use it? One month in the year, and then let it the rest of the time? What's the point? Until I retire we can go to hotels. For the time being I can make a more useful contribution as a Jew from here than by simply contributing my body.'

'As a matter of fact,' Grunwald said, a little bit nettled by the figure of speech but disguising the fact by a look of especial piety as he drew on his cigarette, 'nobody says you have to make such a contribution at all. As a Jew you can contribute just by living as a Jew. We can say it's more normal for a Jew to live outside. In late biblical days, even, more lived outside. How many can the land accommodate, at best? A quarter of us, a third? A Jew's a citizen of the world, Meyer. Perhaps it's only as a citizen of the world that he's a Jew. In Israel he's something else, an Israeli. It's just another country.'

'I thought you were a Zionist,' Ansbach said, not missing the point, and smiling because he hadn't missed it.

'I'm a Zionist. I don't know that it means anything any more. It's already an historical concept. The Jewish people is a bigger entity than the State of Israel, thank God. There are thirteen, fourteen million of us in the world. For me the land is holy and Jews should live in it to preserve its Jewish identity. But that's being done. The people in it aren't going to go away. They've got nowhere to go. It's no longer necessary for people to dis-arrange themselves making serious contributions. I'll tell you, Meyer. The land is holy for me not only because God said so and for what happened in it, but for the view of life it represents, the particular vision, the standards. But standards exist without places. God made all places. We carried the standards around for two thousand years, after all. They exist wherever Jews exist – at least there's a chance. It's all there. It isn't to say that every Jew abides by every small part of them,' he said, looking at Ansbach. 'But at least in acknowledging that he's a Jew – and who forces him? – he *acknowledges* the standards. They're there. It's a line. He can measure by it. It's a question of how to live in the world, a question, fundamentally, of a state of mind. With regard to the land, how many have we got living there – two and a half million? What kind of a country is it that can accommodate such a tiny proportion of its people? It's a token, an indulgence – if you like, a serious joke. Does the Jewish idea need a State? And if so such a crumb of a State? Still, it's a State. But a state of mind is also a state, surely not less important?'

'It's true, it's true,' Ansbach said. 'But still.'

'Yes, still –' Grunwald said, allowing the point with a small shrug. He'd gone about as far as he could in reducing Israel for Ansbach, and he couldn't go any farther. He knew Ansbach didn't really want to go and live in Israel. What could Ansbach have in Israel that he couldn't have here? There was plenty here that he couldn't have in Israel; life wasn't so easy. Also, for a man not by nature prepared to put up with things, for a cultivated man to whom the graces of Europe were a part of himself, there were special difficulties. Grunwald still could experience some heartache for certain parts of Frankfurt; clocks, steeples, first pointed out to four-year-old eyes. Not any of the hideous things that had happened in this land could efface the warm and well-loved landscape where lived the clocks and steeples; his. He could see at this moment a certain gracefully fluted pillar, of blackened and waxy stone, and feel under his trailing ten-year-old hand the familiar seams and pockmarks as he rounded the corner from school. One's consciousness was built of such things. There was an ache sometimes at being so physically distant from them. It was true that what the mind registered in this way continued to exist (quite often he could kiss the smudgy eyebrows of little Ruth, embrace Hannaliese, hold Benjamin's hand as they walked in the park), but not everybody could take solace from the past; not everybody was in the habit of looking backwards to discern unity, identity.

What Grunwald was certain of was that Israel was no place to live for a man who really hankered to be somewhere else and who could afford to live wherever he wanted. You had to have a taste for it; a fairly robust taste. He surprised himself suddenly by the keenness of his hunger for it, the salt and savour of it; the familiar small shops and cafés, the corner sellers, the little synagogues, the square Hebrew script on all sides; the argumentation, energy, life; a high-octane country of tremendously rich character.

There was much selfishness, and serious shortcomings, in the life of Israel; the inhabitants had picked up bad habits from half the world and had a talent for picking up fresh ones from each other. There was too much truculence, arrogance, derision; a certain confusion in the keeping of arrangements; a curious blindness in the field of aesthetics. But yet, with all this, a country of individuals, of basically rational individuals, whose habit was to reason and to assess value – in the wider as in the narrower context – iconoclastic people by no means amenable to authority, yet capable of corporate activity of the most selfless kind; a people at heart sensible, with a realization that all, black, white and yellow, had to make a living on the planet, and an understanding at bottom of what was required of them, and of the human kind.

When Grunwald thought of them he thought of the enigma propounded by Hillel – 'If I do not stand for myself, who will stand for me? But if I stand only for myself, what am I?' – and he saw them often like thickly clustered filings attracted first to one and then the other part of the enigma as to the opposing poles of a magnet, not often finding equilibrium in the difficult centre. And when he thought of Israel he saw it always in a sparkling light – a light of such clarity that many things became plain, including all shades of grey, whose affinities to white or black might be the more finely determined. Determining them, he thought, had indeed been a characteristic occupation of the inhabitants since their first iconoclast Abraham, 'the friend of God', had arrived with his intimations of the magnet.

He was musing on it when Ansbach, mistaking his pre-occupation, said, 'So how much do you still need?'

'It isn't a question of how much. Whatever we have will be enough. It's a question of whether it will be large, medium or small.'

'Can there be so many to benefit – in the terms of the trust?'

'Enough,' Grunwald said briefly.

What it was really a question of was *rachmanut* . . .

They'd been discussing his heart's desire, the Home for the Maladjusted – the maladjusted of South German origin, for it was a project of the Süddeutsche Kultus-Gemeinden-Stiftung. For years it had haunted him, and for years he had urged it at the annual conferences – to see, year after year, other pro-jects given precedence. It wasn't that he didn't approve of the other projects. Who could object to an orphanage, to research scholarships? They were steps in the right direction, all of them, and in accord with his feeling for growth. What growth was there, what sense of seed-time, in a twilight home for the deranged?

But still, *rachmanut*, the spirit of compassion. . . . He had a horror of insanity – of the ailment that reduced a man to a beast. the worst ailment of all, making a mockery of the gift.

In vain he'd pleaded for *rachmanut*, and had met with angry retorts. Who didn't have *rachmanut*? It wasn't a question of *rachmanut*. It was a question of the best use to be made of strictly limited community funds and covenants, maturing on different dates, to meet the objects of the original Hilfsverein der Juden in Süddeutschland, namely the future of . . .

Grunwald couldn't argue. All his life it had been his despair that he was such a poor advocate. And nobody said a home for the maladjusted wasn't a good idea. It was simply a question of priorities.

A kind of weariness, a kind of hopelessness had come over him that the project would never be accomplished in his lifetime. But in the last year or two as the Bamberger bequest had become more and more of a possibility, so he'd gathered more support. Sometimes with, sometimes without, Landsberg's approval – with majority approval, anyway – he'd begun steering strongly. He'd seen to the land. He'd seen to the architect's plans. He'd also seen to it that at least minimal funds had been voted to his steering committee. He'd worked so tirelessly that someone had suggested – and had won applause for the suggestion, whether humorously or not Grunwald wasn't certain but had often thought about – that the home should be called the Grunwald Home.

The Grunwald Home. Yes. Worth the trouble. Worth the trouble in any case, but especially. . . . It wasn't a question of vanity, even though the urge was strong for a man without a line to leave something, some sign that he had lived, that the life had meaning. Not vanity, truly, but meaning. One worked towards meanings. The meanings were always there. He'd lately had a feeling that he'd been groping towards some special one for half his life, discerning its presence, as he'd journeyed, in trains, cattle trucks, camps; sometimes coming close, sometimes losing it. A flavour of it was with him now but he couldn't define it. He thought, because he sometimes experienced the flavour when he thought about these things, that it was to do with valuation, with the necessity to prevent under-valuation; and had a familiar though fugitive impression of himself, never clearly realized, of being a broker in a heartbreaking

243

market where all was confusion, with a responsibility to maintain the value of certain articles, which in some parts were being made valueless; and with this the duty to protect the articles in all their aspects, more even those samples that were not good samples, or imperfect samples, or samples that had turned out wrong in ways that mocked the making of all articles.

The thing as usual went from him quite quickly, leaving a warm disturbed place in his mind as of a comfortable bed from which he'd newly risen, and which still awaited him, the shape of his form in it, if only he could find it again. It was a pleasant feeling – paradoxically of nostalgia for the future, for something that had not yet happened, but that he could almost, if he tried hard enough, remember; and as always it raised tingling energy in him to go forward to meet it.

He found himself looking at his watch at the same time as Ansbach looked at his.

'So what's happend to him?' Ansbach said.

Roused by a pot of black coffee, as arranged, Raison laid himself in a bath and looked seriously at the wall.

The waiter had brought up a note saying that Dr Ansbach had made two further calls and Fräulein Haffner one, but he didn't think about the note. He thought about the perspective. The perspective didn't seem to have changed to any significant degree. He had a good look at it, though. A funny old perspective, he thought, holding himself well in in the presence of the familiar spiritual subsidence.

He had a lurking notion – that never lurked far – that most of them had gone, or were going, or had fallen into the way of processing more or less continuously, round the twist, leaving only scattered pockets of de-energized sanity. He felt himself to be an old occupant of one of these pockets, or depressions, and nodded sombrely at the familiar landscape around and about. The problem at root had never been more complicated than to stop them murdering each other or robbing each other, and it seemed incapable of solution. It seemed rendered perennial by their conflicting notions of life's purpose and by their facility for seeing themselves as participants in an unfolding drama, with special roles to play.

Every now and again Raison wanted to get up and point out to the private court – where from time to time these cases were heard – that nobody had a special role, that all the parties, as they appeared before the court, had the same role. They were life tenants of a rock on which things grew.

'What are the parties' reasons for this fracas, Mr Raison?'

'As I understand, m'lud, some claim they were acting as illustrations of the Lord's work, and others that history had given them a special task to subjugate those whom they considered unsuitable tenants. Very considerable numbers were thrown off the rock, m'lud, on the grounds that they would never make suitable tenants.'

'Do I understand the accused still justify their actions?'

'Apparently not, m'lud. They claim immunity before the court, however, on the grounds that the actions were ordered by a duly constituted authority and had the full force of law at the time.'

'Who elected the authority, Mr Raison?'

'They did, m'lud.'

'I think I'd better warn the court, my patience isn't quit unlimited, Mr Raison. There have been far too many of these cases. If people elect authorities who advocate breaking the law, it's the same thing as choosing directly to break it themselves.'

'Quite so, m'lud.'

'They may entertain whatever notions they please, so long as they don't interfere with the amenities of others. This is a court of quarrels, not of morals, Mr Raison.'

'Hee hee hee,' Raison said. 'Your lordship's wit is well known,' he said.

'The court cannot order them to love each other, Mr Raison.'

'No, m'lud.'

'If they wish they may hate each other. What they may not do is throw each other off the rock. There is a very clear estoppel on that. It's the only guarantee for anybody's rights. We have to have rules, Mr Raison.'

'I could not agree with your lordship more.'

'Very well.'

Raison wouldn't have minded telling someone outside the court all that he thought about everything. But he doubted if he would. There was nobody to tell, for a start. So he addressed the court a while longer, until the bath water cooled. Then he went to Ansbach's and told them about the perspective.

They told him about the perspective their end.

They all decided the best thing to do was to sleep on it. Raison went and slept at Elke's.

He didn't sleep with her. It simply got very late, and he'd been telling her a bit of what he felt about everything. En route he filled her in on the Bamberger situation.

He said, 'It's probably terribly simple, only we made it complicated. It's only a question of his bloody bank account, after all, and how he could have continued it. I thought somebody'd taken it off him and forged his handwriting. But then the experts said the handwriting hadn't changed, so we thought he must have been doing it all along. It didn't occur to us that somebody else could have been doing it all along – that he'd never done any of it himself at all.'

'Adler, you mean?'

'Adler. Anybody. We thought it needed the German army. He had three weeks to himself, you see, in Prague, before the German army got there. But it didn't need the German army, only a specialized branch of the SS. Grunwald had experience of it in Zurich nearly thirty years ago, but it still didn't occur to him.'

'And now it's Adler who says Bamberger will come?'

'Bamberger or son of Bamberger. Vague, you see.'

'And nobody knows if he had a son?'

'Nobody knows.'

'So who is it says he's got one?'

'Adler says he's got one.'

'And Adler's the one you think could have killed him?'

'*Ein zwei drei*,' Raison said. 'He or some other hero.' He told her what else he thought. He said, 'It may be, you see, that bloody Adler is the one we've been so carefully following. He

246

could have been the one picked up by the military police in 1946, and the one who went to Hilfende Hände. He'd have been a wanted man, after all, if I'm right – wanted by the Czechs, anyway, and probably by the Germans also if the truth came out. Perhaps he didn't surface again till he was pretty sure it wasn't going to come out. Then Grunwald and I turned up when he was a respectable innkeeper and local councillor and frightened the life out of him.'

'So why should he want you to go back?'

'You're thinking well,' Raison told her. 'It's that poster instinct. Perhaps he wants to stop investigation elsewhere – Grunwald did point out other sources were available. Or maybe he's realized he's dealing with two separate interests. In the case of the estate the supposed son could be a simple-minded attempt to put us off. Of course, it wouldn't put Grunwald off. Grunwald isn't interested in heirs, missing or otherwise. He's interested in the money. He'll go on being interested till he's got it. So this could be directed at him.'

'How?'

'Well, it's hard to tell with old fighters.'

'You mean it could be dangerous?'

'If all this is right Adler's got plenty to hide. And Grunwald's the only one he's got to watch out for.'

'But this is fantastic. It's incredible.'

'It's a mass of raving bloody lunacy,' Raison said. 'But there you are.'

'So what does Grunwald want to do?'

'He wants to sleep on it.'

'But can't he see the danger?'

'Oh yes, he can see it. He's a bit keen on getting the money, you see. There's always a chance that he will. For one thing, Adler's story could be quite true. All the rest is only hypothesis.'

'James, you can't go into this. It's something for the police.'

'Yes. Well, we can't have the police,' Raison said. 'Not at the moment. The only evidence we've got seems to suggest that the German government paid out an enormous claim in error.

To my client. We can either drop this other claim or stay discreetly with it. Grunwald isn't going to drop it.'

'It's a bit of mess, then, isn't it?'

'You are going to make your mark in the poster world,' Raison said, nodding thoughtfully to his cigarette.

He found Grunwald writing a letter when he looked in to the Ludwigshof next morning. The old man said, 'Ah. I was wondering where you were. Have you been with Haffner?'

'With the family,' Raison said.

'We tried to get Haffner. Ansbach thinks he also should come.'

'You've decided, have you?'

'I can't see anything else for it. We aren't doing anything here.'

'Why Haffner?' Raison said.

'He's a prosecutor, isn't he? Let him come and see.'

Raison lit a cigarette. There were aspects to the coming and seeing of Haffner, including the briefing of Haffner, that seemed to have been forgotten. He said, 'You think Adler really had something to offer?'

'I'm prepared to let him tell me.'

'But not, I hope, to give him the only specimen of Bamberger's writing.'

'He's asked to see it, let him see it. What do you think – he'll steal it?'

'Yes.'

'Let him. There are several attested copies.'

'A bank wants an original, not a copy. It makes it that much harder.'

'On the other hand, Bamberger, or Bamberger's representative, has a right to see it. It doesn't bother me.'

'I'd be very surprised,' Raison said, 'if there should turn out to be a Bamberger.'

'I have to tell you, my young friend,' Grunwald said, 'that nothing any longer will surprise me. I knew the man – a by no means admirable man. It's perfectly believable to me that such a man should have bought his life by unsavoury means and have married and had children there. However, he can still do good.'

'The wife and children are for our consumption, not yours. He'll have something else for you – almost certainly a shot at isolating you.'

'So we mustn't let him. What can he do with three of us there – four, I hope? Ansbach will drive, incidentally. We will go in his car.'

'About Haffner,' Raison said. 'On your advice I've so far told Haffner nothing. He doesn't know about Adler or these other possible claimants.'

'It might make grave conflicts in his conscience, you mean?'

'It might put a strain on it.'

'Well. I have to advise now that you tell him. If something comes of it, he'll have to know, anyway. If it doesn't, the presence of a prosecutor might help reduce the dangers that you're telling me about. But this is something for you.'

'All right,' Raison said glumly and went downstairs. He found Elke hovering. He said, 'Yes, he wants to go. We're travelling in Ansbach's car. It's back to the posters for you, love.'

'But James, I want to help.'

'All right. Find your father.'

'My father? Isn't he at his office?'

'Let's see.'

Haffner wasn't in his office, but his secretary was; a demure German maiden of middle years. She said, 'But he's not been in for two days now, Fräulein! It's this affair of Schonbach.'

'Schonbach?'

'The electrical affair.' She explained a little of Schonbach and the electrical affair. 'He's really been working like a tiger. Today he's in Düsseldorf, but he must return by five for an appointment in connection with Frau General Emmerich.'

'Magda? Isn't she off yet?'

'It's with Dr Wasserman, the Frau General's legal adviser.'

'Five o'clock would be too late for you, wouldn't it?' Elke said to Raison.

'Much too late.'

'But if there's anything *I* can do, Fräulein?' the German maiden said eagerly.

'I'll be sure to get in touch. What pretty flowers,' Elke said.

'I'm afraid my father seems to be out of touch with these affairs, James,' she said, out in the street. 'I hope it isn't going to put you out too much.'

'No. I shouldn't think too much,' Raison said, a bit more cheerfully.

Chapter heading

Chapter 2

A FREILICHT FESTSPIEL

THEY left at two and took the familiar road through Regensburg and Cham, passing the wooden villages and the cuckooclock-type houses. Raison was sick of the sight of them now. The heat was overpowering and Ansbach drove slowly in it in his elderly car. A sombre mood had settled on them.

'We will tread very carefully,' Ansbach said.

'We will take no risks,' Grunwald said.

'We will stay all the time together.'

'We are not fools, after all.'

'Aren't we?' Raison said.

'What else can we do?' Ansbach said irritably.

'We can check our own copy of Bamberger's writing with that of the bank.'

'They are going to rush to show us. Swiss banks are in business with their customers, not those who might have been. If Hans starts an account with Fritz's money, it's not their headache. Let Fritz sue Hans. They won't help.'

'They might stop any movement in the account, in view of everything.'

'In view of everything,' Ansbach said, 'there won't be any money in the account. If you're right, he'll have taken it out and put it somewhere else the minute he saw you. But who knows? What did you find out, after all? That an innkeeper from those parts had a Nazi son. Look wherever you want, you'll find innkeepers with Nazi sons. If you'd dealt with the restitution cases that I have you'd know it's as well to try everything. What's wrong with trying?'

'For one thing, the slight degree of danger,' Raison said, 'and for another the high degree of incredibility. I can't believe an old man would take a trip at a moment's notice, to a place he's anxious to stay away from, without trying to get in touch some other way.'

'As to the danger,' Grunwald said, 'nobody wants to be a hero. And as to what one can believe, I can believe anything. Obviously we need explanations. Adler must be shown we're not complete idiots. Equally, if you're right, he mustn't be frightened on to the first plane to South America. Somewhere, between all the possibilities, there'll be something for us – unless you know of something better?'

'No,' Raison said.

'So?'

There was no reason to go to Furth-im-Wald this time, so they picked another road from Cham and at length bowled slowly out of the humid greenery and into Waldstein. No rain was falling on the place this time, and there seemed to be some other changes. Flags and bunting hung limply across the listless streets and here and there a poster showed charging hussars and the legend *Trotz Kommt!* In the main square, as they cruised slowly round it, a large streamer near the onion-domed church said *Anno 1742 – Historisches Freilicht Festspiel – Trotz der Husar vor Waldstein!* A recollection came to Raison of having heard of this Hussar, and of disagreeable things happening with regard to pigs' bladders, or it might have been something else, and just as they turned into the Goldener Adler's lane he identified it. He said curiously, 'Do you think they really do sleep with their mothers here?'

'With their mothers?' Grunwald said, looking at him in astonishment. 'For what reason?'

'I don't know,' Raison said. But he thought it might still be possible to surprise Grunwald.

There was again nobody in the Gasthof in the dead of the afternoon and they found themselves going through the familiar motions, rapping on the bar and tugging at the cowbell. The cat-eyed old woman appeared, and after a glance at Grunwald immediately disappeared. Adler came out. '*Grüss Gott*,' he said.

'*Grüss Gott*.'

'*Grüss Gott*,' Adler said to Ansbach.

'*Grüss Gott*.'

'I don't think I've had the pleasure.'

'Dr Ansbach of Munich,' Raison said. 'Dr Grunwald's adviser. He's been involved from the beginning.'

'I see.'

'No objection, I hope?'

'Not if it's confidential.'

'Quite confidential,' Ansbach said.

'Then it rejoices me,' Adler said.

'It rejoices me,' Ansbach said.

They were slowly pumping each other's hand.

'Well. Let's sit. Let me get you some beer,' Adler said.

It was cool in the bar and dim after the brassy heat outside and Raison longed to sit with a beer. But when the others refused he thought in the interests of solidarity that he'd better refuse also. Adler pulled himself a beer.

'What are the arrangements?' Ansbach said politely.

'I don't know myself.' Adler seated himself beside them at the trestle table. 'Except that your friend's expected in the next few hours.'

'Here?'

'In the area.'

'It's short notice.'

'Because of the pageant. Without it, it wouldn't have been possible at all. There's always a relaxation of border security – easier visas, more buses and so forth – and he's taking advantage of it.'

'He is coming on a bus?'

'He isn't. It would still mean applying for the visa. But it's apparently a simple matter at this time to organize a diver.'

'A diver?' Raison said.

'For an illegal entry. A guide.'

252

'You mean through the forest?'

'Naturally.'

'Is that the "area" you mentioned?'

'So I would suppose.'

'Yes. I am by no means sure, Herr Adler,' Ansbach said, shaking his head, 'that we would be interested to go into the forest. I think we may say we would not want to go into the forest.'

'Herr Ansbach, I don't make the arrangements. They're made elsewhere.'

'Quite so.'

'It might not be possible to change the arrangements.'

'We would not want to go into the forest,' Ansbach said.

'Also another thing,' Raison said, coughing briskly in the short silence, 'that we're not, Herr Adler, altogether clear about, is who exactly is supposed to be coming.'

'I am not clear, either.'

'Herr Bamberger? His son?' Raison said.

'Bamberger, his son. I don't know.'

'With anybody other than Bamberger a problem of identification would of course arise.'

'I know nothing of these things, Herr Raison. It's all foreign to me. I presume those who know will have arranged something. But I understand,' he said, turning to Grunwald, 'that you also have a piece of identification which I must hand over.'

'No need for you to go to the trouble,' Ansbach said mildly. 'We can do it ourselves.'

'On the contrary, *I* must do it. I must give it to the inter-mediary before a meeting can be arranged.'

'It's something else that has to be changed,' Ansbach said.

'Of course, if you distrust me,' Adler said, going red.

'It's neither a matter of trust nor distrust. It's simply a matter of an original document that we can't let out of our hands in advance of a meeting.'

'But unless you do, there won't be a meeting,' Adler said. 'It's the condition for a meeting. Without it, I can't see what's to be done.'

'You'll think of something,' Ansbach said comfortingly.

'*I* should think?'

'It's after all in your interest.'

'My interest?'

'The hunting lodge?' Ansbach said.

Adler went redder and he began to shake slightly. 'The hunting lodge,' he said, 'I've already explained about.'

'You're nevertheless,' Ansbach said apologetically, 'technically in illegal possession.'

'It brings in next to nothing, the hunting lodge. You're at perfect liberty to go to the devil with the hunting lodge. You told me you weren't concerned about it,' he said to Raison.

'But we're all concerned,' Ansbach said. 'You must be concerned. Who wants to find himself in such an unpleasant position? As an advocate with specialist custodian interests I am naturally concerned at cases of illegal possession.'

'Herr Ansbach,' Adler said in a choked voice, 'I think I should tell you we don't talk to each other in such vulgar terms in this part of the world.'

'It isn't the terms but the situation that's vulgar,' Ansbach said, rather more toughly. 'But there's nothing to argue about. I know you want to correct it. You aren't responsible, any more than for the arrangements. I'm sure you'll put our point of view in the proper quarter. Meanwhile, have you a room at our disposal?'

'There are three rooms at your disposal.'

'One will be enough. With three beds,' Ansbach said.

'But this is ridiculous. The rooms are already arranged. It will take time – '

'We have plenty of time,' Ansbach said. 'We've waited years already. And with regard to Herr Bamberger, I'm sure he'll understand. We only want what we're entitled to. But we won't take risks to get it. We'll stay together. We won't go into any forests. We won't hand over any original documents in advance.'

'Very well,' Adler said. He was still shaking as he got up. They watched him go. They didn't speak while he was away, and he wasn't, after all, very long. In a few minutes he was ushering them up the dark staircase so redolent of pork products, to a doorway that stood open for them. As they reached it, one of the staff came out. He seemed to be carrying a crucifix.

'I'll see what I can do,' Adler said stiffly. 'I can't promise anything. I don't know how long I'll be. It would be best if you didn't show yourselves in the village,' he said, looking at Grunwald's hat. 'It would be best if you stayed here.'

'All right,' Grunwald said.

They didn't speak much after he'd gone, either. It was hot and stuffy in the wood-walled room, and they settled themselves for a nap. Raison fell at once and heavily asleep. It was dusk in the room when he woke and he wasn't sure for a moment whether he was at Schonbach, the Hohenzollernstrasse or the Ludwigshof. He looked at his watch.

'It's eight o'clock,' Ansbach said.

'My stomach advised.'

'Do you want to eat?'

'Yes.'

'Not me,' Grunwald said.

'We'll stay together, nevertheless,' Ansbach said.

They washed, at rather close quarters, with cold water from the jug, and went down together. The bar was crowded, they saw from the foot of the stairs. The cat-eyed old crone scurried along the passage before they got to it.

'Herr Adler's out,' she said.

'Can we have something to eat?'

'The dinner?'

'All right, the dinner,' Raison said.

'Go back. I'll bring it.'

They went back to the room.

Grunwald didn't eat the dinner, but he had coffee when it came. It was quite a long time in coming. Quite a long time after it, Adler still hadn't come. They were bored and restless in the room and it was now dark outside. Ansbach looked out of the window. 'Would we show ourselves so much now?' he said.

'We could take a walk in the cool of the evening,' Grunwald said. They went down the staircase again.

'Herr Adler's out,' the crone said, appearing.

'Tell him if he returns we've gone for a walk,' Ansbach said.

'But you've got to stay in! He said so.'

'For about fifteen minutes,' Ansbach said. 'Is there a back door?'

The crone muttered a little and wrung her apron, but she showed them the back door. They went out of it and a few minutes later were in the square.

The cool of the evening wasn't very cool. It was very crowded. A line of buses was parked in the square and more were arriving. There was a crash of military bands in the air, and enormous mechanical voices, evidently from some part of the pageant. Coloured lights had been strung, and from somewhere floodlamps and flaming torches produced a hazy glow in the air. Swarms of local children, kitted up in little hussar outfits, fiercely engaged each other with toy sabres – engaged any passers-by, too, whose hussar hats or other carnival headgear attracted them, to the amusement of the crowds. It took a few minutes before Grunwald's headgear attracted them.

'Perhaps we should go back now,' Ansbach said.

'Perhaps we should,' Raison said. The smile on his face had become a little fixed. The crowd didn't seem to be quite so amused by Grunwald's headgear. He heard the word '*Jude*' passing. But they shook off their energetic escort of little hussars and presently arrived back in the lane and at the back door.

'Herr Adler's in now,' the crone said grimly.

'Tell him we're also in,' Ansbach said.

'He's up in your room, waiting.'

Adler was smoking a cigar in the room. He was almost livid with rage.

'I told you not to go out!' he said.

'I beg your pardon?' Ansbach said.

'I won't have arrangements broken!'

'Herr Adler, collect yourself,' Ansbach said. 'We're free agents. If we wish to go out, we'll go out.'

'You can go to the devil and be done with it. You can go

and don't come back. I'm sick to death with the pack of you.'

Grunwald looked at him curiously. 'The arrangements have broken down?' he said.

'You've made them break down!' Adler shouted.

'Nobody's coming?'

'They've come. They're here. They're sitting out there in the forest. I've also been sitting out there – like a criminal, doing your dirty work, while you go strolling around the town. I won't have it! I won't have you attracting attention to me. It's all foreign to me. I won't be involved any more.'

'Who's come?' Grunwald said, staring at him.

'Bamberger's come.'

'Bamberger himself?'

'Bamberger and a guide.'

'You know this?'

'Go and see.'

'Not in the forest,' Ansbach said.

'Exactly.' Adler was almost spitting. 'So after all the work it comes to nothing. And I don't intend any longer to pass your idiotic messages back and forth. You can get out, the lot of you.'

Raison had lit a cigarette and he drew in a lungful of smoke. Adler's rage, no doubt about it, seemed quite genuine.

'Did you see him yourself?' he said.

'My friend saw him. He knows him.'

'You didn't see him.'

'He refuses to see anybody, as a matter of fact, except Herr Grunwald.'

In the small silence Ansbach said, 'Why is that?'

'How the devil should I know? He's suffering from a nervous condition. It's taken him a considerable effort to come at all.'

'You didn't manage to discuss the hunting lodge with him, then?'

'He refused to sign the document I wished him to sign.'

'So why ask us to leave if we might be able to get it done for you?'

'If he's not concerned about it, there's no reason for you to be. If I were you,' Adler said darkly, 'I'd watch your own position when it comes to using words like illegal possession. Who knows what you are in illegal possession of?'

There was another small silence.

'So what do you intend to do now?' Raison said.

'I said I'd come back and advise you, and I've done it. I'm going now to tell him it's off.'

'I'll come with you,' Raison said.

'Eh?' Adler said.

'I'll come.'

'I've told you,' Adler said, surprised, 'it's Grunwald he wants. Still, if you want, come.'

Ansbach said woodenly, 'We said we'd stay together.'

'I'm sorry. I forgot.'

'Try not to forget. It's easy to forget.'

'Herr Adler,' Raison said, 'we'd like to discuss this together for a few minutes.'

'As long as you like. I'm going in five minutes.'

When he'd gone, Ansbach said, 'So who was it who was talking about danger?'

'Not for me. He doesn't want to isolate me.'

'Dr Grunwald, then. We shouldn't separate.'

'Lock the door when I'm gone. Bolt it.'

'What do you think you will find out?'

'At least if anybody's there.'

'That, it seems, you won't find out.'

'If I send a message from his daughter.'

They were silent for a while.

'So go,' Grunwald said.

Ansbach said stubbornly, 'If we have a plan we should stick to it.'

'If we stick to it, we can go home right away. At least here there's a chance . . .'

'Do you want me to go or stay?' Raison said.

'Go,' Grunwald said. 'Let him go,' he said. 'We'll lock the door. I want it.'

'All right.'

Raison heard them locking the door, and also bolting it as he went down the passage. The crone was still on duty at the foot of the stairs. A few minutes later, with Adler, he was going out of the back door and down the lane into the forest. They walked without speaking, for several minutes, parallel with the line of felled trees that Raison remembered. Behind them, the mechanical voices and the brass bands faded into a vague murmur. Adler changed direction presently into the almost total darkness of standing timber.

Raison knew – he thought he knew – that he was in no danger, and yet his heart began to pump very unpleasantly. He was certain there was no Bamberger at the other end. He was certain some kind of elaborate trick was going on. He wondered why the devil he'd let himself in for it. He'd been the one to suggest other approaches. He'd been the one to see the danger. At the same time he recalled that the man beside him – he thought it was the man beside him – was a casual murderer, who'd gone quite casually on the run, and who'd often acted first and considered the results later.

'Are you armed?' he heard himself say with marvellous calm.

'What?'

'Are you armed?'

'Why?'

'Are you?'

'Don't talk,' Adler said.

'Dr Haffner of Munich's waiting to hear from me,' Raison said.

'Who is?'

'My colleague Dr Haffner, the well-known prosecutor of Munich,' Raison said. He didn't know why he was evoking Haffner. He couldn't think of anyone else to evoke.

'Good,' Adler said.

They went silently on for several minutes more, Adler now using a small torch to light the way in the dense darkness. 'In a few minutes,' he said quietly, 'I am going to ask you to wait while I contact my friend.' And in a few minutes, carefully flashing his torch about, he did. 'Wait here. Don't smoke. Don't make a noise. Don't move. Stay exactly where you are. I'll come back.'

Raison waited till the soft crackling had passed out of hearing, and then moved. He had to put his arms out to feel his way, but he moved several yards. He got his back against a tree and felt his pupils grow wide as an owl's as he backed slowly round it, trying to see what he could see in each direction. He couldn't see anything. He couldn't see his hand.

As the minutes passed in warm and spicy blackness he began to realize, sinkingly, what a fool he'd been. Ansbach had been right – they shouldn't have separated. Adler was not now trying to contact a friend. Adler was now haring back through the forest to the hotel. He had an absolute conviction of it. The locked door and the two elderly men weren't going to provide any particular problem – not with the noise from the crowded bar below. He suddenly recalled Grunwald's story of the 72 Jews taken off a train and marched into a forest, and had the clearest possible vision of Ansbach and Grunwald shortly making a similar stumbling journey, to this blind place where he'd been left hopelessly anchored . . .

The thing was incredible, of course. It was grotesque. People couldn't be murdered in this way at this date. There were organs of justice around. But yet – who even knew that they were here? Elke knew. Perhaps Frau Ansbach knew. How long would it take them to start inquiries? And what would the inquiries reveal? Adler would say that they had been, and that they had gone. (The car would certainly be gone. The car would be found in Munich.) He suddenly recalled Adler's rage at their having gone for a walk in the village. Adler had not wanted them seen by anybody else. Adler had wanted them to stay in their room. At the same time he remembered Adler's surprised but ready acceptance of his offer to accompany him, and Adler's thoughtful silence ever since . . .

With his back hairs bristling, Raison stepped out in the darkness. He thought if he could find his way back to the line of felled trees he could be at the hotel in a matter of minutes. He hadn't the faintest idea where it lay; had no idea even which way he was moving now, his journey round the tree having disorientated him further. He realized that by moving at all he might well be moving into Czechoslovakia or towards a returning Adler; but even in his scrambled condition found both distinctly preferable to staying where he'd been left.

He moved with his arms out straight in front of him, eyes wide open and aching in the dark. He had the impression his ears had grown out some distance from his head and were independently scanning the night waves. He moved with a somewhat gliding motion through the blackness. He'd covered perhaps a hundred yards when an owl hooted suddenly, practically on top of him, and he nearly fell over with fright. He remained in a crouched position, mouth wide open and sweat running freely, and was still like this when he heard a rather more measured and continuing sound, and looked round and saw the little glow of the torch bob-bobbing towards him, and put himself rapidly behind a tree.

The two men walked past within a couple of feet of him, not speaking. He lost them in the trees, but saw the glow of the torch. Then the torch stopped and started flashing around.

'Herr Raison,' Adler called softly. 'Herr Raison.'

Raison kept quiet.

'Herr Raison, where are you?'

It struck Raison that Adler hadn't had time to go back to the hotel. He'd only had time to do what he'd said he'd do. He seemed to have done it. It also struck him he might have got his friend because he thought he might need his friend. He came out from behind the tree, anyway. He walked towards them, back hairs still bristling.

'Herr Raison,' Adler said. 'Herr Raison.'

'Here,' Raison said.

Adler started swearing. 'I told you not to move,' he said, coming towards him.

'I got tired standing still.'

'We have to keep arrangements. It's impossible!'

He saw the friend had something in his hand, and kept away from him till he identified it. He had a torch in his hand. He tried to get a look at his face. The only glimpse he'd had from Adler's torch had shown a peculiar spread of squashed features, like an imbecile. Then he got another glimpse, and saw there was a nylon stocking over the face.

'Tell him,' Adler said to the friend.

'He wants to see Grunwald,' the friend said.

'Are you sure it's Bamberger?' Raison said.

'Of course I'm sure.'

'Are you sure he won't see me?'

'He'll see Grunwald.'

'Well, it's a pity,' Raison said.

'You mean Grunwald won't see him?'

'He won't see him here. Where is he?'

'About a kilometre.'

'No, he won't see him there.'

'You think I better tell him it's off, then?'

'Yes, you'd better tell him.'

'It's a pity,' the man said. He seemed a bit worried behind his nylon. 'He's sick. They've still got to get him back. He only made the effort to see Grunwald.'

'What's up with him?'

'He has his mouth like this,' the man said, doing something with his mouth behind the nylon. 'It must have been a stroke. He can't talk hardly. He only did it to see Grunwald,' he said, worried.

'How about trying me on him, then?'

'I don't know. Since you're here,' the man said, 'we can try. Have you got anything, have you got any proof?'

Raison had a look in his pockets in the torchlight. He had his driving licence and a letter addressed to himself at Stanhope Gardens. The man didn't seem too happy with the proof. He said, 'I mean, what is it? If you only had this document he wants, if you had that.'

'I haven't.'

'Well, I don't know. There's no sense hanging about. They want to get him back. They're scared he'll bloody snuff it on the way.'

'How many of them are there?'

'One with him, another at the border. I've never seen him like this before.'

'You don't want him snuffing here, then,' Raison said.

'Frigging right. We better get back,' the man said. 'You better come. I'm not running there and back.'

Raison kept an open mind as they walked through the forest. He kept a very open mind. Despite it, he couldn't visualize Bamberger in the forest, so he kept on his toes as well. 'All right, wait here now,' Adler's friend said. 'Both of you wait. What do you want me to tell him?'

Keeping an open mind had brought Raison to a state where he was by no means clear, as he told himself, whether he was on his knee or his elbow. But he said, 'Give me the envelope,' and in the torchlight wrote a few words on it in German. He wrote, 'Frieda loves you. She knows you are alive. Won't you send her one word of love?' He gave the envelope back, and then thought of something else, and added on it, ' – even on this?'

The man looked at it dubiously.

'Is that all?' he said.

'That's all,' Raison said.

He waited quite alertly while the man went, well aware that he might not be going anywhere. But there were no strange sounds in the forest. There were only the footsteps of Adler's friend, and then a whistle, and then an answering whistle.

'We can sit now,' Adler said, sitting.

'I'm all right,' Raison said. He moved away from Adler in the dark.

He could hear voices. He couldn't tell if there were two voices or three. The voices quietly talked. He heard one of them coughing. Then the footsteps returned.

Adler's friend came out of the blackness in a flash of torch-light.

He said, 'He wrote this.'

Raison looked at the envelope in the torchlight. Under his words a spidery hand had written 'HJS'.

'What is it?'

'Don't *you* know?'

'No.'

'Well, that's all he done.'

'Didn't he say anything?'

'He said Grunwald.'

'Look,' Raison said, 'Grunwald isn't coming here.'

'That's too bad, then,' the man said. He seemed nervous and irritable. 'That's about it, then,' he said.

'Won't he come any nearer?'

'They don't bloody want him nearer. He can't bloody walk nearer. They want him where they can whip him back, fast.'

'Are we near the border?'

'We're bloody on the border. We're not supposed to be here. There's bloody armed patrols with jeeps in the forest. He's a big heavy man and they can't bloody move him easy. I'm not staying here.'

'All right,' Raison said, 'listen. I can't promise anything, but see if he'll stay till daylight.'

'You're bloody joking.'

'I can't promise,' Raison said, 'but if he will, and the three of us can see him, we might do something.'

'You're over the bloody top,' Adler's friend said.

'That's the way it's been,' Adler said bitterly, 'all along. One puts oneself out, and they think they're doing favours. This is what I've had.'

'Try him,' Raison said.

In a sort of disbelief, the man did. He was in a nervous rage when he came back. He said, 'Who's paying me, then? Who's paying me?'

'Will he do it?'

'I'm not running there and back. I've bloody had enough,' he said to Adler.

'Will he?'

'Look, you got half an hour,' the man said to him furiously, 'to sort yourself out, no more farting about with mights and maybes. They're shitting bricks there, and so am I. Get back in half an hour,' he said, 'with something definite, which is also fifty extra for me, and they'll let you know.'

Raison walked back with a grimly silent Adler in a state of some bewilderment. There was without any question *somebody* there. And the intermediary's nervousness had been quite genuine. This didn't mean that Bamberger was there. But it certainly didn't mean that he wasn't. He was still trying to decide where he was himself when they got back. He went upstairs and knocked on the door. He said, 'It's Raison, let me in,' and went in and told them. He gave Grunwald the envelope. 'Does it mean anything to you?'

Grunwald said curiously, 'HJS. *Hilfsverein der Juden in Süddeutschland* – it was the name of the Trust before it was incorporated into the SKS. It's the only one that Bamberger would know.'

'Or that anyone who took over his account would know,' Raison said.

'Yes.'

'Yes.'

Ansbach looked at the envelope. 'It *seems* to be the writing of someone old or sick,' he said uncertainly.

'Or the writing of someone writing like someone old or sick,' Raison said.

'Quite.'

'Quite.'

'So what do you think?' Grunwald said.

'I don't know.'

'Is it far in the forest?'

'It's about two kilometres.'

'Do you think, in the daylight, the three of us – ?'

'I don't know.'

'So what do you advise?'

'I don't want to advise anything,' Raison said.

The three of them looked at each other.

Ansbach said, 'If we're in doubt it's best to do nothing.'

Grunwald said, 'It wouldn't be nothing. It would be turning him down. If it's Bamberger,' he said, 'you have the impression he wouldn't do it again.'

'If it's Bamberger,' Raison said, 'it's doubtful if he'll do anything again. They're frightened he won't last till they've got him over the border.'

Adler's footsteps stamped on the landing, and he banged on the door. 'You've got a couple of minutes,' he shouted.

'All right,' Raison said.

'I don't like it,' Ansbach said, 'when I'm rushed. I always suspect it when I'm rushed. It's after all like any other business operation. You decide in advance how far you'll go, and then stop. We already decided how far we'd go.'

'But I've come a long way already,' Grunwald said, 'and I've wasted a lot of time, and it could be the last chance. How much longer have I got?'

'Please God, many years. It's a foolish argument.'

'Tell him yes,' Grunwald said.

'Yonah, be advised!' Ansbach said. 'It's unwise to decide like this.'

'Tell him yes.'

'Are you sure?' Raison said.

'There's still time to think. Meanwhile tell him yes.'

'All right,' Raison said. He went down and told Adler yes. He couldn't see any need to accompany him, so he gave Adler fifty marks for his friend. About one o'clock Adler came and told them to be ready at five.

It was a warm, stale morning, very still. They walked silently down the lane into the forest. Adler had greeted them with a cold nod at the foot of the stairs, and hadn't spoken since. He carried a flask of coffee in his hand. The sun began to get up when they entered the forest, and shafts of light flashed. An enormous chirruping and fluttering went on overhead.

They walked for ten minutes and then Adler curtly said, 'Wait,' and went on himself with his flask.

'I could have done with coffee myself,' Ansbach said.

'Yes.' Raison was conscious of a certain dryness about his own mouth. 'All right?' he said to Grunwald. He'd noticed him taking a pill when he'd got up and his breathing had been noisy as they'd walked.

'Yes.'

They waited.

Adler came back and said 'Very well,' and they walked on again.

'Has he moved?' Raison said, looking about him. He was

266

keeping track of the direction this time. He had no idea where he'd been before but it seemed as well to show an intelligent interest.

'He couldn't be moved.'

'How is he?'

'He's ill.'

'How will they get him back?'

'It's not my concern. None of this would have been necessary if arrangements had been kept.'

They walked a few minutes more and stopped. Adler whistled. His friend walked out of the trees. He still had the nylon stocking on.

'Give him the document,' Adler said.

Ansbach's voice was somewhat hoarse. He said, 'We'll give it ourselves – I told you.'

'And I've already told you, in the greatest detail, Bamberger must have it to prove who you are.'

'Where's the proof who he is?'

'I warn you,' Adler said. 'No more twisted arrangements. You said you'd give the document yourself to the intermediary, and here he is. Any more tricks and the whole thing's off, once and for all.'

Grunwald reached in his pocket.

'Yonah,' Ansbach said.

'There are copies of it,' Grunwald said, handing the document over.

'This is the original?' Adler said.

'It's the original, but there are attested copies.'

'Fine,' Adler said, and the man went off with it.

He was away a long time. He was away much longer than the previous night. Raison couldn't hear any voices. He listened but couldn't hear any. The birds were noisy. He thought they must be farther away from the voices now.

The man came back and said, 'All right.'

'Walk with him,' Adler said to Grunwald. 'We'll walk fifty metres behind.'

'We'll walk together,' Ansbach said. 'That was the arrangement. We said we'd see him together.'

'You'll see him, and he'll see you – from fifty metres. But he won't talk to you. You knew all this. It was understood.'

'It was understood we'd be together,' Ansbach said. 'We're not separating.'

'Then I give up,' Adler said. 'I can't deal with you people. You don't know the meaning of arrangements. Do you want your document back?'

'Yes,' Ansbach said.

'Very well.'

'Just a minute,' Grunwald said.

'Yonah!'

'What's fifty metres? It's not so far, after all.'

'It's nothing,' Adler said, 'but be damned to you. You don't know the meaning of arrangements, and I'm not here to teach you. But at least use sense. If anybody wanted to run away with such a prize as Herr Grunwald, couldn't he take him now? Have you got an army with you? You're frightened of your own shadows. Aren't you going to ask me today,' he said to Raison, 'if I'm armed or tell me some more about your famous friends in Munich?'

'All right, we'll do it,' Grunwald said.

'And get it out of your head,' Adler said with loathing, 'that you're doing *me* favours.'

'So all right.'

'Then move.'

Grunwald moved, with his escort. They went quite slowly. Adler let a few seconds elapse, and then they all moved. As they moved Raison realized, with a pang, that they'd now done all the things they had said they would not do. They'd agreed not to go into the forest, and they were in it. They'd said they wouldn't give up the document, and they'd given it up. And they'd decided not to separate, and they had now separated. Grunwald looked round a couple of times to see how far they were separated, but then stopped looking round. They really weren't separated by very much.

Raison kept alert, all the same. The trees were dense and grew at random and for seconds at a time he lost Grunwald. They skirted a boggy pool, picked their way through some undergrowth and emerged again into a clearer stretch. There was a fluttering in the undergrowth as they passed, but the party in front kept on ahead. They kept on for a considerable time, until Adler's friend raised his arm and stopped, and Adler immediately stopped them, too. They waited for several seconds and then Grunwald turned round. Raison couldn't for a moment see what was different about him. He seemed to be fumbling in front of him. Then he took his hat off and began to urinate in it, and Raison saw what was different about him. Grunwald didn't have a beard any more but he had a fine head of blond hair. As he started running, Raison heard Ansbach, running beside him, moan 'Yonah!'

Grunwald had had all the breath knocked out of him as they went through the undergrowth. He opened his mouth to shout, but found a sweaty sock in it. A greasy hand was pressed hard over the sock, and he gagged over it. He felt his hat pulled off and something crammed down over his head, crammed too far, too low over his nose, he couldn't breathe. Then in a few seconds, gulping, choking for air, he heard the three sets of footsteps tramp past within a few feet of him and the sock was taken out of his mouth and he could breathe. There had been a terrible leap from his heart and a fluttering. He said, 'My heart!' He couldn't see, the thing was pulled down over his face. He could hear them whispering, choking with suppressed laughter. He said, 'My heart!' and fumbled in his waistcoat for the pills. But a hand took the pills from him, and he heard the rustling and the small impact as the bottle was flung away in the undergrowth. They were tying his hands behind him. They were doing something to him. They were unzipping his trousers. He felt himself being sick at the same moment that his heart leapt a second time. He tried to recite the great formula of Judaism but before he got to *Adonai* everything went.

Suddenly it was a carnival. Raison felt the spray of urine against his face as the man threw the hat at him, and then from all about the hussars were prancing and hallooing, materializing from the trees, a dozen, fifteen, twenty of them, galloping imaginary horses, thrusting imaginary sabres. Adler had begun to run with him and Ansbach. 'Where the hell is he? Where is he?' Raison shouted.

'The students. They're quite irrepressible,' Adler said.

'Where is he?'

'We'll have to look. No need for panic, I'm sure. He'll only be mislaid, not lost,' Adler said. 'But I really suppose they must have frightened your friend Bamberger off. I really suppose so,' he said, trying to keep his face straight.

They found Grunwald in the undergrowth. A number of the hussars led them, hallooing, to him, before making off. He was lying like a piece of rubbish with his face crammed in a hussar hat and his hands tied behind him. A stroke of red paint had changed the T for Trotz on the hussar hat into a J. The old man's penis was exposed and a label had been tied to it. It said, *A message to the medical profession – the wrong bit has been thrown away.* There were several other labels tied to him. One said, *A message from the Crematory – I want to be fed.* Another said, *A message from Comrade B. – I want to be alone.* Another said, *A message from departed Jewish Comrades – We want Comrade B. who betrayed us – Hear it in Court.*

Grunwald's nose was somewhat pinched and his face greenish when they got the hat off him. He began to motion weakly when his hands were untied, but they couldn't make out the words on his rustling vomit-coated lips.

'It's his pills. He wants a pill,' Ansbach said. They looked in his waistcoat but they couldn't find the pills. They looked in his pockets.

'He must have left the pills. We'd better get him back.'

The old man's hands continued moving as they picked him up. 'It's all right,' Raison said. 'It's all right.'

But Grunwald was trying to get to his bottle of syrup. He thought if he could get to the syrup he could tell them what had happened to the pills. He couldn't get to the syrup.

'It's all right,' Raison said. He was holding the shoulders, and Ansbach the feet.

'We'll get you the pills,' Ansbach said. 'We're taking you back.'

'I think the best thing,' Adler said, 'is if *I* go ahead and find the pills. Also a doctor. I'll see to that. Don't worry about that.' They lost him quite soon.

Ansbach began to sweat and stumble. 'I'm sorry,' he said.

'You're all right.'

'I'm not well myself.'

'Shall I carry him?'

'I'll continue.'

'I'll carry him,' Raison said.

'If you can. See if you can.'

Ansbach lowered the feet and Raison picked them up. He carried Grunwald in his arms.

'While I get my breath,' Ansbach said.

'It's all right.'

'The bastards,' Ansbach said. 'Abusing him like that. Insulting him like that.'

'They didn't insult me,' Grunwald said.

Nobody heard him, but Raison saw the lips moving and the brown eyes turned to his.

'They didn't insult me,' Grunwald said.

He remembered he hadn't told Raison the story. His heart felt very strange. If felt as if it were encased in foam rubber and the foam rubber was vibrating erratically. He knew this feeling. Once before he'd had this feeling. He'd been talking to Landsberg when he'd had it, and the next thing Dr Rivkin was massaging his heart on Landsberg's floor while waiting for the ambulance. There was no Rivkin and no ambulance here and he saw that if he was ever going to tell someone his father's story he'd better tell it now.

He said quickly, 'There was a young minister who came to a certain town and the rabbi set him various tasks. But after some weeks the minister went to the rabbi and said, "I don't want to stay in the ministry." So the rabbi said, "What is it – you've no bent for religion?" And the minister said, "It's not religion – it's the people. I went to such and such and he kept me waiting, and to so and so and he didn't offer a chair, and

271

this one said he'd send when he needed me, and that one that he had no time to waste. So what with one thing and another," the minister said, "and if it doesn't give offence, I'd as soon find work where people don't insult me." So the rabbi said, "Listen," he said, "I'd like to tell you something," he said, "my young colleague. I've been in this town many years, and I also was kept waiting by such and such, and not offered a chair by so and so, and this one said he'd send, and that one had no time. But they never insulted me," the rabbi said. "Do you understand," he said, " – they never insulted *me*."'

'You'll be all right,' Raison said. He saw the lips fluttering and the face turned restlessly to his.

'Give me his legs again,' Ansbach said. 'I've had a breather.'

'All right,' Raison said, sweating.

Ansbach took the legs.

'Do you understand,' Grunwald said. 'We can't *be* insulted. We're not to be insulted. Insult a tree! It's all God's. We can't insult another, only ourselves. We pile insults on ourselves. Who was insulted in the camps?' The fluttering stopped round his heart; it went dangerously quiescent, a gathering of forces. He knew he had little time to finish so he said urgently, 'They insulted themselves, everything they were a part of, a reduction of everything's value. It's all one, you see. It's a question – ' he said. But it felled him then; a massive plunge into blackness.

'Just a minute,' Raison said. 'Is he all right?'

Grunwald's eyes were shut and his face bluish. Ansbach turned and looked at him, muttering. Sweat was running into his eyes. They examined the old man closely.

'He's breathing,' Raison said.

'Maybe he shouldn't be moved.'

'He can't stay here. He needs a doctor.' They had come to the line of felled trees. 'Look,' Raison said, 'I'll carry him. You run on. Bloody Adler isn't to be trusted. See to a doctor, and if you can find his pills run back with them.'

Ansbach gave him the legs and ran stumbling along the line of tree stumps. Raison walked slowly on with Grunwald. He was almost on his knees as he came out of the forest, and Ansbach was nowhere in sight. He came in sight, racing the old Mercedes down the lane as Raison staggered to the hotel.

'Get him in the car! It's no good here. We'll get nowhere here.'

Raison asked no questions but dumped Grunwald in the back seat, and supported his head as Ansbach took off.

Adler had not been in the Gasthoff. The pills weren't in the Gasthof. The two local doctors had both been called away within minutes to cases outside the village . . .

They couldn't find the hospital in Cham, but recalled having passed one outside Regensburg, so Ansbach flogged the old Mercedes to its top speed, and they got to it a little after half past seven. By eight o'clock Grunwald was in bed in hospital pyjamas, and Raison and Ansbach were discussing his next of kin with an elderly administrative nun. A few nuns seemed to be about.

They stayed in Regensburg for the rest of the day and in the evening went to the hospital again. There was no further news from the hospital, so they decided to stay the night as well.

They ate a glum dinner.

'It was the students from the hunting lodge, of course,' Ansbach said.

'Yes. There isn't any Bamberger, is there?'

'I doubt it.'

'It's a question of laying information against Adler, then.'

'Is it?' Ansbach said.

'You surely don't think he ought to get away with it?'

'It's hard to show murder. It's hard even to show Bamberger's dead. With a reputable Swiss bank saying he's alive, such a case could cause a great deal of trouble if it ever got to court. I mean, of course, with regard to "settlements already arrived at" with the German government. All you're asking for is a big headache – which presumably Mrs Wolff doesn't want.'

'To nail her father's murderer?'

'To have his name besmirched by these allegations?'

'Lying allegations won't put her off, either.'

'Allegations, however lying, have a habit of sticking. Of course you know your client better than I do, but I'd be surprised if she didn't consider it unwise, even improper, to sue in the circumstances.'

'You mean you'd advise *your* client to take all this lying down and go away with nothing?'

Ansbach looked at him with a strange smile.

'We can take it as read,' he said, 'that my client won't be going away with nothing. Dr Grunwald, I have to tell you, didn't come all the way from Israel just to get a label stuck on his penis.'

PART SIX

Amicable settlements shall be permitted.

German Federal Indemnification Law
(*Bundesentschädigungsgesetz*)

Chapter 1

THE GRAND OLD DUKE OF YORK,
HE HAD TEN THOUSAND MEN

'I WOULD by no means say it's an impossibility,' Ansbach said. 'There are difficulties, certainly.'

'The main one being, as you pointed out, that wherever the money is now, it certainly won't be in the Handelsbank Lindt.'

'The action wouldn't be against the bank. It would be him personally.'

'And he won't tell you where he put it.'

'Under the threat of proceedings?'

'He'd buy himself a ticket to South America.'

'Perhaps.' Ansbach's nod implied approval of the performance and his smile that it was always a pleasure to do business. 'From where he could be extradited.'

'I thought you considered it improper to sue.'

'For your client, not mine. Let's for a moment consider the facts. Almost certainly Bamberger is dead. Almost certainly the Handelsbank Lindt doesn't have the money. Almost certainly Adler does have it. But if we're forced to sue him he'll try to protect himself by making poisonous allegations against Bamberger which will be very hard, in open court and in the newspapers, to disprove. Nobody wants that. On the other hand, the money is a bequest to a Trust. Dr Grunwald is an officer of the Trust. I am the legal representative here of the Trust. We have to take *some* steps to recover the Trust's money.'

'Unless it comes to you from some other source.'

'Exactly so.'

'Okay,' Raison said. 'I'll put the point of view. When's he coming up?'

'They're moving him this afternoon.'

'That should cheer him up. He seemed a bit cheesed with the nuns when I was there.'

'It was the bed bath. I daren't tell him there are nuns at the new place. Still, his wife's arriving tomorrow. She can take command. . . . No hard feelings, I hope?'

'No hard feelings.'

'It's a good cause.'

'Of course.'

'So what's the matter?'

'The matter would take a lot of explaining,' Raison said.

Ansbach looked at him, head on one side. 'The trouble with you is you haven't got the temperament for a deal,' he said.

'Is that what it is?'

'You'd prefer it if you were in my position with the possibility to do something direct and uncomplicated. Very often it's best not to do the direct thing. In fact we can say it's always best to do a deal, if we can. Justice is only an abstraction. There are various ways of approximating to it.'

'Yes. Not much of the real stuff around, is there?' Raison said.

He phoned Gunter. Gunter said, ' Just a minute, James, just a minute. She's going to want this exactly.'

He could hear Gunter breathing. He could hear the squeak of Gunter's pencil. It was almost like being in the room with Gunter, which was, all said and done, better than being in a limbo.

'All right,' Gunter said. 'I'm ready now.'

'All right,' Raison said, and told him what there was to tell. Gunter said, 'Yes. . . . Yes. . . . Yes.'

At the end Gunter said, 'H'm. So what are they prepared to take, James, what do you think they'll take?'

'I should think they'll take the lot,' Raison said.

'The what?'

'The lot.'

'A million francs?'

'Why not? It's a good cause, Rupert. Let's not approximate.'

'Yes. Are you all right, James?'

'I'm very well,' Raison said. 'How are you, Rupert?'

'I'm not sure I can hear you very well. I think it's the line.'

'It's a fine line,' Raison said. 'I can hear you breathing. How is everything, Rupert? How is Mrs Wolff?'

'Well, I'll let her know, then,' Gunter said. 'I think you've been going at it rather, James. I think you ought to have a sleep. I won't disturb you any more today. I might just have a word with Heinz. Heinz has a view on this, I suppose?'

'I suppose he must have,' Raison said curiously. 'He has views on everything, Heinz. No sense of humour, though. Quite a good joke happened to him lately, but he won't laugh. I'm not sure he'll ever laugh again.'

'Have a rest, James,' Gunter said firmly, and hung up.

'Herr Gunter, from London,' she said, looking carefully into the room. She saw he'd stopped looking at the wall now. He was looking out of the window, which might be an improvement. 'I didn't say you were in,' she said.

'It's all right, Gerda. I'll speak to him. Yes, Rupert,' he said into the phone.

He listened idly to Gunter for a while, looking at Ansbach's memo again as he did so. Despite himself, his gorge rose slowly, but in a melancholy way. Swinishness, of course; on all sides, swinishness.

'It is by no means my view,' he said heavily, after a time. 'It is the very opposite of my view – not that I any longer expect anybody to – '

' – seemed to think, when I was talking to him a few minutes ago, that there was nothing else for it – '

'Yes. I can't say that I any longer understand James Raison. I am very disappointed in James Raison.'

' – very wildly, a bit under the weather, I thought.'

'What?'

'Talking strangely. I couldn't understand what was the matter with him.'

'I can't say I any longer understand what is the matter with anybody,' Haffner said. 'Which is to say,' he said, 'that perhaps I understand too well.'

Listening in London, Gunter wrinkled his nose and

scratched his head a little. Some puzzling stuff was coming out of Heinz.

'The metaphysical as well as the actual plane,' Haffner was puzzlingly saying.

'Yes, very worrying. Very troubling, I'm sure,' Gunter said. He couldn't make out what Heinz was on about. He seemed to be on about a large amount of swinishness that was evidently in the air. 'I honestly think everybody's been working too hard on this, Heinz, I really do,' he said at last.

'Yes, we work and what for?'

'Exactly. No point in knocking oneself up. You don't sound at all chirpy, old chap, if you don't mind my saying so.'

'What?'

'A bit under the weather.'

'Yes, the weather. It's very heavy here, very heavy.'

Gunter put down the phone presently and shook his head. They certainly were making heavy weather of it there. He was glad he hadn't gone. It was nice weather here. A nice rain had set in. People were hurrying about in raincoats in the rain. They weren't dawdling, pointing their breasts at you, and their little warm bellies, and their mind-reeling legs from ankle to breakfast-time; and you couldn't any longer see in their eyes that disturbing look of rovers that have such an unsettling feeling that a whole other world of activity was going on, a more vital world of offers and acceptances, of animal motivation, from which one was excluded . . .

It wasn't like that at all, really. They were simply people's daughters and sisters and cousins; members of families, members of firms, members, with oneself, of the larger community; all rubbing along, going forward together, a decent sort of progression, to which science made its continual contributions. The thing to do was to continually see them as members, not the frightening anarchs of those illusory moments.

It wasn't easy, of course. A good deal of confusion was about. Age didn't seem to lessen the confusion; it seemed to increase it. There was a sense that the thing was unreeling too fast, had almost unreeled, without one ever having managed to get a proper view. It was entirely a question of view, of course. There were too many things going on, too many factors to be considered, for one ever to find an interpretation that *held*. None of his interpretations had held so far. Still, no point in being morbid. He looked pleasantly out of the window at the rain-soaked tennis courts and the umbrella tops going past. One could always be thankful for small mercies. One could always, when a certain view failed, try another.

'It was having to choose between people and birds that finally defeated him,' Elke said. 'He had to make the choice, you see. They made him do it all by himself. Now he doesn't know where he is. He feels he's betrayed the only thing that really meant anything to him. But he doesn't know what else he could have done.'

'No backbone, you see,' Raison said.

'It's true.'

'As well as being a born loser.'

'Have pity, James.'

'I pity everybody,' Raison said. 'In a way.'

'Except me.'

'Do you want pity?'

'I want love.'

'There's plenty of that about. There's always a good head of love about. That's not the stuff in short supply.'

'Probably you'd better have another drink.'

He had another drink.

'So how do things stand at the moment?'

'At the moment they're after the money. If they don't get it, one way or another, Ansbach says they'll sue Adler.'

'Will they?'

'I don't know. I would. I'd sue, anyway.'

'Would that ensure you'd get it?'

'No. It would probably ensure that I wouldn't.'

'Then what's the point?'

'Probably,' Raison surmised, 'the point is that miscreants have got to be gone after. They've got to be held up as an example.'

'So we have to ask what you want most, the example or the

money. Then we have to ask why you want the money, and if it's a good cause.'

'It's a beautiful cause,' Raison said. 'I don't know where you'd find a better. It's to build a home for mad people; for apparently quite useless people, from whom even medical science has nothing to learn. Where are you going to find a more compassionate use for the money?'

'So it's still a mix-up, isn't it?'

'It's always a mix-up,' Raison said. 'It's a terrible bloody mix-up. Probably that's why you've got to try and make some order. It's why you've got to try and enforce at least minimum rules. Otherwise you wouldn't be able to build enough homes for all the mad people. There's got to be *some* point,' Raison said, 'although I can't at the moment think what it could possibly be.'

'What does my father think about it?'

'He apparently thinks we shouldn't give them it. He says we've got no liability. He thinks it might be an idea to pay them a small gratuity, though, in the way of travel expenses, to stop them making trouble. But he doesn't expect any trouble.'

'What does Uncle Rupert think?'

'Uncle Rupert thinks it's all a bit tricky. He thinks your father's a sound man, though. He thinks it's more or less up to Mrs Wolff.'

'So what does Mrs Wolff think?'

'She's a funny woman, Mrs Wolff. Nobody knows what she thinks. Still, I fear the worst. What with your father being a born loser and Mrs Wolff such a funny woman, I'm in low spirits tonight.'

'Let's make love, then.'

'Not that, love. I'm low-spirited but strong. I feel very strong in that line tonight.'

'Well. If we're not going to make love,' she said, 'I'll make coffee.'

She went and made it while Raison finished off his drink. He found another verse in the chair. It said:

So now we gather to atone
for your transgressions with our own.

(We made you.)
And our vows shall not be vows.
And our bonds shall not be bonds.
And our oaths shall not be oaths.
(We made you.)
But our hopes shall be new hopes
and our dreams shall be new dreams
and our lives shall be real lives.
(We will make you.)
So we think of you tonight
as you were before this night,
our perpetual delight,
our first-born.
We will dream you yet again,
will conceive you yet again.
But the earlier dream is dreamed now.
Earlier bonds have been redeemed now.
Soll er liegen in sein Ruh.
Requiescat in pace, Du.
Shalom, Shalom, Gottenu.

She came in while he was reading it. She said, 'Oh, that. It's Tibor's. There's a lot more of it.'

'Yes, I've read it.'

'Not all. He tore up a lot. He started off hating God and then realized he was hating himself. So he turned it into a requiem for the conception of God we've had so far, and he forgave him.'

'Jolly good for Tibor.'

'He said we couldn't ever know God. He said it was a question of having blind faith in an unknown force. He said all we could do was make representations of what we wanted it to be, and out of our own goodness and mercy we'd made it good and merciful, and out of our own sense of justice and love we'd made it just and loving, but it was time now to make a new one because the last incredible years had taken all credibility from the old, like a chewed-up teddy-bear with only holes and flaps where its eyes and ears should be. He said it was never more than a one-way game, anyway. We could call but Teddy'd never answer. Still, he thought we had to do it because in saying what we wanted it to be, we said what we wanted to be, and when we failed there was always the chance of making good again. I think it's the last verse you've got there.'

'Good,' Raison said.

'Blessed be he who spake and the world existed: blessed be he,' Grunwald said. He had a quick look at the door. His wife was sitting at the door, to keep the nuns out. She'd let one in earlier, though. He couldn't be sure the door wasn't shaking now.

'He reigneth. The Lord reigneth. The Lord hath frustrated the design of the nations: he hath foiled the thought of the peoples . . . who in his goodness reneweth the creation every day continually . . .'

He was late this morning. The nuns had been preparing him for an alleged visit by the doctor. They'd not got him to eat, though. And he hadn't let them wash him. His wife had washed him. He knew they wanted really to catch him at his prayers. He knew his phylacteries exercised an extraordinary fascination for them. 'Our Lord wore phylacteries,' one of them had told him the very first day, confirming him in his suspicion as to what they were after. When he wasn't wearing the phylacteries now he kept them securely under his pillow.

'. . . said I will divide the spoil, my hand shall destroy them. But thou in thy loving kindness has led the people which thou hast redeemed; thou hast guided them in thy strength to thy holy habitation . . .'

The door was certainly shaking. He could even see the knob turning now. 'Let all thine enemies speedily be cut off,' he said, shaking his head severely at his wife. He noticed suddenly that her foot was no longer securely against the door. 'For we have trusted in thee,' he said urgently. 'Blessed art thou, the stay and trust of the righteous.'

There was a knock on the door, and to his fury his wife got up and opened it. Raison's head came in, and after a swift glance went out again. The sight calmed him, and he went quietly on, turning at length to the psalm of the day. The passage of the days bemused him in hospital, but he always knew, first thing in the morning, which day it was. Yesterday he had read the psalm for the third day of the week, so today must be the fourth, Wednesday.

'Lord, how long shall the wicked, how long shall the wicked triumph? They prate, they speak arrogantly: all the workers of iniquity are boastful. They crush the people and afflict thine heritage. They slay the widow and the stranger, and murder the fatherless. And they say, The Lord will not see, neither will the God of Jacob give heed. Give heed, ye brutish among the peoples: and ye fools, when will ye be wise? He that planted the ear, shall he not hear? He that formed the eye, shall he not see? He that chasteneth the nations, shall not he punish, even he that teacheth man knowledge. . . . Hath the tribunal of destruction, which frameth mischief by statutes, fellowship with thee? They gather themselves together against the soul of the righteous, and condemn the innocent blood. But the Lord is become my stronghold; and my God the rock of my refuge. And he bringeth back upon them their own iniquity. . . . O come, let us exult before the Lord: let us shout for joy to the rock of our salvation.'

He knew it so well that the levitical fierceness, the desert zeal, had lost their cutting power, and now the words flowed simply through his mind like healing sense.

But he remained for some moments looking at them before taking off his phylacteries and kissing them. 'He can come in now,' he said, stowing them safely under his pillow. 'The Englishman.'

Raison came in.

'Mr Raison – my wife,' Grunwald said.

'Very glad, very pleased,' Raison said, startled by the apparition with pink hair that confronted him, gold teeth flashing in a smile of enormous amiability. She looked too big, too vital for the frail figure in the nightie. But then he remembered Grunwald wasn't so frail. He remembered he was durable.

'You're durable,' he said.

'God's good.'

'He seems to have given you all you wanted now.'

'I hear it did not make you happy.'

'A passing tantrum.'

'Yes. It's no use worrying about justice, you know. We don't make justice. We make out as best we can. It wouldn't have been best if I'd gone without the money, or tried to get it in ways that made Mrs Wolff suffer. Why should I make her suffer? This way she has the blessing of giving and I have the blessing of receiving.'

'And Adler has the special one of getting away with it.'

'Who knows what he gets away with?'

'We do,' Raison said. 'Don't we?'

'I myself', Grunwald said, 'know less and less about everything. Things that were obvious to me are not now so obvious. Only one thing, on the whole, remains obvious, and that is that everything was created, and with a purpose. The alternative is for me to believe that it was created without a purpose, which I can't believe. I can't even imagine. A strange paradox has happened. Once when we were younger we wondered why we were in the house and what we were meant to do in it, but as we found out more and the mystery increased, we wondered less. Like eccentrics, we became obsessed with particular problems of the house. Mysteries like the plumbing, the wiring, the central heating became gradually comprehensible to us, and the more we discovered the more we realized that everything in the house had a function, and that one function was governed by another, and that by yet another. And in some way, as the house filled up, it became more normal not to inquire what we were doing here, as though the numbers and the activities provided their own explanation. And there grew up a feeling that just as one function of the house was governed by another, and in a sense provided the reason for it, so all the functions combined provided a reason for the house: the house was the sum of all its functions and had in some way brought itself about, and everything in it, including us. Still, even if you believe that – and I can't even understand it – it still doesn't explain what our function is. We come and go and still we don't know. *We* certainly didn't in any way bring the house into being. It was here when we arrived. So despite the mathematical explanations, I don't believe the house brought itself into being, either. I think it was brought into being by whoever brought us into being, and that he knows what goes on in the house, and whether anybody gets away with anything. So the question remains – do they get away with it?'

'They do where it counts,' Raison said, 'and where it hurts, and in the only context where we can know anything.'

'Well,' Grunwald said, 'I can't deny that things have happened in my life that defy explanation, that seem to defy any kind of meaning. But this has always been the case. There's nothing new. What's a mystery in one case doesn't become more of a mystery in six million cases. It isn't a question of scale. And with regard to context, one context is enclosed by another context. Every action we take brings into a major context some minor context. My belief is that what happens here has to be seen in a wider context, and that one day we'll see it. There's meaning.'

'Why do you talk so much,' his wife said, 'when you know you mustn't talk so much, and the doctor will come, and I have my appointment?'

'Everything will happen. Why do you worry that it won't happen? Why do you always worry?'

'I only slipped in to say goodbye,' Raison said.

'You're going now?'

'Haffner's running me to the airport.'

'Then I hope we meet again.'

'When are they letting you leave?'

'If he eats and rests and keeps quiet when they tell him, in ten days maybe. As yet even he's eaten no breakfast.'

'There could be reasons to meet,' Grunwald said. 'It's a wonderful thing Mrs Wolff is doing. Her name will be perpetuated. Why is she giving the lot? I didn't expect the lot.'

'She concluded her father wanted it.'

'A fine woman. You see, it's good to have children. They may be better than we are. You'd better have children.'

'You'd better have breakfast. Goodbye. Get better,' Raison said.

'I'll write to Mrs Wolff. I can't write much at a time. I'll write today.' And he thought about what he'd write when he was alone. He thought about his wife and the clockwork that had brought her here, after all, and her hurry to consult the German specialist – an unnecessary consultation after the verdict of Landsberg's son-in-law. Yet she worried. Why did she always worry? Why did they worry? The stars kept in their courses and the world continued while the creatures slept. It was all so plainly there, so palpable, the design, the evidence of purpose; including the evil, particularly the evil. If it was easy to accept the good without need of interpretation, how much more the evil – otherwise so meaningless. Nothing was meaningless. This was the consolation for it. To accept the consolation was not merely a matter of faith but of sense. To fall out of faith was to fall out of sense. When one did it, in confusion, it was a matter somehow of finding the way back, of somehow making good again. And this was the whole of it.

'The whole of it,' Haffner said. He didn't bother locking the car, even though cars had been taken from the airport lately. Let them take it. 'The whole of it,' he said. 'One feels poisoned with the beastliness of it. It's a kind of grossness, an endemic condition to which all things return. There's a desire for it even. There's no will for order. Observe for a moment over there,' he said with bitter-sweet satisfaction, 'where we can see it says quite plainly No Parking. Yet in just this position someone chooses to park a car.'

'Yes.' Raison said. He recognized the car. 'A poor show,' he said.

'One aspect only.'

They walked into the airport building and Raison checked in. He hadn't any luggage to check in, only his umbrella and briefcase.

'Well. Thanks for the toothbrush,' he said. 'And for the pyjamas.'

'Do you think you will come back?'

'You could keep them handy. But I doubt it,' he said, catching sight of her suddenly.

'Mrs Wolff, of course, has no use for me now.'

'Why not?'

'For my advice.'

'She's a funny woman, of course, Mrs Wolff.'

'Not that I expect it. Nobody has. I haven't myself. There's something in the air. . . . Impossible problems are contrived, artificial dilemmas created. . . . There's something in the times that seems to find peace only in constant senseless movement. What is it?'

'It's the *Wandervogel*,' Raison said. 'Hello, Elke,' he said.

'Elke,' Haffner said. 'What are you doing here, Elke?'

'I rang you at your hotel. They told me you'd already gone,' she said to Raison.

'I had to look in on Grunwald.'

'You were going without telling me.'

'There wasn't anything else to say. What else was there to say?' he said.

'James,' she said. She put a hand on each side of his face and kissed him. Haffner's mouth fell open as he watched. 'There's more than one island, James,' she said.

'It's a question of exclusive arrangements,' Raison said. He'd told her more of the island.

'Nothing should be that exclusive.'

'You can't approximate,' Raison said. 'Some things you can't control, but some things you can. It's a question of need, you see,' he said.

'What need when a person is like that? You can fulfil that need and others.'

'My need.'

But they called his flight then.

'Goodbye,' he said to her.

'Keep smiling,' he said to Haffner.

They watched him go. She took her father's arm as they walked out of the building.

Haffner said slowly, 'I didn't know you knew Herr Raison so well.'

'I don't.'

'But it seems – '

'I only went to bed with him.'

He took his arm away.

She said, 'I'm sorry. I thought you asked.'

'I didn't ask that.'

'It's best to be truthful. Without truth there's no understanding and no love. Father, I'm sorry about Schonbach. I wanted you to know – ' But he was walking away.

'Father, don't go back to the office. Come home with me. Let's talk.'

But he didn't answer. He walked to his car. As he got into it he saw her getting into hers. That, too. All of a pattern. All of a sudden, shoving the automatic gear into Drive, he had a longing so enormous that he knew he couldn't deny it now.

Raison longed for a whisky and he had one. He'd walked from the terminal and loped upstairs in Stanhope Gardens, umbrella and briefcase swinging, smelling the rain on his clothes. There was a pile of post on the floor, but he didn't bother with it. And his jacket was damp, but he didn't bother with that, either. He sat on the sofa with his bowler, briefcase and umbrella beside him and blinked slowly around the loathsome room.

A mixing of minds had gone on of late. He felt a bit battered by the busy world. He seemed to have left one place without having quite reached another. So he sipped his drink in the no-place, and waited for the life that lurked about Stanhope Gardens to exert its old dominion. He had a feeling that he'd detached himself from the screen of a moving picture that continued wearisomely behind him still as he walked away. He'd known intimately while he was in it what it was all about, but now the knowledge was draining out of him like dream knowledge, and the faces of all the characters were also draining, so that all he could grasp was an impression of them without their faces, engaged in a kind of swaying or spinning motion, like so many gyroscopes, toppling and righting themselves, toppling and righting themselves, in response to the directions of various beacons.

He thought they seemed happy when they were up and unhappy when they were down; but it didn't take much on the uncertain surface where they gyrated to send them up or down, and they didn't seem to be up or down for long. They seemed mainly, like the grand old Duke of York's men, to be only halfway up, neither up nor down.

He thought on the whole he preferred them without their faces. But he tried all the same to remember what the girl's had looked like, and got up and gave himself another drink as an aid to memory. The face remained an obstinate blur, as did that of her father, standing beside her in the airport building of sunny Munich, left not three hours ago. He suddenly remembered they'd not even said goodbye to him; he had been the one to say goodbye. The faceless figures merely stood looking after him as he walked away. So he let them say goodbye, and dismissed them, back to their own context, and felt at last the resumption of his own as he took his seat again on the sofa and allowed his wandering eye to rest on the telephone.

A long haul still lay ahead, of course, by way of Haverford-west, or other beacons.

Haffner dug up the Mauser in its little lead coffin, and walked about with it for much of the afternoon, crying. He found the cottage unlocked and he walked about that, too. He couldn't recognize the downstairs, the doors had been taken off, or the furniture upstairs, all new, new all of it, and he cried for this as well, not finding himself anywhere in the place where he'd spent so long. But mainly he walked in the woods, crunching cones under his feet and occasionally stopping to rest, or to thump his head against a tree. He apologized to his father and mother, but mostly to his Uncle Albrecht, for what had become of him. He said, 'You see, I'm no good. In some way, I don't know how, I've spent whatever was any good in me, and got nothing back for it. I've been either short-changed or deceived – a question of judgement, poor judgement. It wasn't always like this – you remember, Uncle, you gave me the gun. I cared. I always cared. Of course, I was unlucky, I was born with too small a will – it wasn't your fault, Mother, an accident of fate. But it always was, exceptionally small, from birth, people could do what they liked with me. And so my judgement was whittled away. It wouldn't have mattered so much if I'd wanted what everybody wanted, but I never did, not at the same time. It's been a fatal lack of timing with me. All my life I've been out of tune – except with the birds. But the birds know, too. They won't go near a dead bird. It's so terribly unfair, my life – so ironic the way the things I love turn on me and destroy me, swinishly unfair,' he said, banging his head.

'We can say,' he said, 'my wife contributed to my destruction, but who chose her? It was my own poor judgement. I married a woman, Uncle,' he said, 'from Vienna, who made me impotent. It's embarrassing to talk of these things, but after all, it happened to me, my life span – soon I'll be with you and the historic dead. People do these things here – an important activity, the most significant and pleasurable they get from their bodies. And she's taken it from me. For years I've not been able to have it or, more important, to give it. What any fox, any beggar, can do in the way of fulfilling and vitalizing its opposite, I can't. My gender's gone,' Haffner said. 'I've tried of course with other women, but it's no good, a painful mockery, something has simply stopped there. When the heart stops, everything stops, but with this things still go on, and yet a death has taken place. For years I tried to tell myself it didn't matter. But it wasn't true. It mattered. It mattered,' he said, banging himself quite dizzy. 'It mattered in every kind of way. People knew, you see. They seemed to know. They didn't respect me any more. They knew something had curled up and died inside me. Sometimes, I looked at my organ – a perfectly healthy organ, by no means dead, quite normal in appearance, but yet hanging there useless for anything except draining the bladder – and I thought I am exactly that organ, I am that walking organ, merely a drain for the food I eat, producing nothing but waste. My whole life has been waste.'

His head was aching and he put a hand to it and felt blood. He had cut the head in battering it against the bark of the trees. He sat on the ground and looked at the ugly Mauser. He opened the square magazine and counted the cartridges placed there by Uncle Albrecht. He wondered if decomposition had taken place within the cartridges and if they mightn't work. But there was no damp in the magazine and the cold metal of the cartridges felt heavy and potent with death: his death awaiting him for fifty years in the spicy ground. 'There's no mess with the Mauser,' Uncle Albrecht had said, 'a clean neat hole, it's nothing. But do for the others first.'

'The thing is, there aren't any others, Uncle,' he said, getting up and walking about again in turmoil. 'It isn't like that. What others? It's life itself. It's all senseless, a swine's dream. There's no honour any more. After all, obedience is a part of honour, isn't it – loyalty? But what's one to be obedient or loyal to? Such things happened here, Uncle – our youngsters running in formation all over Europe chasing people in the high streets, taking them to camps to be murdered – such things you couldn't dream of. How could one be loyal to that? But what could I do about it? They'd only have put me in a camp if I'd tried. And what would have been the point of that? I've got too small a will, you see. Your judgement gets whittled away. I thought I'd be loyal to the idea of decency and justice and afterwards prosecute the criminals. But it isn't so easy. How can you prosecute people for crimes under the law that weren't then crimes under the law? The State that legalizes my activities also legalized theirs – so what's justice as a thing to be loyal to? Justice is the State, and the State's the people, and the people are the ones who connived at these things – swine, swine, all of them,' he said.

His head was racketing so much he thought he'd broken it with battering and had to stop for a moment to lean it against a tree. Blood and tears ran down his face. He felt his knees sag and his words go floating upwards inside his skull as though anxious to be free of him. Not yet, he said to them, not yet.

'You see, I thought,' he said, making an effort to collect the words for Uncle Albrecht, 'that they'd changed, that people do change as their cells change. But it isn't true. The new cells exactly replace old cells. The same rottenness continues. Those who did well then are doing well again now, and I'm still the one out of step. And there's no reason for it now, it's just habit, all the good's gone out of me, wasted, you see.'

He couldn't keep still and walked again in despair, crashing about the trees. He noticed the birds had fallen silent. 'Yes, and I could have borne it,' he said, 'because this was still here, an undefiled thing, still a part of me. You remember, Uncle, my cathedral. But it has to be defiled, you see. It's an essential part of the swinishness that everything must be defiled, preferably by oneself, the ultimate, almost the ultimate, in swinishness. It's so hard with a small will. Nobody says, you see, let's turn a cathedral into a whorehouse. It's never that way. It's an issue now between birds and men – families starving, God knows why, I don't know why. If they didn't come here they wouldn't starve. They could starve elsewhere. But still, you see, people starving – there's a devilish logic in it. One has to make a decision. After all, people – there must still be goodness, a seed of integrity. I met a man of integrity, Uncle.'

He punished his head so savagely he felt consciousness going again and found himself lying over a tree root, bleeding and weeping. The structure of his skull seemed to be of loose plates and girders crashing and grinding together in shellbursts of white pain. He could hardly reach Uncle Albrecht through the shellbursts and had to shout at him. 'I met a man of integrity, and he fornicated with my daughter. Do you understand, Uncle – my only child, a whore, naturally, runs gladly to tell me. Anybody tells me anything. Anybody does anything with me. I don't exist. I'm already dead inside, impotent.'

He couldn't stand shouting any more. He couldn't bear to tell any more. He slipped the catch off the Mauser and lifted it to his head, but it was greasy with blood and awkward to hold in his left hand, for the brain, and he thought he might miss, so he put the barrel in his mouth. His upper teeth fell out, but he sucked the hard gun-metal hungrily, tasting it all over with his tongue, a marvellous thing of reliable potency.

'Heinz, Heinzl!' Uncle Albrecht said. 'Enemies first, Heinzl. Take some with you.'

'There are no enemies,' he mumbled, loving the enormous mouthful that would punch him so neatly to honourable peace. 'Life's the enemy. It's overwhelming me.'

'It could be the darkness before the dawn, Heinzl.'

'No, no. There's no dawn. It's growing darker,' he said. He pushed the barrel hard up against his palate. 'I'm entitled to a Roman death.'

'Very well, Heinzl. I know you love honour. So long as your statement's in order.'

'My statement?'

'As I don't have to ask. I know you'll have written a fine one. It will be a credit to both of us, Heinzl.'

Haffner took the gun out of his mouth, vomiting a little over it. He tried to get up, but couldn't for a while. He put his teeth back in his mouth. When he walked he found he couldn't see, he'd knocked his glasses off somewhere. But there was nothing he wanted to see. He blundered about for some hours, careless of the body that should now by rights be lying over the tree root with a neat, clean hole in it, trying to work out, amid the shellbursts, his statement. He'd left the car up by the cottage, but he fell down a hill presently and found himself on a corkscrew section of road. Somebody gave him a lift, thinking him the victim of a road accident, but he refused to go to hospital. He had to get down to pen and paper, and soon he did. He had the place to himself for an hour, but then he heard her come in, and a minute later try his door.

'Heinz, is it you?'

'Yes.'

'Can I come in?'

'I'm busy.'

'Do you want anything?'

'No,' he said. But he did. He wanted relief from his head. He couldn't write decently with his head hammering so much. Without his glasses he could hardly write at all. He thought he'd better lie down for an hour, and waited till she was out of the way. But she was waiting in the hall when he emerged.

'Heinz – what's happened to you?'

'Nothing. A small accident.'

'But your head – it needs a doctor.'

'No, no. A little sleep.'

'I must clean it.'

He didn't want it cleaned – for what? – but she did it all the same, and bandaged it. 'For one hour only,' he told her. 'Then wake me. No doctor,' he said. 'Is it clear?'

'But I don't understand.'

'It's all right. It's nothing. One hour.'

'Take your trousers off, at least.'

'It's not necessary.'

He lay down on the bed and the plates and girders mercifully slowed. They began to thump instead of crashing, and presently didn't quite touch. He awoke, hearing himself called, and sat up at once. 'Yes, yes,' he said. It was grey in the room. He couldn't think for a moment where he was. Then he saw her beside him. 'Very good. Thank you. What time is it?' he said.

'It's early yet. I didn't call you. Lie down.'

'Early? It's dark. I told you an hour.'

'You slept all night. You needed it. Rest, Heinz.'

All night? He looked in astonishment at the window. It was open, a slim breeze rustling through; the dawn breeze. He suddenly realized that he was in pyjamas and no longer on top of the covers but under them. He said, 'But I told you – But I've got to – ' and stopped, licking his lips. What difference did it make? It was on the whole better. He was calmer. It had to be a credit to both of them, he thought, and as he was thinking it, heard himself called again.

Haffner got out of bed.

'Heinz, what is it?'

'*Lullula arborea arborea*,' he said.

'What? Where are you going?'

He didn't say, because he didn't know. On the way he realized he was going to say goodbye. 'It's all right, Uncle,' he said. 'It's in no sense a humiliation. I don't expect an answer – they know I'm impotent and I understand. It's only my goodbye.'

He couldn't see without his glasses but he leaned out of the window, receiving an impression of fecund trees in a world of recent pearly creation. Cool air washed his naked eyes and his grimy heart. 'Cleanse me and I shall be clean,' Haffner said. 'Heal me and I shall be whole.' He didn't know why he said it, or whom he said it to, but he hadn't said it aloud, anyway. He waited patiently for the woodlark to speak aloud. Presently,

with great ripeness and the utmost clarity – 'Didloi didloi tüttüttü-wiiuui' – it did.

Haffner didn't have his reeds and warblers, but it didn't matter for goodbye, so he pursed his lips.

'Diduli pii-iiüü-ui,' he said to the woodlark.

'Pii-iiüü-ui dwüid,' the woodlark said.

'Eh?' Haffner said, with shock and astonishment. 'Dwüid dwüid didloi,' he said.

'Didloi tüttüttü-wiiuui lulululu-u.'

'Lulululu-u.'

For several incredible minutes, hanging out of the window, Haffner conversed with the woodlark in the pearly creation, till an arm hooked in his drew him back to bed. He went unprotestingly. Extraordinary. Unbelievable. After so many years. To him. But it did not feel like him. It felt like somebody totally different. He felt as if he'd swum. He said, 'Did you hear it?'

'Whistling, in your pyjamas.'

'Whistling? I was talking. Didn't you hear?'

'Rest, Heinz.'

He didn't want to rest. He felt magnificently rested. He felt – How did he feel? In some sense floating. Floating with marvellous softness beside a marvellous softness, never a belt or buckle. He caressed the softness, exulting in his conversation, and found himself presently caressed in return. The direction of the reciprocated caresses obliged him after some minutes to warn absent-mindedly, 'It's no good, Gerda.'

'*Liebchen*.'

'You know it's no good.'

But something very extraordinary was happening. Something even more incredible was happening.

'*Liebchen*.'

'*Liebchen*.'

'*Liebchen*.'

'*Liebchen*.'

To do with the birds; that knowledgeable bird; in a new dawn, a fresh start; with the promise of, at least the desire to; certainly the desire to; one might even say – Haffner thought, falling back rhythmically and frenziedly on the inspiration of the birdsong – that one was coming quite close to; that one was without any question close to coming, to

making

good

again!

MORE ABOUT PENGUINS

Penguinews, which appears every month, contains details of all the new books issued by Penguins as they are published. From time to time it is supplemented by *Penguins in Print*, which is a complete list of all books published by Penguins which are in print. (There are well over three thousand of these.)

A specimen copy of *Penguinews* will be sent to you free on request, and you can become a subscriber for the price of the postage. For a year's issues (including the complete lists) please send 4s. if you live in the United Kingdom, or 8s. if you live elsewhere. Just write to Dept EP, Penguin Books Ltd, Harmondsworth, Middlesex, enclosing a cheque or postal order, and your name will be added to the mailing list.

Some other books by Lionel Davidson in Penguins are described on the following pages.

Note: *Penguinews* and *Penguins in Print* are not available in the U.S.A. or Canada

THE ROSE OF TIBET

'Is Lionel Davidson today's Rider Haggard?' asks Daphne du Maurier: 'His novel has all the excitement of *She* and *King Solomon's Mines*.'

The Rose of Tibet is a story of adventure on the roof of the world, before and during the Chinese invasion. Charles Houston, a London artist, goes out to seek news of his brother, reported dead in Tibet. In India a Sherpa boy tells him of Europeans recently encountered in the mountains and the two set off for the forbidden monastery of Yamdring. Their extraordinary reception there, after weeks in the killing cold, Houston's romance with a reincarnated she-devil, and their violent and tragic efforts to escape the Chinese with a fortune in gems are told with that amalgam of humour, romance, and incredulity that make Lionel Davidson the perfect storyteller for today.

'I hadn't realized how much I had missed the genuine Adventure story – not thriller, not detective, without social significance – until I read *The Rose of Tibet*' – Graham Greene

NOT FOR SALE IN THE U.S.A.

THE NIGHT OF WENCESLAS

On the strength of this first novel Lionel Davidson's work has been compared with that of John Buchan, Graham Greene, Eric Ambler, and even Kingsley Amis. Certainly this thrilling story, so reminiscent of *The Third Man*, is told in the idiom of today with all the imagination and uninhibited will of the true story-teller.

Young man-about-town Nicolas Whistler, whose father had once had an interest in a Bohemian glassworks, really had no choice when he was suddenly 'invited' to make a business trip to Prague. Happily there was said to be no danger in the journey: Nicolas was no hero. But as he becomes more and more deeply engulfed in the seamy underworld of power politics, the reader is bound to go the whole way with this reluctant spy – as if to discover his own fate.

'Fast-moving, exciting, often extraordinarily funny. The freshest first for months' – *Sunday Times*

'Don't miss it. Brilliant' – *Observer*

Night of Wenceslas was chosen by the British Crime Writers' Association as the Best Crime Novel of 1960 and awarded the Silver Quill by the Authors' Club as the Most Promising First Novel.

NOT FOR SALE IN THE U.S.A.